Not yet. To die for duty was honourable. To be killed in the saddle by my own blood was not.

Head down, mane whipping, Jinso plunged through the cracked gates and into the night. Darkness swallowed us, but we kept on without slowing. Every thud of hoof upon road seemed to burst more blood from my wound, but I gritted my teeth in anticipation of arrows. My back tingled, sure the silent death would hit at any moment. Dread turned to hope with every racing step along the moonlit road, until at last I dared to look back. A line of flickering torches lit the top of the wall like watching eyes—the watching eyes of every Levanti I had led to this cursed place. Every Levanti I ought to be taking home.

"Let's start with not bleeding to death and—"

Everything spun as I turned back. The road tilted, and unable to hold on longer, I fell head first to meet it.

Praise for
WE RIDE THE STORM

"With prose that rises above most novels, Devin Madson paints evocative scenes to build an engaging story. Highly entertaining, *We Ride the Storm* is certainly worth your attention and Madson is an exciting new author in fantasy."   —Mark Lawrence, author of *Red Sister*

"Intricate, compelling, and vividly imagined, this is the first in a new quartet that I am hugely excited about. Visceral battles, complex politics, and fascinating worldbuilding bring Devin's words to life."   —Anna Stephens, author of *Godblind*

"An utterly arresting debut, *Storm's* heart is in its complex, fascinating characters, each trapped in ever-tightening snarls of war, politics, and magic. Madson's sharp, engaging prose hauls you through an engrossing story that will leave you wishing you'd set aside enough time to read this all in one sitting. One of the best new voices in fantasy."   —Sam Hawke, author of *City of Lies*

"A brutal, nonstop ride through an empire built upon violence and lies, a story as gripping as it is unpredictable. Never shying away from the consequences of the past nor its terrible realities, Madson balances characters you want to love with actions you want to hate while mixing in a delightful amount of magic, political intrigue, and lore. This is not a book you'll be able to put down."
—K. A. Doore, author of *The Perfect Assassin*

"Darkly devious and gripping epic fantasy boasting complex characters, brutal battle, and deadly intrigue. *We Ride the Storm* is breathtaking, brilliant, and bloody—it grips you hard and does not let go."   —Cameron Johnston, author of *The Traitor God*

WE LIE WITH DEATH

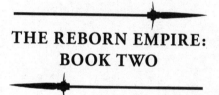

THE REBORN EMPIRE: BOOK TWO

DEVIN MADSON

orbitbooks.net

Copyright © 2021 by Devin Madson
Excerpt from *We Cry for Blood* copyright © 2021 by Devin Madson
Excerpt from *The Unbroken* copyright © 2021 by Cherae Clark

Cover design by Lisa Marie Pompilio
Cover illustration by Nico Delort
Cover copyright © 2021 by Hachette Book Group, Inc.
Map by Charis Loke
Author photograph by Leah Ladson

Orbit
Hachette Book Group
1290 Avenue of the Americas
New York, NY 10104
orbitbooks.net

First Edition: January 2021
Simultaneously published in Great Britain by Orbit

Orbit is an imprint of Hachette Book Group.
The Orbit name and logo are trademarks of Little, Brown Book Group Limited.

The publisher is not responsible for websites (or their content) that are not owned by the publisher.

The Hachette Speakers Bureau provides a wide range of authors for speaking events. To find out more, go to www.hachettespeakersbureau.com or call (866) 376-6591.

Library of Congress Cataloging-in-Publication Data
Names: Madson, Devin, author.
Title: We lie with death / Devin Madson.
Description: First Edition. | New York, NY : Orbit, 2021. | Series: The reborn empire ; book 2
Identifiers: LCCN 2020023563 | ISBN 9780316536387 (trade paperback) |
    ISBN 9780316536363 (e-book)
Subjects: GSAFD: Fantasy fiction.
Classification: LCC PS3613.A2945 W398 2021 | DDC 813/.6—dc23
LC record available at https://lccn.loc.gov/2020023563

ISBNs: 978-0-316-53638-7 (trade paperback), 978-0-316-53636-3 (ebook)

Printed in the United States of America

LSC-C

Printing 1, 2020

To Miss I, for teaching me so much about myself.
And also that the most special and important things in
life are rarely easy.

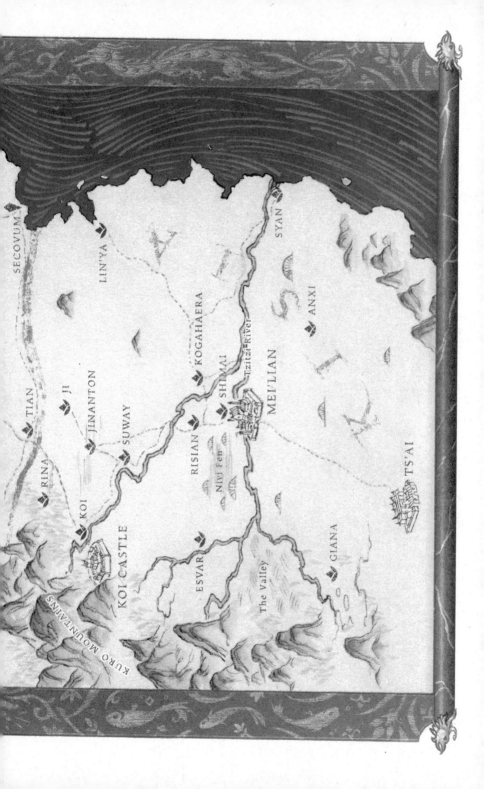

AUTHOR'S NOTE

For those readers who are coming to this book straight from the original self-published version of *We Ride the Storm*, please be aware that there were a few significant changes in the new edition, including the addition of more Levanti characters (Yiss en'Oht, Lashak e'Namalaka, and more) as well as more Levanti worldbuilding, extra chapters (two from Miko's perspective—an introductory one and one of her at the battle of Risian—and one from Cassandra's), some significant tweaks to the way Miko's political arc worked, and perhaps most importantly, a shift in the way the relationship between Gideon and Rah was portrayed. This change in particular may leave a few things in this book feeling odd or undeserved, and I apologise for the confusion. Try to just roll with it.

CHARACTER LIST

Levanti

Torin

Rah e'Torin—ousted captain of the Second Swords of Torin
Eska e'Torin—Rah's second-in-command (deceased, Residing)
Kishava e'Torin—tracker (deceased)
Orun e'Torin—horse master (deceased, Residing)
Yitti e'Torin—healer
Jinso—Rah's horse
Lok, Himi, and Istet—Swords of the Torin
Gideon e'Torin—First Sword of the Torin, now emperor of Levanti Kisia
Sett e'Torin—Gideon's second and blood brother
Tep e'Torin—healer of the First Swords
Tor, Matsimelar, and Oshar e'Torin—the saddleboys chosen by Gideon to be translators
Nuru e'Torin—self-taught translator never used by the Chiltaens

Jaroven

Dishiva e'Jaroven—captain of the Third Swords of Jaroven
Keka e'Jaroven—Dishiva's second, can't talk. Chiltaens cut out his tongue.
Captain Atum e'Jaroven—captain of the First Swords of Jaroven
Loklan e'Jaroven—Dishiva's horse master
Shenyah e'Jaroven—the only Jaroven Made in exile

Ptapha, Massama, Dendek, Anouke, Esi, Moshe e'Jaroven—Dishiva's Swords

Other Levanti

Jass en'Occha—a Sword of the Occha

Captain Lashak e'Namalaka—First Sword of the Namalaka and Dishiva's friend

Captain Yiss en'Oht—First Sword of the Oht, fiercely loyal to Gideon

Captain Taga en'Occha—First Sword of the Occha and Jass's captain

Captain Menesor e'Qara—captain of the Second Swords of Qara

Jaesha e'Qara—Captain Menesor's second

Senet en'Occha, Jakan e'Qara, Yafeu en'Injit, Baln en'Oht, Tafa en'Oht, and Kehta en'Oht—imperial guards

Nassus—Levanti god of death

Mona—Levanti goddess of justice

Kisians

Miko Ts'ai—daughter of Empress Hana Ts'ai and Katashi Otako

Emperor Kin Ts'ai—the last emperor of Kisia (deceased)

Empress Hana Ts'ai—deposed empress of Kisia

Prince Tanaka Ts'ai—Miko's twin brother (deceased)

Shishi—Miko's dog

Jie Ts'ai—Emperor Kin's illegitimate son

Lord Tashi Oyamada—Jie's maternal grandfather and regent

General Kitado—commander of Miko's Imperial Guard

Minister Ryo Manshin—minister of the left, chief commander of the Imperial Army

Lord Hiroto Bahain—duke of Syan

Edo Bahain—duke of Syan's eldest son

Captain Nagai—one of the duke's men

Lord Nishi (Lord Salt)—a wealthy Kisian lord who believes in the One True God

Chiltaens

Cassandra Marius—Chiltaen whore and assassin

The hieromonk, Creos Villius—head of the One True God's church

Leo Villius—only child of His Holiness the hieromonk

Captain Aeneas—the hieromonk's head guard

Swiff—one of Captain Aeneas's men

Others

Torvash—the Witchdoctor

Mistress Saki—Torvash's silent companion

Kocho—Torvash's scribe and servant

Lechati—young man in Torvash's service

THE STORY SO FAR...

Tensions are high between Imperial Kisia and neighbouring Chiltae. Raids along the border have increased the probability of yet another war, and in the hope of calming the situation a new treaty must be signed, sealed with a marriage between Leo Villius, son of the hieromonk of Chiltae, and Princess Miko Ts'ai. To challenge the emperor, Miko's brother attacks Leo Villius as he crosses the border, but fails to kill him and is executed for treason.

Having the excuse they wanted to mount a full attack, the Chiltaens cross the border with an army supplemented with Levanti warriors from across the Eye Sea. Exiled from their homeland, Rah and his people have been forced into the service of the Chiltaens, though to fight the wars of others is against their tenets.

With the help of Cassandra, an assassin capable of reanimating the recently dead, the Chiltaens take the impenetrable city of Koi. Her contract is to kill Leo Villius for his father and she does so, only for Leo himself to return to claim his own head. For her failure, she is sold to the enigmatic Witchdoctor, the only man capable of removing the unwanted voice in her head.

After a failed challenge to wrest leadership of the Levanti from his one-time close friend Gideon e'Torin, Rah is made Leo's bodyguard as the Chiltaen conquest continues south toward the Kisian capital. Intent on protecting it, Miko sides with the emperor against her mother, until he dies, leaving her to face the threat alone. After a tussle for supremacy with the emperor's illegitimate child heir and his guardians, Miko crowns herself empress and rides out to meet the Chiltaens. They are unable to hold off the attack and the Chiltaens take the capital, only to be slaughtered when Gideon orders the Levanti to turn on their masters. Miko escapes before the carnage, and Rah, unable to accept the direction Gideon is leading them, is arrested.

WE LIE
WITH
DEATH

# 1. RAH

Time does not pass in darkness. There are no days to count. No nights to sleep. In darkness you cease to exist as solitude wears your soul to a stub, but nothing could erode the truth in my heart. I was Levanti. A Torin. And this was not how a warrior of the plains died.

"Gideon!" I shouted, pressing my face to the bars. My voice bounced away into the darkness, returning no answer. "Gideon!"

I gripped the bars and, sucking a deep breath through parched lips, began to sing our lament. We sang it for loss. We sang it for pain. We sang it beneath the stars and the scorching summer sun. We sang it when weak and we sang it when strong, but more than anything we sang it when we were alone. Gideon had taught me the words, along with a clutch of other children released from chores at the end of a travelling day. We had sat at his feet, fighting to sit closest as though his worn, sweaty boots were a shrine at which to pray.

"But what does it mean?" one of the others had asked—a child whose face and name had been lost to the haze of time, leaving only gratitude that someone else had asked so I need not look foolish.

"It's a prayer," Gideon had said, smiling at the foolish one. "In lifting your voice to the gods you will never be alone, because they will see you. Will hear you. Will honour you."

He had ruffled the girl's hair and left us staring after him. He might have been the Torin's youngest Sword, just a child to the warriors he served with, but he had been like a god to us. To me.

When I finished, the song echoed on, slowly fading into silence. Gideon did not come.

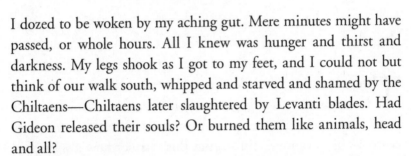

I dozed to be woken by my aching gut. Mere minutes might have passed, or whole hours. All I knew was hunger and thirst and darkness. My legs shook as I got to my feet, and I could not but think of our walk south, whipped and starved and shamed by the Chiltaens—Chiltaens later slaughtered by Levanti blades. Had Gideon released their souls? Or burned them like animals, head and all?

"Gideon!" My voice cracked, thirst cutting like razors into my dry throat. "Gideon!"

No answer came and I paced the length of the small cell, touching each of its bars. Seventeen in all, each perfectly smooth, the six that made up the door slightly thicker than the rest. No light. No breeze. No life. Nothing but darkness, and like the gnawing in my gut, fear began to eat at my thoughts. Had I been forgotten?

"Gideon! Yitti!"

Only echoes answered.

I did not hear footsteps, yet when I next opened my eyes I was no longer alone. Bright light pierced the bars and I winced, shuffling back across the floor until my shoulder blades hit stone.

"Sorry. I didn't think."

With a metal scrape the light faded from noon-sun to gloaming.

"You look terrible."

I laughed. Or tried to, but it came out as a wheeze and my

stomach cramped. "You should have let me know you were coming so I could bathe," I said, every word a dry rasp.

"At least being stuck down here hasn't affected your sense of humour." Sett's customary scowl came into focus as my eyes adjusted. "I'm not sure if—"

"I want to see Gideon."

The only answer was the *tink tink* of the metal lantern growing hot, magnified by the silence. I let the words hang until at last Sett cleared his throat. "You can't."

"He cannot refuse to see me. I am a Sword of the Levanti. Of the Torin. I am—"

"He isn't here, Rah."

I stared at Sett's harsh features like they were lines of script containing answers. "What do you mean he isn't here? He's gone home?"

Sett's explosive laugh echoed along the passage. "No, he hasn't gone home. He's an emperor now, but it's not exactly safe here, is it? The Chiltaens broke the city's defences, and why bother rebuilding them when your empire is north of the river, not south? This is enemy territory now."

"Enemy—?"

"No more questions, Rah. You are the one going home." A key scraped in the lock, and with a grunt of effort, Sett unlocked the door.

Home. I had wanted nothing else since arriving, yet I did not move toward freedom.

Sett folded his arms as best he could while holding the lantern. "Really? After everything that's happened, you're still going to be a stubborn ass?"

"We don't kill. We don't steal. We don't conquer." I raised my voice over his complaints. "And the only way to remove someone from leadership of their Swords is through challenge or death. I am captain of the Second Swords of Torin until one of them challenges me for the responsibility."

Sett growled, his fingers tightening upon the lantern's handle. "Just go home, Rah. Go home."

He turned then and, leaving the cell door wide open, started back along the passage. I followed the retreating light, my legs shaking. "Where are my Swords?"

"With Gideon," Sett said, not stopping or slowing though I struggled to keep up, my feet dragging on the damp stone floor.

"What about Dishiva?"

"The same."

"Leo?"

Sett stopped, turning so suddenly he almost swung the lantern into my face. "The Chiltaen's God boy? Dead. You saw him die. His condition hasn't improved." Sett sighed. "Don't do anything stupid, Rah. I know that's hard for you, but this is your chance to escape this place, to go home, because if you give him trouble again, Gideon won't have a choice but to—"

"To what?" I said as he started walking again, his swaying lantern leading the way like a drunken star. "To kill me?" I hurried after him. "Is that the new Levanti way? To kill those who question decisions without challenge?"

Giving no answer, Sett started up a flight of stairs, each step a frustrated slam of boot on stone. I paused at the bottom to catch my breath, and nearly leapt from my skin as the fading light of Sett's lantern lit the cell closest to the stairs. A man stood as close to the bars as he could get, staring at me, unblinking, in the manner of one committing my face to memory. I fought the urge to step back, to look away, glad of the bars between us. Untidy strands of hair hung around his dirty face, but through the shroud of neglect, familiarity nagged.

Sett's footsteps had halted on the stairs.

"Who is this?" I said, not breaking from the man's gaze.

"Minister Manshin," came Sett's reply from the stairwell. "The man who was sitting on the throne in the empress's battle armour when we arrived."

Minister Manshin, who had taken the empress's place to trick her enemies, now stared at me through the bars of his cell. I wanted to assure him I had never sought Kisia's ruin, that I was not his enemy, but I had fought with my people against his and no amount of words could change that. Words he wouldn't even understand.

"Come on," Sett grumbled, and as his footsteps resumed, the light bled from Minister Manshin's face. I unpinned myself from his gaze and mounted the stairs.

Sett climbed slowly, yet still I could not keep up, increasingly breathless and aching as each step renewed my body's demands for food and water and rest. Had pride and anger not kept me stiffly upright, I would have crawled on hands and knees.

When at last I reached the top, I steadied myself with a hand upon the rough-hewn stone and sucked deep, painful breaths. Sett's footsteps continued on a way, only to stop and return when I didn't follow.

"I'm sorry I left you down there so long," he said, his face swimming before me. "I had no choice. You could only slip away unnoticed at night, and I had to wait for Gideon to leave."

"He doesn't know you're doing this?" I'd had no time to wonder why it was Sett releasing me, but whatever his reason, his expression owned no kindness.

"There's food upstairs so you can eat before you go," he said. "And I've packed your saddlebags. Jinso is waiting in the yard."

Jinso. I had hardly let myself hope I would see him again, let alone be allowed to ride free, but anger overtook relief on its way to my lips. "You're smuggling me out of the city like an embarrassment."

"You could say that, yes."

"While Gideon isn't here to stop you."

He left a beat of silence, before asking, "Can you walk again? Food isn't much farther."

It seemed asking about Gideon was not allowed.

The inner palace had changed. Once bright and filled with dead soldiers, it lay blanketed now in silence and shadows, turning its finely carved pillars into twisted creatures that lurked in every corner. Light bloomed behind paper screens and whispers met the scuff of our steps, but we saw no living soul.

Sett led me to a small chamber on the ground floor where a pair of lanterns fought back the night. A spread of dishes covered a low table, but my gaze was drawn to a bowl of shimmering liquid, and not caring if it was water or wine, I poured it into my mouth. It burned my throat like a ball of fire and I dropped the bowl, coughing.

"Kisian wine," Sett said over my coughs. "I think they make it from rice. Or maybe millet. There's tea too, but don't drink it so fast. It's served hot."

"Why?" I managed, my voice even more strained than before.

"I don't know. When I find one that understands me, I'll ask."

"Is there water?"

Sett examined the table. "Doesn't look like it. They aren't keen on water. They think it's dirty, and maybe it is here, I don't know." He shrugged, before adding in a sullen tone: "They don't cook the whole animal either, at least not in the palace. Instead they"—he waved his hand at the table—"slice it up and ignore all the best parts. I saw one feeding liver to the dogs."

Hunger and nausea warred in my stomach as I chose the most recognisable hunk of meat and bit into it. It was heavily spiced and drowned in a strange sauce, but hunger won and I crammed the rest into my mouth followed by another piece, and another. The sudden ingress of food made my stomach ache, but hunger kept me eating until I had filled its every corner.

While I ate and drank, trying not to slop the food down my already stained and stinking clothes, Sett stood by the door like a sentry. He didn't speak, didn't move, just stood with his arms folded staring at nothing, a notch cut between his brows.

Once my hunger had been crushed, nausea flared and I crossed my still-shaking arms over my gut. The sickly-sweet smell of the strange food clogged my nose and I sat back, hoping my stomach wouldn't reject it.

Only when the nausea had subsided a little did I say, "You're not really going to let me leave, are you?"

"You don't think so? You think I had Jinso saddled for someone else?"

I grunted and got slowly to my feet, still clutching my stomach. "You're really smuggling me out of the city in the middle of the night so no one sees me leave? What do you want people to think? That I'm dead? That you killed me?"

"I don't want people to think of you at all. You've caused too much trouble, Rah. Now it's time you listened. Leave Gideon alone. Leave Yitti alone. They've made their choices, as have the rest of the Swords who want a new home and a better life."

"We already have a home."

"Then go fight for it!"

Silence hung amid the shadowed screens, a silence choked with dust and spiced food and the lingering scent of incense. I could taste the ghosts of another's life on every breath, an ever-present reminder of how far I was from the plains.

I eyed Sett. "Do I get my sword back?"

"And your knives if you want them. If you want a replacement for the sword you dropped in Tian, you'll have to put up with a Kisian blade. Hardly a matched pair, but it's all we have."

I wanted a Kisian sword as little as I wanted to eat their food, live on their land, or conquer their cities, but I nodded and a strained smile spread Sett's lips. "Come, we'll get you some fresh clothes."

We met no one on the way out, the inner palace like an empty tomb. The bodies might be gone, but broken screens and railings remained, and many doors were little more than apertures choked with tangled nests of wood and paper.

Stepping in through another door, Sett swung his lantern before him, revealing not an orderly room but a mess of weapons piled by type amid a sea of cloth and leather and chainmail vests.

"Most of it's too small, but with a few cuts in the right places it's wearable," Sett said, sitting the lantern on a ransacked chest and picking up some green silk. "The Imperial Army uniforms weren't too bad, but most of those have gone."

I didn't want to wear Kisian clothes, but my own leathers had seen more filth than I cared to think about. I had worn them into battle many times, and the cooling blood of many severed heads had dribbled down my knees. Here, despite the disorder, everything was clean and crisp.

Sett tossed me the silk robe and its threads caught on my rough skin as it slipped through my fingers. I let it fall, pooling on the floor like the shimmering green waters of Hemet Bay.

Once more Sett stood silent as I made my way around the room, sorting through the scattered garments. The breeches I chose were too tight, the tunic too long, the leather undercoat too thin, and the cloak too heavy. I needed clothes, but it all cut into my flesh in the wrong places and made my skin itch, and the closeness of the collar around my throat was like a choking hand. So many layers would boil one alive beneath the Levanti sun, but if the Kisian rains were half as bad as the Chiltaens believed then I'd be glad of them. The dreaded rains. If the Chiltaens had been less afraid of a little water, they might have noticed the coup brewing beneath their noses. Or not. I hadn't.

I spread my arms, inviting Sett's approval. "Well? How do I look?"

"Ridiculous. But clean. Now come on, it'll be dawn soon."

Having grabbed a replacement blade and bundled my own clothes into a bag, I once more followed Sett out into the inner palace's silent shadows.

"Where is everyone?" I said, having to walk quickly to keep up.

"It's the middle of the night. Where do you think they are?"

He stepped into the entry hall. Sett was a tall man, yet he shrank as the great height of the palace spire stretched away above him. His last words rose to the moonlit heights, and his steps echoed as he crossed toward the open doors. No, not open. Broken. The Chiltaens had smashed the main doors like so many others, leaving Leo to stride through as though they had been opened by the hand of his god.

A stab of guilt silenced further questions. I had sworn to protect him and failed. Just as I had sworn to protect my Swords. And my herd.

Sett stepped through the broken doors. Shallow stairs met us beyond, and but for the smothering night I might have been walking along the colonnade behind Leo once again.

"What happened to Leo's body?"

Sett didn't turn. "I don't know."

"How do you not know?"

"I didn't ask."

He sped up, striding along a colonnade choked with the scent of rotting flowers crushed beneath our feet. Beyond the tangle of vines the gardens spread away, while above the outer palace a shock of lightning lit the night sky. Inside had been airless and oppressive, but this was worse. Heat pressed in like a heavy hand, its damp touch sending sweat dripping down my forehead.

By the time Sett reached the outer palace I had to jog to catch up, an ache twinging my knees. "Sett—"

"Just walk, Rah, I have no more answers for you."

Thunder rumbled as he hurried beneath a great arch.

"Where are the First Swords?"

Sett walked on, outstripping my cramping gait by half a length each step, leaving me to scramble after him along dark passages and through twisting courtyards. His urgency made his lantern swing sickeningly, its handle creaking as light rocked to and fro upon the walls. Not that Sett seemed to need it. He knew the way. Leo had known the way too.

I tightened my hold on the sack of dirty clothes and caught up. "Sett, tell me the truth," I said. "What is going on?"

"Nothing. Look, just as I promised." He gestured as we stepped once more into the night, the rush of his feet descending the outer stairs like the clatter of a rockfall.

Jinso waited in the courtyard, Tor e'Torin holding his reins. With Commander Brutus dead, the young man was as free as the rest of us, yet dark rings hung beneath his eyes and he stood tense.

"You were just supposed to give the instructions, not stay," Sett said as he approached. "I need you inside to help with the messages. That scribe doesn't understand half the words I say."

"Sorry, Captain," the young man said, pressing his fists together in salute. "I didn't wish to leave Captain Rah's horse alone with the weather so wild. He might have fretted."

Sett grunted. "It's not 'Captain' Rah anymore."

I set my forehead to Jinso's neck and tangled my fingers in his well-brushed mane, pretending not to hear the words that cut to my soul. Not a captain. The strange food in my stomach churned, bringing back the nausea.

In silence I checked Jinso over, more through habit than fear he had been poorly tended. Sett stood waiting, his scowl unchanged with each glance I risked his way. Tor remained too, shifting foot to foot. He licked his lips and pressed them into a smile when he found me watching, but the smile didn't even convince his lips, let alone his eyes.

Thunder rumbled—distant, but threatening. The clouds crowding to blot out the stars made some sense of the Chiltaen fear.

My sword and knives had been stashed in one of the saddlebags—Kisian saddlebags I noted—and though I wondered what had happened to my own, I could not force the question out. It seemed to congeal inside my mouth, glued by the creeping sense that something was very wrong.

"Are you going to tell me what's going on?" I said, thrusting my sack of armour into one of the saddlebags and patting Jinso's neck.

Sett laughed, the humourless sound sending a shiver through my skin. "Get on your horse, boy."

I risked another glance at Tor, but the saddleboy stared at the stones. A fork of lightning lit his untidy length of black hair.

"All right," I said, and saluted him as I would Gideon. "May Nassus guide your steps and watch over your soul."

He barely seemed to hear me.

My legs twinged as I climbed onto Jinso's back, but whatever weakness my body owned became nothing in that moment—for I was a rider once more, Jinso's strength inflating my soul. With his reins in hand I could sit tall and proud despite weakness and doubt, despite guilt and fear and pain. In the saddle I was a Levanti.

"Ride north," Sett said then, the restless clop of Jinso's hooves waking him from his trance. "And don't stop until you reach the Ribbon. When you get back—"

"I'm not going back," I said. "Not yet. Not until I've seen Gideon."

An animal's wounded snarl tore from Sett's lips and he gripped Jinso's bridle. "Don't you ever fucking listen, Rah? Go! Get out of here."

"Not without at least saying goodbye. He's on a path I can't follow, but I cannot walk away without seeing him. Without..."

Sett leaned in close, pressing my leg to Jinso's side. "It's too late for that, Rah. I told you he would need you and you failed him. Failed all of us. I will not let you do it again."

"Failed him?" The words cut into my heart. "I tried to save him. To save us all. I—" I bit down a howl as pain tore up my leg like lightning, mimicking the burning trails of fire crazing the night sky. The handle of a hoof pick peeped between Sett's scarred fingers, its hook piercing my thigh.

"Consider this your last warning," he said. "Leave. Now. He doesn't want to see you."

I tightened my grip upon Jinso's reins until my hands hurt, but it made no difference to the pain swelling in my leg. "Then he can tell me that himself," I said through gritted teeth.

Sett dragged the hook across my skin, tearing flesh. I wanted to cry out, to sob like a child and retch my pain upon the stones, but I pressed my lips closed and breathed slowly. Beneath me Jinso tried to step sideways and I fought to keep him still, to keep the pick from being ripped free.

"Leave this place," Sett said, spitting the words like an angry snake. "You wanted to know where the rest of the First Swords are. Where the Second Swords are? They are all on the walls, waiting to fill your back with arrows if you don't listen to me. So for the first time in your life, Rah, *listen*. Ride north. Ride fast. And don't look back."

He yanked the pick out and I gasped. The courtyard spun. Hot blood soaked my pants and dribbled down my leg, and smelling it, Jinso backed. Before I could calm him, a slap to his rear sent him plunging forward. His hooves clattered across the courtyard and all I could do was hold tight or fall.

The gates passed in a blur as we picked up speed, the effort of clinging on with my legs growing more painful with every stride. I was losing blood fast. The wound needed to be bound, needed to be sewn, but I had none of Yitti's skill and he... How many of my Swords wanted me dead?

Ride fast. And don't look back.

Mei'lian passed in a haze of flickering lights and shadows. Unlike the palace the city was still alive and people leapt aside, cries mingling with the clatter of racing hooves.

The road from the palace to the northern gate was straight and broad, and Jinso followed it toward the brewing storm, lightning mirroring the spears of pain flaring behind my eyes. I flew past burned-out shells of once great buildings, past fountains and shrines and piles of the dead, past barricades and great trees that grew amid it all like hands reaching to the sky. Ahead the walls of Mei'lian emerged from the night, their gates gaping open.

Jinso didn't slow. Blood was pooling in my boot and I needed to bind my leg, but lights flickered atop the wall and I could not stop. Not yet. To die for duty was honourable. To be killed in the saddle by my own blood was not.

Head down, mane whipping, Jinso plunged through the cracked gates and into the night. Darkness swallowed us, but we kept on without slowing. Every thud of hoof upon road seemed to burst more blood from my wound, but I gritted my teeth in anticipation of arrows. My back tingled, sure the silent death would hit at any moment. Dread turned to hope with every racing step along the moonlit road, until at last I dared to look back. A line of flickering torches lit the top of the wall like watching eyes—the watching eyes of every Levanti I had led to this cursed place. Every Levanti I ought to be taking home.

"Let's start with not bleeding to death and—"

Everything spun as I turned back. The road tilted, and unable to hold on longer, I fell head first to meet it.

2. DISHIVA

Itaghai tossed his head as I brushed a day's worth of tangles from his mane. He didn't like having it done, so I took my time, easing each knot with care. It was as good a reason as any to keep an emperor waiting.

Other Levanti filled the stable yard, most sitting with their horses or talking in small groups. No one had approached me all evening, not even my Swords. No one quite knew what to say now the first flush of victory was over. We had won. We had taken the city. We had slaughtered our enemies, those vile men who had beaten and starved us, but...doubts crept in as triumph ebbed. Winning had not made everything go back to the way it had been; it had only made things stranger.

"I don't think they like us," came a voice from the next stall. *Stalls.* Little houses for horses as though they were not used to the rain upon their heads.

"That's all right because I don't like them much," was the murmured reply. "When is your exile up?"

"Half a cycle, you?"

"About the same."

Further questions went unasked, but I doubted loyalty to our herd master was the only reason. Fear had bitten many tongues of late.

"Captain Dishiva e'Jaroven?"

I turned, brush caught in Itaghai's mane. A broad-shouldered Levanti stood in the doorway, the bulk of his arms more than making up for what he lacked in height. He was not one of my Swords, nor one I recognised, but with so many of us gathered in one place that was no longer surprising. "Yes?"

"Herd—Emperor Gideon wishes to speak to you."

"I know he does, but horses do not brush themselves."

The man leant against the door frame quite at his ease, the folding of his arms further bulging his muscles. "No, but they also don't get mad if you keep them waiting."

I sighed. "The rest of your mane will have to wait," I said, resting my hand upon Itaghai's neck. "But don't think you're getting out of it that easily. It's not decent to keep clumps of dry blood and knots, you know."

The Levanti grinned, a smile that made him look as youthful as an untested saddleboy. "Oh, I don't know, he looks quite rakish," he said, but when I turned it was me he eyed appreciatively.

"What's your name?"

"Jass en'Occha, Captain," he said, and pressed his fists into a salute.

"Are you busy, Jass en'Occha?"

His brows lifted toward the short pelt of his overgrown hair, and a corner of his lips twitched. "A captain of the Jaroven has need of me?"

I threw him the brush. "His name is Itaghai and he bites if you pull too hard. I'll be back soon."

"Itaghai?"

I rolled my eyes. "My mother liked collecting stories from travellers and used to tell me one about Itaghai the Dragon almost every night when I was a child. It's not that strange."

Jass laughed, a carefree sound for which I envied him. "If you say so, Captain."

"And you'll stay, won't you? Until I come back."

His grin widened. "I can do that."

He held my gaze all the way to the door where I brushed past into the night. The stall door swung closed, but I must have dragged part of him with me, so physically did his presence cling. All it took was a muscular frame and a willing smile and I had wanted to make Gideon wait even longer, but I kept walking and did not look back.

The Levanti in the yard lowered their voices as I passed, dodging around knots of men and women seated on the stones. Their eyes followed me too, and I was sure they could see into my thoughts, could see the raw, broken edges of my soul.

As I neared the manor house, I passed the remains of some sort of siege weapon, all pulleys and ropes and cracked arms. Remnants of war lay scattered everywhere, as much reminders of how far we still had to go as of how far we had come.

The estate where we had stopped for the night must have belonged to a Kisian nobleman. It had stables and gardens, thick walls and tilled fields and a mansion so full of rooms it was a maze. All the captains had been given rooms inside, but I had escaped its airless passages as soon as I could, preferring the open sky to one made of thick black beams. They looked heavy, as did the tiled roof. Heavy enough to crush me if it fell.

I passed two Swords of the Namalaka on the stairs. Both wore crimson silk over their armour, seeming to smother them in blood. "Captain Dishiva," one said, saluting. I nodded rather than risk speaking, sure my views on their new attire would not be congenial.

Inside, a long, lantern-lit hall greeted me, each wall full of haughty Kisian portraits staring as I passed. I wanted to rip their eyes out, but Gideon had spoken at length about how the Kisians were not the Chiltaens, were not our enemy. They were our people now, our subjects, and had to be respected as such. So long as they showed the proper deference to their new emperor, of course. As with everything, he had a point. I just didn't like it.

As I approached Gideon's rooms, I passed more Levanti dressed like Kisian guards. I outranked them all, but not one saluted. There were no other captains here, no seconds, no healers, no trackers, no horse masters, just Swords desperate for glory and favour, and I glared at every one. The two outside Gideon's ornate doors even stepped into my path, their arms folded. "Who seeks an audience with His Majesty?"

I drew myself up. "I am Captain Dishiva e'Jaroven and you will get out of my way."

"We don't take orders from you."

"Who are you?" I said. "Who is your captain? I will inform them of your disrespect."

One leered, making the scar upon his lip curl into an odd sort of smile. "We don't have a captain anymore. We serve only His Imperial Majesty."

I clenched my hands and hissed through bared teeth. "Well, your Imperial Majesty sent for me, so get out of my way or I will make you." Both my swords hung from my left hip, but I touched my dagger as I assessed the weaknesses of their new armour.

The door opened before either could reply, and they parted for a small Kisian man in white. He bowed deeply, murmured something in their intricate tongue, and ushered me in with an outstretched arm. Both offending Swords stood at their ease, but my heart hammered with anger and I could not make my feet move.

The little Kisian grimaced and gestured frantically for me to enter. From inside came the hum of voices, the clink of dishes, and swish of silk, yet the room appeared empty.

Steeling myself, I unstuck my feet and strode into the large, heavily scented room.

"Captain Dish..." the Kisian said. "Captain Dishava Jar—"

"Dishiva," I corrected. "Captain Dishiva e'Jaroven."

The man muttered it, practicing, but his halted announcement had already caused the hum of conversation to cease. Footsteps sounded from the next room, and Gideon strode in through a pair of thin paper doors. "Ah, Captain Dishiva," he said with a smile. "Exactly who I wanted to see."

I stopped in the middle of the reed floor and, for the first time in my life, grimaced to think I might have tramped horse shit in with me. Even as I looked down, I saluted our new emperor. He too had donned a Kisian silk coat, which hung around him like a bloodstained flag. A very finely embroidered flag edged in gold thread.

Gideon's brows lifted when I did not speak. "Is everything all right, Captain?"

Shadowy figures moved beyond the paper screens. The little Kisian man had disappeared, but unfamiliarity clustered close. Pale sections of wall and floor showed some furniture had been removed, yet a profusion of decorative vases and screens, statues and lanterns, shortened my every breath. "Yes, Herd Master," I said. "I am just uncomfortable in such surroundings."

"Ah." He grimaced. "I hope you will get used to them, because I have a task for you."

He had been summoning every captain and giving each Sword-herd a new purpose. I had known my time would come and dreaded it, but whatever my fears, these were my people and Gideon my herd master. I straightened. "What would you have me do, Herd Master?"

"I would have you and your Swords responsible for my protection and the protection of my wife. I—"

"Your wife? But you are a Sword of the Torin. You are not allowed to marry."

Gideon lifted his brows, his momentary pause enough censure to heat my cheeks.

"I *was* a Sword of the Torin," he said. "I am now Emperor of Levanti Kisia and if I want to remain so long enough to build a new home for us, I must marry a Kisian. We do not have enough Swords to hold this land by force, so we must be diplomatic."

A new home. He had called our plains poisoned, sick, infected with some evil that had gotten into the hearts and minds of our leaders and turned them against us, but although I had seen it with my own eyes and knew it for truth, it could not dampen my yearning. Kisia, with its thick green forests and damp air, its single moon and strange food, was not the plains.

"Do you still wish for this?" Gideon said when I made no reply.

Unspoken was the knowledge he could risk no captain who did not believe in his vision. Rah had been proof of that.

"We need a home that is not under threat," he went on. "We need to survive. To adapt. We are dying back home, Dishiva, *dying*. Our way of life, our people, and our honour—everything that has ever made us great will be our downfall if we cannot embrace change."

Again the unspoken sense that Rah was ever-present. Unbending and unwilling to change.

Gideon began to pace, reeds crackling under his heavy footfall. On a shorter man the tail of his silk coat might have trailed along the ground, but it lapped at his ankles like a restless sea. "We have to fight for a new homeland before there is no place left for us in this world. Before Levanti are nothing but a memory, our groves crushed to dust and our gods forgotten." He spun to face me, hands clasped behind his back in a way that made his sword hilts jut prominently from his hip. "Tell me I can count on your allegiance. Tell me you wish to fight for a future in which our way of life can be saved and perpetuated rather than allowed to die upon the winds of change. If you cannot, I will choose someone else for this task."

He had a mesmerising way of speaking that reached into your chest and twisted your heart, and with emotion swelling, I pressed my hands together in salute. "You have my allegiance, Herd Master. My Swords and I would be honoured to serve in your protection."

"And Lady Sichi's. She requested a female guard and I trust you above all others."

"I am honoured. However, if I may, Herd Master, I thought the reason we had been hoping to find Empress Miko was so you could marry her. Perhaps I am misunderstanding the way their society works."

"No, you're not, but..." He stopped and beckoned me closer, his silence heightening my awareness of the foreign conversation beyond the door.

Close to, his breath smelled of wine and there were dark patches beneath his eyes. "Marriage to Lady Sichi Manshin is the foundation upon which my alliance with these Kisians has been built. We get our empire, they get us, and through family connections to Lady Sichi, the power Emperor Kin denied them. That is why it's important you protect her."

"She wishes for this marriage?"

"She does."

I nodded, and he stepped back. "Their society is old and complicated, built upon shifting power balances and the honour of family names. We cannot expect to understand it in the space of a few days. But we must respect it if we want them to respect us."

"And the empress?"

"We have other plans for Empress Miko when she is found."

He spoke lightly, but the ominous words boded ill for the absent empress.

"Tomorrow we press on to Kogahaera," he said. "We'll be staying there for some time while we plan for the future. You and your Swords will each be given an imperial surcoat to mark you as my personal guards, and while you should assign Swords to me, I want you to ride with Lady Sichi yourself and make her your primary concern."

I had no interest in playing guard to a fine Kisian lady, but being in Gideon's presence had renewed my faith in why we were here and what we were doing. He had led us through the Chiltaen invasion, had freed us from our shackles, had held faith in what we were capable of and what we deserved, and for a long moment emotion suspended my voice and I could not speak, could only salute and bow my head.

Gideon set his hand on my shoulder, and with the gentle weight of his companionship there, it was all I could do to keep tears from spilling down my cheeks. I wasn't even sure what they were tears for, but they pressed on my eyes and constricted my throat all the same.

"It has been a hard road for us," he said. "And I cannot promise it will not get harder, but I can promise I will fight for our people and our right to exist in this world until there is no breath left in my body and no blood in my veins." He squeezed my shoulder. "The only easy road would be to lie down and die, and Levanti do not do that."

"No," I managed. "Levanti do not do that."

While I fought with the lump in my throat, he left his hand upon my shoulder, only dropping it back by his side when I looked up, his gentle manner so completely the embodiment of a herd patriarch that it almost overwhelmed me again to think of the home we had all lost.

"Let me know if there is anything you need, Captain," he said. "As an emperor I must maintain a certain dramatic aloofness for the Kisians to perceive me as powerful, but I am still your herd master."

He let me leave without further speech and I departed possessed of both renewed vigour and renewed hurt. No matter how much I tried to bury the suffering, to kill the memories, they were always there just beneath my skin, so close the smallest cut could send it leaking free.

A rumble of thunder welcomed me back to the courtyard. I had thought nothing could be worse than the mansion's airless gloom, but the increasing humidity made every breath an effort. Lightning cut toward the top of the gatehouse, and as I crossed the yard, Swords muttered and grumbled about the oncoming storm.

Jass en'Occha was waiting for me in Itaghai's stall. The meeting with Gideon had diverted my thoughts and I had forgotten all about him, but not wanting to be alone, not wanting to dwell on the memories that clung like the sticky night, I was grateful for my own apparent foresight.

He had finished brushing Itaghai's mane and moved on to his tail, adding diligence to a list of good traits so far made up entirely of strong shoulders and an impish smile. Jass looked over one of said shoulders and treated me to that smile. "My captain returns!"

"I am not your captain. If you are a First Sword then Taga is your captain."

"And a very good captain she is, but she has never trusted me with the grooming of her mount. He's got quite the attitude, your boy," he added, patting Itaghai's rump. "I have never seen a horse look so disdainful. I don't think he appreciated my stories."

"You told him stories?"

"Why not? I had to pass the time somehow." Jass set the brush down atop my open saddlebag. "Is there anything else I can do for you, Captain?"

I stepped in and the stall door swung closed behind me. Jass's smile became a grin. "Here?" he said, glancing at the straw piled in the corner farthest from Itaghai's hooves.

"Here," I said, and began to untie my belt. My fingers trembled upon the buckle and I hoped he wouldn't notice.

My swords hit the ground and he stepped in close, lips brushing mine. I turned my head, fear like a thousand needles on my skin. "No," I said. "Not that."

He stilled a moment, but it was only a moment before he chuckled and took my hand, pressing my palm to the hard bulge between his legs. "Just this then?" he said, his voice husky by my ear.

"Just that." I pulled my hand away, his gentleness cutting my shell as Gideon's had done. "I don't know you well enough to want anything else."

Jass shrugged and pulled off his breeches, and determined to match his confidence, I tugged down my own. They stuck to my sweaty skin, but I managed to free myself without falling over. He watched me all the while, his smile unwavering. Appreciative. Amused even, in an all too intimate way that filled me with the urge to run. Only Itaghai's presence, his smell, and the restless shift of his hooves stilled my rising panic.

I pushed Jass down into the straw and he landed with a laugh. The free and easy joy in the sound sent my gaze shying toward the door. None of the others had laughed like that. None of them had smiled so. They had only wanted the ride.

Determined not to let fear win, I lowered myself onto him. He groaned as he slid inside me. He crept his hands to my breasts. He gasped and laughed and wriggled beneath me, but I just gritted my teeth, exerting all the control I could over this man who had happily given himself up to me. And trying not to smell him or look at him, not to kiss him or taste him or feel him, we grunted together in the straw. Jass didn't last as long as any of the others and I liked him the better for it. We still both dripped sweat by the end.

"Nefer said you were wild," Jass said, wiping sweat from his forehead and grinning. "You can give me orders any day."

I had dug a rag from my saddlebag but spun back as though slapped. "What? Nefer told you?"

"Yeah, and when Amsu said you'd ridden him too I jumped at the chance to bring the herd master's message. I figured I'd do my part to satisfy."

My cheeks flamed hot. "You thought you'd do your part? Your duty?" I threw his breeches at his head. "Get the fuck out of here and tell your friends I'll have none of you back."

The slap of his breeches wiped away his smile. "What? I didn't mean—hey!" He threw up his arms to keep his sheathed blades from hitting his head, and still naked from the waist down I drew one of my swords from its scabbard. "Whoa! Hey!"

I lowered the tip toward his deflating cock. "I am not a conquest. I am not a joke. I am not a story you tell your friends so they can come fuck me too. I am a captain of the Jaroven and I will cut off your balls if you speak of me with the disrespect one speaks of an animal."

His bare feet scrambled for purchase on the hay-strewn floor as he backed away from my blade. "Whoa! Stop! I didn't say—I just—Get that fucking thing away from me! Are you mad?"

Backed into the corner of the stall, Jass thrust out a protective hand to ward off my blade, the other clutching his breeches to cover himself. Fear had widened his eyes and my anger drained like an ebbing tide. Here I was, a Sword captain of the mighty Jaroven, drawing my blade upon another Levanti in a stable yard far from home while the memory of him still ached inside me. Even Itaghai snorted and fretted, his hooves stirring the fresh hay in with the foul.

My hand trembled. I had drawn my blade. It had to taste blood before it could be sheathed and yet the man staring up from the corner deserved no such wrath. The Chiltaens who did were already dead.

Gripping the blade with my left hand, I spun the sword and offered him the hilt. "I allowed my anger to overthrow my judgement," I said. "The strike is yours to make."

Jass's eyes narrowed before he took the proffered sword. I wanted to clean myself and dress, but I stayed, hands at my sides, and waited for him to draw my blood. Hand? Arm? Throat? He might aim to kill if I had offended his pride as much as he had offended mine.

The blade hovered between us; then, still staring at me, he gripped the steel and ran its sharp edge across the back of his forearm. A thin trickle of blood dripped from the split skin, but he neither hissed nor sought to stem its flow. He handed my sword back. "I'm sorry. I meant you no offence, Captain." He got to his feet and, leaning against the wall, pulled on his breeches and boots. By the time he had finished I still had not moved. "Captain Dishiva," he said, and pressed his fists into a salute. With a pat for Itaghai and a grimace for me, he slid past me, out into the night.

The slam of the stall door sent me scrambling into my clothes, my cheeks burning as self-recrimination flooded my thoughts. What had I been thinking? Drawing my sword on another Levanti. And in such a situation. "Oh gods." I pressed my hands to my face. "What have I done?"

Itaghai made no sound, just watched as I fretted. "I am a fool, Itaghai," I said. "A fool. What sort of captain am I to—?"

A shout out in the courtyard interrupted my muttering. Another followed, and running footsteps passed. Grabbing my belt, I sped out through the stall door, buckling it on as I walked. A swell of excitement surged toward the gates.

"What's going on?" I said, catching sight of Captain Menesor e'Qara, accompanied by his second—a scowling woman whose name I could not recall.

"Someone is at the gates," she said.

"Someone should inform Herd Mas—" Captain Menesor broke off and his scowl became as deep as his second's. "Someone should inform His Majesty. Jaesha, send someone or go yourself if—"

"I am sure our new friends are capable of that, Captain." She gestured at the Kisians atop the watchtower. "If there are enemies, I would prefer to remain."

We reached the crowd of Levanti around the gates, all craning their necks, their hands upon their swords. Worried faces stared around and whispering hissed like shifting sands, but of an enemy there was no sign. Abandoning Menesor and Jaesha, I threaded my way through the crowd toward the sentries, pushing where I had to. Some swore after me, but the majority let me pass. Whatever tenets we'd had to let go to survive, respect for our captains remained.

Just inside the closed gates I found Lashak e'Namalaka already talking to the captains of the Sheth and Oht, along with Captain Atum e'Jaroven, my own First Sword. Captain Taga en'Occha was there too, and thinking of Jass, I found I could not meet her gaze.

"What's going on?" I saluted to Captain Atum. "There is talk of enemies at the gates."

He barked a laugh. "Enemies? No, not enemies. *Enemy.*"

I stared at him, comprehension seeming to travel a long way to be with me. "I am afraid I do not fully understand, Captain. Enemy? There is...only one person outside the gates?"

"So the lookouts say." He pointed up as he spoke, indicating the Levanti doing duty with the Kisians atop the short watchtower. The estate's walls were not tall, but they were thick and sturdy and could survive the attack of one enemy.

"We are worried about one man?"

Captain Taga laughed, but as with Captain Atum's bark there was little humour in it. "It is not the number of enemies we are concerned about."

"Then what?"

"Make way for His Majesty!"

Shouts rose behind us and the gathering parted with a scuffing of boots on stone. Gideon approached, accompanied by a pair of Swords dressed in imperial colours. The little old Kisian from earlier was with him too, his shoulders hunched as though trying to be invisible. I pitied him the cruel twists of fate that had landed him in such a position.

"Open the gates," Gideon said as he halted, his grand silk coat swept so far back that he looked more like the Levanti captain we had followed across these strange lands.

"Are you sure, Herd Master?" Captain Taga said, stroking the fletching of an arrow. "We could just turn him into a hedgehog."

"No. Open the gates."

Captain Atum, never one to delegate something he could do himself, strode forward. Another man might have looked back to check his herd master had not changed his mind, but not Atum. He lifted the bar that held the gates locked and let it drop to the ground with a thud. Distant thunder rumbled in its wake, but no one spoke or moved, the host of Swords gathered before the gates having stilled, ready to fight.

Atum gripped one of the gates, Taga the other, and with twin grunts of effort they heaved. A crack of night appeared between them, growing ever wider as the gates swung open. And in the widening aperture stood a single figure. A shadow against the night.

Whispering spread. Eyes darted from Gideon to the newcomer and back, but neither moved until the gates banged open. The new arrival approached. Slow, deliberate, confident of their welcome. They stopped a few paces from Gideon. A pale hand pushed back the hood.

And there, before the brewing storm, stood Dom Leo Villius. Same hair. Same eyes. Same smile. Even the linen mask hanging around his neck looked the same as the one we had burned. Yet he owned no scars though we had sliced his throat. No disfigurement though we had cut off his lips and put out his eyes—eyes that looked from me to Taga to Atum and around the gathered throng before finally coming to rest upon Gideon with the weight of a hundred lost heads.

"Good evening, Your Majesty."

3. CASSANDRA

The bitch wouldn't stop staring at me. No pretty scenery drew her attention. No amount of noise from outside. Not even the jolting of the carriage. And when day turned to night, her oddly hued eyes went on cutting into my flesh.

"Stop it," I said to no effect. I had tried swearing at her—long strings of colourful language gleaned from the melting pot of the Genavan docks—but she had just stared all the harder. Silent she might be, but she understood just fine. And didn't now look away. I rolled my eyes with a heavy sigh. "Stop staring at me. *Please.*"

A small smile twitched her lips and she turned her attention to the slumped figure of Empress Hana Ts'ai beside me. It was worth asking nicely for ten minutes' respite from those searing violet eyes.

She's schooling you well, Cassandra, She said, speaking in my head for the first time since climbing back into the carriage. Empress Hana hadn't woken at the last stop, but the Witchdoctor had checked on her all the same, ignoring my presence entirely as he put a hand to her forehead and her throat and checked her fingers. *Perhaps I should have tried making you ask nicely.*

"It wouldn't have worked," I muttered.

The violet eyes snapped back to me, the young woman tilting her head as though examining an interesting specimen.

"I wasn't talking to you."

She did not look away.

"Her Imperial Majesty is far more interesting than me. Look, that stuff your god-man shoved down her throat stained her lips purple, and her hair is a mess."

No reply. No movement.

I stared out the window at the rushing night, although the problem with staring at night is there's nothing to actually look at. For a while there had been flickers of moonlit fields and villages and even the glint of light on water, but now there was nothing but darkness. We had stopped only to eat and drink and change horses, this journey all too reminiscent of travelling into Kisia with Leo. How clever I had felt knowing it was me he was trying to outrun.

Light flashed outside, but all that awaited beyond the opposite window was more darkness. The girl must have seen it too for she covered the open face of the lantern, darkening the interior of the carriage as she peered out. Empress Hana snuffled like a sleeping bear. Outside, a great, jagged streak of lightning cut the sky and disappeared into the shadowy trees, leaving a bright flash across my eyes.

It looks like we'll get to see the rains after all, She said.

I'm not sure that's a good thing.

Certainly not for the army if they haven't taken Mei'lian yet.

I nodded my silent agreement as the young woman uncovered the lantern, returning a diffuse glow to the close space. Shielding her eyes, she pressed her nose to the thick glass of the window. It was the most interesting sign of life she had yet shown, but whether satisfied or not she soon sat back, fixing her gaze on nothing.

Afraid of the rains? Perhaps she worried they would hit before we reached our destination, which meant there was still some way to go. Still time to get out of here.

Out of here? She said, riding my thoughts. *This is where we wanted to be. Where you wanted to be.*

I never asked to be sold into slavery. Who knows what horrible things he plans to do to me.

Oh yes, She agreed. *Like feeding you and checking you're healthy and—*

Like an owned animal.

When She made no answer, I leaned against the side of the carriage and tried to doze. I had been awake all day and night and still I could not sleep, could only listen for the patter of rain. Beneath me the coach wheels rumbled and the clatter of hooves made their own distant thunder, but inside there were just the gentle snuffles of a sleeping empress and, after a time, the rustle of turning pages. I shifted my head enough to peer through slitted eyes at the girl. A red leather-bound book lay open on her lap, gold glinting at the top of its spine. Many of Genava's richest men had kept bound books, but in all my time visiting them for one purpose or another, I had never seen one painted in gold. It must have been important.

I managed to doze. I had thought it only a short rest but the carriage was light when I next opened my eyes. It wasn't particularly bright light, rather the sort of weak, watery stuff of misty winter mornings. After so little sleep my eyes ached, but rubbing them was like rubbing sand into open wounds.

"Fuck," I groaned, throwing my bound hands up to shield my eyes.

Cass.

"Go away."

No! Cass, listen!

At the anxious note in her voice I held my breath to listen. Carriage wheels, horses, little rustles from the other corner and—

Rain.

I sat up, blinking. The empress was awake but did not look at me; neither did the young woman on the opposite seat. She was peering out the window at the slashes of water cutting through the air, obscuring her view like a thousand swarming insects.

It would obscure me too as I ran as far away from here as I could go.

No, don't do it, Cass, please!

"I need to piss."

The young woman looked around. So did Her Imperial Majesty, and I could not meet her disdainful gaze. Though the violet-eyed woman said nothing, it wasn't hard to guess the meaning of her frown.

"Yes, I can see it's raining," I said. "But either you stop the carriage so I can piss out there or I'll piss in here."

The young woman just stared at me until I lifted my brows and said, "Well? Street life has given me pretty good aim for a woman."

A flash of disgust animated her expression, and after wrinkling her nose she knocked hard upon the carriage roof. The rap was barely audible over the pounding rain yet a shout sounded outside and the carriage slowed to a jolting stop. A man wrenched open the door and stood there with rain splatting upon the sloping hood of his storm cloak. Behind him the Witchdoctor cut a grim figure on horseback.

"What is required?" he said as rain ran down his face. His head was uncovered, but the weather seemed not to bother him.

"I need to piss," I said, and rose from my seat without waiting for a reply. Bent double, I shuffled past the Empress of Kisia's jutting knees and out into the storm. Fat heavy drops pelted me like stones and within seconds I was drenched through. We were not strangers to storms in Chiltae and I had often wondered why so many traders feared the Kisian rains, but no storm hitting Genava had ever left me feeling bruised.

The carriage door closed, and unflinching beneath the downpour, the Witchdoctor pointed at a hazy clump of trees. "We are too distant from any settlement. It is unfortunate your bladder cannot hold more urine as you will now be saturated for the rest of the journey."

Too stunned by the rain trying to beat me into the ground, I just stared at him. He stared back, his beautiful features lacking all expression.

"You are not moving," he said, shifting a loose lock of wet hair from his brow. "You may relieve yourself here if that is your preference. It makes no difference to me."

I hadn't been desperate to go, but the fierce patter of the rain had increased my need tenfold and I pulled myself together. "Trees are good." I considered asking him to untie my hands but that would only make him wary to my true purpose, so I trudged past him through the sheeting rain. It was like swimming through air, every breath a gasp.

My feet sank into a puddle as I stepped off the road, leaving my boots squelching with every step. Sure the Witchdoctor was watching, I didn't dare look back, nor even think too loudly as I tottered into the trees.

The Witchdoctor followed a little way into the copse and sat watching as I selected a good pissing tree. "Hey, why don't you give me some privacy," I shouted, hooking my bound hands into my breeches. "It's hard to piss when someone's watching."

The god-man didn't answer, but he turned his horse and walked out of sight. His horse's dark-haired tail disappeared with a final limp swish, and I counted three painfully long seconds. Then I pulled my hands from my breeches and ran. My feet slipped on the sloppy loam, but not caring which way I went I sped deeper into the trees, crashing through shrubs and slapping away reaching branches.

Desperation powered my fatigued body on. The sodden trees all looked the same, but even getting lost would be better than being the Witchdoctor's prisoner. How the fuck had I ended up running from a nutter in western Kisia?

Because we need help, Cassandra!

The hollow shell of a dead tree appeared atop a rise and I veered toward it, digging my feet into the muddy slope. Perhaps if I could fit inside I could hide, could wait for them to leave, to—

A sharp pain pierced my leg, stealing my breath. I staggered back, overbalanced, and rolled backward down the slope until the pain in my head and arse almost equalled that in my calf. Hissing through bared teeth, I gripped my leg only to find the smooth wood of an arrow shaft protruding above my ankle.

"Fuck!" I tried to get up, but my feet slid and every movement made the arrow bounce. I gritted my teeth so hard thunder roared in my ears.

Movement flickered ahead and the Witchdoctor calmly regarded me from the back of his horse, bow in hand.

"It would appear that I am out of practice," he said, it a mere curious observation.

"You just put an arrow through my leg, you fucking piece of—" I broke off with a howl as I tried to get up and my head spun.

"If you owned no desire to be hunted then you ought not to have run like common game. Do you intend to attempt further flight, or are you content with having endeavoured to escape once? I surmise to continue would be painful as well as irksome, but many humans own a level of stubbornness that heeds not their well-being."

I stared at him, at this man who called himself a god, who spoke like a pompous governess and sat in the rain like he could not feel it, and all hope of freedom seeped from me. I could hobble at best and the man had more arrows. He was a wall against which I could beat myself senseless, an endless sea owning no shore. Yet he had not killed me. Had not beaten me. Had not touched me at all.

He wanted me alive and well, and that, more than anything else, chilled me to the bone.

My only hope lay in finding a freshly dead body, then She—

Cass, he called you a Deathwalker when he spoke to the hieromonk. He knows.

I looked into those slowly blinking eyes—a dull grey yet sharp as glass.

He can see me, Cass.

But I couldn't just let him haul me back. I could still try, could—

You're the one who took the job to get to the Witchdoctor. You wanted to be free. The only difference is that now I want it too. Don't make me fight you.

Free.

Do you really think there's still a chance? I said.

Yes. I have to.

"I'm done," I said, forcing a smile more mocking and confident than I felt. "But you're right, I feel better for having tried." I gestured to the arrow. "How else could I experience such joy as this?"

The man walked his horse toward me. His intent was clear, though if he expected me to climb onto his horse's back with bound hands and a shaft of wood wobbling in my leg then he too would be subjected to my litany of curse words. But rather than command me to climb up, he sheathed his bow and leaned out of the saddle. He gripped the back of my tunic and lifted me off the ground like a puppy. My collar cut into my throat and my sleeves dug painfully into my underarms, but after a few seconds dangling he dumped me before him on the horse. Before I could complain about such ignominious handling, he set the animal walking, its every step making the arrow bounce.

Emerging from the trees' protective canopy, we were once more hit with the full force of the storm. On the road the carriage waited, water dripping from the horses and the pointed tip of the driver's hood. Behind it stood the covered cart, its load easier for the oxen without the long, heavy wooden box the hieromonk had exchanged me for.

Instead of returning me to the carriage door, the Witchdoctor urged his horse toward the back of the covered cart.

"Kocho," he said. "A companion for you."

No answer, just the heavy drumming of the storm. If I stayed in the rain much longer it would carve ravines in my flesh like rivers cutting stone.

"Kocho."

The cart wobbled and the canvas flaps parted. An old face peered out, the sort of well-aged Kisian man whose skin had much in common with boot leather. "Master?"

Once more the Witchdoctor gripped a handful of my tunic and lifted me from the saddle. I wanted to kick and scream and point out I was neither child nor dog, but before I could think of anything clever to say he had half thrust me, half thrown me through the gap in the canvas. I hit the cart's dry wooden boards with a cry as the end of the arrow snapped off, digging the head farther into my leg. Light and shadows swirled as I sucked great gasps of air.

The cart jolted forward and the rustling of paper mingled with the drumming rain. "Bloody storms," the old man muttered. "And then here you come bringing your puddles and your blood."

"It's not like I wanted to bring either," I snapped when the pain ebbed enough to speak. "You could just let me go and I'll take my puddles and blood with me."

"I'm not stopping you."

I pushed up on my elbows. The man sat at the driver's end of the cart with a small lap table and a lot of papers. A lantern hung over him, hooked upon the cart's frame, and there was nothing—nothing at all—standing between me and freedom. As the cart rocked the canvas flaps fluttered, allowing brief glimpses of the rainswept road beyond, pale in the morning light.

"Have you got a bow stashed here too?"

"No," the man said. "I never was very good with one of those."

He was busy stacking his scrolls and papers as far from me and my puddles as he could and didn't look up. "What will you do if I try to run, then?" I said. "Just shout for the god-man?"

"I could, but I wouldn't bother. He'd hear you. Damn it, where did I put the Boesia?"

"Hear me? Over this rain?"

"Try it if you doubt me."

I stared a long time at the sheeting rain through the crack in the canvas. Surely he wouldn't hear me, whatever the old man said. If I lowered myself onto the road and found a ditch to hide in, I might not even have to run.

"Look, if you're going to do it, just do it," the man said, breaking upon my thoughts. "Thinking about it over and over is noisy and annoying."

"Then help me escape."

"No."

"Why not? I could kill you with a single kick."

"With which leg? The one with the arrow in it or the one without?"

Having finished piling the scrolls, he took up a quill and a fresh page and began scratching words in Kisian. We shared a common oral language, but I'd never understood any of the symbols they used to write it down.

I looked back at the opening.

We're stuck, Cass. Just let it go. It's for the best.

"You should listen to your friend," the old man said. "She's smarter than you."

"What did you say?"

"I said that your companion is smarter than you. Maybe if you listened more often you wouldn't be lying here bleeding near my papers."

"What companion?"

Still writing, the man tapped the side of his head with his free hand.

I tensed like a drawn bow. "How do you know?"

The old man stretched out his arm, the last two inches of his wrist protruding from his short sleeve. In the lantern light a pale red mark glared—a line curved like a snake.

"Did you burn yourself with some sort of iron?"

"No, I was born with it."

"And what is it?"

"If you don't know then you're in for quite the surprise."

Empress Hana had demanded to see my wrist back in Koi and been surprised to find it bare. Captain Aeneas too.

The man tucked his hand back into his lap. Like his master, he left me with the distinct feeling that, injured leg or no, I was at a disadvantage. He knew things I didn't and his bored, superior tone was almost as irritating as the Witchdoctor's.

"So why are you stuck in here instead of getting to ride in the warm, dry carriage?" I said.

"Stuck in here?" He looked up for the first time. "I chose to ride in here rather than get *stuck* with you, but then you went and got yourself all wet and covered in piss, and of course the young mistress's health is far more important than mine. He can't risk her getting wet and sick and dying, so old Kocho has to deal with you instead. And to think I almost stayed home. I'm getting far too old and creaky for these acquisitions, though most of the others aren't as foul-mouthed and unpleasant. It just goes to show what's inside does not always match what's outside."

He returned to his papers, but his words had whipped raw

wounds and I spat at him. I had been aiming for his face but his flash of anger as saliva hit his page made it triumph enough. Without a word he pinched the corner of the paper and lifted it only to let it go over a puddle at my feet. While rainwater consumed it, Kocho dipped his quill in the ink and started a fresh page.

Cass, we need allies, not more enemies.

A smile quirked Kocho's lips and again he tapped the side of his head with his free hand.

If you can't be nice then let me talk to him. I promise I'll let you have the body back when I am done. You could use a break from the pain.

"No." Too well did I recall being merely a passenger in my own skin, and I was in no hurry to relive the experience. So before she could argue, insist, or take control by force, I cleared my throat and dredged up the persona that had gone unused for many weeks now—Cassandra Marius, finest whore in Genava. Politeness and deference were easier to swallow when I knew them to be an act.

"Where are we going?" I said, disliking the knowing twitch of Kocho's lips.

"Home."

"And where is home? Your master appears to be a wealthy man."

Kocho snorted a rough laugh. "Yes and no. He wants for nothing, but that is not the same thing as being rich to your way of thinking. When you've lived out of the world as long as I have you realise how foolish such things as titles and gold are. You begin to measure wealth in knowledge and respect instead."

That sounded like scripture, so I let it go and said, "No fancy palace then. But that doesn't answer my question."

"No, it doesn't."

"You're not going to tell me where we're going?"

"No. We keep it secret. Too many people don't like the master."

"I can't imagine why."

A barb of sarcasm pierced my practised charm, and Kocho gave me a look out of the corner of his eye. "He's not a Witchdoctor. People just like scary stories to explain what they don't understand."

"He put an arrow through me."

"He'll take it out again. *And* he'll sew you up leaving barely a scar because if there's one thing the master is good at, it's bodies. Just leave it in and he'll fix it once we stop."

"In the meantime, I'm just meant to sit here and bleed out?"

Kocho sighed. "If you sit still you won't bleed out."

"I might."

"You won't."

"You're a physician then?"

"No, but the master needs you and he likes his subjects healthy, so he would have fixed it already if he thought you were in danger of bleeding out."

Subject. I didn't like the sound of that word and my gaze once more shied toward the opening at the back of the cart.

Don't be stupid. Running isn't going to work. Besides, we need this man. I thought we just agreed on that?

There is no we, I thought savagely into the safety of my head, my features twisting with silent vehemence. *Your attempts to take over my body are what got us here in the first place. Who knows what he really means to do with us.*

Anything is better than being your passenger forever.

I scowled at the light twisting its shapes upon the interior of the canvas cover. All of this was the hieromonk's fault. He had come into my life and offered me salvation in return for just one more kill. I ought to have ended the job free of Her and rich enough to retire; instead I was lying wounded inside a cart that stank increasingly of piss, with not only my eternal companion but also a grumpy old man. To top it off, we were travelling to nowhere with a god-man and a silent bitch, to be poked and prodded to see how

I worked, no doubt until I died. Or at least until I wished myself dead.

You're really dense when you get in these self-pitying moods.

What do you mean? I asked.

You weren't listening, were you?

I rolled my eyes. I hated her superior tone and She knew it. *Listening to what?*

The man, Kocho, he said "the master needs you."

To test stuff on.

Yes, but why put up with a foul-mouthed old whore who threatens to piss on people and spits on their work if you don't have to? There are thousands of other people he could have picked up. He needs you. Us. Specifically. And that leverage can get us what we want.

I stared at the side of Kocho's face. He had said we were needed. Had said too that his master wouldn't let me bleed out.

Let's see how much leverage I have then, shall we? I said.

I gripped the broken arrow shaft, my heart beating hard at the very thought of what I was about to do.

No, Cass, don't do—

"No!" Kocho dropped his quill as I tightened my grip and yanked the arrowhead out. I felt the flesh tear as though it were sound, ripping skin and muscle and pain. The space spun and flashes of bright light behind my eyes became spreading darkness. But I dropped my head, fighting to stay afloat, regret bitter like the bile in my throat.

"You fool!" Kocho snapped over the hissing swear words leaving my lips like a leaking bellows. "Master! Master!"

As my head spun and blood leaked onto my hands, I managed a laugh. "Guess I am important after all."

4. MIKO

I held Hacho to me like a child, protecting her from the rain. It pelted us mercilessly, the high canopy doing nothing more than collecting the drops so they might fall heavier and harder upon our already saturated heads.

Perched on a nearby branch, General Kitado hunched his shoulders like a sodden blackbird. "It doesn't look like they've left anyone behind, Your Majesty," he said, having to raise his voice to be heard over the rain. It slapped the leaves like drums. "Seems they don't plan to split up."

He scowled through a gap in the trees as the Levanti leader appeared on the road, the distance shrinking his great height. He had donned one of Kin's battle surcoats. My fingers flexed. I wanted to put an arrow through his eye then rip it from his corpse.

"Careful, Your Majesty," General Kitado said as I shifted my weight on the branch. "You kill him now and there'll be no Empress Miko to fight for Kisia."

"I know. That doesn't mean I have to like it."

"It's next to impossible from here anyway."

I smiled. "I know."

At least fifty paces through dancing leaves in the rain, and he a moving figure. Almost the challenge proved too much for my resolve, but I just tightened my hold around Hacho and wondered if my father could have done it.

As the leaves once more swallowed the Levanti leader I relaxed a little. I hadn't enough arrows to hit them all, but had my life been less important I would have revelled in one last glory as I brought down as many of the usurping bastards as I could. But my life was important. My life and my name and my face. I was the last surviving Otako, and Kisia needed me. Alive.

More Levanti passed beyond the gap in the leaves. A few others wore crimson surcoats heavy with rain while the rest looked the same as they had in battle, only wet and bedraggled. They had carts too, their loads covered and drawn by oxen they had certainly not brought with them. And palanquins. Crimson and gold silk peeked from beneath their rain covers while the carriers wore heavy storm cloaks with the Ts'ai dragon picked out in gold upon their backs.

"Do the Chiltaens have so little respect for us that they would give such things away as the spoils of war?" I hissed, gesturing at the silk-clad Levanti.

"I cannot say, Your Majesty, but that is certainly how it looks."

"Why are they leaving? Have they been released from service?"

General Kitado shifted his weight. It caused his branch to shake, but the sound was nothing to the rain. "They may also have left because the Chiltaens didn't pay them enough. Or because the rain is bad for their horses. Better to take their spoils and go."

"Mercenaries," I spat. "No sense of loyalty or honour."

"Better they go. We know how to fight Chiltaens."

I grumbled agreement and for a time we watched the procession in silence. The worst of the thunder had passed in the night, but the rain showed no sign of letting up. I had often watched such storms vent their rage upon the palace, and though I had dreaded their coming for the isolation they brought, they had never caused me discomfort. General Ryoji had set up archery targets inside at my request, and if I chose to ride, I could always wait for brief respites in the weather. Now I was at its mercy, owning no shelter, no storm cloak, no safety or warmth or food, nothing but my sword and my bow and the stoic company of General Kitado.

"So the Chiltaens have taken Mei'lian," I said when the main bulk of the Levanti horde had passed. "And even without the Levanti they have still conquered a huge chunk of the empire. We need a plan. We need allies."

"Minister Manshin said I ought to take you south, Your Majesty. Or to Syan."

I bit at some dry skin on my lip and stared at nothing. "South where? To whom? Who can we be sure won't have given their allegiance to Jie?"

"Then to Syan."

Grace Bahain had been expected at Risian. He had been hoped for at Mei'lian. And he had not come. *Grace Bahain was a loyal minister before he became Duke of Syan*, Kin had said, with almost his dying breaths. *He must be made to remember that. You must help him and his son remember that.*

I went on gnawing at my lip, tugging at the dry skin. "Perhaps." Edo had always shared his news from home on the infrequent occasions his father wrote to him, and no one who had ever heard Grace Bahain's views on Chiltaens and pirates, and more specifically Chiltaen pirates, could believe he would ally himself with them. But why else had he not come to our aid? Why had Edo not written back?

"Either way, we need to decide," Kitado said. "We cannot stay here, Your Majesty. The Chiltaens will be looking for you by now."

The Chiltaens wouldn't know about the tunnel, but once they had scoured the city for me without success they would hunt me outside its walls, might even consider, as I was doing, what places I might seek refuge.

"Perhaps for now it would be safest to find somewhere to lie low, Your Majesty," he said when I didn't answer. "No matter where we travel, being out in the open is a risk."

"That cannot be helped. It is my job to protect Kisia, and to do so I must find allies."

"And it is my job to protect you, Your Majesty, but I cannot do that if you will not listen to my advice."

He did not meet my gaze. I was his empress and he was not allowed to challenge me with a stare whatever our current predicament. "I wish to damn your good advice to the hells, my friend," I said. "No matter how right I know you are. If we could but find out which of our generals are still alive and where our remaining battalions are, if any have survived. We need information and we won't get that sitting here at the edge of the fen."

He didn't answer, just let the heavy patter of the rain speak the hopelessness he could not voice.

Once the last of the Levanti were long gone, I began the slippery climb back down the tree. It was slow going, ensuring a good grip on slick branches while all around me the rain continued, its drops sticking loose clumps of hair to my forehead and dripping down my back. It would have been easier without Hacho, but I kept my stolen cloak wrapped around her and stopped frequently to swap her hand to hand. Kitado made no complaint despite having to slow his own descent to await mine.

At last my feet found firm ground and I kicked away the leaves covering our supplies. In the tree's roots, he had left a single water skin, some dried meat that was no longer very dry, and a pair of blankets knotted into a makeshift satchel Kitado carried upon his back. It was soaked through and I was not looking forward to seeking sleep under a sodden blanket with wet leaves for my pillow. I had slept little the previous night even without the rain. Kitado had insisted I try to rest while he kept watch, but all I had achieved was a fitful doze and an aching neck. Three days since we had escaped Mei'lian through the tunnel and already I felt fractured and raw, like I was held together with fraying twine.

A heavy thud heralded Kitado's return to the ground. He adjusted his sword belt and made to straighten his surcoat only to drop his hand. We had left all imperial trappings behind, thrust down a foxhole where the tunnel had spat us out north of the Tzitzi River.

"If we have scattered battalions left they are more likely to be in the north," I said, as he took up the soaked blankets in place of his surcoat. "And they won't expect us to go that way."

"They won't expect it because it's far too dangerous to risk, Your Majesty. The bulk of the Chiltaen force may be at Mei'lian, but they will have small camps linking them back to the border because that's what Chiltaens do. And they won't just have one scouting party out looking for you, they'll have everyone."

"All right, maybe not north then, but I will not hide."

He grimaced. "Heading east to Syan may serve the same purpose. The eastern battalions must be out there somewhere."

I let out a long breath, hating the itch of worry that struck whenever I thought of Grace Bahain. He had been pleased to meet me in Koi, but that had been before Tanaka's death, before the Chiltaens had poured across the border with their barbarian mercenaries, before everything I had ever known and fought for had come crashing down around me. But Kitado was right. Those battalions had to still be out there.

"Syan then," I said. "Could we use the river?"

"Too risky this far upstream, but east of Quilin we could, and it would beat walking all the way."

"We might even get news from Kogahaera at Quilin."

"Yes, and Grace Bahain is sure to have marched that way if he left Syan. The mangroves along the river are too thick for so many foot soldiers."

I pressed my lips into a grim smile. "I am pleased to have you agree on something for once, General."

He shrugged the shoulder not burdened with soggy blankets. "I do not disagree to be contrary, Your Majesty."

He set off ahead of me, a hand upon his sword hilt and his head always turning, watchful in the downpour. His keen senses had saved us from more than one run-in as we skirted the wild edge of Nivi Fen, though whether we would have encountered enemies or allies or bandits was hard to say. Nivi Fen had always been an ink-blot on the empire's map, a tangled swampland that had rejected all attempts to build on, through, or even near it, and harboured those who wished, for one reason or another, not to come to the emperor's attention. The rains would flush many of its inhabitants to higher ground, which was as good a reason as any for us not to linger within its grasp.

I followed General Kitado at a distance, trying to keep my thoughts upon our situation and my eyes upon our surrounds. The rain made it difficult, falling upon the landscape like a misty curtain while its endless hammering stole all but the loudest sounds from my ears. I couldn't even tell where we were going. Everything melded together, the edge of the fen all tall twisty trees choked with vines that trailed across the path to trip unwary travellers. I saved myself from one's reaching thorns as a road appeared on my left. A road all too like the one we had just watched the Levanti travel.

I stopped. General Kitado walked a few paces then turned back with his sword half drawn.

"We're going south," I said, as he slid the blade back into its scabbard and bowed an apology. "I thought we were heading to Syan."

He readjusted the blankets upon his shoulder. "We will, Your Majesty, but I would rather put a few hours between us and those Levanti heading north. Better to cross the Willow Road closer to the Tzitzi so we can use the mangroves to conceal our passage along the riverbank."

"And you didn't tell me because I'm so impatient I would have ignored your fine advice?"

The general once more shrugged his unencumbered shoulder and, catching sight of my wry smile, allowed himself one of his own. "Something like that, Your Majesty."

"All right, south a bit farther, but then we need to stop fearing to cross the road and just do it."

A sharp nod, a far more humourless smile, and General Kitado continued his long-legged stride south. The tunnel from Mei'lian had taken us farther north than I had expected. We'd rested in its darkness, only to emerge squinting into the light of a new day— no, a new world. I kept thinking it could all be a dream, that if we walked back to Mei'lian we would find a city just going about its day, no conquering Chiltaens in sight. But my hands were covered in cuts from digging clear the tunnel mouth, and whenever I closed my eyes the people of Mei'lian crowded around me in the darkness, offering prayers. We had fought and we had lost, but I would not give in even if I had to fight alone.

That possibility weighed on my mind more than I had let General Kitado guess. Prince Jie, with his three battalions and his true Ts'ai parentage, would easily garner support in the south. He could already be mounting an attack upon our conquerors and succeeding where I had failed. Without allies I could do nothing, would be nothing, and may as well have died gloriously protecting my city than suffer the ignoble fate of merely fading away, powerless and alone.

General Kitado halted, breaking me from my morose thoughts.

We had come to the edge of a track, dual ruts suggesting the regular passage of carts. The ruts were little better than muddy gouges filled with water, but the fresh hoof prints were not.

Crouching, the general held up a warning hand as he examined the prints. "Two horses," he said. "Travelling west not so long since."

"Two? Are you sure?"

He nodded. "Some of the hooves are shod and the others are not."

"Not shod? In this weather?"

"A Levanti horse, perhaps, but it seems unlikely they'd venture into the fen. Might just be a Kisian unprepared for the season."

I peered into the rain-soaked trees, but there were only leaves and trunks and rain, its incessant fall having long since made a mockery of my clothing. It clung to my skin, choking and cold, and for a single, harrowing moment I wished it all undone. What I wouldn't give to be somewhere warm and dry, and perhaps if I hadn't been so determined, so ambitious, so completely *me*, I could have been in Chiltae by now married to Leo Villius. Comfortable. Safe. Kisia still whole.

"They may also be the tracks of Chiltaen scouts," General Kitado said, crouching to trace the hoof prints with a finger. "On the other hand, they could belong to Kisian scouts. If Grace Bahain knows you weren't captured in Mei'lian, he could be looking for us too."

"It may be nothing, but we should check," I said, the lure of potential allies outweighing my fears. "There are two of them and two of us and we have the element of surprise on our side."

He agreed with his one-shouldered shrug and I started along the track. Not far along, a house emerged from the storm haze like an animal hunkered against the rain. Half a dozen outbuildings surrounded it like cubs, and as we approached along the track a horse came into view, owning no rider. "A fur trader, perhaps," Kitado said. "Or a woodcutter."

A burst of shouting halted us in our tracks, and General Kitado thrust out his arm as though shielding me from a rush of unseen enemies. "Trouble," he said, not taking his eyes off the house. "We ought to leave."

"What sort of trouble?" I pushed his arm aside and took a few steps forward, squinting at shadows through rain. A few more steps and grey, misty figures were born from the mire, along with the restless form of a second, larger horse carrying something bulky.

The shouts were indistinct, panic all I could distinguish as I sped my pace.

"Majesty!" Kitado hissed, dashing alongside. "It could be enemies. It could be—"

"It could be Kisians in need of help," I said, thinking of that crowd of people who had looked to me as their saviour, all of whom I had failed. "If I cannot help my own people then what use am I?"

"Majesty, this is not wise."

"What's not wise is you continuing to call me 'Majesty.'"

The grey outlines grew steadily clearer as we approached at a jog. Two figures became three, one outstretched hand became a sword, another an axe, and words that had been just babble became Chilt-aen pleas. "I am not here to steal your gold, my friend—"

"Back, you monster!"

"I beg your help, I—"

"Help so you can attack me when my back is turned?"

I unwrapped the wool cloak from about Hacho and rushed forward, Kitado contenting himself with a grunt of annoyance as he kept pace. Splashing through the puddles, I abandoned stealth and nocked an arrow to Hacho's string.

"Halt!" I shouted. The group stilled to a tableau as I took in the scene. A Kisian man and woman, armed with an axe and a stick, stood before the door. Despite his voice, their assailant was no Chiltaen, rather a young man who looked Levanti but for the length of black hair stuck to his back. A few paces behind him a pair of horses fretted and shook their manes. One was small, its Kisian saddle marked with the Ts'ai dragon, while the other, an enormous animal, carried a second man thrown like meat over its saddle.

The three conscious members of the scene lifted their arms as I levelled an arrow at each in turn, eventually lingering upon the long-haired Levanti. "What is going on here?"

"This barbarian came to rob us of—"

"I did not! I—"

"You threatened us with your sword!"

"Only when you tried to remove my head with your axe! Please." The young man turned to me, his hands pressed together in supplication. "I know I am your enemy, but I don't wish to be. I only wish help for my friend. He is injured. He has lost blood and I fear he will not live much longer."

Without taking my eyes from the Levanti, I nodded to Kitado. "Check he is telling the truth."

"I swear! I seek only shelter and help. I will seek it elsewhere if you will let me go."

"Your friend might die if you do," Kitado said as he examined the unconscious man. "It might be too late already."

The young man sank to his knees despite the axe still threateningly close. I licked my lips. Kitado had been right, not only dangerous to come but a waste of time, playing saviour to a pair of peasants in no danger from an all-but-dead Levanti and his distraught comrade.

I lowered Hacho, annoyed I had exposed her to the rain for nothing. We could have been half a mile closer to the river by now instead of half a mile out of the way.

"You had best say goodbye to your friend and catch up with the rest of your people," I said. "We saw them not long since, heading north to the border."

The young man looked up, grief frozen upon his face. "The border?"

"Yes, isn't that how one leaves Kisia?"

His brows dropped, darkening his eyes. "Leaving? They aren't leaving." His brows sank lower still. "Who are you?"

"I could ask the same question of a barbarian mercenary who can speak the Chiltaen tongue."

My question failed to turn him from his purpose, and he looked me up and down with an intensity even the boldest courtier had never dared employ.

"You say they are not leaving," General Kitado said, stepping away from the injured man. "If they are not leaving, where are they going? Have the Chiltaens given them—given *you*—new orders?"

The young man stared from Kitado to me and back again, his jaw slack.

"Well?" I said when he didn't answer. "You were asked a question. It would be wise to answer it. You are outnumbered."

"No."

"No?" I lifted Hacho again, re-nocking the arrow. "Would you like to try that answer again?"

The long-haired Levanti drew himself up and stared straight at the arrow, daring it to pierce his flesh. "No," he said. "If you want answers then you must help me. Help my friend."

Arrow unwavering, I glanced at Kitado. He scowled. "How do we know your information is worth our time?"

"My information is well worth your time. And so is his." He pointed at the prone Levanti. Rain was dripping from his dangling fingers and the toes of his boots. "This man is Rah e'Torin, herd brother of Gideon e'Torin, the new emperor of Kisia."

The arrow fell from my hand, bowstring slackening as my jaw dropped. I could not have heard him right. Beside me Kitado said, "What?"

"Will you help him?"

"Help you bury him?"

The young man's chin set mulishly, while huddled in the doorway the peasant and his wife were whispering fast. I could feel Kitado's gaze on me but couldn't turn, could only stare at the young Levanti and hunt every line of his face for proof he was lying.

"Maj—" Kitado cleared his throat. "What do you wish me to do? I could make him talk if—"

The young man turned. "You can do no worse than has already been done to me," he spat. "The only way you get answers is by saving my friend."

I glanced at the unconscious Levanti. Brother of the emperor? So drastic a change in the situation made information vital, but to stay and help meant time—time I could ill afford to lose.

Lowering Hacho, I beckoned the general and he came, bending his head close to mine. "We must find out all we can. I fear there is more at stake here than we realise."

"I agree, Majesty," he rumbled in my ear. "But I am not sure we can trust them. They are Levanti."

I looked again at the young man, biting his lip and hugging his arms across his chest. His sword lay forgotten in the mud. Even so, the woodcutter and his wife watched him warily. And me, their eyes equally upon Hacho as the barbarian. Behind them light flickered merrily inside their hut, promising comfort. Dry. There would be food and a sleeping mat that did not squelch.

"We have to," I said. "But I don't think they will accept us lightly. You may have to tell these people you are a lord and I am your daughter. I fear to speak the truth even to my own people."

"As you wish, Majesty."

"Make the arrangements. I will look at the injured one and see what's amiss."

He would have bowed but stopped himself in time, turning it into a nod before approaching the woodcutter with his hands spread wide in welcome. Disliking the man's continuing stare, I picked up my arrow and draped my woollen cloak over Hacho.

The great Levanti horse sidestepped as I approached, but it neither reared nor bolted when I stroked its neck. "Good boy," I said. "I am going to look at your burden now, so don't move, will you?"

The man draped over the saddle looked more like a Levanti than his pleading companion, with all his hair shaved off and a pale raised scar on the back of his head, shaped like a horse and moon. Unlike the other, however, he was dressed in Kisian clothing, a mixture of standard military attire and the finer uniform expected of an imperial guard. None of it seemed to fit him very well, and all of it was soaked through.

"The wound is in his leg."

I touched my dagger, but though I did not draw, the young Levanti took a step back, hands raised in defence. "I did not mean to frighten you. Can you help him?"

"That depends on what he needs," I said, unable to speak the blunt answer that was probably true. "First we must make him comfortable and see what is wrong."

"He was stabbed. In the thigh. I think he has lost a lot of blood, but he wasn't well to begin with."

Fortunately, Kitado joined us before reply became necessary. "They have agreed to let us have the barn and the old house, but they say it's a bit leaky. There's wood in the shed and dry meat in the cellar. That's about all though; it's been a rough summer, they say. I have given them all the coin I can."

"It will have to do," I said. "Ask them to show us the way."

"Yes, Ma—" Once again General Kitado hid his words with a cough and strode away to accept the offered hospitality.

The woodcutter's land bore a collection of low buildings and sheds, and a yard littered in woodchips. Beneath a clump of trees a pair of oxen lay huddled, while two pigs and a scraggly chicken were penned close to the house, enjoying the rain cutting in beneath its angled roof. Across the yard a barn and a second cottage were all but lost to the storm.

"This way," the woodcutter said, drawing up his hood as he bustled past. He nodded respectfully to me, yet looked askance at the Levanti leading both horses in our wake. Quick steps took us across the yard to the farthest cottage. "That there's the barn." He pointed to the nearby building. "We lost our horse in the winter but yours will be dry in there. And here"—he pushed open a thin wooden door that creaked in protest—"is the old cottage. It hasn't been used since my mother died, but you're welcome to it."

I went in first, ducking under the woodcutter's arm. The cottage was dark and small, just a pair of rooms, the smaller curtained from the larger with moth-eaten cloth. Yet barring a couple of drips falling from the roof it was dry, and the fireplace looked sturdy and functional—no surprise in a woodcutter's cottage.

"I'll send my wife with what food we can spare and some blankets, my lord," the woodcutter said as Kitado joined me. "And you can help yourself to the wood in the shed and anything else around the yard that you need. Some of Mother's old pots are still in the cupboard. And I've got...shovels and...well, you know, just in case he..." He trailed off as the young Levanti mounted the stairs.

"Thank you," General Kitado said. "Your generosity is deeply appreciated."

The woodcutter turned pink beneath his hood. "Just good old-fashioned hospitality, my lord," he said, and with a mumble of unintelligible words he turned and walked out, leaving us to the old cottage's questionable comforts.

"All right," I said once the man had gone. "Carry the injured Levanti in and lay him on the floor so I can look at his wounds, then Kitado, you go for wood, and you"—I looked at the long-haired Levanti—"can take your horses to the barn and see them tended."

The young man hovered, unsure whether to argue, but Kitado brushed past him, saying, "Come on, boy," and he followed the old soldier out.

A rummage about the cottage proved it poorly provisioned. The curtained-off room had nothing but a single rolled-up sleeping mat and a gnawed-on old lap table. A small nest of hay in the corner confirmed my suspicion of animals, but there was no time to do more than suppress a shudder. Grunts and thuds from the main room heralded the return of Kitado and the young Levanti carrying his injured friend. As strong as Kitado was, the Levanti man was tall and well built, leaving the pair no choice but to give up at the top of the stairs and drag him the rest of the way. Once he had been laid upon the floor, they both showed signs of lingering. "Wood, horses, go," I said. "I will see to him."

The young man shot me a quizzical look before heading back out into the storm. Despite the assurance I had forced into my words, I could not immediately bring myself to look at the Levanti's wound. Instead I ransacked the cupboards and the single storage chest, pulling out anything that might prove useful. And as I set a pot beneath each of the drips and threw a dusty blanket over the floor, I couldn't escape the hope that when I finally did turn, the Levanti would be dead. It would look like we had tried, the young man could tell us his information, and we could be on our way.

Before either General Kitado or the young Levanti returned, the woodcutter's wife arrived with blankets and supplies all wrapped in a dripping storm cloak, which she hung on a hook by the open door.

"Thank you," I said, but though she bowed once, twice, even a third time as she backed into the rain, she said not a word.

Blankets, old robes, a small sewing kit, herbs, tea, food, and even a few blessedly dry sticks of incense and a worn scroll inked with the prayers of Qi. It seemed she too was not hopeful.

The Levanti groaned. I went to him then, this mess of a man lying soaked and bloody upon the floor, his surprisingly delicate brows drawn into a pained frown. Not dead, but how much easier for us all if he had been. If he had given up and allowed himself the freedom of whatever afterlife the Levanti believed existed. But no, he fought on, and that at least I could respect.

The rain had washed the man's wound clean, leaving only the surrounding fabric stained with blood. A crimson sash had been tied tightly above it, stemming blood loss, and from its silk a Ts'ai dragon roared. *Rah e'Torin, herd brother of Gideon e'Torin, the new Emperor of Kisia.*

I tore the hole in the cloth to better see his wound. Someone had stuck something thin and sharp into his thigh, like a cooking spike, and despite its clean entry a long, shallow gash led from it. He must have lost a lot of blood, but on its own the wound didn't seem enough to account for his weak, near-death state.

I heaved a long sigh as Kitado returned with a load of wood. "Once you have that fire going, see if you can find any wine for this," I said.

"Wine?" The young Levanti stood in the doorway. "You need warm salt water. And cloths. Get the fire going and heat some water over it. Do we have any needles or gut?"

"Gut?"

"To sew the wound," he said, striding impatiently over to look at the little pile of items the woodcutter's wife had brought in. He took the sewing kit from the bundle. "Huh, at least there's a needle, and this thread will do. Can either of you sew? I..." He looked away. "I hadn't learned yet."

Kitado made a rumble that could have been a muttered excuse, and I snatched the sewing kit from the young Levanti's hand. "Give it here. I'll do it." I heaved an irritated sigh. "Whoever thought I'd one day wish I had paid more attention to Lady Yi's stitchery lessons."

5. RAH

Gideon handed me a bowl, its contents all shadows. There was something wrong about him, something I couldn't quite see, his face and his body and his clothes no longer fitting right anymore.

"It's good to have you back." His voice was overloud too, but it was my thoughts that shouted, writ large in thick, gouged strokes.

"It's good to be back," I said, the words a whisper beneath the roaring inside my head. "I missed you. Missed this." I gestured to the distant herd gathered for the evening meal.

"Missed it so much you want to be out here on your own?"

His gaze had been shrewd but kind. Always kind. "No, I just..."

"I imagine adjusting back is hard. Do you want to talk about it?"

I closed my eyes on tears I did not want to shed, sure that when I opened them he would be gone. Who was I to have earned such care from him? Whatever childish promises he had once made my mother, he was a Sword now and I was not even a saddleboy, was nothing but a failure in the eyes of many. The boy who'd never be a horse whisperer, who had brought shame to the Torin.

The weight of his arm fell upon my shoulders and he was beside me, warm and strong and smelling of salt water. "I know what you're thinking and you're not, Rah. You're not a burden or a failure. You have nothing to be ashamed of. The way of the horse whisperers is hard. Not everyone makes it. You did your best."

"I didn't."

"What?"

He hadn't moved away or lifted his arm from around me, and before I could think better of it, I was spilling my truths into the safe space he had created. I told him about the lectures and the routines and the expectations, the unquestioning obedience, the pretension and the endless, crushing silence. I ought to have been proud to serve my people, to bring honour to my herd, but every day I had lost a bit more of myself and every day I had yearned to be free, yearned to throw duty to the wind and run, whatever the shame, whatever the weight it would add to my soul. And then one day I had. Everyone had assumed I had been sent away for not being good enough, but I had run. I had just walked out and not looked back.

And now the shame of it, the sense of how deeply I had failed myself and my herd and my people, weighed upon me like a mountain.

When I finished speaking, Gideon closed the circle of his arms and held me while I cried, his head upon my shoulder. He did not run under such weight as I had, not then and not later. Not ever.

A crackle rose over the soft song he hummed by my ear. It grew louder and louder, swallowing first his voice and then his presence, only his warmth and the memory of his touch remaining.

In his absence, pain struck fists upon my body. The stink of Jinso's wet hide was there and gone, while the patter of rain was endless. A familiar voice overhead was soon joined by others. A room spun. Sharp pain tugged at my flesh and I cried out, the sound no more alive than the rattle of a corpse.

A voice exclaimed, but I could not understand its words. Footsteps shuddered the floor beneath my head and a face appeared. A familiar face belonging to the familiar voice.

"Tor?" I punctuated his name with a cry as the piercing pain returned, shocking me to movement.

More words I didn't understand, fast and angry, and Tor's hand was all that kept me from trying to rise.

"Don't move," he said. "A girl is stitching you up."

"Girl?" I croaked and licked dried lips, staring at him as I reached for understanding. "Why?"

Tor looked around. His face filled my whole awareness. "Sett ripped your leg open with a hoof pick," he said, lowering his voice to a hiss like quenched coals. "Don't you remember?"

His words tore the darkness back like a curtain, shocking the room into focus. A small room, lit by candles and a smoking fire, with meagre light creeping through an open door beyond which rain poured like a waterfall. It battered the roof and dripped into pots, and the smell of damp choked every breath. Clothes hung drying by the fire. The blanket beneath my head smelled musty. And filling the space around me was a sea of strewn herbs and little bowls, needles and thread. And the girl. Not a girl, too tall and well built to be a girl, but a young woman of similar years to Tor. She knelt, bent over her task, a few strands of damp, dark hair escaping from a messy bun caught to the back of her head. Paused with needle and thread in hand, she looked at Tor and spoke in clipped Kisian.

"What did she say?" I wheezed.

"She wants to know if she can keep stitching or if you're going to faint on her."

I met her sharp, assessing gaze. No pity there, no apology. The hardness of her expression only increased with impatience, waiting for Tor's reply. "Tell her to continue," I said, hating my dry croak. "Levanti endure."

Tor repeated my words, and the young woman's lip curled cynically. But she turned her bright gaze back to her task, once more sticking her needle into my leg. I gritted my teeth, clenched my hands, and stared up at the flicker of light upon the ceiling. It was no new sensation, but Yitti had always made it easier with banter and old stories, with food and drink and good company.

Tor crouched at my side like an animal prepared to flee. "I am sorry for having to accept the help of these people," he said. "But I had no choice."

"Who are they?" I didn't turn my head again to watch her, but the young Kisian woman filled the corner of my vision. And footsteps behind me meant there was at least one other in the room, possibly more.

"They were dressed like soldiers," Tor said, throwing a wary glance at the woman. "They are well armed, but I don't think they are who they say they are. The peasants who own this place bowed to them a lot, so it's possible the man is a lord."

I winced at the awful feeling of thread tugging skin. "And where are we?" I said, trying to take my mind off the deep ache in my leg that seemed to cut to the bone.

"I don't know." Tor grimaced. "I found you on the side of the road and I was sure Sett would send Swords after me, so I just kept riding." He forced a brittle laugh. "Damn but these Kisian horses are poor brutes."

"Jinso?"

"In the barn. He's fine. I've even brushed him and made sure he has dry hay."

More questions clogged my mouth but I could not spit any of them out, fearing the answers. Silence fell, tense and fragile. Only the rhythmic prick and tug of the needle broke the string of my thoughts, a relief though it made my gut churn.

A deep voice spoke from behind me. Kisian again. The young woman answered without looking up. Tor looked from one to the other as the conversation continued, then perhaps catching my confused expression, he said, "They are talking about you. She says it seems you may survive after all and he is warning against optimism. Such wounds, he says, can still fester."

The young woman ended their conversation with a shrug and a few final words, which, only after I said "Well?" did Tor translate.

"She said that would be a greater waste of her stitching than—I am not entirely sure of the word because we were not taught finery, but I think she is making reference to..." He made a vague stitching gesture as he hunted words. "Cushions? Pictures stitched on cushions. Like our embroidered saddle blankets."

No one spoke again until she had yanked the thread tight for the last time and snipped it free.

"Can you sit up?" Tor translated when she spoke to me for the first time. The young woman pursed her lips as she waited, and never had I wanted to understand their language more than in the face of such impatience. "She says it will make the wound easier to bind. And there is water. And meat. And rice if you feel up to eating." He offered me his hand, but I did not take it. With shaky arms I forced myself upright, sending the room spinning once more. The young woman snatched something out of the way as I almost knocked it over, but apart from clicking her tongue in annoyance she said nothing. Her companion, a middle-aged Kisian with a scarred and expressionless face, passed her a handful of linen strips, their ragged edges recently torn. The man met my curious gaze, but he too said nothing, and soon went back to tending something by the fire.

"These are Kisians," I said, finally giving voice to what was bothering me. "We killed and burned and conquered our way through their lands and took their capital. Why are they helping us?"

Tor handed me a ceramic cup painted with tiny flowers. I sipped from its chipped rim, afraid I might break it with hands that seemed suddenly far too big.

The boy didn't answer.

With my leg propped upon her knees like a stool, the Kisian woman began to wrap my wound. Curiosity got the better of me and I looked down before she could cover it. Yitti had always been good at his job, but she had achieved double the number of tiny stitches he had ever managed *and* left it cleaner. With the same deft hands, she soon had it tightly bandaged.

I looked up at Tor. "Why?"

"They want to know what happened. In the city. They thought we were hired soldiers. I promised to tell them everything if they helped you. It seemed a small enough thing to offer."

It was my turn not to answer. Every part of my body ached and I wanted to sleep, but for the second time in as many days my stomach growled its sick hunger. This time I picked at the food they gave me, sure I would be ill if I ate any faster. The only thing that could be worse than the woman's impatience was her disgust.

Having finished her task, she disappeared into a second, curtained-off room. I heard her moving around over the crackle of the fire and the pelting rain.

While I ate, Tor talked.

"—and blood was going everywhere, I really didn't think you'd make it," he was saying when I drew my attention back. "I thought maybe you'd fallen from the saddle and smacked your head, because you were so slow and limp, but I guess with having been locked up and starved and all, well...But we'll strengthen you up. You'll be riding again soon."

He paused a moment, then pushing back his long hair, went on, "I wish I'd known he meant to do it. Sett. I could have stopped him."

I laughed around a mouthful of rice. "Stopped him? How?"

"Threatened to leave. He needs me, you know. I don't know what he's going to do now he has no one to translate for him." Tor gave a short, satisfied laugh. "I was going to leave anyway, but I'm glad I waited."

"So am I."

Between the wound and the starvation I would surely be dead had he not come along, might even have been killed by my own Swords had I fallen within sight of the city walls.

At the memory of that line of torchlight, the rice turned to a sticky mass in my mouth and I could not chew. I put the bowl down. In the silence a drip from the leaking roof fell into a pot with an overloud *plink*.

"You're lucky you didn't hurt yourself more when you landed," Tor said after a short pause, but the words meant nothing beneath the recollection of how completely my Swords had turned against me. How completely I had failed them.

You're not a burden or a failure. You have nothing to be ashamed of.

If I closed my eyes, I could almost imagine the weight of his arm across my shoulders.

"I'm sorry we got stuck here," Tor went on. "I'd heard whispers that a group of Levanti had left after Gideon claimed the city and were setting up a camp in this area. I tried to find them, but I was worried you wouldn't make it if I didn't find help." He scowled. "It would have been better if I'd found them."

His inability to do so seemed to be preying on his mind, and thinking of Gideon I dredged up enough effort for a wan smile. "You did your best to look after me, and no one could do more than that. Thank you."

It was nothing to what Gideon had given me just by being present that first evening back with my herd, but it was all I had and it lightened Tor's scowl.

"Well, we can find them when you're—"

He broke off as the young woman pushed the curtain aside. She had changed out of her wet armour and into a plain robe. It was worn and faded, and yet she wore it with a fierce pride that dared anyone to think poorly of her. She moved toward the fire without glancing at us, and now standing with her companion I could see they were of a height, both built like fighters despite Tor's doubts. The woman even held a bow, which she indicated as she spoke, glancing every now and then at Tor.

Her companion growled an answer, also glancing at Tor, but though I could have asked him to translate, I stared at the bow instead. At its blackened arms and great, tall curve. I had seen it before.

"When you're strong enough to ride we can find the camp," Tor went on, lowering his voice. "Then go home."

Home. Without my Swords I had no reason to stay, and yet the idea of riding away from all this sent a chill through me I could not explain.

The Kisian woman's approach saved me from having to reply. She addressed Tor with the directness of a command and annoyance clouded his face. I heard my name. Heard Gideon's name. A question. Plaintiveness in her look if not her voice. Her companion joined her, standing a step behind and beside—a protector. Tor eyed both him and the woman's bow with disfavour as he replied.

Whatever he said did not please. Again I was gestured to, glanced at, more object than individual, and never had I hated my lack of understanding more.

"What does she want?" I asked.

Tor broke off what he was saying. "She wants to know what happened at Mei'lian."

"Then tell her."

"But we cannot leave yet. Once they get what they want they will take our horses and kill us if we try to stop them."

The Kisian woman looked from me to Tor as he spoke, her sharp scowl returning when I said, "Ask if that's their plan."

"They will deny it."

"Just ask."

Tor did so, and while he spoke, I watched the woman's face. Her eyes widened only to narrow, lines hardening around her lips. And when she replied the words were curt and she held herself stiff, hands clenched upon her bow.

"She says they will not kill us. She says we can trust her because Kisians live and die by honour, though that is something barbarian mercenaries wouldn't understand."

The laugh came unexpected to my lips and shook my whole body, setting off pains in places I had forgotten even existed. And while I chuckled in a way that sounded delirious even to me, the woman's scowl darkened and she snapped a question at Tor.

Before he could translate, I said, "Tell her no silk-clad city dweller could understand why I am laughing. But I believe they mean us no harm. Tell them what happened."

Tor was so pleased translating the first part that he didn't refuse the second, and however much the woman looked like she wanted to poke out my eyes with an arrow, she peppered Tor with questions instead. I could only guess what she asked, could only listen for mentions of Gideon's name, of the city and the Chiltaen leaders, of myself and my comrades. And Leo. Even as Tor told the story, I relived it. The dead blanketing the streets. The blood. Gideon sitting on the throne with Leo's broken body tossed like refuse upon the floor. And only I had refused to bow. To kneel. To accept that this was what we had become. Schemers. Killers. Conquerors.

It had been her city. The longer I watched her the more sure of it I became. She was not just a woman deposed from her home, she was an empress deposed from her empire. The bow. The assurance. The man standing deferentially behind her like her guards had upon the battlefield. She needed only a suit of gleaming armour to be the golden dragon once more, to be Empress Miko Ts'ai. And every word Tor spoke, every detail he gave, was a punch to an open wound. Yet there she stood, proud and determined not to break.

Tor seemed oblivious, owning neither enough deference nor enough belligerence for a man who knew the truth. He had changed since Risian, a zealous light now shining in his eyes.

When at last the empress had no more questions, she turned to her companion. No words passed between them, but in that brief look they shared such pain I wished it all undone. This was not our land. Not our home. We had no right to its souls.

The silence stretched, then the empress once more disappeared behind the curtain and her companion poked the fire viciously, sending sparks flying. He threw a new log on, and asked a short question of Tor, who answered with a shake of his head. Sure he was moments from renewing the conversation about going home, I set my water cup aside and tested my leg. It ached, every movement pulling at skin stretched too tightly over my flesh. I set my jaw against the pain. Movement was freedom, and as Herd Master Sassanji had often said, only while we were free could we be wise.

Footsteps thudded on the stairs and all three of us tensed, eyes on the door. A Kisian man in a big cloak entered carrying a box, and both Tor and the empress's companion relaxed. Words were exchanged and the man bowed and went back out.

"Who was that?" I said.

"The man who owns this place. They are calling him the woodcutter."

"The woodcutter?"

"His job, I think. Chopping wood."

"For fires? But—?" Even as I began to ask why, I thought of the big Kisian cities where no food or trees could be grown, cities that had to rely entirely on resources from outside. The city states were the same, yet still people chose to live there, crammed inside the walls like so many nuts in a crate.

Empress Miko returned from the curtained-off room. She seemed restless, flitting in and out with short words to her companion and annoyed looks at us.

"Did you thank her for helping me?" I said, drawing Tor's attention away from the rip in his breeches he was picking at. "She seems annoyed."

"They were travelling east and worry they are losing time."

"Tell them I no longer need their care and they can go."

Tor shook his head. "I don't think you're the only reason they're here. They speak a lot of half-finished sentences, so I cannot be sure, but I think they don't have anywhere else to go."

An empress without an empire. How she must hate the very sight of us.

Whatever her feelings toward us, Empress Miko and her companion checked my wound twice before evening fell, neither appearing to find Tor's continued observation sufficient. He rolled his eyes at this, but seemed to have decided no good would come of aggravating our hosts. They cooked more rice and let me eat as much of the dried meat as I could stomach, and slowly I began to feel a little more alive. Yet pain had settled in my bones. Exhaustion carried me into dozes, but I could not recall what it felt like to exist without the deep ache of torn flesh.

For the most part we all sat in silence, my companions breaking it only for short stretches of strained conversation punctuated with grimaces. When the rain eased around sunset, the empress took her bow and stepped outside to disrupt the evening with the rhythmic twang and thud of loosed arrows. From where I sat propped against the wall, I could not see her, but I listened to the speed and precision of her drawing action and doubted I could best her.

"Tomorrow we'll see if you can ride," Tor said, returning again to the conversation about our future like an itchy scab. "The camp can't be too far away and you can let Jinso do all the work."

A Levanti camp was a good place to recover my strength so I agreed, but asked for more water before he could again broach the topic of going home. No doubt he would soon sense a pattern in my reluctance, but for now the boy jumped up without complaint and, throwing his long, straight ponytail over his shoulder, strode out to the rain barrel, cup in hand.

He ought to have been back in seconds, but minutes passed. Under the watchful gaze of the empress's companion, I dragged myself to the door. Tor had frozen on his way back from the water barrel, full cup in hand and his eyes caught to the empress loosing the same ten arrows one after another into the rotting wall of an old building. Once the tenth left her string she strode to pull them out, showing no sign at all she knew or cared that we were watching.

"She'd best all but the finest of our archers, I think," I said. "At least while stationary. If she could do it while riding, I would really be impressed."

Tor flinched and looked away. "Sorry." He glanced at the cup in his hand as though surprised to find it had water in it already, and held it out. "Got distracted."

"Knowing she could put an arrow through both of our eyes in the space of a breath is very distracting."

He crushed the beginnings of a smile with a shake of his head and turned away. "If only they thought as much of our skills."

That night the empress's companion laid out four stale sleeping mats, one in the curtained-off room for her, the other three in the main room for us. The little moving about I had forced myself to do had exhausted me more than I had thought, and no sooner had I lain down properly than I fell asleep.

Whether it was the pain that roused me or something else, I woke to the hiss of whispers. The main room was dark and beside me Tor was a shadowed lump curled upon himself like a dog before a fire, but the Kisian man was missing. I rolled to look at the curtain to the other room. Light crept around the edges of the heavy fabric, and behind it their whispers were little more than the shifting of sand in the wind. Curious, I would have shaken Tor awake had the empress's voice not broken on a sob. I stilled, listening to her companion's comforting murmur, and felt a stab of guilt. A foolish, ridiculous stab of guilt, I told myself, given how little control we'd had over the Chiltaen conquest, but a stab of guilt all the same.

For a long time, I lay awake staring at the ceiling and listening to a grief that was nothing like my own and yet the same in every way.

When Empress Miko checked my wound the following morning, I found I could not meet her gaze. No matter how furiously she scowled upon the world, the memory of her sorrow stuck in my mind.

She lifted the torn wadding from my leg, ignoring my wince at the way it stuck to the dried blood and stitching. Her fingers worked deftly, examining her handiwork but making no move to clean it.

"It needs salt water," I said, and she looked up as though surprised I could speak. "I can do it myself if you'll get some for me." She switched her gaze to Tor, who translated.

Once he had finished, he added in Levanti, "I've had to keep telling them that's what it needs. You'd think they've never had to keep a wound clean before. Maybe they haven't. She's definitely never stitched someone up."

"That's surprising given the work is neat."

"She's used to stitching, just not skin."

The empress looked from Tor to me and back as we spoke, and the concerned creasing of her brow showed the first visible crack in her assurance. Tor sighed. "I'll heat some water once the fire is going. At least it's not raining anymore."

The morning had dawned misty and grey, but any hope of seeing the sun died all too soon. Before Tor had finished cleaning my wound, rain was once more pattering on the roof. It stuck around into the afternoon as I dozed off and on and ate whatever was given to me, slowly feeling life return to my flesh. Tor had decided I was still too weak to ride, but he brought me a comfortable account of Jinso from the stables and assured me we would soon be back with our own people.

For the most part the empress and her companion kept to themselves, the four of us a dour group each caught in our own dark thoughts.

Until a scream cut through the rain. My gaze snapped to the door. Too well did I know the difference between a scream of shock and a scream of pain. And the sound of hoofbeats. They rose from the drumming rain only to break rhythm as they slowed and circled.

Empress Miko stood, bow in hand. Her guard followed. They were at the door before I could speak or even recall that speaking Levanti would have no purpose. I had no weapon, but I struggled up and limped after them as fast as my injured leg would allow. "What is it?" Tor said, a hunting knife appearing in his hand. "Horses?"

"That's her!" came a shout—a shout I understood, for out in the pelting rain three horses circled the yard while a fourth stood near the barn, the only sign of its rider a foot caught and twisted in the stirrup. The empress nocked a new arrow, while before her on the steps her guard drew his sword.

"Stop!" I shouted, a steadying hand upon the door frame. The faces of the Levanti were lost to the storm, but their heads turned as an arrow leapt from the blackened bow, missing a fretting horse by a hair.

I gripped the next arrow as she drew it. The empress snarled and ripped her hand free, but a fragile moment of peace settled on the strange scene and she did not immediately draw again.

"Rah e'Torin?" a voice called through the rain. "Twice a traitor now?"

"A traitor? Never to those who live with honour. Why are you here?"

The speaker slowly walked their horse close enough to make out a vaguely familiar face, one I had seen around but could put no name to. She pointed at the empress. "That one. Emperor Gideon requires her."

"Dead?" I asked, not that the answer would matter. What I had seen of Empress Miko was enough to know she would not go willingly. The fragile peace was already straining, pulled taut like the empress's bowstring.

"What does it matter to you?" The woman sneered at me. "Going to stop us? Whatever orders I have don't extend to protecting your life."

Tor shoved past me into the rain. "Rah is worth ten of Gideon," he shouted. "What is a Levanti without honour? A Levanti who forgets who we are?"

"I don't know, but a castrated runt would be more leader than you could ever be, you unmade little bitch."

"Get down off your horse and say that again," Tor snarled, his hand clenching and unclenching upon his hunting knife.

"Tor," I said. "These are our people, they—"

"They are not *my* people."

He strode past the empress, who looked from the riders to me and back, fingering the feathers of another arrow.

The challenged rider leapt from her horse, drawing both her blades before Tor. He still had the long hair of a saddleboy, but he was well past Making age. He was a true Sword of the Torin and did not tremble to face a foe. To face his own blood.

"Tor, don't!" I shouted, but he did not turn. The empress loosed. Her arrow slammed into their leader's shoulder, jolting her back. And before she could regain her balance, Tor was on her. Heedless of the death that might await upon those curved blades, the young man charged in, burying his shoulder in his opponent's gut. Together they fell to the mud in a tangle of limbs and steel and rain.

Another arrow cut past a Sword's ear as she turned to charge. The guard stepped to meet her, and the whole scene became a rain-soaked nightmare. He dodged the first swing only for her second blade to slice his arm, ripping free a spray of blood. He staggered but drew a dagger as the Levanti circled back to charge again. In a shower of mud the horse bore down upon him. He stepped left, then right, feigning indecision though he held the dagger steady until the very last moment—the moment he buried it deep in the animal's neck. Blood gushed and the horse's knees buckled, throwing its rider.

And all the while, I had not moved. Empress Miko's sword hung before me, its hilt within reach. I could take it. I could fight. But for who? For my people? Or for those who had done nothing to deserve the devastation we had brought to their lands?

I had to choose, but I did not. Could not. Not when the second rider charged. Not when his blade slashed her guard's side. Not even when the empress screamed and drew the sword I hadn't as she charged into the rain.

The second rider leapt from his saddle to land in front of her, no doubt intending to capture her unharmed. If he had hoped for an easy task, what he got instead was the onslaught of a furious warrior.

Tor had their leader pinned to the ground, but I only had eyes for the avenging force of Empress Miko, pushing her enemy back with strike after strike, not seeming to care about protecting herself from retaliation.

Beaten back to the other side of the yard, the Levanti man ducked clear and ran for his horse. The empress didn't give chase. Dropping her blade, she drew her bow and nocked before the man covered half the distance.

"No!"

Even had she heard me, even had she understood, it would have been too late. The arrow leapt from her string to bury itself in the Sword's back, throwing him forward onto his face where he twitched in the mud.

A heartbeat of shock held everyone frozen. Gideon's Levanti were all dead or dying and still I had not moved from the step. Tor stood, chest heaving, in the middle of the yard while with a sharp cry the empress ran toward her injured companion. She knelt, patting his chest and babbling, her voice catching on a sob as she gestured to the cottage. Tor, covered in equal parts mud and blood, darted to obey, disappearing inside.

On stiff, aching legs, I staggered toward her. She had managed to help her companion to sit and was talking fast and moving even faster, trying to stem the bleeding.

"We should get him inside." I gestured to the cottage out of which Tor now sped. "We should get him inside," I repeated to him. "Help me."

He nodded, and bent so her companion could put his arm around his neck. Gritting my teeth, I made to help, but the empress shouldered me out of the way and aided the man herself. Lifted between them, the guard cried out as he was half carried, half dragged past me to the cottage steps. They edged him awkwardly inside in silence, two heads of long, dark hair bent about their task, their arms meeting across his mud-stained back.

Inside they set him down and the empress began cutting away cloth with her dagger. Tor had the water back boiling over the fire and was putting his time as a healer's aid to good use. All saddleboys and -girls learned the basics as part of their training. Mine was all a little hazy, but Tor prepared strips of linen with ease while the empress worked.

Soon the wound was exposed, a bloody mess sliced from hip to underarm. His ribs seemed to have protected his upper torso from worse damage, but the lower part had not been so lucky. Blood oozed beneath the empress's shaking hands. For a moment I met Tor's gaze. We had both seen wounds like it—impossible not to when your purpose is to fight and die for your herd—we had just never seen people recover from them. Determination and good care often kept them going for a while, but not even Yitti could have fixed this.

The empress dipped the linen in the hot water, but every time she cleaned some blood, more returned. She spoke as she worked, Tor's reply a shake of his head. She gestured to the needle and thread, and again he shook his head. She raised her voice, tears spilling, and I could not watch. Could not stay, so immersed in her suffocating hope.

Retreating into tradition, I went back out and sank into the mud beside the closest body, ignoring the searing pain in my thigh and the weight of my exhausted limbs.

I drew a blade from the dead Levanti's belt. Its hilt felt wrong just as his head felt too heavy. I did not recognise him, but a branding like that of the Jaroven or the Oht stood proud on the back of his head. Without paint it was hard to be sure. One of Dishiva's? Nausea swelled at the thought. I swallowed it and made the first incision. Blood flowed onto the already sodden ground. Better not to look at it. Better not to think. Better to just let my well-practised hands take over.

With one finished, I moved to the next—the one Tor had fought. Taking the head ought to have been his responsibility, but he was occupied trying to save life; it was the least I could do to save souls.

The babble of his heated conversation with the empress lapped at the edge of my awareness as I slid my blade into the woman's throat. Tor had made a mess of the body, thrusting his blade again and again into the woman's chest, arms, and stomach—anywhere that might vent some of his fury. Fury that had overcome respect.

With each body my progress slowed, my arms tiring and my leg stinging with angry pain. But I could not let their souls Reside, so I worked on, no matter how long each took, no matter how much I had to suffer to see it done. Deep down I knew I deserved it. That I was still that boy who had run.

The third Sword's neck was thinner than the others, and the fourth's had snapped. Her horse lay in the mud like a discarded sack of meat. It might have been little else to most people, but to us a horse was life. Freedom. Everything. This one's glorious soul had fled its broken body to run upon the spirit fields and I sang while I worked upon its master, a song to guide its way home.

By the time I had finished the fourth head, Tor had emerged from the house and was raiding the Levanti saddlebags for supplies. We did not speak as I piled the heads in the centre of the yard, moving so slowly that Tor had finished his task long before I had.

With them all gathered, I walked toward the woodcutter's house in search of a sack or crate in which to carry them. Yet there by the open door I found a fifth body. The woodcutter lay face down upon the muddy earth, an axe in his hand and a great split upon the back of his skull. His wife crouched nearby, rain mingling with the tears running down her cheeks.

Hardly thinking anymore, I unsheathed my knife and, dropping soaked knees to the mud, rolled the dead man into my lap. The woman spoke, her words meaning as little as rain upon already soaked skin. Blood burst from my first incision. I had taken enough Kisian heads to know their blood was the same as ours. We were all the same once life fled, all just as fragile. Alive one moment, dead the next, the weight of each individual soul upon the world as fleeting as a sparrow.

The woman spoke again, sobbing as I slit muscle and skin and tendons with the serrated edge of my blade. My arms ached and my wound burned, but it needed to be done. Just this one and I could rest.

Someone shoved me sideways, but pinned by the dead body I did not fall. Empress Miko Ts'ai stood over me, her brows caught in a scowl as fierce as her dragon mask. Blood stained her hands and she was talking fast, gesturing to the dead woodcutter and his wife. Unable to understand a word, I continued my task.

Pressing her muddy foot to my shoulder she kicked me, and I hit the ground hard enough to knock my teeth together.

"His soul must be offered back to the world!" I said, wiping mud from my face.

She shouted something else, gesturing wildly.

"Tor! Tor!" I called, and after a moment the boy appeared, his lips set in a grim line. I pointed to the woodcutter's body. "Tell her I have to do this or his soul will be trapped. Even a Kisian cannot be allowed to Reside."

Only when Tor spoke did the empress stop shouting, but his words did nothing to lighten her expression. She replied and Tor's face reddened. "She says this is barbaric," he said. "She says you are... dishonouring this man by mutilating his body."

"This *is* honour." I spoke directly to her, not Tor. "You said we didn't understand honour but you are wrong. To us, this is honour. Honouring the dead by releasing their souls so they may be born again. I do this out of respect."

Tor spoke as I did, and when he finished her eyes narrowed.

"He is already dead," she said, her voice coming from Tor's lips. "His soul is already gone. Let him be."

"I cannot," I said. "I—"

She interrupted with a few curt words, and Tor said, "She says you are upsetting his wife."

The crying woman was rocking back and forth now, rain running down her face and over her silently gaping mouth. My stomach dropped, horror seeping in as I realised her grief was not just for the loss of him, but for what I was doing.

The empress spoke again. "She wishes to perform the burial rites," Tor said for her. "She wishes to wash her husband's body and lay him out, she wishes to—"

"But...But he will be lost!"

"Then let him be lost. The dead are dead. The alive need to grieve their own way for they are the ones who remain."

My bloodstained hands clenched into fists and loosened again, every joint aching. This was what we did. This was how we ensured souls did not get trapped, unable to be reborn. But how could I explain that Residing souls clung as surely to those left behind?

The empress lifted her brows, daring me to keep cutting.

When I did not move, Tor spoke her damnation. "You come into our lands and you kill our people. You mutilate their corpses whether they want you to or not. And after you've forced these horrors upon us you have the gall to call it honour? Put down the knife. Now."

6. DISHIVA

Riding behind Lady Sichi's silk box was dull and irritating. Her carriers moved half a beat slower than Itaghai's natural walking pace, meaning he had to stop every few steps and let them pull away. Beside me, Ptapha didn't appear to be struggling with it as often, while the two Swords leading the way were trying to set the carriers a quicker pace and failing. Beside the silk box rode Nuru, the only Torin saddlegirl who had learned the Kisian language—not from the Chiltaen commanders like the others, but from talking to the female slaves in the Chiltaen camps. I could not tell what she was saying, but she kept up a constant conversation with the invisible lady within like they were good friends.

I could have borne the slow journey better had Leo Villius not been with us, the whispers containing his name as pervasive as his presence. Like Lady Sichi, he travelled to Kogahaera surrounded by Levanti, though whether we were protecting him or protecting ourselves, I wasn't sure.

We ought to have killed him the moment he stepped through the gates, but the highest of high priests had offered himself to Gideon as a hostage, claiming it to be the will of his god, and Gideon had agreed. Having buried his knife in Leo's flesh once, he seemed unwilling to do so again. Whatever the reason, the protection of Dom Leo Villius had been added to my new duties, and every time

I looked back I couldn't but be reminded of how Rah had ridden with him once, had served as his protection, and been led astray.

I kept my gaze firmly forward despite the itching at my neck. "Do you remember the puppet shows the missionaries put on when we were kids, Ptapha?"

The young man's head tilted in question. "Vaguely, Captain. Why?"

"They used to tell stories from their holy book, years ago before everything started to turn nasty. There was one about a man whose god brought him back from the dead." I resisted the urge to look around at Leo. "And each time he was brought back, more and more people believed he was special, that he had been chosen for a purpose, and eventually the belief was so powerful he became a god himself. Do you remember that one?"

Ptapha shook his head, but I could remember the puppets all too well. The missionaries had long since been forgotten, as had the crowd of children I'd watched the show with, but the puppets... The reborn one—Ven? Vent? Veld?—had worn the featureless mask that seemed to represent their priesthood, but the fractured pieces of obsidian they'd used for the eyes had looked so real, glittering dangerously as they cut a warning into my soul. The puppet that had repeatedly killed the chosen one had been coarse and dirty and covered in furs as though stuck halfway between human and bear, while the god that brought him back to life had been represented by a prettily painted paper lantern. A smaller such lantern had been attached to the reborn one's head at the end, after he had been brought back enough times to become a god himself, imbued with the power to rid his homeland of all the people who had come to conquer it.

"It had creepy-looking puppets," I said. "Creepier than usual. With...obsidian eyes and the whitest of robes. I wonder how they kept them so clean out on the plains."

Seeming to have no opinion, Ptapha said nothing. I scratched the back of my neck, all too aware of Leo behind us. "Do you think he's really been brought back from the dead?"

The taciturn Sword shrugged. "We believe in rebirth."

"Of the soul, not the body. And only if the soul has been properly released to the gods." Leo Villius had been given no such honour.

"I guess."

I gave up and risked a look back. Leo Villius rode with eight of my Swords in a square around him. Between their heads, he met my gaze, eyes glittering through his mask's slits. I repressed a shudder and turned back, intent on not looking again.

In the middle of the afternoon, Kogahaera appeared through the misty rain, little more than a dark blot upon the horizon. My imagination had failed to predict the size of any city, of any army, even the intensity of the rains, and what little idea I had formed of Kogahaera was as laughably incorrect. It was a city, much smaller than the two capitals but larger than anything else we had seen, its inner core of clumped buildings surrounded by walled compounds. Each of these was like a smaller city on its own, possessing a grand central building and a flotilla of smaller ones caught within a protective circle of wall.

The biggest had two tall stone towers rising from the walls like straight horns, seeming to proclaim ownership over everything around them. The compound had belonged to a Kisian lord and was now to be our home, a place from which Gideon could build the empire he envisioned. Others would house the allies Gideon had gathered, while the remnants of the military camp would be put to good use. I had been unsure how I felt, listening to such plans, but looking upon it now, a seed of hope pierced the surface of my ill-ease. If anyone could make this work, it was Gideon. It was a hope worth cherishing, because without it we had suffered for nothing. Without it we had nothing. Were nothing.

Lady Sichi's rooms inside the manor house were palatial, or so they seemed to me even as she ran a critical eye over them. She would have guards with her at all times and had three Kisian attendants in addition to Nuru, but the trio of rooms could have fit many more without lessening her comfort. Still she pointed at things and her attendants bustled about shifting screens and chests and tables until at last she pronounced it acceptable with a shrug.

"If Lady Sichi is comfortable now, I will see to my other responsibilities," I said, addressing Nuru. "Inform her I will ensure she has two guards on her door whenever she is within her rooms, and it is Herd Mas—His...Majesty's wish that they accompany her wherever she chooses to go as well."

Nuru spoke a few short sentences in Kisian, and I was impressed, as ever, at her fluency. To my ears at least. Perhaps to a native Kisian speaker it sounded like a cat being tortured.

"She says that is acceptable to her." Nuru translated while the lady stared intently at me, her penetrating gaze unnerving. "But when you are free from your other duties, Lady Sichi wishes you to return and have tea with her."

There wasn't much I wanted less, but with her staring at me like a lidless bat I could only nod and excuse myself. Before I could escape someone tapped on the open door.

"Captain?" Ptapha stood awkwardly in the doorway, looking like a giant in so low a frame.

"Yes, Ptapha? What is it?"

"It's...Leo Villius, Captain. Where...where should we put him?"

I wanted to say in a hole somewhere, but Gideon had said to treat him with respect until we knew what use he could be. "A... room? He is going to require at least...four guards at all times and—"

Lady Sichi interrupted me in Kisian, and everyone looked to Nuru. She squirmed in discomfort. "She asks why a Chiltaen priest gets more guards than your—*our* future empress."

How to admit I was frightened of a priest? That this pale-faced, mild-mannered man of faith turned my blood cold for no reason except that he should not exist?

"If it's more guards she wants then let's increase it to six," I said, more snappishly than intended. "We can have two outside under the windows, two in the hallway, and one hiding in each of the other rooms. I will see to it. In the meantime, I have a dead man walking to find a bed for." Forgetting the right protocol in the heat of the moment, I saluted to her as I would to a herd master, and turned to depart with Ptapha before anyone could call me back.

Despite my desire to escape, I almost turned and went right back in, for standing in the hallway, flanked by Levanti, was Leo Villius.

"Ah, there you are, Captain Dishiva," he said in that mild way of his, the Levanti words never ceasing to sound strange on his lips. "I'm afraid no one quite knows what to do with me. Perhaps you could clarify whether I am a guest or a prisoner. It would make it easier to direct your Swords to the right place."

"You do not direct my Swords," I said. "If it were up to me you would be in a cell, but as it is not, we will find you a moderately comfortable room."

He touched his hand to the pendant he wore around his neck, giving thanks to his god. "I like you, Dishiva. You say what you think, which is a rare trait."

"Only to people I dislike."

"That you are more honest with people you do not care for and pretend with those you do is a great tragedy." His words were a blade thrust into my soul, but he pointed along the hall as though he had spoken mere commonplace. "Shall we? There appear to be a lot of rooms. Your Swords could surely find the most uncomfortable one for me."

"Yes, they can, but do not presume to understand me, priest."

Leo's brows rose. "It is not presumption if it is truth. You wish to feel in control and that is quite understandable given the circumstances. So very little is within our control, however, as we are nothing but leaves drawn upon life's currents. Our purpose is not to fight against them but to become one with the direction God chooses for us. All you control is your ability to love and thank him for that life and purpose."

He had started walking, but I gripped his arm. "How are you alive?"

"My task was not done, so God sent me back."

"With a whole new body that looks exactly the same as the last."

"It can hardly be the same body given what you all did to it."

He spoke pleasantly, but shame niggled. Ptapha shifted his weight.

"How do you know what we did?" I said, defiantly meeting his gaze.

"The soul does not leave the body immediately," he said, a flicker of pain behind the smile. "There is time enough to know one's fate. To live it. But unlike the decapitated head I proudly showed your friend, I will be a happy man if I never see that body again."

His hurt deepened my stab of shame, but I scowled to keep it from escaping. Whatever we had done he deserved no remorse or apology, this man who had led Rah astray. Who would lead us all astray.

"I would be happy if I never saw *you* again," I said. We had deliberately left his head attached so he could not be reborn, yet here he stood, faintly smiling in the dusty hallway of a manor outside Kogahaera.

"That's unfortunate since I quite enjoy your company," he said. "And there is much I have to do here before my task is done."

He made to keep walking, but I gripped the front of his plain robe and yanked him back. "I don't know what you're up to," I spat into his face. "I don't know how you come back to life, but if you hurt any of my people, if you twist Gideon the way you twisted Rah, I will test how many bodies your damned god has sitting around spare for you, do you understand?"

He didn't flinch, and that alone made me want to punch him. "Yes," he said. "I understand far more than you, enough to warn you to take care how you threaten me."

"Or what?" I scoffed. "You'll kill *me*?"

"Oh no, I would never do that. That is not the path God has set before my feet. I am a pious man, Captain; I wish no harm upon others. But not everyone who shares my faith shares my temperament. I am willing to die for my faith, others are willing to kill for it, and such true believers are everywhere. Even in places"—he gestured around at the empty passage, its heavy beams as oppressive as the dark clouds outside—"you would least expect."

I tightened my fist. "Is that a threat?" The fabric of his neckline cut across his throat, but Leo Villius's eyes only widened in disbelief.

"No! Not at all," he said. "It is merely a warning to take care lest you accidentally upset people who consider me worth killing for."

I let him go with a snort of disgust and he almost fell back into Ptapha. "I am not afraid of you."

"Good. I would like us to be friends, Dishiva, not enemies. I might be the only person here who misses Rah as much as you do."

I felt the heavy weight of my Swords' attention at that, and repeating my disgusted snort, I waved them forward. "Come, let's find a place to stash this body too, shall we?"

———————◆———————

Once everyone was settled as well as could be, Gideon called a meeting in his new imperial hall. When I arrived I was shocked to find Kisians joining us. They were part of our future now, I reminded myself, as I took in the confusing number of people present.

Aside from Gideon and myself there were ten Levanti, a fact the Kisians seemed to find unnerving. Many flicked glances at the gathered captains as though expecting them to pounce. There were captains from every exiled herd: Captain Atum e'Jaroven, my First Sword; Captain Yiss en'Oht, who had been here almost as long as Gideon and was fiercely loyal to him; Captains Menesor e'Qara and Taga en'Occha, both quiet scowlers; Captains Bahn e'Bedjuti and Leena en'Injit, both new to their positions after their Sword-herds had suffered heavy losses; Captain Dhamara e'Sheth, one of the many Levanti named for the popular children's story; and Captain Lashak e'Namalaka, who had slowly become something of a friend as we travelled. She smiled now, a tight little expression that communicated shared discomfort.

Without Sett or Yitti, Gideon himself appeared to be speaking for the Torin, two translators rounding out our numbers. Both had long hair, but only one looked young enough to be unmade. Oshar e'Torin must have been the youngest exiled with Gideon, his chin owning only the faintest dusting of fine hair, while Matsimelar e'Torin had thick stubble. Unlike most Swords he was slender, years spent learning words having failed to build up his physique.

Both looked tense. As did the five Kisian men who had joined us. And they were all men, each a variation on the theme of fussy little beard, long tied-back hair, bright expensive silks, jewels, and proud expressions. Only one I knew by name, the man in the double layer of blue, with his hands caught behind his back and an expression of utter calm. He was Lady Sichi's uncle, Grace Bahain, our strongest ally.

Not a man to anger lightly.

Stepping into the centre of the gathered circle, Gideon spread his arms and smiled, speaking first in Kisian and then Levanti. "Welcome," he said, "to the first joint council of Levanti Kisia. Working together in the way of a Hand, we will build this new empire for all of us.

"As it has been a long day, we will keep this meeting to our immediate plans." He put a gentle emphasis on *our* as he turned to look at all present. It was unusual for Levanti to meet standing, and by the way a few of the Kisians kept shuffling I wondered how they normally met and whether Gideon was trying for some middle ground. When he began his next sentence, in Levanti, I was sure of it. He was treading a very fine balance.

"The first piece of news is that there has yet been no sign of Empress Miko."

After he had repeated this in Kisian, Grace Bahain stepped into the circle and spoke, his hands remaining behind his back as though he feared the secrets their gestures would betray. From his place at one end of the room, Matsimelar began to translate.

"A complete search of the city found no sign of her, which is... was a surprise—unexpected"—the young man cleared his throat—"with the gates manned. There are tunnels, however, and she may have gotten out disguised. Regardless, we will find her."

"Why is it so important she be found?" my First Sword asked in the calm way he had.

Oshar translated this into Kisian, but before he had finished, Yiss en'Oht had turned a scowl on the Jaroven. "Because there is only one throne and we wish our emperor to continue sitting on it, preferably without having to keep fighting."

When he shifted to translating her words, Oshar pointed at her to indicate the speaker. Yiss visibly bristled, but this was the price for communication now.

"And what will happen to her when she is found?" Lashak asked, and the Kisian next to Grace Bahain stepped forward. He wore a similar robe to the others except it only reached his knees, leaving a pair of loose breeches sticking out beneath. He wore a belt around his waist too rather than the usual sash, the sword he carried looking well forged. "It would be easiest to kill her, as with all unneeded leaders," he said through Matsimelar's lips. It seemed to be his job to translate Kisian to Levanti while Oshar translated the other way. "But in the case of Empress Miko there is value to be had in marrying her suitably."

"She would be an ideal wife for our emperor," said another Kisian at the opposite end of the circle. "Kisia has a long history of marking new alliances with a political marriage."

Barely had the translation finished than Grace Bahain faced his countryman. "Ah, but you forget, Emperor Gideon is to marry my niece, Lady Sichi, for exactly that reason. But no matter, a use can be found for Empress Miko." He turned to look upon the circle. "And we will find her. I know enough about the allies she is likely to shelter with that it's only a matter of time. Of more immediate danger is the boy south of the river calling himself Emperor Kin's heir. He appears to have the loyalty of the southern battalions."

"I have heard of this," spoke the Kisian I had started thinking of as Breeches, his hand resting upon his sword pommel. "Prince Jie. The events that took place in Mei'lian in the days before it fell are muddled, but from all I can discover it is true. The boy really is the old emperor's bastard heir."

Muttering accompanied the end of the translation, while a few of the Levanti captains shared doubtful looks. "Do you mean this man is not an emperor but rather an emperor's son?" said Taga en'Occha, scowling her question at the gathered Kisians.

Grace Bahain smiled and made a little bow to her. "It is one and the same, Captain. The rights of emperors have traditionally been passed from father to son, only interrupted by conquest."

"That is a foolish way to decide leadership."

"Given all you know of him, is it likely he will attack us?" Gideon stepped in before the scathing translation could be completed.

Maintaining a forced smile, Grace Bahain shook his head. "We do not know much of him, Your Majesty. He seems to be no more than a child, so it's likely he is not in command at all, but which general has the strongest influence over him is hard to say."

"Either way it is unlikely they will mount an attack until the snows melt," Breeches said, still resting his hand upon his sword. "Battles are hard in such weather, and they are safe south of the Tzitzi."

"A child," Taga scoffed, and Oshar wisely decided not to translate. The Kisians scowled at her all the same.

"A child who stays on the other side of the river need not trouble us for now," Gideon said. "The Chiltaens, on the other hand, are on this side of the river."

At mention of the Chiltaens every Levanti captain shifted their weight, preparing to fight, Lashak going as far as to grip one of her sword hilts. "They must suffer for what was done to us."

Grace Bahain stepped forward again, closing the circle a little tighter. "We have destroyed every one of the Chiltaen support camps," he said, his words continuing to emerge through Matsimelar's lips. The young man's eyes glazed as he went on: "They have no presence in Kisia south of the city of Koi, which they continue to hold and which it would be...unwise to attack."

"Then we attack *their* cities."

A few rumbles of agreement met Lashak's words, but nothing seemed capable of dampening Grace Bahain's sense of superiority. "Attack their cities? You will happily leave a contender for the throne south of the river but wish to cross the border to attack another country?"

"This boy across the river has not wronged us." Lashak drew herself up as tall as Grace Bahain had. "The Chiltaens have."

"Is not a whole city choked with dead Chiltaen soldiers enough revenge?" he said with a little laugh, looking to his fellow Kisians to join his amusement.

But even if they would have laughed, Lashak had already mimicked his move and stepped into the circle. "We know how city states work. It is not the soldiers who make decisions and give orders, it is the rich men sitting at home in their fancy clothes." She jabbed a finger at Bahain and went on: "They are the ones I want to be revenged upon, the ones who witnessed us arrive on these shores and saw nothing but a resource to be exploited."

Barely flinching, Grace Bahain said calmly, "That's as may be, but the snow season is far worse for waging battles, and now is hardly the best time to be starting a further war with the Chiltaens."

"Aren't we already fighting a war?" Captain Menesor e'Qara said, entering the conversation for the first time.

Grace Bahain replied, but the translation was lost amid a flurry of angry agreement, Oshar failing to keep up with which captain was speaking. The Kisians looked from one scowling face to another and, getting nothing useful from Oshar, eyed their emperor. A little of the hope I had been carrying since arriving died within me. We needed the Kisians, more than they needed us it seemed, and yet how could we ever build here, have power here, when language was such a barrier to understanding? There were only four Levanti in the whole of Kogahaera who could speak Kisian. If something happened to any of them the struggle would become insurmountable.

It was a daunting prospect, but there was little time to consider its full implications as the volume in the room increased.

"Yes, but a long war, Levanti, not a quick skirmish," Matsimelar translated for a frustrated Grace Bahain.

"We suffered at the hands of the Chiltaens while you sat this out and left us to it," Taga snapped.

"Exactly! Our people died for your ambitions," Lashak threw at Bahain.

"As did our own!" he spat back.

"But that was by choice."

Oshar and Matsimelar were having to shout to be heard over the growing noise.

"Waiting while we grow strong will only allow them to grow stronger too."

"The rains are nothing to the snow that is coming!"

"Do you really want to wait for them to attack us first?"

Through it all Gideon stood watching, turning from speaker to speaker. In someone else it might have looked like disinterest, or a love of chaos, but the intense way he watched, his heavy brows drawn close, was the look of a hunter waiting for the right time to strike.

Yiss was the only other person who had said nothing, and I was doubly glad to be standing on the sidelines when Lashak turned on the older woman. "You have been silent, Yiss. You cannot tell me you are content to leave our enemies unchallenged."

"I am content to put my faith in the decisions of our emperor. He has been here the longest and gotten us this far."

Lashak reddened, her hands tightening to fists as eyes all turned to Gideon.

Called upon, he finally stepped into the middle of the circle, spreading his arms. "I appreciate the passion with which you speak your minds," he said, speaking more to us than the Kisians. "We suffered many losses to get to where we are now. If we want to hold this land, if we want to take revenge on those who used us, then we have to regroup. Rebuild. Grow strong. I share your desire to see the people responsible for our suffering destroyed, but we must do it when we are ready, when the weather is what we are used to fighting in, when we have time to make a plan that will result in their complete defeat. Whatever our pain and our suffering, caution has ever been our way, because we are not only thinking about ourselves but our herds. We are the herd masters now, we are the matriarchs and the patriarchs and we must survive above all other considerations."

By the time he finished speaking even the Kisians had turned to him like wildflowers to the sun, the measured, moving way he spoke inspiring everyone to make him proud. I had seen the effect on Levanti before, but had not expected to see the same look worn by men with such different experiences of life, with a different language and a different culture.

"I will address everyone in the morning so there can be no doubt over our plans," he went on after a brief pause, Oshar continuing a little behind him. "So all can hear from me and understand the reason for my decision."

He let out the smallest of sighs. "Anyone wishful to discuss this particular decision further, I feel it will be more useful to do so in private. And I hope next time we will be able to keep things a little more organised, for the sake of our translators if nothing else."

It was a dismissal, and despite their respect for him, I was surprised how easily the Kisians allowed themselves to be so dismissed. Perhaps because they had, for the most part, gotten what they wanted, while some of the Levanti captains still looked unsure. But Gideon had already stepped back from the circle and there was nothing to do but salute and file out along with the bowing Kisians.

In my capacity as imperial guard, I remained while everyone else departed, leaving the hall an empty, echoing space. Gideon did not move.

"Well?" he said when we were alone, not turning but staring at the floor where the joint council had stood. "Did I disgrace us all, Dishiva?"

"No, Your Majesty."

He turned, the quirk of an amused smile on his lips. "That title sounds so strange from you."

"It feels strange to say too, but you carry it well. Even the Kisians seem to like you. But I worry."

When I closed my lips upon the words he lifted his brows. "You worry? I may be an emperor now, but I still value the opinions of my people."

"I worry you... *we* are putting too much trust in them. Especially in... Grace Bahain."

"We need him. You wince and I hate to admit it as much as you hate to hear it, but we need him. Herds have little need or understanding of money. We trade goods and services, not coin unless we are dealing with merchants from the city states. Here everything is done with coin and influence. I could wear as much crimson cloth as I liked and sit upon a dozen thrones, and it would do no good without a man like him bowing at my feet. Once we build wealth and influence in our own right, we will not need him."

"He knows we need him."

"Of course he knows." Gideon's smile was strained. "That is why I agreed to marry his daughter, and haven't sought to challenge him. Let him think me an easy puppet, I don't care so long as it gets us what we need."

The pragmatic words were both the most honourable and the least honourable thing I had ever heard anyone utter. They were demeaning of his pride and yet he had chosen to put himself beneath the needs of his herd, and that was worth every shred of my respect.

"You understand me," he said, perhaps seeing something of my thoughts in my expression. "If only Rah had possessed your comprehension, perhaps..." He trailed off with a sigh and I wondered if I was the only one he spoke to about Rah, the only one he knew had struggled with Rah's defection as he had.

"I do not think Rah lacked…understanding," I said, unable to look at him as I attempted to voice my thoughts. "Have you considered that…Dom Villius is…" Gideon frowned, but I had come too far to stop now and hurried on. "That he is the reason Rah turned from us? He was dead, Gideon. He cannot now be walking and talking in that same body like nothing happened."

Gideon's frown hardened. "I don't know what he is, but he is the only bargaining tool I have that is entirely out of Grace Bahain's hands. That alone makes him valuable enough that the rest is unimportant."

Even Rah? I almost asked and stopped myself, so fierce was his expression now.

"Still, ensure you have plenty of guards on watch tomorrow," he said at last, shaking some of the scowl away. "We need everything to run smoothly."

"Yes, Your Majesty."

He made to depart, but stopped as he drew level with me and set his hand on my shoulder. "Have faith in me, Dishiva. We need a future. A place where we can exist. And if it's not here, then where? If not now, then when?"

———————◆———————

As though the gods themselves had parted the clouds for him, Gideon stepped out into a hazy dawn free of pelting rain. He stood on the manor steps looking every bit an emperor while the Levanti gathered in the damp, cloaking mist. My Swords stood at either end of the steps, inside the door, and at strategic places around the yard. Not all were Jaroven, which was taking some getting used to. Swords from all different herds had chosen to join Gideon's guards, but most were Oht who, like Yiss, followed Gideon with the same fervour the Chiltaens had shown Dom Villius.

Having positioned myself out of the way behind Gideon, I had a good view of the gathered crowd, shaking out its morning restlessness as it settled.

"Swords of the glorious Levanti Empire," Gideon said, raising his voice over the rustling. They fell silent, all attention caught to the man upon the steps. "We were too long in Kisia as slaves, but today marks seven days since we threw off our masters and rose free. Not just as warriors and healers and hunters from the plains, but as leaders of a new empire, a new world, one in which we will not be hunted down and slaughtered, in which we are an inextricable piece of a new whole."

A barrage of rhythmic clapping broke the morning's peace, before fading as Gideon lifted his hands.

"Seven days of freedom is worth celebrating," he went on. "But there is still a long way to go before our children can safely call this land home. We won the battle, we routed our slavers, but there are enemies all around us, and we must strive to show our new Kisian brethren that they are safe under Levanti rule. We are not cruel masters like the Tempachi and the Korune. We do not live in decadence while others starve. We take care of our herd as we have always done, only now that herd is much larger. So do not look on your Kisian fellows and see an enemy; look upon them and see your brothers and your sisters—your blood."

Murmuring began to grow, the restless shuffle returning. My eyes darted about the crowd, watching for pockets of dissent as I had once watched my own Swords. No leader stands atop the cliff without keeping an eye on the roiling sea below.

"We are all angry at what the Chiltaens did to us, but now is not the time for revenge upon their people, not the time to honour our wounds with their blood. Now is the time to build, to heal, to strengthen ourselves for the fight we will take to them before long. For now let us build our temples anew. Build our lives anew. Let us welcome new blood and share our ways with the world and be all the stronger for it."

There were no claps now, but his words seemed to swell the gathered Levanti as every breath he drew swelled his chest. He was promising them blood and vengeance, but first he was promising life. Whether or not they had heard every word or understood all he wanted for them, the sight of Gideon standing proud before them could not but be heartening.

"I cannot build this great future without you," he said, appealing to them with outstretched arms. "I need you. All of you. We must fight together for this future, and for Levanti greatness."

He lifted both hands and cheers were followed by the rising beat of his name chanted over and over, fists punching into the misty morning air. "Gideon! Gideon! Gideon!" In that moment he was as much a god to us as Leo was to his people, and we could achieve anything.

Until the arrow struck Gideon in the shoulder. He staggered back under the force, and fearing a second, I shouted gods only know what as I tried to push him out of the way. My boots slid on the slick step and I fell into him as a second arrow hit the stone.

Cries swirled from the crowd as my Swords sped to surround their injured emperor.

"Find out where that arrow came from!" I shouted at no one in particular. Upon the top step Gideon sucked in breaths, trying to slow them even as he struggled to his feet. "We must get you inside," I said. "Get—" I snapped my jaw shut, not sure which healers we could trust when only a moment ago the Levanti had felt united at last. "You can't go out there!" I darted in front of Gideon as he tried to push through my Swords. "Someone just tried to kill you."

"That is . . . exactly why . . . I—"

Running steps pounded toward us and I shoved Gideon back

as a Levanti leapt up the stairs, crashing over the defensive line of guards. Blade out, eyes crazed, he lashed at me with a snarl, landing hard enough to throw me against the door frame. My head struck wood and pale patches burst across my vision. In that stunned moment he had all the time he needed to kill me, and I knew myself lost. Yet a choking hack broke through the noise, followed by a gulping death rattle. The Levanti stood before me, blood oozing down his chin as life leached from wide, glassy eyes.

Gideon withdrew his sword from the man's gut, leaving the body to fall dead at his feet. No one spoke. No one moved. Then Gideon waved my Swords aside causing the arrow in his shoulder to wobble. White lipped with pain and rage, he turned once more to face his people.

"This," he said, pointing down at the dead man, "is not who we are. Wherever we live. Wherever we die. Whatever our purpose, *this* is not who we are. We do not kill in the dark. We do not stab in the back. I am your leader until someone challenges me for the responsibility of all this." He lifted both arms and gestured around, once more making the arrow in his shoulder shake. The only sign of pain was the tension in his jaw as he held out his hand to me. "Your knife, Captain."

I handed it over and all eyes watched Gideon take it. Without ceremony he knelt upon the step and pressed the tip of the blade into his attacker's neck, sending blood dripping onto his knees.

"We are better than this," he said as he began severing the man's head. Every movement cost him his own blood, yet he did not stop. "We are stronger than this. We are *Levanti*."

7. MIKO

Kitado barely kept up. I had sewn the wounds upon his arm and his leg, but the gash splitting his side was too big. It needed time we didn't have and rest we couldn't take. All we could do was clean it with the warm salt water the Levanti recommended and bind it well. The young Levanti, Tor, had done that part, wrapping the makeshift bandages around the general's chest with more gentleness and skill than I had expected.

We had ridden east from the woodcutter's hut, and under the cover of clouds and darkness had crossed the Willow Road, no one there to see us but night birds and frogs. Open land met us on the other side and we were able to pick up speed, the rush of air against my face making up for the endless bite of the rain. And the heightened fear that tainted all.

I was being hunted in my own land. If I didn't find allies soon, I would not only die but worse—fail at everything I had set out to do.

Syan was the only option.

Kitado had agreed, yet I watched him and I worried. Every now and then his head would sag upon his chest, and though he did not speak our language it was always the shorn Levanti, Rah, who swept his horse up beside Kitado's to see how he was.

I had feared to leave the Levanti behind knowing all they did, but not for a moment did I think they would come with us unless threatened. Yet they did. A dozen times I had been on the verge of asking Tor why, but every time I swallowed the words, at first because I feared to scare away valuable hostages I could trade if Grace Bahain was no longer loyal to my cause, and then because I feared to be alone. Levanti they might be, yet here they were, riding front and back of our strange little cavalcade like guards, helping make camp of a night and caring for Kitado. And with each passing day a resentful gratitude grew within me I wished I could dash.

But why had they come? Did they think me their prisoner? Did their honour code require return service? Neither seemed likely from their behaviour. In fact the only sensible answer was that they were following my horse—Rah's horse. The horse Tor hadn't wanted me to ride.

"You cannot have Levanti horses," he had said when I entered the woodcutter's barn laden with heavy saddlebags.

I had dropped them, meeting his scowl with a hand upon my sword. "No?"

"Even if you kill me you still cannot have Levanti horses," he had said, sounding self-satisfied. "They do not let any but a Levanti upon their backs."

Rah had spoken then, and while their exchange turned into a series of snapped and hissed words, I examined the great animal he had been tending. It looked the same as any other horse, only larger and stronger. Even the saddle and bridle were the same, only a few of the knots and decorations odd to my gaze. Did he think no one else could ride such a grand animal?

I gripped the reins. The horse backed and tossed its head, almost lifting me from the ground. The young man stopped arguing with his companion to sneer. "I said they do not let you ride them. Levanti only."

Rah pointed to another horse. Agitated talk ensued, and like when he had tried to take the woodcutter's head, his temper flared. Rah thumped his chest with his fist and spoke with great feeling, his words weighing down his young companion's head with shame. He spoke with fervour and assurance, and for a fleeting moment I saw Tanaka once more standing in the throne room, appealing to the masses, spilling his heart in the moments before losing his head.

The discomfort of being present for such a dressing down only increased when he gestured to me. I had looked at the ground rather than acknowledge Tor's embarrassment, but in the end, Rah had led the other horse toward me, talking to it all the way as one might to an anxious child.

"Jinso," he had said, indicating the grand animal.

Tor rolled his eyes. "This is Rah's horse, Jinso. Rah says Jinso will let you ride him with Rah here."

More snapped Levanti followed, but Rah shook his head. And after a moment of silence the translator went on: "He will hold Jinso's reins while you try. None of the others will let you ride them, but they will let him. Your companion can ride the Kisian horse. It is very tame and will give him less trouble with his wounds."

Comfortable sounds gathered around us—the clink of a bridle, the snuffle of a nose in hay, a shifting hoof. The horse was taller than Kin's war charger, but ignoring the fear wriggling in my stomach, I took hold of the pommel and lifted my foot to the stirrup.

Jinso had snuffled and moved his feet in the straw, but Rah held his reins as I climbed into the saddle. And while Rah crooned to his horse, Tor said nothing. He was scowling again and would not meet my gaze.

At last Jinso stilled. Fretful tension remained, but when Rah stepped back, his horse did not buck me off. After a few more minutes Rah took another step, then handed me the reins over Jinso's

head with a nod suspiciously like a bow. My heart sped to a panicked tattoo as he stepped clear and Jinso backed, tossing his head.

"Rah says you must stay calm."

I knew how to ride a horse and my back stiffened. "Step away,"
I said. Fear gnawed, but I squeezed Jinso's sides with my knees
to set him walking, his only protest a toss of his head as we went
from the dusty dry out into the rain. There he lengthened his
stride and exhilaration beat aside my fear. He moved with such
ease, with such unspent power in the bunching of his muscles. In
that saddle I could forget my troubles. Could feel invincible. No
wonder the Levanti lived as they did. Fought as they did. Died as
they did.

We stopped at Otobaru Shrine, the resting place of the old Otako
emperors. Once a place of pilgrimage, it now sat tucked away in
the woods between Shimai and Quilin, the contingent of guards
that once tended and protected it disbanded long before my time.
The graves were overgrown and the statues worn, and though there
were signs that others had camped here over the years, the tracks
were old and the fire pit filled with grass and kanashimi blossoms
drooping in the rain.

Rah crushed a clump beneath his foot as he eased himself from
the saddle. Almost I snapped at him to take care, shocked anyone
could see those flowers and not step over them. I could explain, but
neither Levanti would understand.

I took an exaggerated step over a clump, looking for somewhere
to tie Jinso's reins. Rah, having left his horse untethered, pointed at
the shrine and spoke.

"Is that a holy place?" Tor translated.

"Yes," I said. "It is a shrine to Qi. And this is the resting place of
emperors."

Tor passed my answer on and Rah nodded. He untied the blood-stained sack from his saddle and carried it toward the shrine.

Kitado slid from his horse only for his knees to buckle, landing him in a tangle of long, wet grass. I went to him but he shook his head.

"General," I said. "You cannot deny me the offered opportunity to check your wounds."

He forced a grim smile. "Your handiwork is very fine, my lady," he said, indicating the gash on his arm I had sewed. "Whatever would Lady Yi say if she could see you stitching skin instead of silk?"

"It has something of the same resistance, the same…force required to push the needle through and pull it out the other side. But I will not allow you to hide behind Lady Yi. You know that isn't the wound I wish to look at."

"It is, however, the only one you shall see, Your Majesty."

He wore his jutting jaw proudly. "Very well, General," I said. "You are safe for now. Can I get you something to make you more comfortable there on the ground?"

Kitado looked up at his horse and its bags, a battle seeming to rage behind his eyes. "I hate to request anything of you, Your Majesty, but I don't think I can unload or tend my own horse just now. If one of the Levanti—"

"I can carry bags and tend horses, my friend. Have I not proved I am made of flesh and blood, not porcelain and gold? I am a capable woman, not just an empress."

"You will always be a god to me, Your Majesty."

Had I not laughed at the silent apology in his eyes, I might have cried.

An old stone altar sat at the base of the shrine's wide stairs, and kneeling before it with a dirty, decapitated head in his hands, Rah began to chant. As with the way he had spoken to Jinso, it was a musical sound, rising and falling with a poetic cadence that almost transcended language. There was grief in every word and yet the whole came together with a sense of joy that filled my heart with hope.

"What is he saying?" I said, looking to Tor, who was tending his horse.

"He is singing a lament. He will pray as well and offer each soul back to the world. The lament is not required, but as this is not an altar to Nassus he wishes to first draw the attention of the gods."

"Nassus?"

"The god of death. He rides with us. We are branded in his name that he may always know our sacrifice. We are the Swords that hunt so your hands may be clean. We are the Swords that kill so your soul may be light. We are the Swords that die so you may live."

"And why the heads?"

My question crushed Tor's fervour to a scowl. "So the soul may be taken to a holy place and released. If not, the soul gets trapped in this world, in the cage of its flesh, never to be reborn. It is dishonourable to leave a soul to Reside, even an enemy's."

General Kitado shifted in his seat of mud and flowers. "Reside?"

"To stay here. Unable to be reborn. That is why he tried to take the woodcutter's head."

Tor had said so at the time, but I had been too furious at the desecration and the woman's pain to give it any thought. I had sat with the woodcutter's wife as she laid out his body. I had lit the incense. I had prayed with her and offered reparations I could not yet pay, but all she had said was "Thank you, my lady" and "You are too kind, my lady" and looked dead inside. Despite her loss I had fretted. It was dangerous to linger, yet guilt pinned me in place like a butterfly to a board. Minister Manshin had scarified himself that I might live to fight another day, but everywhere I went I brought nothing but more death to my people.

All the while Rah had hobbled about the yard, tending the horses and cutting off heads. He had collected them in a sack, blood oozing through the hessian. It had seemed a lot of work to go to for trophies likely to rot by the day's end.

"Why heads?" I asked once more, my gaze sliding toward Rah as he knelt chanting before the altar. "Why not fingers or toes? They would weigh a lot less."

Tor sneered. "What use would it be cutting off fingers and toes except for sport? The soul resides in the head, not the hand or the foot or the nose. That is why we brand and paint the back of the head."

"But you don't have a branding. Or shave your head. Why?"

For a brief moment he met my gaze, before turning back to his horse without an answer. I glanced down at Kitado, dripping with as much sweat as rain, and he gave an infinitesimal shake of his head.

I did not ask again.

———————————◆———————————

While General Kitado rested, Rah built a fire from the wood Tor gathered. I had been against having one, but the shrine had a stone entryway and we needed hot water, so I gave in and hoped no one would notice smoke leaking through the shrine roof.

I carried all the saddlebags inside and set pots to catch rainwater, but none of the Levanti horses would let me tend them, not even Jinso though I had ridden on his back all day. I hated leaving the job for Tor, but the horses gave me no choice. The young Levanti had headed back into the trees in search of more firewood, but he soon returned empty-handed and sped over with what I had come to think of as his permanent scowl. "There are people coming."

I tensed. "People? What sort of people?"

He made a gesture part shrug, part impatient hand wave. "I don't know. People. Kisian people."

"Kisian? Where?"

"On the road, heading this way."

I couldn't tell if fear or excitement owned more of my thoughts. People meant news, but the wrong people could mean trouble.

"Should I kill them?" Tor said, the words spoken in so innocent and helpful a tone that it took me a moment to register what he had said.

"Kill them? No! Don't kill them, I mean…not yet. What have they done to harm us that your thoughts jump so quickly to death?"

Tor's cheeks reddened and his scowl returned. "You're hiding. Killing people is safer," he said a little petulantly. "Or I could go welcome them. I'm sure that would go well." He gestured to his face and he had a point. Explaining to anyone why two Levanti were travelling with two Kisians would be a feat.

"How far away are they?"

"They'll be here any minute."

I touched the covered form of Hacho. "Armed?"

Again with his odd impatient shrug. "Not obviously, but knives are easy to hide."

Almost I snapped that I was well aware of that, but instead I pointed to the horses. "They won't let me tend them. You do that and—"

Voices sounded on the road, followed by hoofbeats, and I swallowed the urge to pull my bow from its place on my back. The road that led to Otobaru Shrine went nowhere else. As a road of pilgrimage, it bore signs of old glory—cracked and weathered statues, writing etched into the stones, and overgrown flower beds that must once have looked beautiful.

Three young men were approaching, their horses overladen with supplies.

"Good evening," I called out. "Have you come to shelter at the shrine?"

"Evening!" one of them returned. "Indeed we have. There is little other shelter to be found, so it's no surprise to find others here in such weather."

"No indeed." I waited until they drew closer before adding, "I hope it will not trouble you to share your shelter tonight."

The seeming leader—a young man of means by the look of his horse and his attire—smiled and made a respectful bow. "Not at all, good lady. We must all come together at such difficult times."

He looked around the clearing, and although General Kitado was out of sight resting inside, both Rah and Tor went about their tasks, wary eyes upon our newcomers.

"These Levanti are not our enemies," I said, pre-empting questions. "Whatever part they played in the Chiltaen attacks."

"Were forced to play," one of the other three muttered—a young man with a finely manicured beard bisecting his chin. "They are also our liberators."

"Yes," the third said, shocking me with his suppressed vehemence. "And if Dom Villius trusts and follows them then who are we to doubt."

As though those words closed the conversation, all three dismounted and began to settle in. I stared at them as their words washed over me. They didn't all make sense, but I ought to have picked up the signs they were followers of the One True God— no family sigils, simple clothing despite their fine cut, and each wore a silver necklace around his throat. Two wore them tucked beneath their robes, but the bearded man had the silver mask sitting proudly atop his clothing for all to see.

Belief in the One True God had never been popular at court. Kisian believers tended to hide their religion, all too easy was it to equate with treasonous support of our enemies. The world was full of nuance, but a lifetime at court had taught me that power lay in convincing the masses it wasn't. Us and them, good and bad, right and wrong—the most powerful messages were the divisive ones.

"Did you say Dom Villius?" Tor said, as Beard carried his pack under the shrine's portico.

The young Kisian lifted his brows, no doubt as surprised at the question as that Tor could speak our language. "I did. We heard of his return and are on our way to Kogahaera to join him."

"Return?"

The man dropped his heavy pack and straightened with a little groan of stiff joints. "The One True God has blessed him with new life, finally proving the long hoped-for truth that Dom Villius is Veld Reborn. We go to serve him as is called upon by all followers of the True Faith."

Before Tor could ask further questions, Rah turned from the fire. "Leo?"

The resulting interchange looked heated, with Rah sitting forward and gesturing to the newcomers and Tor grumbling back, and I thought of Dom Villius sitting atop the hill at Risian surrounded by Levanti. They had seemed to value him, preferring to protect him themselves rather than leave the job to Chiltaens.

Whatever had troubled Rah, he settled into scowling silence while the newcomers unpacked their belongings on the other side of the shrine. There were a dozen things I ought to be doing, but while Tor went back to tending the horses I just stood awkwardly, all too aware of standing between worlds. They didn't know me for their empress, their god, yet even so it was a Levanti emperor they rode toward and a Chiltaen man they worshipped. Was this what all Kisians would soon look like, if I failed? If the empire fell? Was it already too late?

We had not ourselves been a chatty group, but when the three pilgrims joined us around the fire that night the silence was so deep and awkward that I wished my people would go away again.

I might not understand their language or their ways, but the Levanti made sense. Kisian believers of the One True God made me uncomfortable.

"We have wine and meat and bread we are happy to share," said the one I thought of as their leader. "It would give us joy to help others."

Back at the woodcutter's house, General Kitado had shown me how to smush all our leftover rice into patties, wrapped up in waxed paper. We had little else and still had far to go, so it was with reluctant relief that I accepted their offer and offered none of our food in return. It was not the hospitable way, but I had two injured men and farther to go.

The trio's meat and bread were still fresh, and the sight of them spread beside the fire made my mouth water. How many days had it been since I'd eaten good food?

Rah pointed at the meat and spoke low. Tor replied with his impatient shrug. More conversation passed between them, and after watching them for a few moments, the pilgrims began their own low-voiced conversation about how many days they thought it would take to reach Kogahaera. They were still discussing the point when Tor took a piece of the Chiltaen-style flatbread and lined it with meat before rolling it up. This he showed to Rah, seeking a nod of approval, before handing it to General Kitado sitting propped against the shrine wall a few paces back from the blaze.

My cheeks reddened with the shame of not having thought to see what he needed myself, so caught up had I been with the strange newcomers. General Kitado thanked the young Levanti, not seeming to realise Rah had instigated the provision.

"How long have you been camping here?" the head pilgrim asked, despite the answer being obvious.

"Only tonight," I said, sure they actually wanted to know who I was and where we were going. Did they suspect? I didn't recognise them, but if they came from Mei'lian there was every chance they would recognise me.

I shifted my weight and sought a change of subject. "You said you were joining Dom Villius in Kogahaera. You are not afraid to go there with the Levanti present?"

"The deeper the faith the shallower the fear, good lady," the man replied, touching the pendant hidden beneath his simple robe. "Besides, the Levanti emperor is receiving Kisian oaths and gathering allies; he has no reason to harm us."

Receiving Kisian oaths and gathering allies. The words pierced my heart with icy fear, and it was all I could do not to glance at General Kitado. My mother had spent years cultivating alliances, but almost all of them were in the north—the north that had been decimated in the Chiltaen invasion, the north that had been burned and broken, the north that was bowing now to a foreign emperor. The feeling that walls were closing in on me intensified and I could not shake it, could not shake the fear that I had already lost, that my empire had moved on without me.

"I've heard talk that he'll marry Empress Miko," the young man continued, sublimely unaware of the second jolt of fear he dealt me. "That should help people accept him."

"You want a Levanti emperor?" General Kitado asked from the shadows beyond the fire.

"We want an emperor who will not repress our religious beliefs as the Otakos and the Ts'ai have been doing for generations."

His tone was belligerent and his chin jutted, challenging the injured soldier to argue. Whether in possession of his full health Kitado would have done so or not, he countered with a gentle "You do not fear that Levanti rule will destroy all that makes us Kisian?"

"A lot of the common people seem to have that fear," the leader said, proving I had been right about their social standing. "But if he marries a Kisian and allies himself with Kisians, eats like a Kisian, talks like a Kisian, and lives like a Kisian, is he not Kisian?"

Tor scowled darkly and set his teeth, but made no comment.

"I can see there is fear in you," the bearded pilgrim said, leaning toward me with a smile. "But you need not be afraid of change. We are all in the hands of God and always have been despite our insistence on worshipping spirits of the water and the moon and the forest. It is time to let go of these things and be free."

He held out a pendant, its silver shining almost gold in the firelight. The Mask of God. When I did not take it, he shifted it closer, his smile a sweet, helpful thing as though he was aiding a lost child. "As we do not control this world, to fight change is to kick and scream at the dark."

"Is that what your god demands?" I said, my voice sounding unlike my own, so constricted was my throat. "Capitulation? Surrender? That you do not strive?"

"Not at all, good lady, merely that we strive to build anew rather than fight to hold on to the old."

I flinched as he took my hand and pressed the pendant into it. "For when you are ready to listen, good lady."

———————◆———————

Despite the presence of the pilgrims, I slept better that night than any other since leaving Mei'lian. Perhaps I was getting used to the hard ground and the interminable rain, or perhaps I had been calmed by the presence of the gods. Our gods. I had not been able to refuse the gifted pendant, but I had shoved it to the bottom of my pack where I need not look at it.

When I woke, the shrine's thick, dusty beams were shadowed in dawn light. I could hear the three pilgrims packing their things and speaking in low voices, while beyond the lattice screens rain struck the ground with the force of hatred. Not wanting to face the trio of traitors, I pulled my damp blanket tighter around myself and sought more sleep, but all I could think of was that pendant and the indifferent shrugs with which they had discarded generations of Kisian leadership. I tried to tell myself these three were an anomaly and did not speak for the rest of my people, yet all the same fears and doubts assailed me. Had I any allies left?

A fevered whimper levered me upright. A few paces away General Kitado lay in the tangled remains of his own blanket. He let out a cry and rolled, leaving a patch of blood behind.

On hands and knees, I shuffled to his side. "General?"

He twitched but did not answer. I patted his shoulder and Kitado flinched and opened bleary eyes, staring at me like he had never seen me before. "Majesty?"

I looked around to be sure our unwanted companions were too far away to hear. "General, you are not as well as you would have me believe."

"Merely fatigued, Your Majesty," he said with a strained smile. "The ache makes it difficult to sleep."

"You are bleeding again. You need a physician. I can ride to Syan on my own while you—"

"No."

I scowled at him. "You are no use to anyone dead, Kitado. I will order you to ride for the closest town if I must."

"Your life is my concern, not the other way around. One does not become the commander of the Imperial Guard to prolong their time in this world."

"But—"

"Miko." His use of my name shut my lips even as it twisted a smile from his. "I am going to die whether a physician looks at me or not. Whatever game we play, whatever pretence we allow ourselves, we both know that whether I stop and rest or press on, my days are limited. No, let me finish, please. The wish of this dying man is not to wallow in false hope but to see my task done. We may not be sure of his loyalties, but Grace Bahain is an honourable man and his son is your friend. If I could see you safely to them in Syan, I could die knowing some part of my duty to be discharged."

I looked at the deep gash oozing blood through its torn bindings. He had kept it hidden each day beneath his armour, had let Rah clean and bind it each night with fresh strips ripped from a spare blanket, and their silence had allowed me hope.

"I am sorry, Your Majesty," he said, all attempt at a brave smile sliding from his face.

"No, I am sorry. I ought to have left Rah to bleed out back in the fen." Bitterness stained every word. "If we had kept moving, we might have stayed ahead of the Levanti search parties."

"What is done is done. Look forward, Majesty, never back." Kitado nodded to Rah, sitting nearby, watching. "He repays the debt, at least. He knew, though you did not. There are some wounds even the great Master Kenji cannot fix."

"He stopped Kin from dying when half his body was burned."

Kitado managed a smile. "Emperor Kin was a god, Your Majesty. I am merely a soldier. Now we ought to keep moving if we are to reach Syan."

I wanted to argue, to tell him it would be all right because I was a god and I willed it, but they were the words of a child and I kept them to myself as I helped him sit. From the other side of the shrine, Rah watched. Kitado met his gaze and the two men shared a nod full of understanding and respect I could not but envy. They might come from different places and worship different gods, but a warrior was a warrior, carrying the same honour and fortitude with them like a cloak. Tanaka and I had play-acted such things, but while he would have earned that respect, it seemed I would always be a princess in need of protection.

We ate what little was left of our supplies, drank rainwater as it gushed from the eaves, then left Otobaru behind. Rah and Tor had to help Kitado into the saddle and Jinso was unsettled, but the moment the two Levanti mounted they became one with their horses, leaving me all too conscious of my own shortcomings.

The rain seemed intent upon drowning us and hammered with increasing fervour as we rode east, yet there was a panicked rush to our pace that had nothing to do with the weather and everything to do with Kitado. I was not the only one watching him with a wary gaze. I tried to tell myself he would make it. That he would be all right. Rah had re-bandaged the wound before we left, the two of them speaking together while he worked though neither could understand the other.

It had been days since we'd left the enemy Levanti behind, days since we'd seen anyone but the occasional traveller, long enough that I had stopped looking over my shoulder. But not so long I didn't almost choke on my heart at the thundering of hooves behind us.

Rah and Tor caught them at the same time and a quick flurry of conversation passed before Tor gestured off the road. "It sounds like at least five riders. We have to hide."

At the sudden halt, Kitado swayed in his saddle, but held out his hand to show he was fine even as I reached for him.

"Quick," Tor hissed, waving an anxious hand. "They'll be in sight any moment. Get into the trees and keep the horses quiet. We'll cover the tracks."

I urged Jinso off the road into the thick undergrowth. General Kitado followed, brushing through reaching greenery toward a small clearing, but no sooner had he drawn level than he slipped sideways, his weight dropping onto my leg like a falling tree.

Panic swept me, but I held Jinso firm and shook the general's shoulder. "General? General!"

He lurched up like a man shaken awake, his face pale with pain. "Hold there," I said. "I'll get you down."

I dropped from Jinso's back and dashed to Kitado's other side, hardly caring we were being pursued or recalling the rest of the world even existed. Only the crush of undergrowth beneath boots made me turn. Rah was leading both his and Tor's horses, Tor nothing but a dark shape farther back in the trees. The approaching hoofbeats grew close, hammering at my ears, but Rah dropped his reins and hurried forward to help me.

He caught General Kitado as he fell, and I closed my eyes as the roar of approaching hooves crashed over us like a wave. It seemed to last forever, my heart thudding to the same frenzied beat, until at last they began to fade. I opened my eyes upon a heavily breathing Tor, staring after the retreating sound. He met my gaze only to look away. "They didn't even slow."

Rah had laid Kitado upon the ground and I went to him, patting his pale cheek. "General? General!"

His eyes fluttered open only for him to flinch and squint at the endless bombardment of the rain. Rah stood and a moment later the rain ceased, landing instead upon Rah's tunic stretched over us like a badly made tent.

"Sorry, Your Majesty," Kitado croaked, blinking fast. "I'm afraid I am going to fail you."

"No, never, General," I said. "It is I who has failed you. And I do most humbly beg your forgiveness."

His chuckle became a wince. "You honour me, Your Majesty, but I will pretend...I did not...hear that. You are...our empress. You cannot...fail. You...cannot be wrong."

A shadow fell and I glanced up at Tor.

"We need a physician," I said. "You must ride to the nearest town and—"

The young man shook his head. "I will prolong the suffering of the dead no longer."

"But he isn't dead!"

"He has been dead for days. Let him go with honour."

I made to argue, to shout him down, but Kitado gripped my hand and I had no further thought for Tor. "Majesty," the general said, his eyes wide with sudden desperation. "Let them take my head."

"What?"

He lifted a shaking finger at Rah standing half-naked beside us, unmoving despite the rain now dripping through the tunic he held aloft. "I want him to . . . release my soul. To the gods."

"But—"

"Please, Majesty. I don't want to be trapped here, in this broken body. If there is even a small chance they are right . . . Promise me, Your Majesty, I beg of you."

"Yes. Of course. I promise."

Even with more time I would not have argued, but as I gave my word the intense light drained from Kitado's dark eyes like a sigh from his lips and he slumped back into the mud. His hand fell from mine and he slid into peace, the exact moment of his passing lost to the tears that filled my eyes.

"He wants Rah to take his head," I said.

When no answer came I looked up to be sure Tor had heard me and found a notch cut between his brows. "Is it what *you* want?" He jerked his head at Rah. "He won't do it if you're going to scream at him again."

"Do it," I said. "It was his wish."

Tor shrugged like it meant nothing to him and spoke to Rah. Their discussion passed over my head while I wiped tears on my sodden sleeve, then Rah withdrew his tunic leaving the storm to once more drown me in its sorrow. He drew his short knife but awaited further permission, and I knew not whether to honour him for the respect or hate him for forcing me to give it.

I nodded and moved back, letting him take my place at General

Kitado's side. I could not watch, could only stare at the endless storm and think of Tanaka's severed head lying separate from his body.

Whether or not the Levanti were right about freeing the soul, from the moment Kitado ceased drawing breath, I was alone.

8. CASSANDRA

Despite Kocho's lecture on wealth, I had expected better of the Witchdoctor's house than a tumbledown mansion, its drive so full of potholes the whole carriage jolted. My injured leg banged against the door and a pained hiss escaped before I could catch it.

"Fuck."

The girl stared.

I had been allowed back inside the carriage after the god-man stitched me up. Kocho had summarised the situation for him in a few terse words, and without comment or complaint, the Witchdoctor had set about his work. It had hurt more than I expected, but after a stop for food, water, rest, and fresh clothes, we had been on the road again, the watchful gaze of the silent woman on me at all times.

The rain had poured endlessly upon the carriage and now it drenched the run-down house, trying to wash it off the hillside. The surrounding terraces owned waterfalls, and the steep drive was little better than mud.

"What a shithole," I said, though I might as well have kept my thoughts to myself for all the acknowledgement I received from either companion. Even She had been quiet since the arrow.

Empress Hana had been awake more and more as we travelled

west, but although she was awake and seemed stronger, more often than not she stared at nothing as she did now, uttering not a word.

As the carriage climbed the drive the house disappeared from view, only to reappear around the next curve. An enormous tree standing in the grounds had moved with it, and I leaned closer to the window.

"There is a tree growing through the roof," I said, frowning through the wobbly, rain-streaked glass. "Why the hell would anyone let a tree grow inside their house?"

"Tree?" Empress Hana said, speaking for the first time. She didn't so much thrust me aside as insert herself before the window, forcing me to make space. We drew closer, proximity removing all doubt the tree was indeed growing straight through the roof of what must once have been an elegant country manor.

"So, there's a bad storm and the roof collapses, letting rain inside the building," I said. "Leaves fall in and compost down, and after a decade or so there's enough dirt for a seed to take root. But surely if you see a sapling in your house you pull it out, even if you can't afford to fix the roof. Unless they thought the tree's canopy would make a good replacement, and hadn't yet realised the damn thing was deciduous."

Empress Hana started to laugh. It began as a throaty chuckle and I prided myself on having amused her, but she laughed for so long and with such an increasingly manic tone that I began to doubt she had even heard me. When she turned her bloodshot eyes upon the silent young woman, I was sure of it. "Why here?" she demanded, as imperious as if she still sat upon the grand throne in Koi. "Why does your master bring us here? It does not belong…" The empress trailed off, all assurance draining out through her slack mouth. Her eyes widened and her gaze darted about the silent woman's face as though seeing it for the first time. All at once the carriage seemed not to have enough air.

"Saki?" the empress said.

The young woman cocked her head to the side as the carriage slowed. It halted with a jolt and the driver appeared at the door still hooded in his storm cloak. Another figure stood in the open doorway to welcome us, just like it was still a lord's residence and not a rotting remnant.

Kocho appeared, his grizzled grey hair stuck to his forehead. "Mistress?" he said, looking from her to the empress and back. "The Deathwalker isn't being foul again, is she?"

The young woman shook her head. She shot another glance at the empress then, with the flicker of a smile, took the wrinkled hand Kocho held out and stepped into the rain. Not seeming to care whether it drenched her, she ambled the short distance from the carriage to the house with Kocho harrying about her heels like a dog rushing her to safety.

"After you, Your Majesty," I said, gesturing to the open door in through which the swirling wind blew dustings of rain.

"I am no empress anymore, Miss Marius, and I know whom I have to thank for that. I will not show you my back that you might stab me in it. Again." She made a mock little bow. "After you, Miss Marius."

I could have explained myself, have begged forgiveness and pledged to serve her in reparation, but they were the actions of someone with a heart and a conscience, the actions of a woman who gave a damn what the world thought of her, and I was not that woman. I had done what I needed to do, and the moment I got what I wanted here I would move on again.

So, with a grim little smile, I stepped out into the rain. After two blissfully dry days I shivered at the cold, clammy touch of the storm. The tight bindings around my wound wouldn't allow me to run, but I quickened my hobbling hop toward the door. Despite the damp air, the front hall was thankfully dry. My experience of Kisian manor houses was limited, yet even the most stark entrance hall should have owned more than a few mouldering watercolours and a pot so cracked it looked to have sprouted teeth. A single passage led away into the building, full of shadows. One slowly coalesced into the approaching form of Kocho.

The servant holding the door looked me up and down as I hobbled in, making no attempt to hide his curiosity.

"What are you looking at?" I snapped as Kocho arrived.

"Don't mind her." He thrust a pair of walking sticks at the startled young man. "She seems to have made it her life's purpose to be as nasty and miserable as possible. You'll get used to it."

He stepped back out into the rain to offer his arm to Empress Hana, all respect and deference.

"Where am I supposed to go?" I said, leaning upon the wall to ease the strain in my good leg.

"Umm…" The servant opened and closed his mouth and looked around for help. Finding none, he said, "I don't know. There are rooms for each of the…of the…the…" He trailed off, leaning even farther back into the dark shadows behind the door.

"The subjects?" I suggested.

"Yes, subjects." He let out a relieved breath. "Yes. I don't know where yours is. I'm sure…Kocho—" He leaned out to address the old man as he and Empress Hana stepped beneath the portico. "Ah, Kocho, where is Deathwalker Three supposed to go?"

"I have a name, thank you. Wait—Deathwalker Three? There are others like me?"

"Not at present, but in the past…And the…the master does not use names for his subjects. It is simpler if everyone is referred to by their soul anomaly."

"Their what?"

The man shrank back again, his gaze flitting to Kocho.

"Don't answer that, Lechati," the old man said. "Leave her to me."

"Lechati?" I said. "So he gets a name but I am Deathwalker Three?"

"A few days ago you didn't even want to be here." Kocho turned to Lechati. "Here, you show Her Majesty to the room beside Mistress Saki's. I'll see to this one."

The empress's gaze snapped to Kocho. The name meant something to her. Saki. An old Kisian story spoke of a Saki, but this young woman with the sharp violet eyes was very real.

Heaving a relieved sigh, Lechati handed the walking sticks back to Kocho and bowed to Empress Hana. The movement brought him fully into the light, showing his skin to be even darker than it had first appeared, darker even than the Levanti. People from all different lands traded along the Ribbon, but in all my time in Genava I had never seen someone quite like Lechati. "This way, Your Majesty."

Kocho watched them go without a word, then thrust the walking sticks at me. "You'll want these to help you get around," he said. "And let me give you a word of warning. This place is as easy to get out of as it is to get into. There are no gates or walls or guards. You can, in theory, leave at any time. Most of the master's subjects are here voluntarily—he prefers it that way. But you"—he poked a finger into my face—"you heard me right in the cart the other day, he needs you. He needs you alive and he needs you well and if you do what he asks he might just give you what you came here for. If you don't do what he asks then that wound in your leg won't be your last."

"I've heard better threats from drunkards in Genavan gutters, old man."

Kocho grinned. "But I know something those drunkards don't. I know you're nowhere near as cold and nasty as you try to be, so let's just play nice and get this done without all the snark, shall we?"

He walked away along the passage without looking back. For a few seconds I considered not following, but with one walking stick gripped in each hand the prospect of attempting a getaway in the rain was not enticing. I hobbled after him.

The passages of the run-down house were thickly swathed in shadow. Dim light filtered through open doors and lattice-screen windows, but the endless pitter-patter of the rain found no holes in the roof. It must once have leaked, for the floor owned dark blotches of scrubbed mould and the ceiling had been patched with a distinct lack of craftsmanship. Better an ugly roof than no roof at all, yet Kocho averted his gaze from each hasty repair like they upset him.

"It didn't always look like this," the old man said, half turning his head to address me as I clunked gracelessly along behind him. "It was grand in its day."

"The Witchdoctor isn't as good at taking care of houses as arrow wounds then?"

Something like a sneer twisted Kocho's lips. "He doesn't own this place. He just uses it. I grew up in the nearby town, Esvar, at the bottom of the hill. As kids we used to dare each other to run up here. There were all sorts of stories about the Laroths. They ate children. They could turn into bats. You'd die if you ever met one's gaze. Silly stuff. The manor was getting worn out back then too, but you could still see the glory of it. If we'd come in through the front doors you would have seen the Wisteria Court, overgrown of course, and flooded at this season, but nobles used to come from across the empire for Errant tournaments."

"What happened to the family?"

"A decaying bloodline."

I stopped beside a faded portrait of an expressionless young woman, and a few steps farther on Kocho halted too. "You make it sound like the family started rotting like the house."

The old man shrugged. "It's as good an analogy as any. They

certainly didn't like each other very much by the end, nor were any of them entirely sane. Misunderstood soul anomalies do that to a man, and by the look of their records they stopped birthing Normals a few generations ago. The master found it quite fascinating, which means it's probably unusual."

He walked on, and as though caught to him by a string I followed, eyes lingering a moment on the portrait. "So a falling-down house and a dead family. Why are we here?"

"Rumours keep prying eyes away."

"So do walls and gates and locked doors."

Kocho took a corner and veered deeper into the building. Light had been following alongside, but it called to us from ahead now, its glow faint upon the floor. "You're not going to tell me why, are you?"

Again a shrug without turning. "If you're curious you might not need as many arrows to keep you from running."

"I am here against my will, old man," I said, my irritation turning the words into a snap. "If I get the chance to run you can be damn sure I'll take it."

"If you say so."

He walked on in silence, past closed doors and more patched sections of roof, the light getting steadily brighter until it filled the passage. With it the scent of dust thickened into something sweet, and I coughed. "What is that smell?" I said, wobbling on my sticks as I tried to lift a hand to my nose.

"Flowers."

"What flower smells like that?"

"Rotting ones."

I stopped breathing through my nose and I could still taste its stink. "Even rotting flowers don't smell that bad."

Another shrug. Kocho seemed untroubled by the smell, though when he turned to glance at me his eyes were watering. "You get used to it," he said in the stuffed-up way of one holding their nose.

"Get used to it? You're crying."

"All right, it's fucking awful and doesn't get any better, but it's impossible to get from one place to another without going through the central hall so just... cover your nose with your sleeve and keep moving."

I gestured to the sticks. "Not so easy when I'm injured."

"Consider it payback then," he said through the sleeve of his plain robe.

"Fuck you."

His eyes crinkled in amusement.

From the passage it had looked like nothing but a grand room, brightly lit, but hobbling out in Kocho's wake, I stopped and stared up. The tree stood taller than both floors of the house, its canopy so broad it spread beyond the broken hole in the roof. It had spread inside too, limbs and roots covering everything from the floor to the balustrade of a great staircase, the wood twisting around it like snakes. And what I had at first taken to be a patterned carpet upon the floor was a thick spread of rotting flowers. Great iridescent purple and blue blooms rotting to dross upon what might once have been a wooden floor now turned to earth.

Holding both sticks in one hand, I bent to pick up a flower. It was much heavier than I had expected. The flowers on the tree looked heavy too, weighing down their host boughs like fruit.

"What is it?" I said.

"A tree."

I let the shimmery flower splash back into the water and gave him a look. "A tree? All this talk of souls and rotting bloodlines and that's your answer?"

"Best one I've got. Come on. You're upstairs."

Kocho picked his way across the floor, following a path of solid stones through the mire. On each he stopped to sweep away rotting blossoms with his sandal, muttering that they would be slippery beneath my sticks. While he worked, I watched raindrops ripple the surface of the water, plinking far more musically here than outside.

A patter of fat drops followed us all the way up the staircase. It wound around the great, enthroned tree, every bump upon its knobbly trunk like the features of an ancient face.

At the top of the stairs two passages branched away. "This way," Kocho said, taking the one straight ahead. As we left the tree behind the smell faded fast as if too heavy to follow, leaving every breath choked with dust and old incense once again. But for the shimmering pollen upon my fingers I might have imagined it all.

"Here we are." Kocho stopped outside a door that looked no different to any other, except for one paper pane missing like a rotten tooth in an otherwise orderly smile. "I'll have a fresh sleeping mat sent up. Food comes three times a day and when the master needs you, someone will fetch you."

"And when he doesn't, I just sit here like a prisoner?"

"You can wander the house if you like, but it has some unpleasant parts that haven't been fixed or cleaned and it's easy to get lost. There's a library downstairs. If you can read."

I gave him a look and he held up his hands in mock surrender. "A lot of people can't," he said, sliding open the door. "I make no assumptions."

"I want to see the Witchdoctor."

Kocho shook his head. "It doesn't work like that. He decides, not you."

"I'm not here to be his plaything. I'm here so he can fix me."

The old man laughed, and gestured to my room. "Get comfortable. You have a lot of disappointment in your future."

My room was nothing more than an empty space owning fresh matting. No furniture, no sleeping mat, nothing but a high, narrow window, its original shutter closed to stop any rain blowing in beneath the overhanging eave. "So that's it? I just get to—?"

But Kocho's footsteps were already fading away along the passage.

Almost I followed, but I knew better than to harry him for more information now. Better to wait, to tease it out of him slowly, to play along.

Then you've finally decided we're staying? She said, breaking Her long silence.

"For now. But once the Witchdoctor takes you out of me, I'll be gone."

Kocho said—

"I know what he said," I hissed, checking whether the shadows still hid the old man. "But if he thinks—if they all think I am cooperating they'll let their guard down. I'll be a good little girl until then."

She laughed a bitter, sneering laugh and said no more, and not for the first time I wished I could see Her thoughts as She could see mine.

I hopped into my room and closed the door, shutting myself inside a calm, quiet box smelling of fresh matting and rain. Outside the storm continued unabated and while I listened to it pour upon the roof, I checked each wall for hidden doors in the panelling, checked under the matting for hatches, and dragged a storage chest from the passage to beneath the high window so I could see into the garden below. There were no lower roofs or nearby trees, which meant even if the window was large enough to escape through, it was two floors straight down into overgrown bushes. Better to just walk out the door. Cassandra Marius had enough confidence to do it, but then Cassandra Marius would already have stabbed all these weirdo bastards and been on her way, seducing anyone more intractable to get what she wanted. Clearly Cassandra Marius was losing her touch.

Why are you thinking about yourself like you're someone else?

"Shut up."

Why should I? We might not be together much longer, but I still deserve better than shut up *and* fuck off *after all we've been through.*

"If you wanted better treatment you should have hijacked someone else's body."

This is my body. This has always been my body.

"Bullshit. It's mine. It's always been mine and it always will be mine. Now shut up while I go find the Witchdoctor."

I had expected her to argue, but she slid back into silence as I took up my sticks and hobbled into the passage. Lechati appeared at the top of the stairs carrying a sleeping mat, but rather than bring it toward me he took the other passage and disappeared from sight. By the time I reached the corner there was no sign of him, but a distant hum of voices filled the air. With Lechati busy, it was the perfect time to go in search of the Witchdoctor, and yet curiosity caught me. I crept along, moving slowly with my sticks to keep them quiet. Step after soft step the voices grew louder, only to be punctuated by the thud of the sleeping mat hitting the floor. Fussing footsteps followed as it was unrolled and made. I crept closer. A door halfway along the passage stood open, the weak light from its own shuttered windows diving through the doorway to fall upon the passage floor.

"It is beyond the Sands, Your Majesty," Lechati was saying when I drew close enough to make out his words. "A very long way from here."

"Then why are you here?" came Empress Hana's voice, ever imperious.

"I'm here with Master Torvash. Normally we move around a lot, but for the last year or so we have been here. It is very beautiful, but I cannot say I like the cold."

I stepped within the spreading arc of light and out of habit reached for my dagger, only it wasn't there. Even the one I had so often relied on hiding in my boot was long gone. I was unarmed in an unknown place with unknown people. My heart hammered with rising panic as Lechati spoke again.

"Food shall be delivered soon, Your Majesty," he said. "Is there anything I can get you in the meantime?"

"No." A weary answer. "I will rest."

Footsteps sounded, and I stumbled a few steps toward the aperture, not wanting to be caught lurking.

You were *lurking.*

"Shut—"

"Deathwalker Three!" Lechati said, falling back as he almost walked into me. "I didn't see you there."

"I'm sorry, I did not mean to startle you," I said, once more making use of my well-practised routines. I smiled at him, my body naturally falling into its accustomed stance only made more difficult by the walking sticks. Breasts out, hip jutting—Kocho might be too old and jaded to take an interest, but young Lechati could be the weak link I needed to get what I wanted.

The young man's eyes slid down my body and he swallowed hard. I made no sign of noticing, though there really was nothing more obvious than an inexperienced young man. "I came to see the empress," I said. "But if she intends to rest perhaps you could show me around instead."

He opened his mouth, already nodding, but Empress Hana's voice emerged from within the room. "I am not yet resting, Miss Marius. Leave the poor boy alone and come pick on someone closer to your own age."

Lechati squirmed, glanced back through the door, and with a bow to me instead of the empress, he darted off along the passage in a mire of confusion.

Empress Hana strode into view, her arms tightly folded and an eyebrow lifted. "Although," she said, "I think that for all your beauty you are significantly older than I. Your face owns many lines if one looks past those oh-so-perfect features. You would have been quite the beauty if you'd ever learnt to smile properly." She smiled herself, and gestured regally for me to enter. "You wish, perhaps, to apologise for the deaths of thousands of my people and the destruction of my city?"

I did not move from the doorway. Her smile did not reach her sharp blue eyes and her lips were pressed into a thin line, yet despite the palpable anger I did not want to run. My own anger flared, and clenching the handles of my walking sticks, I stepped into the room. "I am not here to apologise. We all do what we must to survive, you should know that as well as I do."

"There are limits. How many dead innocents is your life worth, Miss Marius?"

"As many as it takes because there are no limits. Honourable sacrifice won't keep you warm at night once you're dead. Go on, tell me I'm wrong. Tell me you wouldn't let a whole nation die if it meant getting your son back."

She fixed me with a hard stare. "What do you want?"

"You looked at my arm. Back at Koi, in that stone room with the dead."

"I did."

"Why? Were you expecting to see the same mark Kocho has?"

Genuine surprise lit her features and her eyes darted to the doorway almost fearfully. "And what symbol is that?"

"A long curve, like a snake."

Relief? She certainly seemed to sag. "I don't know what I was expecting to see on your arm, Miss Marius, but I know what I feared." The empress pointed at the shuttered window. It owned the same carved pattern as the shutter in my room, but no matter how hard I looked at it, it meant nothing.

"That," she said, when it became obvious I did not understand, "is the one I fear. Do you see it? Once you notice it you will see it everywhere in this house, because the Laroths were exceedingly proud of it. They thought themselves gods amongst men. And Kisia nearly burned for it."

I tilted my head. It was just a pattern of lines, some straight and some diagonal. "What does it mean?"

"Is this the information you were hoping to get out of Lechati?"

"An easy enough method."

Empress Hana once more folded her arms. Her room contained some simple furniture, even a small table, but she had not invited me to sit or made any move to close the door. I was an unwelcome intruder in her space despite her imperious invitation.

"If I tell you will you leave that young man alone?"

I laughed. "I wasn't going to torture him. I assure you, Your Majesty, I am very good at my job. He would enjoy it immensely."

"He is young enough to be your son."

"And Emperor Kin was old enough to be your father. In fact…" I tapped my chin, feigning an attempt at recollection. "Wasn't he in love with your mother? I'm sure that was why all the rich folk in Genava laughed when news of your marriage reached us."

She kept her expression impressively impassive, even as I went on. "And then when you gave him bastard children, well!"

The empress lifted thin brows. "Are you finished?" she enquired, coldly polite.

"Yes, I think so."

"Good. You will have to try a lot harder than that to hurt me, Miss Marius. You are hardly presenting me with facts and assumptions I have not heard a hundred times before. It has, however, been all too long since I traded insults without also having to serve tea and smile and hope my headdress would not pull loose from its pins and tumble onto the table, so do, by all means, find some more. At least, whatever my transgressions, I am not a freak like you."

My words might have glanced off her armour, but hers cut me deep. That single word, *freak*, contained within it all the jibes of the hospice kids, every time I had been kicked or spat on, the horrified looks upon my parents' faces, and a whole lifetime of putting up with Her. And by Empress Hana's faint smile, I knew it showed on my face. "Ah," she said. "More weaponry at my disposal. I really thought you would be a more worthy opponent."

I clenched my walking sticks, wishing more than ever for a bottle of Stiff to relax my muscles. What I wouldn't have given for a whole flask of it to drown my troubles.

Footsteps sounded in the passage outside and we both turned, more in accord in that moment of sudden unease than we had been in every one preceding it.

Kocho appeared in the doorway. "There you are," he said, something of relief showing in his face. He turned his gaze to the empress. "I'm sorry to disturb your rest, Your Majesty," he said, wryly emphasising *rest* with a glance flicked my way. "But the master wants to look at you."

"Has he some more foul-tasting medicine for me?"

"Very likely, Your Majesty."

"If he wishes to waste his time on so pointless a task then by all means I will come." This the fiery empress who had first received me in Koi's throne room, regal and frightening in a space that echoed with power. Now she was being summoned by the Witchdoctor.

"I am coming too," I said. "I will see the Witchdoctor now."

Rather than remind me I had no power here, Kocho shrugged. "As you wish."

I stopped in the doorway. "He already asked for me?"

"No, the mistress wants you. Just for a few preliminary tests so she knows what to expect and how well you respond."

Out in the passage, Empress Hana stood waiting, but I did not move. I wanted the Witchdoctor to free me, but the word *tests* conjured every horror story I had ever heard about him, stories of bodies in vats and people going missing in the night only to return twisted and broken. Kocho was kind enough, but the Witchdoctor had sat proud and perfect upon his horse, bow in hand, and stared down at me as though I were but an interesting slug he had deigned to help.

If you don't walk down there, I will do it for you.

"I can do it on my own, thank you," I said, not caring that I spoke aloud now they knew me for what I was. That freedom brought an unexpected rush of joy and as I stepped out, I added, "Besides, you aren't as good at things like walking."

I would be if you ever let me practice, you body hog.

Kocho laughed, leaving Empress Hana to look from him to me and back again. "I do not understand what is amusing."

"Kaysa."

"Kaysa?"

The old man pointed at me. "The second soul inside our Deathwalker. She's lovely. Shall we go?"

I lingered, frozen there in the passage outside the empress's room. "Can you always hear Her?"

"I hear lots of things." Kocho turned and strode off along the passage. "Come on, they're waiting."

Kaysa? I said, setting off in his wake.

Yes?

That's your name?

I... think so? I've always liked it. I think it suits my face better than Cassandra.

Uneasiness stirred, but shoving it down, I hobbled on.

◆

Mistress Saki and the Witchdoctor were waiting in a well-lit room containing a pair of workbenches, some shelves, and two real chairs that reminded me of home. Despite their well-worn appearance they looked out of place in so Kisian a house.

No sound greeted us beyond the distant roar of the rain and the faint scratch of quill upon paper. The Witchdoctor and the young mistress sat perched side by side upon stools at one of the workbenches, their heads bent over the same large scroll of parchment held down at either end by jars. Neither spoke, yet each looked at the other while they wrote, engrossed in their activity.

Kocho cleared his throat. Neither of our hosts turned, but the Witchdoctor lifted his hand. "Thank you, Kocho. You will stay to assist Saki."

"Yes, Master."

The old man gestured to the chairs, inviting us to sit and wait. Empress Hana didn't seem to notice, too busy staring at Mistress Saki's profile. I looked from Saki to the empress and back and saw no likeness. Despite her loyalties and her reputation, the empress looked more Chiltaen than Kisian, while Mistress Saki was as classically Kisian as it was possible to look, saving only her oddly coloured eyes.

"It is an interesting theory," the Witchdoctor said as Mistress Saki rose from her stool. "We may not have time to test it, however. The empress—" He broke off as Saki placed her hand upon his arm, shooting a warning look at us in the doorway.

The Witchdoctor came toward us without a welcoming smile— it seemed not to be a part of his facial repertoire. Perhaps he really was the statue he had first appeared, perfect beauty hewn from rock.

"I want you to fix me," I said, stepping in front of him. My heart raced at my own daring. "I want you to take this...thing out of me."

I am not a thing.

The Witchdoctor looked me up and down and never had I felt

so assessing a gaze. "That is not why you are present today. Nor will I discuss my intentions or the specifics of my experiments with any subject."

He made to walk past me, but again I stepped in front of him, thrusting out one walking stick. "If I don't get what I want, I will not be staying."

So much for lulling them into a false sense of confidence.

The Witchdoctor deigned no reply, just gestured to Kocho.

"Come on, let it go," the old man said, gripping my elbow and guiding me into the room. He grabbed one of the chairs and drew it across the wooden floor, its legs clunking as he dropped it in place.

He pointed to it. "Sit."

"Is that required?" I said, clenching the handles of my walking sticks.

"No, but if you prefer not to hit your head it's wise to listen."

"Hit my head?"

"Just sit down."

Do it, Cassandra. This is what we came here for.

I sat, unsure if I had made my legs collapse beneath me or She had. Kaysa. The name echoed in my thoughts and I tried to thrust aside the fear that came with it. She had taken over so easily that night outside Koi.

Don't think about it, I told myself, hoping She was not listening.

Mistress Saki turned from the bench and, having passed her gaze over Kocho, let it fall upon me. Curiosity lit the young face and she rubbed the thumb and fingers of her right hand together rapidly like someone trying to conjure flame. Then, as though afraid it might sting, she slowly reached her hand toward me. Soft, cool fingers touched my cheek and somehow tugged me forward, dragging me across the blurring room. Everything became shadows and echoes like a woollen blanket lay draped over my head. And then, a background hum became voices and I was looking at myself through the fog. Myself, sitting in the chair looking stunned and confused, blinking rapidly and pressing fingers to my own face.

Well, someone said, and it was not Her, but another voice. *That's new.*

I did not hear a reply but felt it, a sense of agreement, of excitement, and the image of me tilted as though being examined from a different angle. Kocho appeared through the same fog, his mouth open as he looked from me to . . . me.

I tried to shift the confusion muddying my mind.

Don't worry, you get used to it, spoke the new voice. *Although it can be hard to hear when it gets crowded.*

Crowded? Where am I? I asked, but as I looked down at a hand rubbing thumb and forefinger together, I needed no answer. It came anyway.

Welcome to the body of Saki Laroth.

9. DISHIVA

Tea bowls clinked as the tray was set between us. With a tiny gesture full of authority, Lady Sichi dismissed the maid, leaving us staring at one another over the steaming pot. Tea was not common on the plains. It could be bought in Tempach and a few Levanti had taken a liking to it, but it was still just a drink. Here it was a ritualised part of every day in the same way we tended our horses and checked the water levels in the barrel wagons—little things that any day would feel wrong without.

I shifted my weight on the matting. I was used to sitting for everything from meetings to meals, but the Kisian way of kneeling was different and I wondered if it was rude to cross my legs instead.

Lady Sichi stretched her hand across the table toward the teapot, her arm encased in shimmering silk. "Thank you for joining me, Captain Dishiva," she said in creditable, if stiff, Levanti.

I glanced up at Nuru, standing to the side of the table—she the only member of the empress-to-be's retinue who was present. "She wished to memorise a greeting phrase to make you feel more comfortable," the girl said a little snappishly. "Just say thank you."

"Thank you, Lady Sichi."

The Kisian woman stretched a thin smile and poured a steaming bowl of tea for me. It smelled floral and a little bitter, a surprisingly pleasant mix. As she poured her own bowl she spoke again, this time in the lilting Kisian I was used to hearing.

"It is a great comfort to know you are in charge of our protection, Captain," Nuru said, translating so smoothly as she went that I wondered how much of this had been rehearsed. "It is a fine thing to be able to trust in one's safety."

I answered with a nod, unsure if she meant it or it was a thinly veiled hint she didn't trust me at all. The Kisians were not expressive and she might have been a sculpture for all her face moved.

"It is also very pleasant to have a female guard upon whom I can rely," Nuru went on a few beats after Lady Sichi. "I am sure you have noticed, Captain, that women in Kisia do not bear arms or hold such positions."

"I did notice that, yes. Except for Empress Miko, who I saw ride into battle at Risian."

The flicker of some emotion crossed the lady's face so fast it was impossible to tell what it meant. "Yes," she said, and Nuru mimicked her cool tone. "Empress Miko ever strives to be an exception."

When I didn't answer, Lady Sichi took up her tea bowl in both hands and drew a deep breath of its scented steam. She blew on it. Once. Twice. Three times. Then lowered it to say, "You have perhaps also noticed that Kisian women are not allowed to be present at discussions of politics, even when they are to be an empress. Even when..." She looked at me directly for the first time since she had begun speaking. "The entire alliance by which we sit here today was brokered upon my marriage."

It was all I could do not to squirm beneath that clear, unblinking gaze, the kneeling position suddenly three times more uncomfortable than it had been before.

Feeling called upon to answer, I said, "I have, yes."

Once again, she lifted the bowl and gently blew the steam from the tea's surface. "It is not in my nature to allow myself to appear weak or desperate without good cause, so I hope you will appreciate how difficult this is for me, Captain. Power comes from knowledge and survival comes from power, and I wish more than anything to survive. Whatever information you are able to give me about the shifting alliances in the meeting room would be very useful. I do not wish to put my faith in the wrong people."

Despite her lack of expression there was a vibrancy to her voice I could not ignore. A deep pool of emotion lay behind the mask and I pitied her, yet this woman was Kisian, the niece of Gideon's most powerful ally, and not someone I ought to trust.

I shifted my bowl for something to do, something to look at that was not her. "If…if Gi—Emperor Gideon has not chosen to take you into his confidence then I do not feel it is my place to go against his wishes."

To my surprise, she smiled at that. "I believe His Majesty is rather too busy at present to have even considered my future part in this. I have come to doubt I will get any…attention from him until the consummation of our marriage."

A faint blush coloured her cheeks, but she looked at me with a directness that belied, or perhaps defied, any embarrassment. I considered replying with the same degree of honesty and explaining Gideon's disinterest, but I had been in Kisia long enough to see just how different their society was and kept my mouth shut. I could not tell how she would take it.

Not receiving an answer, Lady Sichi put her bowl down. She hadn't taken a single sip. "I have done you the courtesy of being honest and open. It is not a common thing in Kisia, you will find, Captain. Lies and manipulation are far more useful tools and most nobles are well used to the game. All I request in return is that you are equally honest with me. If you have been warned not to communicate with me and not to trust me, then say so."

I had not, and yet despite her show of vulnerability and how much I disliked the way the Kisians treated their women, I could not risk trust, not even of information that to me appeared to have little value.

I set my tea bowl from me, equally untouched. "I'm sorry I cannot be of more use," I said. "I am not unsympathetic to your position and will continue to do all in my power to ensure your protection, but it would be against my honour to speak information Gideon has not himself divulged."

A brief nod, lacking all surprise, before Nuru had made it even a few words into her translation. "At least in that I hope I may rely on you, Captain Dishiva."

Was she questioning my loyalty? Suggesting I would let harm come to her by deliberately turning my back? It was impossible to tell but there was a hard, assessing look in her eyes I found it difficult to meet. "Of course, Lady Sichi" was all I could say, and was grateful that the following nod was a dismissal in every language.

Performing the task usually left to Lady Sichi's servants, Nuru slid the door open and ushered me out into the dim passage. Rather than closing it behind me she stepped out too, shutting Lady Sichi in alone.

"She is not plotting against us, Captain," Nuru said, her hushed whisper cutting straight to the point. "Whichever Kisians you fear are our enemies, she is not. It is hard for us to understand, but in Kisian society the act of marriage means she is wholly in Gideon's power and reliant upon him for protection. The wives of failed emperors are not well treated and she will not be spared for being Kisian if he falls. Keep that in mind next time. Please."

She was gone before I could reply, her fierce sentiments echoing in my chest even once she'd closed the door behind her. Needing to escape the oppressive manor, I strode away, determinedly not looking back at the door to what I now couldn't help but think of as Lady Sichi's pretty prison.

Rain had been steadily beating down since we had arrived in Kogahaera, with only occasional breaks for the world to draw breath, but sunshine peeked through the clouds now, flecking the mud and stones with dazzling gold. From the front steps I caught sight of Lashak standing by the stables and made to join her, only for Jass en'Occha to appear before me.

"Captain Dishiva," he said, owning a solemn look.

"Jass en'Occha," I said, striving for aloof pride though I had not been able to think of that night without a stab of shame.

When his cheeks flushed and he looked over my shoulder I knew he had recalled it too. Despite his broad musculature and the seriousness of his features, I added blushing to the list of ways he appeared young, along with his twitch of a smile and his carefree laugh.

Having expected him to greet me awkwardly, salute, and move on, I lifted my brows when he remained hovering. "Is there something you wish to say, Sword?"

"I... understand you are short a full complement of Swords to protect the emperor. I wish to offer my blades in service."

"Have you spoken to Captain Taga about this?"

"I have, yes. She understands and respects my desire to protect Emperor Gideon and gives her permission."

I was still at least a dozen Swords short despite having taken on many, but I had hoped to make up those numbers with Levanti who did not make me feel uncomfortable.

"Then by all means," I said, having no good reason to refuse him. "I am glad to have you. We are quartered in the barracks within the manor. If you keep walking along the main passage to the far stairs you will find it. Keka, my second, should be there."

Jass saluted. "Yes, Captain. Thank you, Captain."

I made to move on, but he sidestepped into my path only to step back out of it again. "Sorry, Captain, I just also wanted to say..."

He gripped his hands behind his back, standing to attention, his look something of a challenge. "I just wanted to say I was sorry for the other night. I have great respect for you and regret my words."

I ought to have returned the apology. He had given me the perfect opportunity to make amends now we would be working together, but I could not spit the words out. He had gifted me too good a chance to sidestep responsibility for my actions, and I grasped at it like a drowning woman sucking down air. "Thank you," I said, and before he could say more, before I could say more or even think about it a moment longer than I had to, I nodded and walked away. I was halfway across the yard, walking blindly, before Lashak's voice recalled me to a sense of my original purpose.

"Di! Don't wander off on me, you dreamer."

She waved when I turned around, and grinned as I joined her beneath the eave of the main stable. "Sorry, my mind had wandered."

"Yeah, I could see that." She nodded in the direction of the steps where I had stood talking to Jass. "That boy has been hanging around for the last hour."

"He is hardly a boy."

Lashak shrugged, picking something out of her teeth. "All Swords still in their first terms of service are children to me, Di."

"He wants to be one of my Swords and guard Gideon."

"Oh yes, and that's all?"

I thought of the night in Itaghai's stall and made fists upon fidgeting fingers. It had not been possible to find new partners, my cycle having shifted into fertile days and there being no supply of epaya here. There had been a lot of other things on my mind, but it had added a layer of frustration at this strange society we were to become a part of. Did they just... have babies whenever they liked without thought to the consequences?

Lashak set her hand on my arm. "How are you?"

The understanding of a fellow sufferer always made a lump form in my throat. "Fine. I keep busy. Don't think about it."

Tightening her grip, Lashak bent her lips to my ear. "I heard yesterday that it happened to Yiss as well," she whispered, and I turned, hunting untruth in her face. But there was just a twisted half smile full of apology it should never have been hers to give.

"That makes it even more surprising she voted not to attack the Chiltaens," I said. "Did they...*all* the captains?"

"All the females at least. The only men I've heard tell of are young bloods and saddleboys."

I gave a grunt of understanding but in truth I did not understand at all. It made sense to demoralise captives by shaming their leaders, but that the Chiltaens had chosen only to attack and degrade female leaders was irrational.

Knowing Lashak would no more be able to explain it, I shrugged, the action as much an attempt to dislodge the thought from my mind as dismiss it from the conversation.

"I did what you asked," she said after a moment's silence.

I looked around. The only Levanti close enough to hear was Loklan e'Jaroven, my horse master, but he was humming as he checked his Leiya's hooves. "Oh yes?"

"Given the angle the arrow struck Gideon's shoulder, it must have come from the northern side of the compound. The tower there isn't used but is accessible. Mostly Qara Swords are camped in that area along with a smattering of Bedjuti, assuming of course it was actually a Levanti who attacked him."

"The man who came at him with a knife certainly was."

Lashak bobbed her head in agreement. "I worry."

"So do I," I said. "I'm not sure we can do this without him."

As she agreed I thought of what Nuru had said about Sichi's future, about her safety being tied to Gideon's success and survival. In a way it was true for all of us.

Despite the attack, Gideon continued to walk about the compound like any other Levanti. Almost any other Levanti. He wore the imperial surcoat at all times and was often accompanied by messengers or Kisian supporters, but for the most part he still looked like a herd master.

I had offered to have my Swords walk behind him as they did with Lady Sichi, but he refused, even when I reminded him his attacker had been Levanti.

"If I judge all by the actions of one, I will soon be at war with my own people," he said. "Tell your Swords to watch from a distance, but I cannot lead if I am not safe without them."

Within a few days, Lady Sichi was doing the same. I saw her first while talking to Lashak over a morning cup of pottun. It had become our little ritual, a brief respite after the chaos of the morning meal. She had stashed away a whole pouch when exiled and had been rationing it ever since.

We stood leaning against the stable wall in the morning mist, each holding a battered tin cup that to anyone else would look like water. "Is that Lady Sichi?"

I'd had my eyes closed, enjoying the bite of the pottun on my tongue, stale as it was. "Lady Sichi?" She was crossing the yard, not toward us but toward the main stable, Nuru beside her and two of my Swords a step behind. They still looked odd to my eyes in their crimson surcoats, and even more odd to be walking behind a lady like she was a newborn foal. "Yes, that's her."

"I haven't really seen her yet; she's always shut away in another room or that silk box." Lashak narrowed her eyes. "Hmm, Gideon is almost to be envied."

"You think so?" I took another sip of pottun and swirled it around my mouth before swallowing. "She's to your taste?"

"It's the decision in her walk. And that proud way she lifts her chin as though daring us to think little of her. Yes, decidedly she is quite to my taste. But then so is Gideon, so..."

She gave a wicked grin and I dug my elbow into her side. "Don't even think about it. We need less trouble around here, not more."

Lashak cackled and downed the last of her pottun as Lady Sichi approached a Levanti in the yard. He was rubbing down one of the horses taken out for exercise, a strange enough concept in itself, but not as strange as watching Lady Sichi hold out her hand for a horse brush and begin working.

"What is she doing?" I said. "Does she think we're not capable of looking after our horses properly?"

"Looks more like *she* isn't capable of looking after horses properly."

The Sword was, with Nuru's help, now showing Lady Sichi how to use the brush more efficiently. She was watching, listening, smiling, and some others in the yard gathered to give advice. "Nothing can get a Levanti talking faster than a debate on horse care," I said. "I think maybe she's a smart woman."

"Or that Nuru is."

"Both, I think. It looks like Gideon has more of an ally there than I thought."

Lashak looked around, holding her cup just below her lips. "You think she's deliberately seeking our approval?"

I nodded in Lady Sichi's direction. A Sword had her hand on top of Lady Sichi's and was showing her how to make the curled strokes that promoted good circulation in cool weather. "If that's not a deliberate show, I'm looking at the most charismatic accident I've ever seen."

"And here comes Gideon," Lashak said, swirling the dregs in her cup. "It'll be interesting to see what he thinks."

"He'll probably approve, but—" I swallowed the last of my

pottun. "Either way, that's my cue to go lurk about and make sure no one kills him." I handed Lashak the cup. "Thanks."

"See you tomorrow morning?"

"For as long as you have pottun, yes."

She pressed a hand to her heart. "Oh, how you wound me. I am slain. It was just the pottun you loved, not me."

I winked. "Always."

With a salute and a demure "Captain," I left her chuckling and strode across the yard unable to suppress my grin.

I hadn't even made it halfway to Gideon before a gong rang at the main gate. Trusting him to the competent eyes of my Swords, I walked over, already twitchy at the thought of new arrivals. Day by day the compound at Kogahaera had grown busier. When we arrived, it had been little more than a residence surrounded by out-buildings and tents pitched in mud, but each day brought more allies, messengers, and supplies. And more Kisian lords. They came to bow at the feet of their new emperor and jostle for position.

"Who is it?" I called up to the pair of sentries on the gates, one Kisian, one Levanti. The Kisian pointed and spoke, but I waited for the Levanti to talk over him.

"There are ... non-fighting people who want to come in."

"Kisian?"

"Some of them."

"What do you mean some of them? Who are the others?"

The Levanti glanced at his Kisian companion, and despite the language barrier they seemed to share a moment of ill-ease. "Well, there are a few Chiltaens, Captain."

"Chiltaen soldiers?"

"No, not soldiers. Peasant folk. And there's a pair of, well ... honestly, Captain, I don't know where they're from."

I scowled up at the man, his worried face encircled by the stiff hood of a storm cloak. "Well, what do they want?"

"I think Ryo"—he indicated the Kisian soldier—"is trying to say they want to see Dom Villius." He tapped his collarbone where Leo wore his pendant.

Levanti had been known to travel long distances to seek the advice and guidance of a horse whisperer, or embark on pilgrimages to the great shrines. That believers in Leo's god felt him important enough to travel so far was troubling. I thought of the puppets again with their shining eyes.

"Pilgrims." I sighed at the closed gates. Chiltaens I could understand, but Kisians too? How far did belief in this god stretch?

"Do we let them in, Captain?"

A voice cleared its throat at my side, and the Levanti sentry got caught halfway between a bow and a salute.

"If they are devout enough to travel here unsure of their welcome, they will just camp outside if we refuse them entry," Gideon said. "Better they are where we can see them, don't you think?"

Better we loosed arrows into each of their throats and left them to rot rather than give Dom Villius allies, I thought. But killing innocent pilgrims would not serve Gideon's ends.

I called to the Swords hovering nearby. "Open the gates."

They grumbled, but with staggered salutes a small group of Qara and Jaroven unbarred the gate, scraping a layer of mud flat as they hauled it open. Outside stood a small, mismatched, wary group of pilgrims. For a moment they looked at us as we looked at them, and they might have remained frozen there, unsure of their welcome, had not three young men on horseback led the way in. Another man leading a mule followed, along with a pair of women in ragged robes travelling on foot, their gazes darting. Behind them came a covered box like the one in which Lady Sichi had ridden north. Its four carriers were damp with rain, or sweat, or both, as was a fifth man in the same-coloured uniform leading a pair of mules piled high with packs. Two armed guards brought up the rear, they the only ones who looked at all comfortable.

The creaking of the gates faded, leaving a hushed camp in its wake. Where there had been talk and bustle there were now hundreds of staring eyes and whispering tongues. The two women stepped close together, but the servants bearing the silk box pushed forward. One carrier wheezed at the nearest Kisian soldier and was pointed in the direction of a stone block outside the manor. I had thought it a relic of some long-broken statue, but Lady Sichi had been set down in exactly the same place. A mounting block for silk boxes? How could two such different cultures ever become a cohesive whole?

"I will meet these people inside *before* they see Leo Villius," Gideon said in a low voice and slipped away, no doubt so he could make a grander first impression.

Which made dealing with the newcomers my job. Reluctantly, I followed the silk box to the stone mounting block, keeping my eye on the Kisian guards walking with it. Catching sight of Loklan in the crowd, I signalled for him to join me, and the quietest of my Swords shouldered his way through the gathering onlookers. "Captain?" he said.

"Find Nuru. I need her to translate for me. Quick as you can."

"Yes, Captain."

He ran off while the carriers lowered the box so slowly their arms shook and their legs twitched. A voice spoke from inside— Kisian, but rich of tone like a fat Tempachi merchant. Yet the hand that pierced the curtains was slim and soft, only its gesture a coarse demand for attention. The uniformed man with the mules hurried forward and bowed, speaking quickly, every word tinged with apology. There were plenty of Kisian soldiers watching, but those who heard his words only glanced at each other, unsure.

The curtain parted in a flap of silk and a fine spray of water. A wooden sandal met the wet, sun-sparkling stone, followed by a second, each leg encased in the skirt of a shimmering blue robe. The servant's hand shot out to help, but it was ignored as the box shifted with its owner's weight and a man far younger than I had expected emerged. Despite his cushioned vehicle, not a hair stuck out from his severe, slicked-back topknot, a knot pulled so tight his skin owned not a single line or wrinkle. At least not until he squinted against the bright sunlight.

Lifting a hand to protect his eyes he looked around, gaze alighting on my crimson silk.

Taking two steps forward, he pointed to my surcoat and erupted into a stream of hasty Kisian. By the way he stood he considered himself superior, and part way through his speech he made the sign of Leo's god, but there my understanding ended and all I could do was stand proud like a stone buffeted by the veldt winds and wait for Nuru.

She came eventually, her long hair tangling as she sped across the yard. She slowed as she approached, breathing heavily, and saluted to me before bowing to the newcomer.

"This man appears to be a pilgrim," I said. "Here to see Leo Villius, I—"

His high priest's name sent the man off on another speech, and Nuru narrowed her eyes in an effort of concentration. Her reply when he finished made him throw up his hands and gesture rudely at me. Nuru spoke my name, then said, "His name is Lord Nishi, Captain. He *is* a pilgrim here to see Dom Leo Villius, but he is… confused by contradictory reports as to whether the emperor has killed his high priest or not."

"Perhaps it isn't wise to say both are true," I murmured. "Who are the others?"

Nuru looked over my shoulder to the gaggle of new arrivals

clustered in the muddy yard. She pointed them out to Lord Nishi, whose answer made him look so lofty and pompous I wanted to throw him back in his silk box and send him on his way.

"Other pilgrims who fell in with him for protection. All are one in the eyes of the One True God, he says."

"Damn it," I said, hating the weight of so many eyes upon me. "Well, Gid—His Majesty says he will see them before they see Leo Villius. Tell him so and see what he says."

Nuru did so, but the annoyance I expected didn't come.

"He says he came here with the object of bowing to any emperor who treated... 'Veld Reborn' with the respect and reverence he deserves in the eyes of the One True God. And something about being gifted with donkeys, but that might have been a quote."

"Veld?" The name struck a memory. "Does he mean Dom Villius?"

"I am not sure, Captain. Would you like me to ask?"

"No, no, just get them out of here." Loklan had returned with her and again I gestured him forward. "Go warn Gideon they're all coming to see him. Tell him they want to know Dom Villius is safe before they support Kisia's new emperor."

The young Jaroven repeated the words back to me in his low, nervous voice and, receiving a nod, hurried off again like a hare tearing across the plains. "Nuru, tell Lord Nishi the emperor will see him and the other pilgrims soon, and take them to that big hall with all the padded bed seats to wait."

"Divans?"

"Whatever the fuck they're called," I snapped. "Take them there so they can stop causing a scene here."

Nuru saluted. "Captain."

I fell back as, with something like the courtly grace Lady Sichi managed, Nuru gestured and invited our new guests to step inside. All the pilgrims went, Lord Nishi with enough confidence that he left his two guards and his servant behind. The servant looked me over with disdain before addressing the closest Kisian soldier, who pointed in the direction of the stable yard. I followed him and the two soldiers to ensure they made no trouble.

"Captain," Nuru said, catching up halfway across the yard. "His Majesty wishes to greet the new guests and waits on you to join him before—"

"Then let him wait a few more moments," I said as Lord Nishi's men disappeared into one of the stables. "Come with me. I need your mouth."

"But, Captain," she protested as she tiptoed after me, afraid of soiling a pair of shiny wooden sandals far lighter than the colour of her feet. I lifted my brows at them, but Nuru just clicked her tongue in annoyance and tried to avoid the mud. By the time we reached the stable I could barely see her feet for the splatter.

The two soldiers and Lord Nishi's servant had halted not far inside the door as though waiting to be served, but the only Kisians present were two men wearing Grace Bahain's sigil who eyed them as warily as they eyed us.

"Address these men for me, Nuru," I said, standing to my fullest height. "Ask them how long they expect to stay. Be nice."

"I'm always nice, it's you—"

I cleared my throat and forced a smile to my lips that didn't like being there. Nuru broke off her complaint and spoke instead to Lord Nishi's men in halting Kisian. The servant answered, his surprise at being accosted fast becoming a sneer.

"He says they stay as long as their master stays."

"Why are you stammering when you talk to him?"

Nuru's gaze flicked to me and then down. "I'm trying some of Lady Sichi's tricks, Captain," she said, sounding like she was hiding a smile. "Men here are different. I think this one wants me to be small and silly so he will feel big and powerful and answer more easily."

I bit back the urge to tell her not to be small and silly for anyone. "Ask if they are all pilgrims or are only here serving their master."

"Captain, what use—?"

"Just ask them. I need to know what their purpose is to understand what threat they are."

Nuru let out a breath and smiled at each of the men in turn as she asked the question. Clearly, she had been watching Lady Sichi very closely. To simper at anyone was disgusting, but I had to admire the skill of her act. She might still be a saddlegirl, but riding with the First Swords of Torin would have taught her how to fight and hunt and kill, how to sever the heads of the dead and release their souls to the world. Had Lord Nishi's servant known what she was capable of he might not have leered at her so foully.

At least he answered my question easily enough, unlike the guards who had to be asked a second time. One replied with a little shake of the head. The other a nod. Nods touched something at his throat as he answered and glanced toward the heavily-laden mules.

"The man says of course he is a believer, he—"

"What's in the packs?"

Nuru looked at me, but I didn't take my eyes off Nods, squirming where he stood. Nuru relayed my question, a little more stiffly this time, and the servant drew himself up, launching into a diatribe. Without waiting for her to translate, I said, "Tell him I am the commander of the Imperial Guard and if these packs are not opened for inspection, they will all be thrown over the walls."

The man jabbed an angry finger at me. Dropping her weak act, Nuru snapped my threat. His tirade died in a snarl and he untied the first pack with a rough tug. The scent of incense punched out from a tightly packed collection of rolled silk robes, tied sandals, and linen. I patted the sides in search of odd shapes, more to annoy him than because I expected to find something hidden, before letting that one pass with a nod. While he retied the pack and opened the next, Nuru hissed in my ear. "His Majesty wanted you to attend on him straight away, Captain. What are we doing examining Lord Nishi's clothes?"

"Making a point," I said, though it was only half the truth. I was thinking of the calm way Leo Villius moved through the world, and of the way his eyes glittered through his mask like the puppets all those years ago.

The second pack contained much the same, and a third what looked more like the gathered belongings of the two soldiers. The other mule wasn't carrying soft packs, rather a pair of wooden boxes slung either side of the beast's body, both painted in a sticky black substance to protect against the rain. I pointed to them and with a reluctant sigh, the servant tugged one of the lids open. Inside, nestled in a protective bed of straw, sat dozens of small books. The Tempachi missionaries had brought books just like them into our camps and I stepped back in revulsion. No wonder Nods had looked at their cargo. The holy book of the One True God. My fingers itched to burn the lot of them. It seemed Lord Nishi had come not only to see Leo Villius, but to make converts.

An icy fear settled in my stomach.

"How many?"

Nuru asked and received an answer. "A hundred," she said.

I pointed at them. "Tell them they must seek Emperor Gideon's permission to have these here. They must be taken to the manor. Now."

The message was relayed. They argued. Nuru reminded them they were guests of the emperor, and eventually the servant acquiesced. Wringing his hands, he took the non-believing guard with him and led the mule back toward the manor. Nuru took a few steps after them, in a hurry to leave, but I looked at Nods who once more touched the pendant at his collarbone.

"Ask him if he is well versed in the faith of the One True God."

"Captain—"

"This would be a lot faster if you stopped complaining and just did as I asked, Nuru. We will go in a moment. Ask him the question."

She did so, tangling her long fingers together. The man lived up to the name I had given him and nodded.

"Ask him if he knows anything about Dom Villius."

Again Nuru asked. Again the man nodded.

"Does he know why they called him Veld?"

Another nod.

"Tell him I am...curious about the faith. Ask him if I might meet him later to learn more about it."

"But are—?"

"Just ask," I snapped, worry fraying me at the edges like a worn-out saddle cloth.

She did. Again he nodded, albeit more slowly. Then he spoke the first words to pass his lips and glanced at me only to look away as his soft voice rumbled on. At last he stopped and Nuru cleared her throat. "He says to know the faith one must be humble and prostrate oneself before God. He says he is not a very good teacher, to learn at the feet of Dom Villius would be the greater privilege, but if you wish to learn he will do his best to set your feet upon the right path."

"I have plenty of things I wish to learn from Dom Villius, but his faith isn't one of them. Thank him, and tell him I will seek him out tonight so we can talk more."

Nuru did as I asked, and finally I let her drag me back toward the manor, though only after extracting a hasty promise that she'd join me later to translate.

———————◆———————

Gideon's meeting with the pilgrims was short. Leo Villius was already there when I arrived, smiling as he accepted the reverence of each traveller in turn. They all looked overawed to see him, to kiss his hand, to touch the hem of his shapeless robe, crawling on the floor like grovelling worms while he blessed them all. Even Lord Nishi prostrated himself upon the floor, confusing me all the more. He sounded old and looked young, appeared pompous yet belittled himself before a Chiltaen in the plainest of robes.

Gideon watched it all from the padded chair he used as a throne, his face impassive. Grace Bahain was present as always, bent low beside his emperor whispering words for his ears alone. Nishi might have brought a hundred holy books, but Bahain had brought a hundred ships and the loyalty of many soldiers. Whatever his intentions ultimately were, avarice and a hunger for power were easier to work with than faith.

I tried to dispel my uneasiness but it only tightened when Leo glanced my way, a beatific smile turning his lips.

"Majesty," I said, cutting off whatever Grace Bahain was saying. "You need to send these people away."

Gideon's brows lifted in surprise. "Send them away, Captain? Why?"

It all made so much sense in my head, but when I tried to explain my words tripped over one another on their way to my tongue. "Look at them!" I managed and, lowering my voice, added, "Dom Villius is dangerous enough without giving him allies. Did you see the books Lord Nishi brought with him? This is exactly how the Tempachi sent their missionaries into our herds, surely the Torin experienced this?"

"You will be glad to know Grace Bahain agrees with you," Gideon said, leaning toward me. "He would very much like me to send them all away." He looked up through his lashes, something mischievous in the quirk of his lips. "Because he can't control them. And this... Lord Nishi... Apparently, he and his father avoided the Imperial Court. The whole Nishi family are fervent believers in Leo Villius's god, something about their lands being in close proximity to the Chiltaen border. Most of the Kisians call him Lord Salt, at least I think that's what the word means. Some of the translations are a bit strange."

"Lord Salt? The sort of salt that goes on meat or heads?"

"Meat, I believe. I think salt mining has made him one of the richest men in Kisia. If I comprehend Bahain correctly, the man lends money to people on the understanding they will give it back when they have money of their own. With extra as thanks."

The words made little sense, but the subtle hint of a thrill in Gideon's voice twisted my stomach. He had said we needed to keep Leo Villius because he was the only bargaining tool the Kisians had no control over. Now here was a source of money not connected to Grace Bahain, which meant Gideon would not send them away whatever my fears.

He must have guessed some of my thoughts, for he went on: "While it's important to think of Kisia as a herd in here"—he pressed his fist to his heart, then pointed at his head—"it is too big to be a herd in here. We can't expect farmers to give us their whole crop when we cannot feed and shelter their families. A portion of it has always been paid to the emperor, but what little comes in will not keep an army fed and supplied, will not feed our people and our horses, will not ensure we have enough lantern oil and parchment, enough arrows and meat and tea and wine and silk. And if they are not paid the servants will not clean and the cooks will not cook, and—"

Gideon broke off as Lord Nishi approached.

"Your Majesty." He bowed, not just a bow of acknowledgement but total obeisance with his forehead lowered to the floor. There he stayed until commanded to rise.

And while Lord Nishi bowed to the first Levanti emperor, Leo stood at the back of the room, his pendant gleaming in the light.

He had worn the same necklace on his last body, and I wondered if his god sent him back with one already in place. A chain of servitude, perhaps, rather than a gift.

As I stared at him, he stared at me, and the lump of cold fear in my stomach returned, or perhaps had never gone away.

One day, when Gideon no longer needs you, I will kill you, Leo Villius, I promised in the silence of my head. *I will kill you as many times as I have to and in as many different ways as it takes until you don't come back.*

At the other end of the room, Leo just smiled.

———————◆———————

By the time the audience broke up, I had envisioned six different ways I could kill Leo Villius. Most were far from subtle, ranging from slitting his throat when I next passed him in the passage to picking him off with my bow, but it would be better to poison him. So easy to imagine him face down at a table, his tea bowl smashed and froth drying at the corners of his pale lips from a dose of redcap.

I imagined the scene all the way to the kitchens to join my Swords for the evening meal. The rowdy chatter died as I entered, leaving salutes and murmurs of "Evening, Captain" to circle the firelit room. Hazy clouds of smoke and steam hovered around the ceiling, yet the scene beneath looked so like a campfire gathering that I smiled. They were not all Jaroven, but they were all Levanti. Here around this table we ate and drank as one, and even the strangeness of the food and the wine could not steal the fierce joy from my heart.

As I slid onto a bench their talk resumed. I let the noise wash over me, grateful for a place where I recognised everyone's words and didn't have to put up with Leo's existence. My stomach rumbled and I reached for the wine jug, catching sight of Jass en'Occha a few seats away. He had stopped eating to watch me.

"Captain," he said, perhaps hoping I wouldn't notice he'd been staring. "Thank you again for the opportunity to protect Emperor Gideon. Keka says—" The young man looked momentarily confused because *says* was never the right word for a man who could not talk. Jass decided to stick with it anyway. "He *says* you'll need more Swords though, especially since you lost one today. So if I can recommend—"

"Lost a—?"

I hunted Keka along the table. He was already watching with his sharp gaze and nudged Loklan, who hastily swallowed a mouthful of wine with a wince. "Ptapha left, Captain," he said, not quite looking at me.

"Left?"

The table quietened. Loklan shrugged. "Deserted."

"Fuck," I said, and seeing so many firelit faces turned my way I added, "When?"

"Not sure. Baln saw him this morning."

I looked along the table. "No one asked the sentries? They aren't meant to open the gate without a captain's say-so."

"I asked," Loklan said. "But they said it was only opened for those pilgrims this afternoon."

"Then someone is lying."

There was desultory movement up and down the table, a shifting of spoons in bowls and bums on benches. When no one answered I let a few more curse words hiss between my teeth. "Change doesn't happen in a blink. Empires aren't built in a day. This was always going to be hard in the beginning."

Muttered agreement met this, but the previous good cheer was lost and, whatever my stomach might say about it later, had taken my appetite with it. Leaving my bowl empty, I sipped my wine and waited for conversation to return. I wanted to leave, but a captain had responsibilities.

"Loklan," I said, swirling the last glittering mouthful of wine in my bowl. "How are the horses?"

"Fine, Captain," my horse master said. "They need more exercise than they can get in the yard, but I've been taking them out as much as I can. A few of their hooves have started splitting too."

"So, actually not fine at all."

He murmured something that might have been an apology. Young he was, but he was more attentive about his duties than any horse master I'd yet had, so I asked, "What can be done?"

"I think the problem is the damp weather. They are used to dry, hard ground to wear down their hooves, so all this rain and mud is making them soft." His eyes widened and he seemed to quiver in his seat as the thrill of his art overtook him. "Munn thinks it is the change in diet, but I've never heard of this happening anywhere on the plains before. I think...I think it's why the Kisians and the Chiltaens shoe their horses. There might be other ways, but I've been trying to talk to one of their horse masters and he seems keen enough to teach me. If I could just understand what he was saying."

"I'll ask Gi—His Majesty if you can have Oshar or Matsimelar tomorrow. You need to tell him these things too. We are nothing without our horses."

Loklan grimaced. "Yes, Captain."

Conversations once more lapped around us like a tide. "And our supplies? How are we for food? Water? Redcap?"

"All good, Captain. The water from the well here is good, and hay and oats come regularly. Some of the herds got low on redcap so we've had to share it around, but we've enough so long as all our horses don't suddenly get sick. And honestly, Captain, if that happens, I think we have bigger problems than a redcap shortage."

Murmured agreement met this, though at the end of the table Jass en'Occha remained silent. He was watching me, either waiting for me to kick him out or thinking, as I had been trying not to, that a second romp in the straw wouldn't be so bad.

Time to escape. I got up, mumbling something about walking a circuit of the yard, and left the room.

It was cold and wet outside the manor, the drenching rain cutting diagonally through the last of the hazy grey light. The few people in the yard huddled beneath their storm cloaks. I had left mine inside and I was too restless to go back for it. It was an hour until I was due to meet Nuru at the building set aside for the pilgrims, so I walked slow laps in the sheeting rain. I met no one as it grew steadily darker and darker until I could barely see my feet. I gave up. Without Nuru, I wouldn't be able to understand everything Nods said, but better to make a start in the dry than wait for her in the rain.

Lord Nishi had been invited to dine with the emperor, so unafraid of meeting him, I pounded on the door and waited, booted feet sinking into the mud. No one answered and I hammered harder. Still nothing, but the door was not locked and swung easily when I lifted the latch. Lantern light spilled onto my muddy boots.

"It's Captain Dishiva e'Jaroven," I said, taking a few steps into the silent building butted up against the walls. "Commander of the Imperial Guard. Is anyone here?"

No one answered. I walked in, stepping heavily to herald my presence. Mud from my boots splattered onto the clean floor. "Hello?"

Lantern light glowed through the screens of a nearby door, accompanied by a deep, all-absorbing silence. I slid it open, meeting the scene beyond with a hastily swallowed cry. It was exactly as I had imagined it down to the shattered teapot, the spilt tea shining on the wood, and the dried foam at the corners of pale lips.

But it was meant to be Leo, not Nods. The poor man looked

as though he had been taking tea by himself and failed to notice the slightly odd taste of redcap on the rim. Or if he had, there hadn't been time to do anything about it. Twitching spasms, frothing mouth, then dead before he'd taken more than a half-dozen breaths. A quick kindness for injured horses. Not for people.

Yet wherever he was, I was sure Leo Villius would be smiling.

10. RAH

The castle stood upon the edge of a cliff, more like a great stone spire than a palace. It owned the same winged roofs and curling decorations as the palace in Mei'lian, but here they had been carved whole from a monolith. In Levanti, *syan* was the name of a tiny flower that bloomed in patches across the steppe, so I had expected something beautiful, not a stark, grim fortress. Even the city lying in the castle's shadow looked to be little more than a rockfall tumbling toward the ocean.

Empress Miko did not stop to admire the view but continued toward the city gates with the same unwavering focus she'd had since the loss of her guard. It had been all we could do to make her stop and rest each night, for the sake of the horses if nothing else.

"We should stop here," Tor said as the walls grew closer. Narrow rays of sunlight gilded the castle from behind. "She can finish the journey on her own."

He had argued all the way. She was not our empress. My duty was to my own people. This was a waste of time and if we weren't careful would get us killed. He was not wrong, yet guilt spurred me on. If I had drawn her sword. If I had fought. If I had stood up to my own people, then her companion might still be alive and she would not need our protection. But I had not and he was dead. Now I would see his task through and get her to safety. My conscience demanded it of me, not just my honour.

Tor knew this, so rather than repeat myself, I said, "I will not leave without Jinso," and followed the empress through the lingering drizzle.

Rain had trailed us all the way. It had soaked into everything, into the short stubble of my hair, my clothes, into my very skin. Even my saddle seemed to squelch. I had begun to think longingly of the dry, parched summers back home, when even the air needed a drink. In the dry, my clothes did not rub my skin raw.

The gates of Syan stood open and people were coming and going as though there had been no war. Even the farmers in their muddy fields followed our progress with curiosity, not fear, more interested in the lone Kisian woman we rode with. It seemed whatever destruction we had wrought at the hands of our Chiltaen masters, none of it had touched these lands.

Tor had thought the empress wary of coming to this place, yet there was no sign of anything amiss. No soldiers awaited us inside the gates, only more staring eyes that shifted from me to Tor to Empress Miko, whispers rising.

Syan looked to be a large city, but only a small portion of it lay squeezed between the outer wall and the castle, the rest tumbling down the slope to a waterfront thick with ships. I caught glimpses of it between buildings as Empress Miko made her way along narrow streets, the air full of a salty tang and the screech of seabirds.

"We should leave," Tor said again, urging his horse alongside mine as the castle gates appeared ahead. "We can take Jinso and she can walk the rest of the way. We need to get back to our people now, not risk trouble by going farther."

"Would you cut all the way through a neck only to leave the last threads of skin attached?"

"No, but—"

"You ought to take every tenet of our honour code as seriously. She saved my life, we owe her this much."

The castle gates loomed, the interminable rain having darkened the wood until it looked almost black. "I do take them seriously, but I am worried," Tor said, not looking at me as he spoke. "I fear we may not be as welcome here as she is."

"No, but they have no reason to harm us for protecting their empress. All we need to do is see her to safety, get some supplies, then we can be on our way. If you wish, you may turn back now and I will meet you outside the gates when the task is done."

Tor did not argue, but neither did he turn back. The clop of his horse's hooves on the road kept pace with mine until at last the empress stopped outside the gates.

Someone shouted down to her, and stiff-backed upon Jinso she called back, chin lifted and pride sounding in every word. I remained a length back and Tor slunk behind me, yet still the sentry upon the walls pointed to us and spoke again. She lifted her chin even higher, but whatever she had said to the second challenge seemed enough, for another did not come.

A few minutes passed. The horses were restless, but Empress Miko just sat and waited until the castle gates opened. And without checking we would follow, she rode Jinso through.

An open strip of sun-speared grass met us on the other side, across which a pair of horses cantered from yet another gate set into yet another wall. Here again Tor hissed his warning, but I did not answer. The empress had not slowed. She sat tall in Jinso's saddle and urged him on at a confident pace, facing down the incoming riders.

The welcome party slowed, their horses kicking up mud as they came to a halt halfway between the castle's inner and outer walls. Empress Miko did the same, Jinso's height leaving her staring down at the heavily armoured men. They looked much like standard Kisian soldiers, except their mail had plates and the leather at their throats and arms was thick with padding. Different due to the weather or because they were better provisioned? It was hard to know. Each man also carried a spear, one decorated with a damp flag whipping in the sharp sea wind.

The flag bearer spoke, and in an under voice Tor translated. "He says he is Captain Nagai of the Fourteenth Battalion under Duke Bahain. He's demanded to know who she is."

Tor sounded amused, but the empress spoke her name so clearly Tor had no need to translate. "She has demanded to see the duke," he went on afterwards, and when the captain replied, he continued, "The duke is not here. But his son Edo Bahain is. Is that a close enough ally to leave her with? Can we go now before we cannot get out?"

As though drawn by his plea, a second soldier indicated us as he spoke. His words elicited a quick snap of a response.

"She says she takes responsibility for our actions. I'm not sure what she means, but I don't like it. Come on, Rah, we have done the task we set out to do, now let's go."

It was not the friendly welcome I'd hoped she would receive. There were no smiles here, no relief at finding their empress alive. Kisians seemed cold at the best of times, yet the calm these men sought to display was not shared by the fretting horses beneath them.

Before I could repeat my intention to stay until I was sure of her safety, Tor spoke to the empress, no respect in his tone. The empress's cheeks reddened and she snapped an answer. The boy glowered.

"She says I am free to go, but if you wish your horse back you will have to ride to the castle with her. She will not so dishonour her name by walking the rest of the way in the mud."

"And what did the captain say?"

"That he has no desire to keep filthy barbarians."

"Then I imagine he will let us go once our duty is fulfilled."

Despite the opportunity to leave, Tor rode with us toward the castle. It towered over us, looming larger and larger until it blocked the sun from view. And in its shadow the endless damp was all the colder.

The slope steepened toward the open gate and Empress Miko urged Jinso not to slow. He had never been one for hills and would not appreciate it, but he carried her up and through the stone arch with regal stoicism.

"This is a bad idea," Tor said, but together we passed through the gate, from day to night and back out the other side. An empty courtyard met us, echoing the clatter of hooves until it sounded like there were a hundred horses instead of five. The gates thudded closed behind us.

No fanfare. No welcome. Just a man standing upon stairs spewed from the base of the castle like a crinkled tongue. At first glance he was like every other grim-faced Kisian nobleman in stiff, regal silks, but as we drew closer it was a face no older than Tor's that solemnly watched our approach.

"Edo," the empress said, and a smile softened her face as she leapt from Jinso's back. The duke's son smiled too, though even half hidden in the castle's shadow it looked strained.

Friendly Levanti meeting again after a long time were more likely to crush one another in a hug rather than stand awkwardly, barely speaking, but Kisian customs seemed to involve touching as little as possible.

After a strained pause the grandly dressed young man bowed to his saturated and mud-splattered empress, but when he straightened, it was over her shoulder he looked at Tor and me. She followed his gaze and spoke. The young man nodded. Replied. The words were loud enough to hear, but not a single one beyond *Levanti* did I understand.

The captain kept glancing my way but he spoke to Tor, and while Tor translated, intent stares prickled the back of my neck. "They have offered us food," he said. "And a chance to rest and dry before the fire in the kitchens. They will tend our horses." He paused a moment, everyone staring as they awaited an answer. "Don't do this," he added, his voice low. "We can leave now."

Tension hung about the empty yard. The great castle and its walls protected us from the worst of the sea wind but none of the rain. It dripped from the stripped branches of a large tree and left the courtyard glistening. It made every flag and flower droop, yet the guards were stiff statues with their eyes on me. Waiting. A smart man was one getting out of here as fast as possible. But they had closed the gates. And atop the inner wall figures moved, all but unseen.

I forced a smile to my lips. "We can't. Don't look up, but there are archers on the wall and that soldier by the tree has his hand on his sword. Tell them we accept their hospitality with thanks."

Tor's eyes darted, but to his credit he didn't turn to either soldier or wall. He managed a calm answer, and the soldier by the tree took his hand from his sword and clasped it behind his back. The silk-clad lord on the steps smiled and, bowing once more to the empress, invited her to go before him up the stairs. Even had I been able to speak her language a warning could not be uttered. Too many watching eyes. I had to hope I was wrong and only we were in danger. These were her people, after all.

As the empress disappeared, Captain Nagai gestured for us to follow him, and before I could set my horse walking, he reached for Jinso's reins. Jinso stepped back, snorting, and I slid from my saddle. "Calm, boy, I know," I said, striding up to him and pressing my hand to his neck. "We're in yet another strange place, but I'm here." He calmed at my voice, but when I made to lead both horses, the captain stood in my way. His hand had frozen outstretched, his smile bemused.

"Tell him we will tend the horses," I said to Tor. "Tell him they do not like the hands of strangers."

Tor spoke. The captain answered. Shrugged. And turning on his heel, led us toward a wide opening in the inner wall. A second courtyard sat beyond, and against the base of the castle clustered a great many outbuildings in stone and wood, each with a wavy roof down which the rain trickled, pooling along the eaves.

The man pointed to a building in the castle's shadow, its entryway carved with horses emerging from crashing waves. There were few buildings on the plains, and upon first arriving in Chiltae I would have called such a construction a fine house; that the Kisians went to such trouble to house their horses was impressive.

Inside the building was comfortable and dry, with feed and fresh straw, brushes and combs and picks. For a few blissful minutes, I lost myself in the task of tending both Jinso and the other horse, taking off their saddles and rubbing them down, humming all the while. No one disturbed us. Tor did not speak. The rain drumming on the roof ebbed and flowed in its ferocity, but even when no sunlight made it through the doors, lanterns kept the shadows at bay. Yet doubt ate at my comfort like my wet clothes rubbing on drying skin. I had come this far only to repay my debt, to atone in what small way I could for having been part of Kisia's destruction, not to get caught up in disagreements between the empress and her people. I had my own people to get back to, my own people to serve.

"What's your plan?" Tor said, breaking his anxiety in upon mine.

"To get out of here as soon as we safely can," I returned, and caught his little sigh of relief. "I say we wait and see what they expect of us before we make any moves. If we show ourselves to be unthreatening and calm they may let us go after we have rested."

"Or they might slit our throats in our sleep."

I looked at him over Jinso's back. "You think we are in that much danger?"

"It's hard to tell from what they say; they may only fear us as supporters of the empress. Either way I won't be comfortable until we're outside those gates."

He didn't remind me of the half-dozen times he'd warned me not to walk through them in the first place, but even had I known how we would be received I wouldn't have done differently. Stubborn, Gideon would have called me, that wry, almost pitying half-smile turning his lips. But I had failed my people once, failed myself, had walked away from responsibility and weighed my soul heavy. I would not do it again.

We stayed working quietly in the hope we would be forgotten, but after a time the captain returned, renewing the offer of food and a warm fire. His smile was friendly, though it tightened to a grimace as Tor translated. Seeing it, I accepted, glad at least of the opportunity for some warmth and a hot meal.

"Are you sure?" Tor said.

"I'm sure. Patience."

Tor pursed his lips but accepted the invitation and went to grab his second hunting blade from his saddle. "Don't," I said, risking a glance at Captain Nagai's stiff smile. "Don't make it look like we're arming for a fight. If we have to fight our way out of here, I'd rather fight relaxed soldiers than tense ones."

"Fight our way through a closed gate? With no weapons?"

"Let's hope it won't come to that."

"Yes, let's, because I don't know about you but I haven't developed the ability to kill with a glare yet."

"No? You need to train harder."

He snorted a laugh and I patted Jinso's neck. "I'll be back," I said, hoping it would be true. "You rest and I'll be back."

We followed Captain Nagai to the kitchens, a series of large stone rooms in the bowels of the castle, their high, domed ceilings stained black like the night sky. Smoke hovered overhead in clouds, and through the haze servants bustled from fireplace to stove to table and back, grazing past us with grunts of annoyance as the captain led us to a table near an open fire. Feeling like a giant, I crouched at the little table lacking in stools. Tor knelt and pointed to a rough cushion half obscured. "You kneel on it. They sit on the floor, that's why the table is so low."

I knelt opposite, amid the clattering pots and chattering voices. Captain Nagai had removed to another table nearby, where a dozen soldiers knelt with bowls. Laughter rang to the high ceiling.

Two bowls landed on the table and before I could thank the girl who'd brought them, she hurried off into the spice-laden steam.

"Our reputation precedes us, I see," I said, looking at the bowl's contents. Vegetables floated in an off-colour liquid.

"I told you we shouldn't have come."

"Oh, did you? I mustn't have heard you."

He gave me a sullen look. "Funny."

"I know you think this was a bad idea and maybe it was, but I had my reasons. You need not have followed."

He said nothing for a time, just let the sounds of the kitchen swirl around us. Then, snatching a piece of carrot with his fingers, he said, "I saved your life too, you know. You'd be dead if I hadn't picked you up and found help."

Guilt cut deep. The boy had left Mei'lian for me, had hoped at last to find a herd he could be a real member of, to go home, and here we were putting a balm to my heavy soul.

I pressed my fists in salute. "You're right, and for my life you have my thanks. And for staying with me while I carried out a task that was important to me."

"As long as you know it says nothing good that you felt helping a Kisian was more important than helping your own people."

I had been about to lift my wine cup, but I let it go and stared at him across the table. "Your assumption that I do not care about both does you no honour."

Tor scowled at the table. "My apologies, Captain."

Captain. That stung as much as the guilt. Without my Swords I was no captain, nothing but an exile in service to no herd.

"You have every right to be angry at where circumstances have landed you," I said. "I'm sorry I can do no more to make amends than help you get safely back home now we are finished here."

He nodded and pulled another piece of carrot from his soup. With nothing else to say, we fell into silence while we ate, letting the gentle hum of conversation rise and fall around us in the smoky kitchen. As I was finishing my soup, a new group of Kisian soldiers strode in damp from the rain. They made for the nearby fire, eyeing us as they passed. I could have asked Tor to translate what they said as they sniggered, but their expressions left me in little need of specifics.

Tor stiffened. His hand stilled upon the table and he tilted his head ever so slightly. "What is it?"

He lifted a single finger just off the table and went on listening. I waited, watching his face rather than the men as they went on talking, though to call it talking was generous. It was more jeers punctuated with laughter. At the next table, Captain Nagai seemed to have forgotten about eating. Worry twisted inside me, the weight of my sword belt my only comfort.

Tor crushed his fingers to a fist.

"What is it?" I said again, and this time he glanced at me only to look away.

"They are talking about Gideon."

A hand squeezed my heart. "What about him?"

"They are laughing at the Levanti emperor who thinks himself so powerful, who thinks he rules Kisia. They say..."

"They say what?" I demanded in a desperate hiss as Tor trailed off.

The sudden directness of his gaze was like a challenge. "They say it was oh so good of him to get rid of the Chiltaens for them, but Grace Bahain—the Grace Bahain who owns this castle—is the real ruler of Kisia and Gideon is but a puppet. Until his usefulness runs out."

A strained silence fell, beating to the rapid thud of my heart. "Are you saying that Gideon, that *our people*, have been…used? That all of this…" I could not bring myself to finish the sentence. The ground seemed to shift beneath me at the enormity of the very idea that Gideon had been manipulated, that we had been nothing but a means to get rid of Kisia's enemies whatever the cost to Kisia itself.

"I think…yes," Tor said, that last word a damning monosyllable. In its wake the room lacked air, my every breath not great enough to fill my lungs.

A hundred thoughts swirled at once through my mind, but the first words that found their way to my tongue were "He has to be warned."

Tor's mouth hung open a moment. "Gideon? Warn Gideon? After everything he has done, he deserves whatever is coming to him."

I tried not to think of the young man who had sat with me in silence, letting me spill my grief until I was empty. He was not that man anymore. He had left Levanti behind to die, he had given saddleboys to the Chiltaens, he had ordered a whole town killed, women and children and all, and called it necessity.

"Rah," Tor said, reaching across the table. "Gideon has made his choice. The Levanti who chose to follow him have made their choice. All we can do is help those who want none of this to go home."

It would be so easy to leave, to call my exile done, but every thread of me resisted like a tree rooted to this troubled land. An exile of exiles I might be, but my Swords had been my family too long, Gideon my world, and the thought of leaving without either turned my blood to ice.

"No," I said. "No, I can't go back without my Swords; whatever happened I owe them that much."

"Rah, the last true Levanti," Tor said, a hint of a sneer in the words.

The last true Levanti. How had I put myself so far above others? Guilt and shame fought for dominance, but what made me sick was the thread of pride I could not let go.

"You haven't heard what people say of you?" Tor's brows lifted. "Many hate you for shaming them. For beheading their kills when they did not. For clinging to your duty and reminding them of a time they can never return to. But for every one that hates you, there's one who would follow you to death and beyond." He set his elbows on the table and leaned closer, his young face lined from lack of sleep and his long hair hanging damp. "Think of what you could do if you went home. The plains are poisoned. Our herd masters have lost their minds, but you, you have the power to unite people, to bring herds together to fight the evil back, and you owe it to every Levanti that ever lived to at least try."

You owe it to your people, Rah. It is an honour to be chosen. It is an honour to serve. Herd Master Sassanji's hand had been so heavy on my shoulder, like the weight of the whole herd's expectations and pride. What Levanti would ever run away from that?

Tor leaned closer still, lowering his voice. "You are the leader we need, Rah. You can save us."

I had stood at the edge of the grove and stared out across the plains, imagining my herd was just over the horizon. I had dreamed of running back to them, fear tingling through my stomach and down my legs like an army of tower ants on the move, but every time the memory of Herd Master Sassanji's hand seemed to crush me into the ground, breaking me with shame. I felt the same tingle of fear in my limbs now, and it was that frightened child who met Tor's gaze across the table.

"No. I can't."

Tor slammed his fist down, making the ceramic bowls jump. At the nearby table the Kisian soldiers stopped their conversation to stare. "Damn you, Rah, you are not listening to me. I—"

"I am listening to you. Every word you say fills me with more fear than I have ever felt."

"You're afraid of change? Of fighting for what is right?"

"For what is right? Think about what you are asking me to do. The Levanti are not a people in the way the Korune are a people, in the way the Kisians are a people. We do not have one leader, but many. Do not have one way of life, but many. Do not have one land, but many. To fight against so great and all-consuming an evil, even if we knew what it was, we would have to fight together."

"Yes, and you could lead—"

"And to truly fight together we would have to destroy everything that makes us Levanti. We would have to become one people with one way of life and one land. We would have to turn away from our tenets and perhaps kill some of our own. Can you tell me you are not afraid of that?"

The question rang into a room of quiet whispers. Eyes still watched from all around, but I no longer cared.

Tor clenched his jaw, glaring at me. "I would do whatever it took to save our people."

"That is a very…Gideon thing to say." I ran a hand along the regrowth sprouting from my scalp. "Perhaps it is too much, Tor, perhaps it is too late and there is no saving us, no going back."

"Then you support Gideon's plan?"

"No! No, this is not our land, these are not our people."

"Then what? You cannot tell me the great Rah e'Torin would rather just lay down and die, would let the Levanti just lay down and die? Where is your pride? Where is your honour?"

"You ask me to commit atrocities against my own people and then talk to me about honour. If I did what you asked, our hearts would be so heavy upon Mona's scales that our souls—*my soul*—would be lost forever in the darkness."

He slammed his fist down again, even harder. "The gods have abandoned us, Rah! They have let the city states hunt us, have let them poison our leaders' minds, have—"

"If they have abandoned us it is because we were no longer worthy. We abandoned them first."

Tor's jaw dropped. The whole kitchen was silent but for the crackling of fires. Eyes shone in the gloom.

"And so that's it?" he said, recovering from his shock. "We are not worthy and so you will abandon all hope? Will you stay here with them?" He pointed at the watching Kisians. "Perhaps stay for an empress who can't even understand what you're saying? Who will never let a *barbarian* like you so much as touch her hand, let alone her—"

Exhausted rage surged and I threw my soup bowl at Tor's head. Most of the remaining liquid splashed onto the table, but enough hit him in the face to leave him gasping as the bowl struck his forehead. It fell, smashing into tiny pieces on the stones, but before remorse could hit me, Tor did. Dripping soup, he lunged over the table and swung. I was too close to escape his fist and it caught my ear, toppling me back onto the stones.

The silence erupted into shouts. Cheering Kisian faces filled the smoky gloom behind Tor, sitting on my chest. Pain sparked white bolts of lightning as he clutched his hands around my throat. "I believed in you! You are the only one who can fix this. Can save us. And you won't even try!"

His grip on my throat tightened and his snarling face swam. After running away from Whisperer Jinnit, I had lain down beneath the hot sun prepared to die for my shame, but the thirstier and hotter I got the more alive I had felt, the urge to live infusing me. The same determination overrode all the guilt and shame Tor had thrown at my head and I dug my fingernails into his arms, drawing blood. He yelped, and when his grip loosened, I ripped his hands from my neck.

"Stop this," I rasped, throat raw. "I know you are hurting. I know you want everything back the way it used to be, but—"

He lashed out, but I slapped his hand away and bucked him off into the forest of legs.

"Listen to me, Tor!" I staggered to my feet. "This is not the way. This is not—"

His fist struck my jaw and I reeled back. The faces in the smoky blackness spun and I lost balance, falling into them as blood filled my mouth. The ringing pain in my skull spread down every limb as I landed against something hard, a song of cracking wood and smashing ceramic booming like thunder over the Kisian cheers. And through the chaos lunged Tor, his hands grasping toward my neck like desperate talons. His hair hung around his twisted face and he seemed to have run out of words. He tightened his grip around my throat again and as the room darkened, he was all I could see, spit glistening on his lips and his bared teeth as he squeezed his thumbs hard into my neck. I couldn't remember gripping his wrists but I held them now, my forearms trembling to hold back the force of his anger. Every breath shortened to a gasp. My vision faded to just his wild, staring eyes, and tasting death I knew a moment of peace. Nothing would matter anymore if I died. Except that I would die dishonoured.

Blood roared in my ears like crackling scrolls as Mona loaded my deeds upon the scales.

I tried to push him off, to lock my elbows and force him back. To tear at his skin. To kick and thrash and slam my knee into his body again and again, and still his rage held him firm. Light was fading.

Tor's fingernails scored my neck as he was wrenched away, and I rolled onto my side sucking agonising breaths. Words swirled around me, no longer cheers but upraised shouts. Someone gripped my shoulder. The captain's face appeared, concerned lines marring his brow. They vanished as I blinked blearily and he let me go, calling something to his men. More words whipped around me like a storm. More faces. More noise. Water came but I could not drink it. Wine, but I would not touch it. Even air hurt like knives. Tor had brought me all too close to the darkest of futures.

The boy started to laugh.

I turned my aching neck. He stood close, blood smeared on his hands and manic glee brightening his eyes. "Do you hear that?" he said, gesturing to the soldiers around us. "No, of course you don't. Well, I'll tell you, great Rah e'Torin, I'll tell you what they are saying." He pointed up at the ceiling. "Your empress has fucked you after all. She thinks you're Emperor Gideon's brother and has bargained you as security. But don't worry, they're only interested in what fee you might fetch."

He took a step toward me, but one of the soldiers thrust out an arm to bar his path.

"It's the empress Grace Bahain wants. If he marries her he won't even have to wait for Gideon to consolidate power, he can just get rid of him as soon as he's not useful anymore. Well? What's your plan now, last great Sword of the Levanti?"

Knowing nothing of what Tor had just said, Captain Nagai clapped his hand on my shoulder and once more offered me a bowl of wine. This time I took it and his face relaxed into a smile. A few of his men laughed as he glanced expectantly at them, the ease so forced they must have thought us truly naive.

"My plan," I said, unable to draw my imagination away from a scene in which hundreds of Levanti lay slaughtered, Gideon with them, "is not to run when I can help. It is not my place to judge, only to fight for my people. Even those who have done wrong."

And before he could retort, I dropped the wine bowl and punched Captain Nagai in the face. The man reeled back with a shocked cry, opening space around me, space in which I ripped my knife from my belt. The sharp blade slit skin as I pressed it to my own throat. Every soldier in the dimly lit kitchen froze.

"Tell them it is not dishonourable for me to kill myself," I said. "Tell them I demand to be taken to the empress, or I will bleed out here and they will take the blame for the loss of the emperor's brother."

11. CASSANDRA

Bile splattered into the bowl, leaving me spent. My limbs trembled and my stomach cramped, pain the only reason I knew I was in my own skin.

"Nothing is taking," the Witchdoctor said, a slight frown marring his sculptured brow. "I am not yet able to make sense of this."

"I think that's enough for today, Master," Kocho said, and his concerned face swam before me as I looked up from the bowl, damp hair sticking to my face. "You're pushing her too hard."

"I am well aware of the factors limiting the fortitude of the human physiology, Kocho."

The old man's brows knitted and he disappeared from view, leaving me staring at the blurry contents of the room. I had lost track of how many times I'd been pulled free of my body and put back that day. On its own the sensation might have been bearable had I not also temporarily inhabited a number of other bodies. The corpse had been the worst, its stiffness constricting and the taste in its mouth like—

Ash. It's weird, isn't it?

I had no energy to even think a reply. Until today, She had spent more time inside dead skins than I had.

Conversation continued overhead.

"Make a specific note about Saki's inability to move one of

Deathwalker Three's souls into a corpse and have it remain," the Witchdoctor was saying. "Given that is the reason why a Deathwalker is so called, I find this development both fascinating and frustrating."

A quill scratched as I swallowed the urge to puke again.

"I spoke no word of blame," he went on after a pause. "The frustration is born from the illogical nature of such a situation. Why is it possible for a Deathwalker to pass one of its own souls into a corpse and let go, but you are unable to assist the transfer manually?"

More scratches upon the paper. The room had finally ceased spinning.

"That is possible. The connection to you is stronger than the connection to the corpse. If that is so then we must find a way to strengthen the bond to the host body."

"When I said I wanted a body of my own," She said through my lips, "I did not mean I wanted a dead one."

"As you see, Kocho, Deathwalker Three is uninjured."

The old man appeared once more. "That's the other soul, Master."

"You can tell the difference?"

"Yes, Master."

"Be sure to make a note of that in your file."

"Yes, Master."

Ignoring Her comment, they went on talking over my head.

"Saki, are you removing the same soul every time, or not?"

A brief beat of silence, I could only imagine she filled with a nod.

"Then it is possible one is the host and one is the guest and if they are unequal, they may take differently. I posited this hypothesis before I lost Deathwalker Two but was unable to test it. Remove the other one and try it with Deceased 17-1390."

"Lost?" I said.

"Master, I really think we should let her rest."

"Just one more test, Kocho, then you may make them soup."

"Soup, Master?"

"I have observed the human belief in soup. You seem to have imbued it with a magic it hardly deserves, but as I believe the mind has much more control over the body than even I have yet proved, I shall not seek to make you disbelieve in its undeserved properties."

I would have laughed had I not ached all over.

"Saki. Continue."

I braced for the dizzying whirl of being pulled free, but her touch lingered, burning like ice, then she drew her hand away.

Footsteps. Rustling paper. She bent over the worktable. The Witchdoctor watched her write for a while then glanced at me over his shoulder. "That has not happened before."

She wrote again. And again he answered. "I do not understand."

What are they talking about? I said, summoning the energy to speak despite the throbbing ache in my head.

No answer came. Yet I knew She was there, for the yearning song of the nearby corpses continued unceasing.

"Try again."

Saki shook her head. More writing. She stabbed at something on the page with the tip of her quill.

Why is she upset?

Because I wouldn't go with her, She said.

What do you mean, you wouldn't go with her? It's not like you get a choice, she just yanks you out.

No answer.

Hey! What do you mean you wouldn't go with her?

I clenched my hands upon the arms of the chair.

Kaysa! Answer me.

Amusement filtered through my thoughts. *So I have a name now? I am allowed to be a person and not a disease?*

Just tell me what you meant.

I meant what I said. You can't hide from her but I can.

But if you don't let her move you, you'll never get a body of your own.

I already have a body of my own. It's you who needs a new one, Cassandra.

The Witchdoctor was still talking. Saki still writing. And in my head my pulse thumped like a drum. *No,* I said. *This is mine. I was born in it. I—*

I was born here too!

Breath came and went fast and I pressed a hand to my thrumming heart. *But this is* me.

She made no answer.

You can have another one.

Nothing.

Kaysa? "Kaysa!"

The three occupants of the room turned, but it was the Witchdoctor who spoke. "Attempt to remove both," he said. "One after the other. We are yet to find a soul that has been impossible to remove from its shell."

"Tomorrow," Kocho said, with far less deference than usual. "She needs to rest."

A silent moment went by like an age as the Witchdoctor looked first at me and then at Saki. "Very well. Tomorrow."

I sank into the bath with a sigh. The hot water was almost as wonderful as the first sip of Stiff after a hard day, and I had lived through many a hard day. Difficult clients, jobs that did not go to plan, arguments with Mama Hera that shook the walls, but none of them had left me feeling quite as empty. As broken.

The hot water eased my aches. The day had been a confused whirl, all ash and bile and the endless scratching of Saki's quill. Even now my mouth tasted dry, and I lowered my jaw into the bathwater. Some spilled inside, but though it was warm and wet my tongue, it was not Stiff. I let it trickle out, down my chin and back into the bath. Someone had dropped petals into the water, dry white ones that floated on the surface like flakes of skin. They might have given off a scent, but it was impossible to tell through the choking fug of incense. Someone had lit the vile stuff beyond the edge of the wooden tub, but I had not even the strength to complain, let alone move.

Saki had pulled me from my body. The first time I had been sure it was a trick, then she had done it again. Three times. Out and back. Out and back. Out and back. Each time without a word or even a look that displayed anything beyond mild interest. That had been the first session.

Today's session had been much longer. Out and back. Out and back. Out and into a corpse, with its ashen-tasting tongue and its stiff limbs. Out of a corpse and into Saki, her mind a glowing lantern overhead while I wallowed in her darkness. And always that other voice for company. It didn't often speak, but when it did it was kind.

When did you ever care about kind?

I shifted my aching limbs in search of hotter tracts of water, sending the dry petals bobbing like boats in a storm. No voices penetrated my thoughts. No footsteps. Nothing at all seemed to exist beyond the edge of the bath.

I swallowed more water to chase away the memory of ash. "Is it always the same?" I said, my voice a husky croak as water spilled down my chin.

I don't know.

"Has it been every time you've walked in the dead?"

She did not answer immediately, but just as I was about to ask again, She said, *I have never walked in the dead.*

I frowned at the play of light upon the water, beneath which my legs looked like pale, drowned flesh. "What about Jonus? And that commander at Koi?"

You walked in those. I have never left this body.

"Bullshit."

I thought about Jonus, about running to him down the hillside, feet skidding, and heart thumping. Of crying out. Of touching him. Of leaping forward, yanked into his flesh. I had panicked, but when I realised I could move his body that panic had birthed a wild idea. And throwing wide his arms I had shouted to the Kisians below.

"I should have stayed in Genava," I said, needing to speak, to say something that might waylay the memories that followed. Of Jonus's body stiffening around me like a tightening shell until it became a rotting cage from which I could not escape.

Part of me insisted I'd never experienced that pain, and pushing my thoughts toward Her, I tried to read Her mind, to know Her in that moment of doubt, but there was nothing.

I told you not to take the job. Either job.

Back in Genava I would have had my endless stream of clients, Mama Hera's biting complaints, and Gergo's knowing smile as I stopped by every few days to refresh my stock of Stiff. That routine had become my life. Unvarying. Safe in its own way. And what other life was there beyond survival?

What other life? A shocked silence rang in my head, clearing it of all thoughts. *What other life?* She repeated. *Any life would have done. Any life would have been better than the one you forced on me. Any life better than taking joy only in how easily you could manipulate people and take their lives, better than being drowned in that cursed Stiff. You could have travelled. You could have seen the world. You could have given yourself to the One True God and helped people, Cassandra, you could have done anything. Remember that lord who wanted to marry you? Yes, he was a silly old fool but what a life that could have been. I could have had children, Cassandra.* Children. *Oh, the things I could have done with this body if you had not been here, if you had not pushed me into the dark corners. Children!*

Children. It had almost happened a few times, such being a danger in my profession. Yet all it took was one evening drinking Mama Hera's foul babybane tea, and in a rush of blood and pain those unwanted lives had poured out upon the floor.

"No child deserves me for a mother."

No one deserves you for anything.

The water was getting cold, or perhaps it was just the ice in my bones winning. Either way the bath was no longer comforting. All the aches returned, along with nausea made worse by the angry swirl of memories I could not avoid. Of bodies and bloody floors, and the ashen tongues of the dead bloating behind cold lips.

Someone must have helped me out of the bath. Someone must have helped me dry and dress, but I heard no words and felt no touch, just found myself sipping something hot from a blue-rimmed bowl while footsteps shuffled around me. The sleeping mat had been warmed, but the pillow smelt damp.

I lay down to sleep but it brought no rest. The moment I closed my eyes I was back in Koi, forcing the body of the commander to walk and talk and lie, sure at any moment someone would see the gash in my throat. *My* throat? The fear felt real yet I had never seen the back alley before where I stripped a dead man of his clothes, never seen the gatehouse and the guards who stared at me open-mouthed as I cut the gate's counterweight.

Koi had to fall. We had to find the Witchdoctor. I needed to be free.

The disjointed feeling followed me to the workroom the next day. Saki and the Witchdoctor were already present, while Kocho was settling himself at a bench, quill in hand.

"Deathwalker Three," the Witchdoctor said. "Report."

I looked from the god-man to Saki perched upon the stool behind him.

"I'm..." The Witchdoctor's gaze bore unblinkingly into me. "Sore and tired, but...fine?"

His eyes narrowed as his gaze shifted about my body, not with the lascivious attitude most men possessed, rather with the cold, dispassionate eye of a doctor. It was a new experience, almost as unusual as being asked how I was.

"Begin entry. Fourteenth day of the storm season, 1390. Deathwalker Three appears to be in consistent spirits, although fatigued by the exigencies of yesterday's session. The wound on her calf, inflicted by myself upon the road, looks to be healing well, and now she has improved in her use of the walking sticks, it troubles her less." As the Witchdoctor spoke, he gestured to the chair I had occupied yesterday.

I sat, leaning my walking sticks against the arm of the chair. Yesterday had been unpleasant, today would likely be more of the same, but the chance of freedom still felt real, just out of reach.

"Saki, you will once more attempt to draw the host soul out on its own," the Witchdoctor went on. "And should that fail a second time, take out both. Attempt to replace them in a different order and see what works and what does not. Kocho, is your line of sight sufficient?"

"Yes, Master."

"Good. Begin."

Mistress Saki appeared in front of me, her brows knit in concentration. I flinched at her touch, but as with the day before, nothing happened bar the darkening of her frown. She switched hands, touching my other cheek. Still nothing. Gripping the arms of the chair, I tried to sense what she was doing, but like with Kaysa's thoughts there was nothing. Then a gentle tug pulled me forward only to let me sink back into the chair, back into a body that had not moved at all.

The young woman straightened and shook her head. The room was silent but for the scratching of Kocho's quill.

"Move on to the second test."

"If you'll allow me a moment, Master, to finish this up."

The lack of answer appeared to be a grudging assent, and in the moment of peace afforded, I looked toward the window. Sunlight streamed in, sending shafts of gold across the closest workbench. The shutter was open a crack, and outside, birds chirped far more merrily than the situation warranted. Nature had never held much appeal for me, but I yearned for the touch of that sunshine, and the feeling of being disjointed increased. I ought to run, to leave, to get out of this place before it was too late, and yet...

Freedom.

"Ready, Master."

Again Mistress Saki crouched before me, touching her cool hand to my cheek, and again I was tugged forward, but this time I was pulled all the way, carried, weightless to the warm, hazy darkness of Saki's head. Above, the great machine of her mind worked on, while through her eyes I could see myself. My mouth opened to speak, but as Saki reached out a second time my body slumped in its chair.

How crowded it is getting in here, the host voice said. *Welcome to the body of Saki Laroth.*

Kaysa was with us, but she made no reply, just hid in the shadows around my stifled awareness.

Without a body time meant little and I don't know how long I hung there, neither part of Saki nor of myself, just a collection of floating thoughts and memories. She returned me to my body long enough for me to revel in the renewed solidity, only to yank me free again, in and out, juggling us like an entertainer. She must have stopped every now and then for she wrote, dipping her quill to scribble at a furious rate. When the Witchdoctor spoke he sounded distant, but his words were no less precise for arriving in my mind via someone else's ears. And after he spoke, she would write again, on and on until the chill air of the workroom lapped at my skin and I sat upon the hard chair, all aches and fatigue, as Kocho said, "Lechati is bringing the bodies now, Master."

"Good." The Witchdoctor stood before me. "Deathwalker Three," he said. "You have one soul that is easy to remove and one that is not. I wish to determine the reason for this. When you split is it always the same soul that takes over the dead body and the same soul that remains behind?"

The word *yes* formed upon my lips only to be ambushed by doubt. I could remember seeing Jonus shout to the Kisians as clearly as I could remember shouting the words myself. His arms had resisted at first when I tried to spread them, as though the muscles had thought themselves no longer needed.

"I...I don't know."

A frown marred the Witchdoctor's perfect brow. "I fail to understand how you cannot know. You, the soul to which I am speaking at this moment, have you ever walked in the skin of the dead before now?"

Again I wanted to say I had not, but doubt clouded everything. "I don't know," I said. "I...remember doing so, but I also remember not doing so."

The Witchdoctor straightened and met Saki's gaze over my shoulder. Then, turning, he addressed Kocho. "Make an additional note," he said. "To design a series of tests by which I might determine the degree to which the souls inside a Deathwalker meld and share their experiences. It did not appear to be the case with either Deathwalker One or Two, but three subjects are not a sufficient sample from which to draw conclusions."

"Yes, Master."

"Saki," the Witchdoctor went on. "For now we must be satisfied with testing to see if either soul takes inside a corpse if both have been removed."

She must have nodded or bowed for the Witchdoctor strode away, the snap of his sandals upon the floor as precise as his words.

As with the day before, Lechati brought in two bodies and the dance began again. At any given moment I knew where I was, whether in my own skin or the dead flesh, but the movements between them blurred and the workshop spun. On and on until the Witchdoctor called a halt and I sat licking ashen lips with a dry tongue.

"Then neither takes," the Witchdoctor said, pacing now with a furious gait. "That is... unexpected. I see no reason why you would not be able to move the soul of a Deathwalker from its host and set it inside a corpse, since, unlike the souls of Normals, it is a journey they are well used to. What," he seemed to demand of the world at large, "is the difference between the method you use to remove souls from their bodies and the method a Deathwalker uses?"

Silence met this question. He stopped pacing. "I need to consider what we have learned. The session is over. Have Lechati take the bodies away."

The Witchdoctor strode from the room, passing the dark-skinned young man in the doorway. Lechati gazed after his master before looking a question at Kocho, who had dropped his quill and was now rubbing his wrists. "Not good?" he asked.

"No answers, more questions."

"Ah." The young man seemed to chew on his next words, his look wary enough that after a few moments Kocho stopped rubbing.

"What is it?"

Lechati cleared his throat. "I... I picked up some news when I was in town."

"Bad news?"

"I suppose that depends on your point of view." He fiddled with the hem of his tunic. "We can always leave, so it doesn't matter to us who rules Kisia, but the empress…"

Kocho sighed. "Spit it out for those hard of hearing, boy."

"Mei'lian," he said, "was taken by the Chiltaens, who in turn seem to have been slaughtered by the Levanti, and one of them has proclaimed himself the new emperor of Kisia. I…I heard too that it wasn't Emperor Kin who led the Kisian army into battle. It was Empress Miko, Her Majesty's daughter."

"Her Majesty will be glad to hear she's alive."

Lechati pursed his lips. "I'm not sure she is since she lost, that's why I haven't told Her Majesty yet."

Silence filled the room, and despite the fatigue that bent my spine, something of the empress's impending suffering bit through my selfish fog.

"Tell her," Kocho said. "Better to hear it now than later."

"But the master said we ought to do our best not to upset her, as it could affect her condition."

"Then don't tell the master. The empress has a right to know."

Lechati parted his lips to argue, but Kocho broke in, saying, "Damn it, this is her daughter we're talking about, boy. Wouldn't you want to know if it was you?"

The young man nodded and looked to Saki. "Mistress?"

She gave a single, sharp nod and turned away to continue tidying her work. Lechati hesitated, rocking on his heels in the doorway before finally departing along the passage. A moment later Kocho's voice shocked me from my stupor. "You can go rest now. He won't ask for you again until morning. Perhaps longer. The master is unpredictable when he gets in these moods. Once he was gone for half a year." Kocho laughed, but I disliked the prospect of waiting so long. So it was in a despondent mood that I hauled my aching body out of the chair, took up my sticks, and shuffled, like a broken old woman, out into the dark maze that was, for now, my home.

———————◆———————

I considered running. I considered it seriously enough to walk a lap of the house noting its exits, from holes in walls to doors and court-yards, some locked, others sitting open goading me to attempt escape. I kept my eyes open for a weapon, just in case, but all I found was a collection of decorative clubs and two barbed sickles tucked away in a gallery off the Wisteria Court. I eyed the pair of sickles, but they were too big to carry concealed.

With the onset of evening I returned to my room and sat on the matting, listening to the seemingly endless patter of the rain falling upon the roof. The Kisian storm season really was as bad as people said, and for the first time, thinking about their adapted architecture and clothing, something like admiration stirred. These people dealt with yearly rains of this magnitude, with flooding rivers and thick drifts of snow, and yet they still functioned as well as Chiltae. I wondered whether the Chiltaens who had once lived here had done as well.

The light steadily faded, and as the room filled with shadows, someone knocked on the door.

"Who is it?" I said, reaching for a dagger that wasn't there.

"Kocho," came his muffled voice. "I have food."

"Oh, come in."

The door slid and Kocho, awkwardly manoeuvring through the narrow space he had made, sidestepped into the room. "You're sit-ting in the dark?" he said, sliding the door closed with one foot.

"It wasn't dark when I sat down."

The old man set the tray upon the matting with a tinkle and clink of ceramic. I could not see what was on it, but a delicious waft of warm food made its way to my nose. My stomach grumbled.

After some fumbling around in his serviceable brown sash, Kocho lit a length of tinder and moved around the room lighting the lanterns. He'd brought rice and fish, some green vegetable or other, and a stewed peach. A teapot sat to one side of the tray spewing its steam in dainty curls, and my dawning respect and appreciation for the Kisian way of life grew a little more.

"How is Empress Hana?" I said when Kocho showed no sign of departing.

The man grimaced and clicked his tongue. "Not good. She took the news about her daughter pretty hard."

"You sound surprised. That's both her children dead now." I waved my hand through the steam, not wanting to look up.

"Yes, I know," Kocho said. "But it's not just grief, it's...well, she blames herself. There is a lot for her to regret."

With nothing to say, I waited for him to leave, but the moments passed and Kocho made no step toward the door. The silence grew deeper and more awkward, and I was about to tell him to go when he said, "You have a lot of questions. Shall I stay and keep you company for a while?"

And before I could refuse, I had accepted—for the answers, not the companionship.

Kocho grunted as he knelt on the other side of the tray, all stiff joints and clicking knees. I had no table, but he settled himself as though I did and began serving the tea. There were two cups, I noted, and gave him a shrewd look. "Planning to stay all along, I see."

"Yes, well, you're a tough bird, but none of the master's subjects gets through this without a struggle. No one grows up understanding it. He always says that's the problem. No one comes here knowing the soul is anything more than an idea perpetuated by their religion. Perhaps if they knew it was not only *their* religion but every religion, they might realise it has to be more than just an idea to have spread so widely."

He poured as he spoke, but the liquid spilling from the pot was darker than tea. I pointed at the brew sparkling in the bowl. "What's that?"

"Roasted tea," he said, and waggled his eyebrows. "It's a delicacy and worth a damn fortune so don't wrinkle your nose like that until you've tried it. I found a stash of it here when we first arrived and have been waiting for a good time to use it."

I snorted. "You chose poorly."

"No, I didn't." He took up his bowl and shifted position, settling with his back against the wall and his bowl on his paunch. "Usually I don't bring food trays, you know. I've been with the master too long for things like that and I'm too old to be running up and down stairs. But no one wanted to bring yours so they asked me."

I looked down at the food, tensing in anger. Did he think I cared what they thought of me?

"Because, you see," he went on, "while you were born with two souls in one skin, I was born able to read the thoughts people don't speak. I can see the Cassandra everyone else sees, but I can also hear the Cassandra no one else knows."

He smiled, all his wrinkles crinkling as I glared at him. "You can read my mind."

"Yes."

"But that's ridiculous," I said despite all the times I had been sure he was doing it.

"More or less ridiculous than being able to reanimate the dead with a second soul who shares your body?"

I left a beat of silence rather than admit his point. "Prove it."

"All right. Think of a word. Or a number. Or a poem. Anything."

"Fine. What am I thinking about?"

A little notch appeared between his brows. "A crass limerick about bumblebees. Or the number eight. It's a little more complicated with two souls but based on personality I think I can guess which was yours."

Mine had been the number, but the vague warmth of amusement radiating from Her meant he had gotten both right. I stared at the old man as he took a sip of tea and let out a sigh. "You should try it while it's warm," he said. "It's good."

I didn't touch my bowl. Nor had I touched the food. "How do you do it?"

"See your thoughts? I don't know. I've spent my whole life finding ways not to and taking care no one found out I could. It scares people."

"But...how? Why?" I said, all the questions that had been burning inside me emerging in a rush. "Why can you do that? Why do I have two souls? I can't believe I'm even saying that. What *is* a soul?"

"A soul is you. Your whole personality and experience and life essence. Everything that isn't physical that you think of as yourself. That is your soul. That's why even when Saki removes you from your body you still feel like yourself, just in a different place with a different skin. Your body is a shell, let's say, a physical construct you need to interact with the physical world. Without it you would be unanchored and would dissipate."

"To nothing? Is that what happens when we die?"

"Yes, but when a soul is freed, it is reincarnated."

The food was going cold, but in that flickering, golden space I felt no hunger while his voice held answers.

"Seven reincarnations," Kocho said, after another sip of tea. "Each time growing more...wise, more..." He waved a hand. "Self-aware. Oh, not of their previous incarnations, most people don't remember one to the next, but I imagine you've met the sort of simple, uncomplicated people who are first incarnations."

I could certainly have named a few, and one I'd seen reincarnate with his memory intact. Leo had not even seemed confused when he'd taken his own severed head from my hands.

"But we were all that soul once. Everyone starts there. And it's meant to end at seven. The master says after the seventh incarnation most souls don't come back, but...some do. And they're different." Balancing his half-drunk bowl of tea upon his gut, Kocho pulled up his sleeve just as he had back in the cart, displaying a birthmark like a winding snake. "I am an Overincarnation. To be precise, according to the master, I am the tenth incarnation of a soul only meant to be returned seven times. A Thought Thief."

Kocho let the sleeve fall and steadied his cup.

"All tenth souls are like me, some stronger or weaker in their ability, but all Thought Thieves. Eighth incarnations are Prescients. Nines are Empaths. Tens are—" He indicated himself. "Elevens are Ghost Hands. Twelve, Time Burners. Thirteen—"

"Are Deathwalkers?"

"Oh no." Again he gestured to the mark on the inside of his wrist. "You don't have one of these. You're not an Overincarnation like me. You're different again."

"How? Tell me."

Kocho's brows lifted. "But you already know. You are two souls born into one body. An anomaly as unusual as any Overincarnation. Two Normals, each of you somewhere between your first and your seventh incarnation, accidentally dropped into one body instead of two. There are people who are the opposite, you know, one soul born into two bodies. They are able to share their thoughts over great distances and are...less when they are apart than when together. You can see why the master studies this. Why he studies *us*. It's fascinating. And so few people understand it or even know there is something to be understood."

Once more letting go of his tea, he gestured to the house. "The

Laroths were Empaths. Generation after generation of Empaths who struggled with their lack of understanding and ultimately died out because of it. Saki is the last Laroth. Rare and unusual because females almost never survive birth."

"She can remove my soul from my body."

"Yes, not a common Empath trait, but something a strong female is able to do. The master has never met another and already has whole shelves of notes dedicated to her. Empath Forty-Four." A slight note of bitterness there, but I bumbled on with more questions.

"And the Witchdoctor, what is he?"

Kocho's excitement faded. "I don't know. I've been trying to find out, when I'm not needed here, but there are so few texts that reference anything like him. And those I can find are in languages I don't understand, so waiting for translations has been slow." He gnawed at his lower lip, staring hard at the floor as though seeing through it to a whole world beyond. "But he's old," he went on. "And not old like me but old old. Over a thousand years old. He never ages. He is never ill. When he's injured, he heals so fast it's like it never happened. He has notes about every soul anomaly he has ever come across. He has notes about every disease and injury he has ever treated. He has diagrams of the inside of the body, not only of us, but of every animal he has ever found. He drinks knowledge like we drink water and he never dies."

The roasted tea sat untouched, teasing me with its colour all too like that of Stiff. "So, he *is* a god?"

"I don't know. I don't think so. He's not without his flaws. And if there's something this job teaches you, it's that our ideas of gods and souls and heavens and hells are all ridiculously narrow-minded. Did you know there used to be a tribe that worshipped a turtle that got caught in some reeds near their village, and when it died they all killed each other because the world had come to an end? And there was a whole civilisation in the north that believed every bad thing that ever happened was punishment from their gods. The master isn't cruel like that, he's just curious. He doesn't see individuals as anything more than information."

He laughed and went on telling tales from the Witchdoctor's journals, but my mind seemed to be full and unable to take in more. Reincarnation abnormality. Two souls born into one body. Had I entered it first? Or had She? Who did it really belong to?

At last Kocho sighed and drank the dregs of his tea. He seemed to have talked himself out, and I had to wonder, then, if he had actually stayed because *he* had wanted someone to talk to. When he set his tea bowl back on the tray and stood, I was sure of it. He had the look of a man well satisfied. He had given me answers, but I was not satisfied. I just had more questions, increasingly complicated and unable to be given form.

"There are always more questions," he said. "I have been very fortunate being able to work with the master. To know something of the inner workings of life, of people, to know things no one else might ever know, and yet I will have to let it all go. Because one day I will die with questions unanswered, and even if my soul is reincarnated for an eleventh time, I won't remember any of this."

He turned his face away. "I'm a tired old man. Save the rest of your questions for another time," he said, and slid open the door. "Goodnight, Cassandra. Goodnight, Kaysa."

He left. And in his wake, there could only be silence.

———————◆———————

Despite the setback, the Witchdoctor returned within a few days, and after all Kocho had told me I watched him closely, looking for signs of age in his perfect face. But it truly was a perfect face, not the foulest expression able to mar its precisely hewn beauty. Though like stone it rarely formed such expressions, instead seeming to watch the world with a detached half interest, owning nothing like the fire that had burned bright in Kocho's eyes.

When I arrived, the old man was sitting in his usual place at the bench, quill and paper at the ready.

"We shall not be taking notes as we go today, Kocho," the Witchdoctor said, looking up from where Saki was writing. "You are required for the initial test."

"Ah, like that, is it," the old man said, and I added yet another question to my ever-growing list. Could Kocho read his master's mind? Or was it so unlike anything he was used to as to be impossible?

I sat in my chair and prepared for another session of tests in the hope I might one day be free, might one day be alone in this body. *She* had been increasingly quiet. I tried not to think too loudly, but it worried me. Every time Saki took me from my body, I feared She would get up and run.

"Today we will attempt the relocation of each of Deathwalker Three's souls into a living host body, to see if there is something about them that more easily allows for cohabitation," the Witchdoctor said. "Kocho, you will be the first, before we move on to others across a broad range of ages, abilities, and races to see if there is any difference in how well, or poorly, it works. Are you ready?"

"Yes, Master."

No one asked if I was ready. I was just expected to sit and let Saki work her magic, pushing and pulling me around like I had no more power over my soul than a leaf caught upon a current. And like a limp leaf I sat and waited for her to pull me from the bright, noisy world of my head and thrust me into the comforting warmth of someone else's. The swirling nausea at being suddenly disembodied seemed less pronounced today, and the voice inside Saki's head had no time to utter a greeting before I was sent flying toward Kocho. Where I hit bright, searing noise.

The soul is taking only while I hold my hand here, just like with the deceased bodies.

You are getting as anxious as your god.

All the words melded together like a symphony of the room, every person's thoughts adding layer upon layer atop Kocho's—an ever-swelling song without end.

He's going to be frustrated.

Because he doesn't want to lose you.

Not yet. Not yet. I must be patient. When least expected.

Before I could get used to the noise, I flew free, returning in a whirl of movement. I blinked as brightness pierced my eyes and a loud bang rang through my skull.

"What is it?" the Witchdoctor snapped. "We are working."

"It's the Empress, Master," came a voice through the thick workroom door. "She's . . . She's collapsed."

"Bring her in." He took long strides toward the door as Lechati entered, half carrying, half dragging the limp form of Empress Hana. Her long blonde hair fell in ropes over her face and her robe hung loose about her thinning form. Lechati had struggled, but the Witchdoctor lifted her like a doll, just as he had lifted me onto his horse with a single hand.

Over a thousand years old, Kocho had said. He never ages. He is never ill.

The god-man laid the empress down upon one of the cleared benches more commonly occupied by a corpse, but for all her ill appearance, Empress Hana was not dead yet. Her eyes fluttered, trying to focus on Saki's face.

"Her temperature is low," the Witchdoctor said, and pressed fingers to her throat. "Slow heart rate. Limp muscle tone. The body appears to be going into a state of torpor."

"She was a little tired, but well enough when I took her breakfast in this morning," Lechati said, hovering like a worried fly. "I was late going back for it because…well…and I found her slumped over her writing desk."

Ink smeared one side of her face and stained the fingers of her right hand.

"We need to infuse her system before she dies."

I got to my feet but even as I stepped toward the bench, I knew there was nothing I could do. I could not fix her body. I could not help her fight this.

I had no reason to care for Empress Hana's fate, no reason to care for her grief or her loss or her legacy, yet the thought of Kisia's Dragon Empress fading to a whisper in some mouldy corner of her empire was so wrong, a poor chord struck on the strings of history. And it was my fault. My fault this woman had lost her empire. Lost her daughter. I ought not to have cared about that either—one doesn't get far as an assassin with a conscience—but I could not but think of Aunt Elora whenever the empress gathered her pride and refused to break.

You think of Aunt Elora like you gave a shit about her.

"I did."

"You didn't," She said, wrenching away control of my tongue. "You are the reason she suffered as she did. You're the poison that was born into my skin and ruined my life. You made me every-thing she would have hated."

She had spoken aloud, but the others were too busy to pay any heed and I wallowed in guilt alone, knowing deep down She was right. Aunt Elora had lost so much because of me, just as Empress Hana had, and I had not been there to fight with her.

"Kocho, fetch my"—the Witchdoctor looked down as I gripped his sleeve—"restorative box." Still looking at my hand, he added, "Something you wish to say, Deathwalker Three?"

"Put me inside her head." Doubts assailed me the moment the words left my mouth, but I rushed on. "She hasn't got a reason to live. She has lost her daughter. Her son. Her empire. She needs someone to give her a good kicking, but I can't do that from out here if she can't hear me. Let me talk to her. Inside."

Saki looked to the Witchdoctor. His moment of frozen thought lasted only a second, during which the door opened as Kocho ran for the restorative box. "Yes," the Witchdoctor said. "Yes, Saki, it will also allow us to test whether the proximity of the host body to death has any impact on its retention of other souls. As I theorise the body opens up to release a soul at death, so it might be more open to absorbing another."

The young woman scowled at him but pointed me back to the chair. I sat, gripping the armrests with shaking hands. I was going inside Empress Hana's head.

You're not afraid of her. You're afraid of me. There was triumph in Her voice. *Don't worry, Cass, I think Torvash will need a bigger distraction than a dying woman for me to take my body and run.*

Saki pulled me from my body. *My body.* The only body I had ever known and ever wanted to know, smiling at me now as I was drawn away. It sat back in the chair, stretching out its legs as though settling in to watch an entertaining play.

It was too late to go back, and no sooner had I reached Saki's head than I was moving on to Empress Hana's. From comfort to pain, from darkness to a biting cold and fatigue that dragged upon every part of my body. It marred every sense and distorted every sound, turning the world from the sensible workroom I had left to a feverish nightmare in which people ran screaming. Everywhere I looked something was on fire—no, not something, a city. A burning city. The flames danced upon the dark surface of a river at my back, while before me a crowd tugged at my arms and legs, shouting and screaming. If I could just jump into that river of fire, I would be free.

No! I shouted to the flaming darkness closing in upon me. *You can't do that. You can't give up.*

Fear swirled like a storm, and disembodied as I was, Empress Hana's voice replied, *I failed. Just let me die in peace.*

The only way to fail is to give up. You can still fight for Kisia. You can still save it.

What for? came words more moan than speech, each one seeming to crackle from the flames. Still people pushed and pulled at every part of me, edging me toward the river. *There is no one left to give it to. My children are dead. I made a promise and I failed him.*

"You killed us," hissed the figures around me. Each grew a face, the same pair of faces repeated over and over—Miko and Tanaka Ts'ai. They bared their teeth and peppered me with sprays of blood and accusations. "You let them kill me," the boys said, all at the same time, their lips moving as one. "I was so scared, Mama, but I knew you would save me. I knew you wouldn't let him do it. But you didn't save me. You didn't."

One by one each of their heads rolled forward off their necks, torn free to land with heavy thuds of finality upon a glossy black floor.

Even as the heads rolled, the collection of Mikos hissed their own diatribes. "You ignored me though I was smarter. You ignored me though I was the better fighter. You ignored me though I had as much ambition and all the political sense Tanaka lacked."

But where the grasping figures of Tanaka had died and fallen, the Mikos stilled their lips and their hands and stood like a silent, endless army with their accusing gazes fixed upon me. The river was so close. I could just step back and—

No! You are the Dragon Empress. You must do your duty before anything and your duty is to Kisia. Your children might be gone but your empire is not. Its people are not and they need you.

A moment of peace batted back the chaos, and in its stillness I shouted over the scowling Mikos. *They found no body. That means there is still a chance your daughter is alive. And if she is then she needs you now more than ever. Don't let her down again.*

The gathering of Mikos repeated my words. "Don't let us down again."

You can still redeem—no!

Saki's skill tugged. I shouted and clawed to stay, but spun away from the fire, away from the city and the army of broken children. I must have returned via Saki's head, but I did not open my eyes until I was sitting in my chair once more.

"The needle, Kocho," the Witchdoctor said, as the three of them continued to crowd the unmoving body of Kisia's empress. Her stillness belied the chaos inside.

"Is she going to make it?" I said, hating the croak of my voice, overused, I told myself, not emotional.

"Still losing her," Kocho answered, something like apology in his tone.

My head spun and I wanted to be sick. Why had I come to this wretched place? There were no answers here, no future.

"The will to live is a frustrating variable, unable to be calculated or reset to a constant," the Witchdoctor said. "External work can only take a body so far, leaving the last leap of effort to be made inside. For some the leap is too great. For others no matter the ease of crossing it, no effort is made. I apologise for being unable to do more," he added, turning to Saki. "Her condition is manageable only while she wishes to manage it. We ought, I feel, to leave her in peace."

"No!" I leapt from my chair and hobbled to the bench without the aid of my sticks. "No!" I thrust Kocho out of the way. "She was going to fight for her daughter, just in case there's a chance. No, damn it!" I gripped the empress's slack shoulders. "No. You are going to fight, you hear me!" I shouted. "You are going to survive and you are going to fight for your daughter because she needs you. If she's out there then she needs you alive, not dead. You're no good to her dead."

"Deathwalker, there is not—" the Witchdoctor began, but I gripped Empress Hana's pale cheeks.

"Fight, damn you!" I shouted into her face. "Fight for—"

Then as though Saki had gripped my soul, I tumbled into darkness—a darkness that sucked at my very being, closing me in its cold, suffocating grip. No fires now, no accusing stares, just an endless pull of water dragging me screaming into its depths.

12. MIKO

Stairs followed still more stairs as Edo and I climbed the heights of Kiyoshio Castle in silence. In the main hall he sent servants bustling with low-voiced orders and a faint smile that didn't reach his eyes. He turned that smile my way when he found me watching. "I imagine you must greatly desire a warm bath and some fresh clothes, Ko—Your Majesty."

"If I have learnt anything since we parted it's that there are many things more important than warm baths and clean clothes. We need to talk."

He grimaced. "And if I have learnt anything it's that there are certain honours due one's name and rank. It would do neither of us credit to converse when you are at the disadvantage of being ill-attired and hungry."

"Nor would it be wise to bathe and eat while unsure of where I stand. You answered none of my letters."

Surprise widened Edo's eyes and he hovered like a wary hare at the bottom of the next flight of stairs. "I have received no letters and can only apologise for having given you reason to doubt me."

Despite his stiff formality, relief flowed through me. I was shocked by the strength of it, at how much the hurt of his betrayal had been eating at me even though I had not acknowledged it.

"And your father?" I said, trying to keep hope out of my voice. "He isn't here?"

"No, he is with the eastern battalions."

More relief, and I closed my eyes a moment to stop the swell of exhausted tears. "I am glad to hear it, Edo, I confess. I am not entirely empty-handed myself, you know; despite everything I am still capable of bringing something to the bargaining table. That Levanti I brought with me is brother to the one calling himself emperor and may be of some use to us."

Edo glanced at the guards standing around the main hall. "Ah, he will be interested to hear that, I'm sure," he said, but although his smile stayed in place it looked strained and my renewed confidence waned. This was not the Edo I knew, not the Edo I needed. Something was wrong and he could not or would not tell me what it was. Too much had changed perhaps, the weeks since we'd last met in the throne room at Koi having made different people of us both.

"Shall we?" He gestured for us to continue and together we climbed the next flight of stairs. Kiyoshio Castle appeared to have them in abundance. It was hard to tell without them side by side, but at first glance it appeared taller even than Koi, narrower, more like a continuation of the cliff than a castle. Roofs and balconies jutted all over, and where there was neither bolthole nor window, there were carvings of Ichio the water spirit, lifting his hooves from the roiling sea.

Despite the castle's grand scale, its passages were narrow and dim. There were lanterns aplenty but few had been lit, perhaps because, apart from Edo, no one appeared to be home.

"Have you heard from your father recently?" I said as we reached the end of an upper passage where weak daylight spilled through an archway.

"A messenger two days ago," he said. "But nothing since."

"Did he say where he was camped?"

A pause. "Not far from Kogahaera, I believe."

I tried to read in his expression whether he knew the Levanti court had removed there, whether his father had some understanding with them or was planning an attack, but another pair of guards watched us from the end of the hall and I shut my lips on every question.

Edo bowed, inviting me to go before him into the room at the end of the passage. "You have not seen the Cavern before, Your Majesty. I remembered it vaguely from living here as a child, but no memory, no matter how strong, could ever have done it justice."

"I have heard of it, of course. How nice to see it for myself."

From the narrow passage we stepped into a grand room that stretched all the way to an open balcony and the crashing sea beyond. Matting covered the floor, but the ceiling was no criss-cross of thick wooden beams, rather vaulted stone like the interior of a cave. Dozens of stone spikes dotted its surface, each a knife blade poised to drop.

"It is believed the other half of the spire tumbled into the sea a long time ago, leaving this cave open to the sky."

"And yet someone chose to live here. In this half," I said. "I admit I would not have had the courage to commission the building works knowing the cliff might crumble at any moment."

Edo laughed, and though it was not the laugh I remembered nor the smile I knew, it brought life to the dead shell who had met me upon the stairs. Foolish to have expected a warmer welcome. Losing Tanaka had changed us. Had changed Kisia.

"I don't think they knew," he said. "Perhaps they might have chosen differently if they had."

I stared beyond the balcony at the grey sky streaked with rain. Waves crashed and warming coals crackled in their braziers, but Edo's voice must have been as clogged as mine for he did not speak again until a servant scuffed into the room.

"Ah, good, your bath is ready, Your Majesty," he said, bowing to me once more. "When you are finished there shall be food and we can talk. It's been...too long since we last met."

Almost I refused the bath and the clothes, but his voice had cracked on the words and he turned to stare out at the rain with the stance of one determined not to be drawn back. To someone who did not know him he looked to be staring at nothing, his thoughts far away, but I could see grief in the way he bent his fingers far back, in the curl of his shoulders and the press of his lips. Yet I could not speak, could not comfort, sure the acknowledgement of Tanaka would break us both beyond bearing. It felt wrong to even be in the same space as Edo without Tanaka lounging nearby.

Needing space, I went with the serving girl, crushed beneath a new guilt whose weight knew no bounds. I had not thought of my brother for days, weeks, had not grieved, had not prayed, had done nothing but keep fighting for the throne that ought to have been his. A throne he now could never take. And Mama. I had no reason to believe she had survived the sacking of Koi, yet I had not lit a single prayer candle for her or any other members of the court. So many dead. So much gone. But not me. Not yet.

The serving girl offered to stay and wash my hair, but I sent her away and sank alone into the hot water, letting it melt the ice stiffening my bones and bring feeling back to my aching limbs. And there in the small stone room, so deep in Kiyoshio Castle I could not hear the crashing waves, I took up one of the candles. Wax pooled around its flaming wick, and forcing myself to recall my brother's face—frustrating, confident, dearly beloved Tanaka—I tipped a drop of hot wax onto my arm. I hissed, surprised by how sharply it burned when I had thought myself prepared. Meaning in that, perhaps.

Once enough wax had built up, I pictured my mother, Kisia's Dragon Empress, and tipped another drop of wax beside Tanaka's penance. The next was for General Kitado. Then General Ryoji. For Minister Manshin. For Master Kenji, Chancellor Goro, and Yin, on and on until I needed four candles sitting upon the edge of the bath to keep up with the names of those I had failed even to remember, let alone respect, in death.

———————◆———————

A silk robe felt strange after so long in damp armour. As a princess, most of my robes had been decorated with dragons and pikes, but this was white and adorned all over with deep blue embroidery like the raging sea, horse heads visible amid the waves. Like the Ts'ai, the Bahains were intent on stamping their mark upon everything it seemed, even me.

Once again, I refused the help of the maid. I was too restless for paint and combs, making do with three jewelled hairpins stuck through a rough bun. Edo, of all people, would forgive my lack of formality.

He was waiting back in the Cavern, but though he threw me his warmest smile yet, it was a flurry of tan fur and scratching claws that made my heart leap. I dropped with a squeal of delight as Shishi dashed toward me, her tail wagging so fast it blurred with excitement.

"Shishi!" I scruffed her fur as she sniffed furiously at my face and licked my proffered cheek, her scent so reminiscent of a life I had lost that my throat contracted and I blinked back tears.

"She must have heard your voice," Edo said as I buried my face in Shishi's fur. "She came trotting in looking for you not long after you went to bathe."

I nuzzled Shishi, murmuring to her until I could command my voice without it trembling. "Thank you for looking after her, Edo."

"You're welcome, Your Majesty," he said, and I realised he had not once used my name since I had arrived. It was like we had never played in the gardens together, never chased one another down the long halls when we thought no one was looking, like those children were long gone. "It would have broken my heart too had she come to harm."

My sleeve covered the wax burns on my arm, but still I tugged it as I joined him at the table, regally spreading the skirt of my robe. Shishi settled beside me.

"Lord Edo," I said, acknowledging him with the same formality with which he had greeted me. I could not repress a bitter smile.

He looked up and for a moment our eyes met across the sea of delicate dishes filling the air with the scent of spice and memory. "It seems strange to be on such terms of formality," he said as a serving girl poured wine. "I used to wonder how it would be when Tanaka became... But I think after everything we had... well, I don't think it could have changed us."

The words plunged a dagger into my heart, twisting as he finished with a sad, wry smile. I had spent so long listening for the hidden meanings in words that I could not stop now, could not keep my doubts from blooming anew. Had all that childhood play, all that friendship, been for nothing because it had not been me he loved?

"You're right," I forced myself to say though each word was a hammer strike to a heart already cracking. "Tana would never have let you bow and call him fine titles."

He would have been informal with everyone; it had just been his way. I had none of his assurance. The title I claimed hung by a thread, owing its existence to nothing but the continued mention of it. I had no palace. No crown. No throne. No empire. No people. Nothing but the name.

Edo's lips trembled and he said nothing. I wanted to talk about Tanaka. To mourn him with the only other person who had loved him as dearly as I had, but I had not come to Syan to open such a wound. Not while there was no time or strength to do it justice.

There would be time later. Always later.

I had been ravenously hungry when we had arrived, but could only stomach picking at a few slices of fish. "You must not have been home long before your father left with the battalions," I said, choosing my words so carefully it might have been a minister seated across the table.

"Not long, Your Majesty, no."

Night was falling beyond the balcony, bringing renewed storms. The blustering wind sent waves crashing against the cliff and whistled through the room, making the candle flames dance. Sandals scuffed matting. Ceramic clinked. Coals hissed in their braziers. They ought to have been comforting noises against the background roar of the storm, yet I felt more tense than Hacho's string. We were just eating a meal, yet my fingers twitched at the absence of my bow, left in my room with my sword and armour. I touched the knife hidden in my sash, but it brought little comfort.

Pressed against my side, Shishi lay still, only her tail stirring restlessly.

We ate in silence for a while, though I seemed to be doing most of the eating and Edo most of the drinking. Due to a tendency toward headaches, he had never been much of a drinker, but headache or no he was drinking now. I sipped at my wine, more in an attempt to burn away the lump in my throat than because I wanted it. It didn't work. The lump remained. And only the warmth of Shishi against my leg kept the tears at bay. Why couldn't I just ask him what had happened? Ask what his father was doing and whether we could ride to meet him? Why could I think the words but not get them past my lips?

The answer might have been unfathomable at any other time, but by my thudding heart and queasy gut I knew it for fear. I had been so sure of so much, only to have it torn away. Edo was all I had left. Whatever happened next, I wished to prolong our friendship as long as I could. Even if it was just one more minute in silence. Followed by another. And another.

Outside the wind howled.

"I assume you heard about Koi," Edo said as his wine bowl was refilled. The serving girl returned to her place kneeling just inside the door.

"Yes," I said. "Word came to us in Mei'lian. Did you hear about the capital?"

"About the Chiltaen massacre? Yes."

I cleared my throat and forced out more words. "I understand the Levanti *emperor* has removed to Kogahaera." It was like treading very quietly around a cave lest I wake a sleeping bear.

"I believe that to be true, yes."

"I must admit surprise then, that you have had no recent messages from your father."

"He has little reason to communicate with me here unless to pass orders to his steward." Bitterness? Edo had never had much of a relationship with his father. "I am but a caretaker." He spread his arms, indicating the room. "Ensuring the great Kiyoshio Castle does not fall into the sea."

The creeping fear something was amiss strengthened. "Edo," I said. "I..." I glanced at the servant kneeling by the door—the very best of spies, Mama had once told me, for no one pays them any heed. Too many servants made their living from the pocket of more than one master and I had lived too long beneath the court's watchful eyes to trust anyone's discretion.

Edo seemed to follow my thoughts, for he cleared his throat and gestured to the girl. "Bring tea. Her Majesty is not fond of wine."

The girl rose, bowed, and uttered, "Yes, my lord," as she backed out of the room. It had no door for her to close in her wake, leaving the sound of her footsteps to fade as she scuffed away down the stone passage. As soon as she was out of earshot, Edo fixed me with a look so full of fear that my mouth dried.

"What is it?" I breathed, the words barely owning enough strength to be heard above the storm.

"My father is not the ally you think him," Edo hissed over the top of his wine bowl. "Did you never wonder why he did not ride to your aid? Why he replied so late to Minister Manshin's call to arms? He—"

Edo broke off. Footsteps were already returning along the passage. He was not fool enough to turn and look, but over his shoulder I watched a new servant enter bearing a pail of coals. Wordlessly the man moved around the room from brazier to brazier, taking his time stirring the coals and adding more from his charred pail.

Edo did not watch the man, but tapped his wine bowl between mouthfuls, drinking so regularly he had to refill the bowl himself. Before the man finished his task, the serving girl returned with tea, ending any chance for further unheard conversation.

Edo's words gnawed at me. I had wondered time and again exactly what Emperor Kin meant when he said I had to remind Grace Bahain who he was loyal to. Lacking other options, I had come to Syan wary, sure at the very least that no man possessed of such hate for the Chiltaens could ever ally himself with them.

Still without answers, a cage closed tighter around me.

Edo downed the rest of his wine and the serving girl refilled that too, slow and graceful about every task. I had to bite back the demand she leave us. She would have to obey, but another servant would just take her place.

At last she returned to kneel by the door, her eyes lowered. Checking the coal man had gone, I cleared the dishes from the centre of the table and tipped up the rice bowl. With my knife I spread it, still steaming, into a flat surface. *Who?* I wrote, using the tip of the knife to carve the word into the rice.

Edo took up his own knife, and having glanced around the room, he smoothed out the rice and wrote *Levanti*.

I had considered Jie, or even that Grace Bahain had merely been working in his own interest, but that he had allied himself with the Levanti was far more frightening. That he had not ridden to our assistance meant their alliance was of long duration, and the massacre of the Chiltaens in Mei'lian no crime of opportunity. I caught my breath at the enormity of my ignorance.

I longed to be able to speak openly, to tell Edo everything, but I clamped my lips and took up my knife. *Trap?*

He nodded.

Unable to eat any more, I took up my tea with shaking hands, trying to take comfort from the warmth of the bowl and the habitual act of blowing away the steam. Across the table Edo stared at the rice as though he could burn a message into it with his eyes. Beside the door the serving girl knelt statue still.

"This storm season has been uncommonly bad so far," I said, proud my voice didn't shake as much as my hands. Small talk came naturally after growing up at court and it seemed to snap Edo from his reverie.

"It has," he agreed. "But I have never spent one on the coast before, so perhaps it is always this bad. The castle weathers it well."

"It does. I am surprised more rain doesn't get in through your open balconies."

Edo frowned, looking through me rather than at me. "Yes!" he exclaimed after a time, and began throwing handfuls of rice back into the bowl. "Yes, isn't it marvellous? It's due to the overhangs. The castle might look like a natural feature, but the people who built it were really clever. You see the angle of the rain—damn, it's too hard to explain without a picture." He turned his head. "Bring paper and ink. I left some over on the writing table."

The serving girl rose, bowed, and moved across the room to retrieve paper and ink. While her back was turned, Edo swept the last few grains of rice off the table with his hand. Shishi padded over to snuffle and lick at the matting.

Edo moved his bowl as the serving girl set paper before him, along with a brush and ink that needed more water. He poured wine onto it and stirred, taking as long about the task as it took for the girl to retreat to her place by the door.

Then he started writing.

"So if the rain is coming in at an angle like this," he said as words bled from the end of his brush, "which it often does off the sea because of the winds, then"—he paused as one might if drawing, but he kept on writing, the words messy and frantic—"by putting the balconies here and having little roofs jut here..." Another pause as his brush swept to the end of a line and stopped, quivering an inch from the page. "...then the rain will hit only the balcony and none of it will get inside. The matting does have to be changed more frequently at that end of the room, but it's mostly because we tread the damp inside." He slid the note across the table, only to begin illustrating exactly the scenario he had just described on the next page. I had no eyes for it, only for his messy lines.

Father wants the throne. He allied with the Levanti to get rid of the Chiltaens and wound Kisia. Now he will marry you and get rid of them. I'm to take you to Kogahaera and if I do not, his soldiers will. Go to your room. I will come for you in the night and smuggle you out on a boat I have ready.

"There are balconies like it all over the castle," Edo went on, the words washing over me as though spoken in a foreign language. Marriage. How deep did this plot go? And how far back? "Some are natural formations, but most were carved from the stone and I marvel they don't fall. Apparently, it hasn't happened once in the recorded history of the castle. At least it's not in any of the Toi family records and they lived here for hundreds of years, you know, until both the old duke's heirs died in a particularly bad season of pirate raids."

Edo barked a bitter laugh that drew my gaze from the page now trembling like an aspen leaf in my hand. "Duke of Syan," he said. "Half reward, half punishment, Father has always said. It's no wonder the old duke tried to leap from one of the balconies."

I folded the hastily written warning and shoved it into my sleeve. "I am sure your father is more than up to the task, Lord Edo," I said, trying to thrust the idea of being made to marry him from my head. No wonder Edo had been so stiff and quiet. To have thought one thing of his father and found the truth otherwise must have been a heavy weight to add to his already oppressive grief. I had only anger, and a return of my disgust at how readily two power-hungry men had sought to claim my body and my name, usurping my freedom to further their ambitions. I had already refused the fate once. I would refuse it again.

Too anxious to eat, I considered whether it would be safer to make a feigned escape to my mat now or attempt more conversation. There was so much more I wanted to say to him, but this revelation had put everything else from my mind. I patted Shishi, grateful for her comforting warmth.

An irregular patter of footsteps rose above the crashing waves, not one set but many, approaching along the passage. Edo's hands clenched to fists. He dared not turn, but he leaned so I could see through the archway while his eyes scoured my face. A crowd of figures blocked the passage, its leader owning a distinctly military stride.

"Is something wrong?" I said, not having to feign a note of worry. "Has something happened?"

Edo turned then, getting to his feet. "Captain Nagai, what is—?"

The soldier took one step into the room and bowed, leaving the rest of his men bottled in the passage. "There has been an incident," the captain said, his voice sounding stuffy. Blood crusted his nose. "The two Levanti have demanded to see the empress on terms it seemed…unwise to refuse."

"How so?"

"The tall one, the emperor's brother, threatened to slit his own throat if he was not allowed to speak to her and given his…value to His Grace…" Here the man's gaze flicked my way, expecting a reaction. Was this a trusted man left to ensure I made it into Grace Bahain's hands?

"Could you not sort this out yourself, Captain?" Edo said.

The captain's eyes widened in mock innocence. "I could have done that, yes, but I thought you said you were the master here in your father's absence, not me."

He stepped farther into the room, uncorking half a dozen soldiers and two Levanti from the passage. They crowded in around the serving girl, Rah and Tor in the middle of the pack. Like the captain had said, Rah had a blade pressed to his throat and blood oozed from a cut, a warning he would make good on his promise. Had anyone else threatened such a thing I would not have believed them, but I had seen enough of Levanti determination to be sure he would. The guards seemed to have felt the same, though the lack of respect apparent between Edo and Captain Nagai might have played into Rah's hands.

I rose to my feet, forcing a welcoming smile despite wishing I could send them all away. The situation was fraught enough without adding still more variables I could not control.

"Rah. Tor," I said as the two Levanti stepped forward, Rah's blade unmoving and Tor's expression a dead mask. "I am sure whatever you have to say can wait until tomorrow. I was just about to retire for the night and—"

Rah spoke, his confident words filling the space. Eyes swung to Tor, and the young man's lip curled.

"As your *protector*, Rah would like to know if you are ready to depart as planned. He can have Jinso saddled at once."

So calm a speech was at odds with the blade he kept pressed to his own throat, such that even without the emphasis upon the word *protector* I couldn't have missed their meaning. Somehow they knew, and whatever I had feared, neither could have had anything to do with it. That ought to have been a relief, a joy that these two men had risked their own safety to warn me, but it could not but throw into sharp relief the actions of my own people. The people I ought to have been able to trust.

"Now would be good," I said, fiercely hoping it might for once be that easy. "I have done all I came here to do and would prefer not to be a burden upon Lord Edo's hospitality any longer."

"I'm afraid that's not possible," Captain Nagai said. "His Grace requires your presence in Kogahaera, Your Majesty."

If there had been little air before, it all dried up then and I could not breathe, could only stare from him to the Levanti to Edo, heart hammering. They had come to warn me, but had brought with them six armed soldiers intent on my capitulation.

My options were painfully slim. Agree to go and end up married to Edo's father, the very man who had let all this happen, or refuse and fight.

The captain lifted his brows, mocking my indecision.

I drew myself up. "That, Captain, is not how one makes an invitation to an empress. If His Grace is desirous of my assistance, he ought to send me a formal request or, even better, make it himself. And you, Captain, ought to be disciplined for daring to tell me what I can and cannot do."

Shocked silence met this speech, cocky assurance wiped from every watching face. A moment passed in which I thought I might have won them, hoped I might get out of this with words instead of steel, but they saw no empress, just a gangly girl in their master's colours claiming a throne she could never win.

Captain Nagai smiled, but all kindness and humour had drained from his face. "A fine speech, Your Majesty, but I have my orders. You'll go to Kogahaera whether you want to or not."

Rah had not shifted the blade from his throat but his eyes darted now as he hissed at Tor, demanding answers. The young man seemed amused, detached enough from the scene to care nothing for the outcome.

"No," I said. "I will not."

The captain lifted his brows. "No?"

"No."

My pounding heart beat loud against the silence. A smile twitched the captain's lips, and his gaze flicked over my shoulder.

Rah dropped his blade. "Empress!"

I spun, catching a flurry of linen to the chest as the serving girl leapt. A small blade slit a searing line across my cheek as I stumbled back, slamming into a wall of sweat and armour and all too many arms. Shocked gasps and cries stuffed the air, but I dropped before anyone could grab me, and scurried on hands and knees across the matting. Shouts and pained cries erupted behind me. Thudding footsteps. A crack of something hitting stone.

The serving girl lunged, her blade coming at me like the fangs of a silent but determined snake. It bit the matting by my ear, only to be torn free and plunged into where she thought I would go next. But I rolled into her legs, knocking them from under her. She toppled over me but gripped my ankle as I sprang for freedom. No words. No threats. She just dug her fingertips into my leg and yanked me off my feet.

My chin hit the matting first and every sound in the room melded with the stunned ringing in my ears. I needed to move but could not. Somewhere Shishi was barking. Footsteps juddered the floor. Light flickered and I blinked and blinked and tore through the shock until at last my arms moved, dragging me up, my head throbbing. The serving girl was screaming. Shishi had gripped her ankle and she was trying to shake the dog free, hissing in pain as long teeth sank through her skin.

Forgetting the dagger tucked into my sash, I charged, locking my arms around her waist and pushing her back so fast her feet scurried to maintain balance. With one great kick she sent my dog flying, but though I let her go, she dragged me on by fistfuls of silk. Together we barrelled through the open mouth of the one-time cave and out onto the slick stone balcony. She hit the railing first, sending it ringing like a gong, and had I not been bent low she might have thrown me right over. Instead she gave a grunt of effort, levering against the railing as she strained to haul me up. I tried to drop, but her grip on my robe was too strong and my feet lifted from the stones. Panic washed over me. With handfuls of silken decadence she was going to throw me to the jagged rocks, and there was nothing I could do.

I thrashed, but the serving girl seemed to have the strength of two men and both of their determination. I kicked every part of her I could reach, but she just tightened her grip on my collar and arched back over the railing. I screamed as we drew face to face over the dark abyss. "Goodbye, *Majesty*," she said, a manic light shining in her eyes.

She smiled, and in that single moment of calm I pulled the knife from my sash. My arms were too caught to strike her, but as she twisted to throw me over, I sawed through silk. The sash was thick, but my weight helped to snap the threads. And throwing up my arms, I slid out the bottom of my robe.

I dropped, stunned, as the silk robe flapped like a flag in the ferocious wind. The railing juddered. Followed by silence.

"Miko!"

Edo's sandals skidded upon the wet stone as he slid to a halt at my side, a bloodied table knife clattering from his stained fingers. "Miko, are you all right?"

Dazed, I tried to swallow my lump of fear. There was no sign of the serving girl or my robe, only darkness beyond the edge of the balcony.

"Miko?"

I looked around. "Shishi?"

"She's fine."

The Cavern opened behind him like a golden-lit maw, the figures of Rah and Tor standing in the place of teeth. "We took them by surprise," Edo said, perhaps thinking it was the sight of the bodies that stung my eyes with tears. "They didn't expect all three of us to attack, and you running into them like that knocked them off guard." His voice trembled as he went on. "More will come when they don't report back. We have to get you to a boat. Now."

"My bow," I said, letting Edo help me to my feet. "And my sword. I'll get—"

"No, it's too risky. Servants will see you in that part of the castle. We have to go now."

He dashed back into the Cavern. I hated to leave my father's bow anywhere, but he was right. To risk everything for it was madness.

"I thought you said your father wanted to marry me," I said, feet still caught in place.

"He does." Edo's expression darkened. "My test of loyalty was to take you to him at Kogahaera."

"Then why did that woman try to kill me?"

"I...I don't know."

"Was she one of your servants?"

He shook his head slowly. The guards had made no threat against my life, had sounded shocked even as the woman lunged for me, yet now they all lay dead and I had no answers.

Edo walked to the door. "We should go before anyone else comes."

I looked at Tor, standing with Rah in the middle of the floor, blood splattering their already mud-stained clothes. "You need to get out of here too," I said. "Lord Edo has prepared a boat." It was not quite an invitation, not quite a question, but Tor seemed to understand it all the same and gave a short nod. He did not meet my gaze, however, or translate my words for Rah. Neither seemed to be looking at the other.

With no time to wonder what could have happened to them, I walked to the door, Shishi at my heels.

Rather than risk meeting more guards or servants in the upper castle, Edo led us into a narrow side passage ending in tight, spiral stairs. They spun down into the rock, a lantern at every bend all that kept the darkness at bay.

More darkness met us at the bottom, and doubling back, Edo brushed past me to snatch the bottom-most lantern from the stairwell. Its trembling light filled yet another narrow passage echoing with the thunder of crashing waves.

"Without going through the front gates there are only two ways out of the castle," Edo whispered as he walked, his voice bouncing off the stone. "Through the drain that leads out into the city, which won't be safe enough, and by boat. Syan is a busy port. Ships come and go at all hours. No one will notice one more."

The breaking of the ferocious waves grew louder and wind blustered down the passage from an archway at the end, sharp with the tang of salt and seaweed. Firelight called us on, but Edo stopped. "There's a lookout," he said, without turning to face me. "On a platform above the jetty. There's no way to take him out without raising the alarm and no way to take a boat without him seeing you. So the moment you step through that door you have to get in a boat and be out of here as soon as you can. I'll hold them off if I must."

"Edo." I reached for his shoulder only to clench my fingers to a fist and let it drop. Too much history. Too much heartbreak. "You have to come with us."

He turned, the lantern lighting his pained face from below. "No, Koko," he said, and my heart broke anew at his use of my old nickname and his wry, twisted smile. "I cannot run from this. I only ever wanted two things out of life. One is gone and can never come back. The other is here. This is my home. This is my heritage. This is the only place I have and the only way I can help. If I leave now my father will disown me, and how then will I make a difference?"

Unable to speak, I nodded. Without him I would be rowing out into a storm with only two Levanti for company. I might have laughed had I not been so close to tears.

"I will take the drain to the city."

The unexpected words spun me around. Tor stared back, his features more like a collection of shadows than a face. "I have already come too far upon this foolish errand and I will go no farther."

Edo lifted his lantern and I looked to Rah, but the shorn Levanti was watching Shishi milling around our feet, her tongue lolling. "I am sorry you got caught up in this," I said to Tor. "The city may be dangerous. If you come in the boat I can set you down wherever you wish. It would be safer."

The young man gave a determined little shake of his head and looked at none of us.

"Very well," Edo said at last. "The grating is on the far side of the jetty. If you let Empress Miko step out first the lookout will run for help and you might be able to get through unseen."

The young man did not thank Edo, but he nodded and kept his gaze averted from Rah as Rah kept his averted from me. One Levanti for company then. I tried to tell myself I needed no one, but the thought of rowing out into that storm alone made my stomach clench tight. "Remember," Edo said, glancing from me to Rah. "Be quick and don't stop. Let's go."

He walked on, stepping through the archway with the stiff-backed pride of a man intent on seeing this through.

The jetty was no outdoor harbour, rather a cave cut in beneath the weight of the castle above. Water dripped from the stone ceiling and the wind blustered in, sending the oil-soaked torch flames streaming. Waves washed in from the stormy sea, bobbing half a dozen small boats—the largest owning ten oars and a mast that almost touched the low ceiling, the smallest a one-man rowboat.

No guard. No sign of where the lookout hid. No shout as we entered, though no doubt the man was already running for help before Edo even closed the heavy door behind us.

"Quick, to the boat," he said, waving us toward the nearest, a small craft with three sets of oars and a mast at least twice my height, its sail tightly furled. "Don't touch the sail; you won't want it in this storm." He reached into one of the many barrels and withdrew a satchel, thrusting it into my arms. "Take this. Some supplies I packed while you were bathing. I couldn't get much at short notice with so many people watching, but it should help. Go south. Father's influence as good as ends at the mouth of the Tzitzi since he's not well loved by the southerners."

Almost I pointed out that neither was I, but with a rough shove he pushed me toward the boat. Rah stood beside it, eyeing the rocking hull warily.

"That's the drain," Edo went on, pointing to a grating at the opposite end of the slick stone jetty. "It comes out in the city. I can't guarantee someone won't follow you or that you'll be able to get out if they lock the gates, but perhaps if you lie low or put on some Kisian clothing—"

"I can look after myself," Tor said, and strode toward the grating. Rah had climbed inside the rocking boat and eyed his companion as the young man unhooked the drain cover. He spoke and was ignored. He repeated himself, louder, but Tor did not reply until Rah made to get out of the boat. Whatever the words he snapped back made Rah scowl, his face reddening, but before he could speak again or move at all, Tor slid into the drain and was gone.

I threw the satchel into the boat, just missing Rah's feet. He seemed to have frozen in place staring at where Tor had disappeared. Shishi panted beside me.

"I'm sorry, girl, but you have to stay," I said, and though I had known this moment would come, tears bit at my eyes as I knelt to once more bury my face in her fur. "You have to stay and be safe, my one and only friend."

Something slammed against the door, shattering the peace. It came again like the fist of a giant beating upon the wood.

"Shit," Edo hissed. "You have to go. Give her to me and get on that boat. Go!"

Another boom. Frenzied words poured from Rah's lips. He was working the mooring knot loose and beckoned me to hurry. Sucking one last deep breath of Shishi's fur, I rose and turned away, blinking back tears as I stepped into the boat. The sound of shattering wood filled the cave.

The boat rocked as Rah freed it from its moorings, but before he could push us away from the jetty Shishi squirmed from Edo's grip.

"No! Shishi!"

A strangled cry left my lips as she leapt, landing in the boat with a clatter of claws to abase herself at my feet, her tail wagging. She licked my toes as the shattering wood melded with the storm. The head of a maul was sticking through the door.

"Sorry!" Edo called over the crack of the maul being ripped out. The roar of the waves and the wind grew as Rah used the oar to pole us clear of the cave mouth. "I'm sorry!" Edo shouted again, but the warm snuffle of Shishi's breath against my feet lightened a heart too long weighed down with dread. Even as Edo turned away to face his father's soldiers, the tears spilling down my cheeks were tears of the fiercest joy.

13. DISHIVA

They buried the soldier the following morning with his head still attached. It took two men many hours to dig a hole outside the walls, and while they lowered the body into it, all but one of the pilgrims gathered in the rain to watch. That was how those of the faith farewelled their dead. Leo had been given permission to leave the compound and speak blessings over it himself.

A tragic accident, it had been pronounced, and every horse master told to keep careful watch over their redcap supply. Yet still there were whispers. Had it been a Levanti? Someone intent on harming Gideon's image? Or someone, like Grace Bahain, who didn't like the arrival of Leo Villius and his supporters? I was sure it had been Leo himself, but Gideon blamed recent Levanti deserters and his words were pinpricks of doubt upon my certainty. Ptapha *had* left that day. And he had been close to Loklan, our horse master, who had a supply of redcap. It fit very neatly together, yet still my gaze shied toward the man they called Veld Reborn.

But why? Why kill one of his own people? The question had plagued me half the night, tossing and turning on my sleeping mat as I revisited the sight of Nods dead upon the table. Because of me, was the reason I kept returning to, because he didn't want me to talk to the man. But what could the guard of a Kisian nobleman say that Leo didn't want me to hear? Didn't want us to know.

I needed an answer, so while Leo was busy saying prayers over the dead man's grave, I took Matsimelar to visit the pilgrim who had remained behind. The pilgrims had been quartered in a sprawling building within our compound, and there we found the Chiltaen woman huddled in a mound of blankets beside a low brazier. Last night's rain had not abated and we entered with water dripping from our storm cloaks. We left them by the door but couldn't help tramping mud along the narrow passage.

The stink of burning herbs hit as we entered the main room, and Matsimelar screwed up his nose in distaste. He halted, seeming to want to keep distance between himself and the trembling ball of blankets. Peeking out of it, the woman smiled in wan welcome.

"I'm not sure it is safe for us to be here," the young Levanti said, twisting his long, slim arms before him like a nervously woven shield. "She looks sick."

"We won't stay long. I just need a few answers."

Matsimelar glanced back at the door, wistful. I hated I could not do this without his help. But how much more must he hate having no other purpose but to facilitate other people's conversation.

"Introduce us," I said. "Please. Just names, not titles. I don't want to frighten her."

Letting go a small sigh, Matsimelar pointed to himself and spoke his name, then mine, before saying something that sounded like a greeting. The woman's reply was split by a sniffle.

"Her name is Livi," he said. "And she welcomes us with God's blessing to her home."

Hardly her home, but I let that pass. "Ask her why she is not with the others and if there's anything we can do to make her more comfortable."

"I'm sure Dom Villius or Lord Nishi has already—"

"Just do it, Matsi. Please."

He scowled at the shortening of his name but did as I asked.

"She says she has a chill upon her lungs. She wished to go, but the rain would have been bad, so Veld blessed her remaining behind. She is sure it will pass, though some warmed wine and soup would be appreciated."

"Tell her we shall send someone back with both when we leave."

The translation of this was met with another wan smile and many thanks. That was one of the few words I did recognise, though the Chiltaens and the Kisians said it slightly differently, determined not even to have a language in common.

"Now tell her I have a few questions about the faith and ask if she will answer them."

Matsimelar hesitated but translated my question. I had expected the woman to scowl and shake her head, to be as skittish as an untested colt, but her smile broadened to show yellowing teeth and she nodded.

"Anything you wish to know, she is more than happy to share the knowledge and the blessing of the One True God."

Once more biting back a sarcastic reply, I knelt across the brazier from her, preferring the smell of the burning herbs to that of her sickly-sweet sweat. "Tell me about Leo Villius," I said. "You called him Veld, why is that? Is it just another title for a religious leader?"

No sooner had the translation left Matsimelar's lips than she was off, words spilling and her eyes overbright. It was too long a ramble to wait until she had finished, so he translated as she spoke, haltingly, staring at her lips and her gestures as he fought to catch her meaning if not the exact definition of her words. "No, the hieromonk is the head of the faith," he said. "And his...position is passed down generation to generation. Not in the same family. To a Defender. Guided by the spirit of God." Matsimelar's lips moved even when he wasn't speaking, as though it helped him understand her words. "He...no, Dom Leo Villius is special. He is as Veld.

The foretold one—no, not foretold. The old one. One who has been before, I think."

"Veld Reborn. Is that because he keeps coming back from the dead?"

"Probably?"

Livi had paused to look from me to Matsimelar and back.

"Ask her," I said. "See if that's what she means."

"Captain, can we just—"

"I know you don't want to be here. I know this shouldn't have to be your job, but I need you and I'm sorry for it. Please ask the questions then we can go."

He looked away, a hint of a flush upon his cheeks. "I just don't see what purpose this serves."

"Wise is the warrior who learns first and kills second. If His Majesty is intent on accepting Leo Villius into his court I must know all I can about him. My duty is to protect."

In the silence Livi continued to look from one of us to the other, unsure. Then Matsimelar asked my question and once again translated as she answered. "In their...holy book"—the woman touched the worn cover of a book beside her on the floor—"Veld was the founder of the old holy empire, conquering divided heathens to build a glorious, unified people in service to the One True God. It was the purpose he was sent into the world to achieve, and he was killed six times and sent back by God six times before his purpose was complete." Matsimelar halted a moment then added on his own, "So I think she means both. Dom Villius was reborn by their god, but Veld was a...historical figure who has been before. Who was also brought back by their god."

"And they think Leo is here to do that again? Veld...reborn."

"I guess so."

"I remember the missionaries telling us the story, but just in case I have recalled it wrong, please ask her how Veld built an empire?"

Again the woman touched the cover of the book, drawing comfort from its presence. And when she spoke, it was with her eyes closed and her face upturned to the dark shadows lurking above. "By living God's truth and God's way," Matsimelar translated. "By bringing people together rather than dividing them. By...gifting sight? I think she is saying, and wisdom, mercy and justice and love for all regardless of wealth or rank or people."

She was in raptures now, blankets falling from her pale, scrawny arms as she held them aloft, trembling with the effort. "Peace can be possible in the empire of the One True God, and all who turn toward his benevolent sight shall be rewarded by his love. To the One True God we gift our bodies and our souls, our hearts and our—" Matsimelar winced. "She's going too fast for me, but it sounds like all the sorts of things we say about our gods and isn't very...practical."

After a few more moments of rising pace her words became a chant and we let her go until her religious fervour burned itself out and her arms dropped. As though realising she had done a lot more than answer our questions, Livi pursed her lips in a sheepish little apology and once more drew the blankets around her shoulders.

"God is everything to me," Matsimelar translated over the woman's now husky voice. "God ought to be everything to everyone. If they but knew the peace he gifts to such devotion."

"Then you came here to worship Le—Dom Villius," I said. "Because you believe he will do the same thing Veld did in your book and create one unified empire under God, by...dying repeatedly to become a god."

Livi started nodding before Matsimelar had finished. "He will. It is written," she said, and I heard the conviction in her voice that words alone could not translate. "He will die again before it is complete and we will be there to protect and honour his fallen body, for there will be many disbelievers."

Footsteps sounded in the passage and all three of us turned, Livi with the same weak smile she had worn upon our arrival. I tensed, fearing the very man we had been speaking about, but another Chiltaen woman walked in, dripping rain. She looked from Livi to us and also smiled in welcome. I still had questions, but her arrival meant the return of Leo to the compound and it was time to go.

Matsimelar spoke thanks for the hospitality and the conversation while I watched the interaction between Livi and her companion. There was nothing of suspicion there, nothing of silent communication, each as open and friendly as the other. Both entreated us to return should we ever wish to talk about God again. Livi's hand never strayed from her holy book.

"Ask if I can borrow her book," I said, not stopping to wonder if it was a rude question.

With the prospect of freedom so close, Matsimelar translated without argument, but Livi shook her head. "She cannot do without it," he said. "But she believes Lord Nishi brought some copies with him for those interested in studying the faith."

With nothing else to say, we left. Matsimelar let out a huff as we stood together on the steps, drawing up the hoods of our storm cloaks. "I don't hate it," he said after fussing with his long hair, trying to get it all beneath the hood. "I mean...I do hate it, but not for the reasons you seem to think."

It took me a moment to realise he was talking about translating. "I've always loved languages," he went on. "And I feel...special, I guess, needed, valued. This would be impossible without me and Oshar, but..." He stared out at the rain. "It isn't a job, within a herd. Translating. I don't know about the Jaroven, but the Torin had traders who knew enough to speak to merchants, but their job was to buy and sell and they were valued for bringing back goods we needed, not for just...speaking. We haven't had...time to develop appreciation and value for what I do. It is not even valuable enough to warrant being Made." Those were bitter words, but he folded his long arms over his cloak and looked no accusation at me. "Change takes time and important work is never easy," he added, and I wondered if he was quoting Gideon, if he had asked to be Made and been denied the opportunity.

I wanted to tell him I was sorry, but what good would it do no matter how much I meant it?

Nearby, Lady Sichi and Nuru stood amid a circle of Levanti, snatches of laughter floating our way. It sounded as though she was practicing Levanti words and phrases to much acclaim, and I didn't have to turn my head to know Matsimelar scowled. These were the very same Levanti who did not value our translators though they held all our dreams together.

"I'm sorry," I said, wishing there were better words.

He shrugged like a man shaking off a troublesome fly. "It's fine," he said, his tone betraying him. "It's good one of them is trying to talk to us rather than expecting us to learn their language. Grace Bahain hates it, you know. I heard he's forbidden her from making these...displays, he calls it, says she is demeaning herself." Matsimelar turned a smirk my way. "Really I think he just hates that she's becoming far more popular with us than he is. Oh, look, the man himself."

Grace Bahain strode down the shallow steps from the manor, with a man in uniform whom I often saw in his company. They looked to be having a heated discussion, or at least the duke was, his companion weathering all without comment. Lady Sichi looked up as they passed, the slight straightening of her back and rolling of her shoulders the only sign of recognition she showed. His step faltered and I thought we were to be entertained with the sight of them shouting at one another in the drizzly courtyard, but Grace Bahain gathered himself and strode on. He and his companion passed close by, the duke's low grumbling like the growl of an animal.

I looked at Matsimelar before I could stop myself. He rolled his eyes. "He's just complaining about Dom Villius. He dislikes the priest's influence with Gideon even more than he hates Lady Sichi's popularity. It sounds like Dom Villius is in there now and Bahain is having to wait for a meeting."

"In there now? They're back?"

Grace Bahain's head snapped around at the sound of my voice. He did not stop walking, but he stared at me until the wall of the building stole him from view.

"I have to go," I said. "But thank you. I'm sorry not enough people value what you do, but for what it's worth, I do."

He gave me an awkward nod and a strained smile, and unable to go on standing beneath the weight of my own self-conscious embarrassment, I mumbled another thanks and hurried away.

———◆———

Returning to the manor, I found Jass in the entrance hall. Catching sight of me, he tucked his hands behind his back in a way that accentuated the muscles in his arms, although in truth anything he did tended to have that effect.

"Captain."

"Waiting for me again?" I said, deciding I had energy only for bluntness.

"No. Yes." The gods only knew how a man who looked strong enough to rip off limbs could appear so awkward. He had been all easy confidence when we'd first met, but it seemed to have abandoned him. "Yes, I was waiting for you, Captain. I had something else I wanted to say the other day and I didn't so I'm just going to say it now." He glanced briefly along the narrow hall, but for all the distant sounds of activity farther into the manor, we were alone. "After I got over myself the other night and realised I'd been a total ass, I also realised you wouldn't have been so upset at me unless you were already upset at something else and maybe you needed someone to talk to. And I..." He sucked a breath and let it out hard. "Want to be that someone."

I stared at him, his words still not quite sinking in.

"To make amends!" he added suddenly, his blush making him look barely older than a saddleboy. "You know...for what I said."

"Right."

"Yeah. So...are you...is everything...all right?"

Lashak asked me that question every day, and every day I had a different answer, but we were working through our hurts in our own way together and I had no desire to give the hurt the Chiltaens had forced upon me more space in my mind. Yet I didn't want to walk away either, to decline his offer, when it had taken a lot of courage to make it.

"I was on my way to see His Majesty. Walk with me?"

With a relieved smile, Jass fell in beside me, regaining something of his earlier confidence as we strode in time along the passage. "Tell me what you think about this sudden spike in deserters," I said.

"Oh, um, I haven't really given it a lot of thought, Captain."

"Then give it some thought. I admit I am not entirely able to make sense of it. This is not easy"—I gestured around to indicate a general everything that we were doing—"but then whenever has life on the plains been easy? We are used to challenge and adversity. In many ways it has shaped who we are."

"But there is the challenge and adversity of survival, and there is challenge and adversity that gains one nothing," he said. "Who chooses hardship fighting the unfamiliar when the familiar still exists? The longer we are away the more sentimental we become and many have begun to forget the troubles that landed us here in the first place."

I gave him a sidelong look as the last of his impassioned words faded away. "That is a very pretty speech for someone who hasn't given the subject any thought."

He met my gaze with his mischievous smile. "Isn't it?"

"Have you given as little thought to the presence and rebirth of Leo Villius?"

"The things I have given little thought to are endless, Captain."

"Well?"

"I thought we were going to talk about you."

I glanced at him again, and again he met my gaze with that smile. "You asked what troubles me," I said. "These are the things that trouble me."

Jass saluted an acknowledgement and I stared ahead rather than at the bulge of his arms or his smile or his broad shoulders. "I think I am not alone in saying the presence of Dom Villius here makes me uncomfortable," he said. "Many of us may be forgetting the specific pain of what brought us here, but no number of lived days will scrub the memory of missionaries from my mind."

"Did they ever perform puppet shows for you?"

"Yes, I recall that."

I stopped walking at the end of the passage to Gideon's rooms, outside which two of my Swords were ant-sized figures standing guard. "Do you remember the story about the man who died again and again only to eventually become a god?"

"Yes. The puppet had creepy eyes."

"Yes!" My exclamation echoed along the passage. "Yes," I repeated more quietly, gripping his arm. "I think about that puppet every time I see him now. The pilgrims think Dom Villius is the man from their stories, that he will die again and again until he ascends to godhood and builds them an empire."

I lowered my voice to a harsh whisper, but though I expected Jass to laugh or tell me it was just a story, he nodded. "Definitely something worthy of your concern, Captain. Especially since if he has designs on this empire he'll have to get rid of Gideon to do it."

I had barely been able to voice my concerns at all, let alone so succinctly. "Exactly." I heaved a sigh, wishing the answer was as simple as *kill the bastard*. I looked along the passage to the door at the end. "Thank you for listening to me and for your...unconsidered opinions about things you've clearly given no thought."

"You're welcome, Captain. My unconsidered opinions are yours whenever you have need of them."

"Generous. Now go on, I have to see Gideon."

Jass saluted. "Captain."

Baln and Tafa en'Oht were on duty outside the emperor's door, both members of the original dozen guards Gideon had gathered before appointing me the task. As such they had not chosen me as their captain and showed me less respect, a fact I hoped to change over time as I earned it.

"Emperor Gideon is occupied, Captain," Baln said as I approached.

"With Dom Villius, yes, I know. How long has he been in there?"

Baln and Tafa shared a look. "Maybe half an hour?" Tafa said, shrugging her shoulders. "Since he came back from outside the walls. Lord Nishi was here too, but he left a little while ago."

"They both came straight here?"

"I don't know, Captain, I—"

She broke off as a serving girl shuffled toward us along the passage, her eyes lowered to her tray of food. She risked a glance up at the two guards, then at me, before lowering her eyes again and saying something none of us could understand. Baln sprang to open the door for her anyway, sliding it all the way. Warmth seeped out of the room, and while the serving girl awaited permission to enter, I leaned in, catching sight of Gideon and Leo kneeling at the table.

I cleared my throat. "Your meal is here, Your Majesty."

"Send it in," Gideon said, not looking up.

Leo, however, turned his head and smiled in welcome. "Commander Dishiva."

"Captain," I said.

"Oh yes, of course, do forgive me. At least I did not make the error of calling you General e'Jaroven, which would be your title under true Kisian conventions." He swept his happy smile first to me then Gideon and, getting no response from either of us, settled on sipping from his tea bowl. The serving girl went past into the room and began setting each dish upon the table.

Baln kept the door open, his hand on the frame, but I shook my head and gestured for him to close it. He did so with a shrug, the soft tap of the sliding doors meeting as definite as the click of a lock.

Gideon looked up, making a small gesture used to halt herds, and said, "And you bury them?" as though picking up the thread of an interrupted conversation. "Without doing anything else to the body beforehand."

"Yes," Leo said, cradling his tea bowl. "The body was created by God and gifted by God; it would be wrong to desecrate it in any fashion."

I was glad to see a frown of annoyance cross Gideon's face at the term *desecrate*. "Why bury them though?" He seemed genuinely interested, a curiosity I recalled many feeling during our early interactions with the missionaries. "They rot in the ground and so the gift is ruined just the same. Burning would achieve the same effect faster and involve less digging."

"Because to burn would be to lose that gift. Buried in the ground it can be...I cannot think of the most appropriate Levanti word, but *digested* is not too far wrong if a little unsavoury. Broken down. Then rebuilt. Made new. Just as you believe the soul is reborn and made new."

"And that is the basis of your religion? Bodies instead of souls?"

"To be of our faith is to serve God's purpose; burial is but one part of that." Again Leo looked my way. "I believe Captain Dishiva has something she wishes to say to you, Your Majesty."

Gideon looked up. "What is it, Dishiva?"

Leo met my gaze with steady, polite interest, and the urge to throttle him was alarmingly strong for a man who was doing nothing, who I could not even be sure was truly our enemy. Time, perhaps, to see how he would react. I drew myself up, hands tucked in the small of my back. "I wish a copy of the holy book of the One True God, Your Majesty. I understand you had them confiscated from Lord Nishi, but—"

"Confiscated?" Gideon's brows dropped low and he parted his lips to keep speaking, only to close his jaw so fast his teeth snapped. He stared down at the table.

"Your Majesty?" I said after a lengthy silence. I glanced at Leo, engrossed in his tea. "Herd Master?"

Gideon looked up. "Pardon, Captain Dishiva? I am afraid my thoughts wandered."

"I...requested a copy of the Chiltaen holy book. I wish to use it to begin learning their written language and gain a better understanding of our...new arrivals."

"Admirable plans, but I am afraid I do not know where they are or what happened to them."

Leo looked up from his tea bowl. "It might be wisest to ask Lord Nishi."

Again with the mild, polite response and kind smile. Yet the revulsion I felt was stronger than I had ever felt even for a Tempachi. I forced something like the same smile to my lips and told myself that despite what Jass and I had spoken of in the passage, despite the dead guard and the story about Veld and the gods-damned creepy puppet the missionaries had carried with them, he was important to Gideon. Here was a man that, properly used, could perhaps outweigh all Grace Bahain's military might.

With a little grunt of effort, Leo Villius got to his feet. "I can ask Lord Nishi about the books on your behalf, Captain. I ought to be getting back to my people as it is. Your Majesty." He bowed and was most of the way to the door before Gideon seemed to come out of his reverie. He made no attempt to call Leo back, seemed satisfied to see the back of him, and I wondered where his thoughts had wandered to so suddenly.

Once the door was closed behind Leo, Gideon heaved a sigh, and having let go so heavy a breath he looked up at me, brows raised in question. Troubled lines cut his forehead and dark circles hung beneath his eyes. I realised in that moment that in the absence of Sett, or Rah, or any of the First and Second Swords of Torin, he had no member of his herd to confide in. Despite the length of time she had been here I could not even imagine him confiding in Yiss, because her loyalty was too important to risk on truths. Somehow, strangely, I had become his only confidant.

"Is something worrying you?" I said, fear twanging my every nerve.

"Everything. Is that not the part a leader has to play?"

"Anything specific then. You look troubled."

He let out another sigh, shifting his weight on the silk cushion. "I am troubled. It appears I am going to have to send out most of our Swords to hold the north through the winter. I had hoped the Kisians would be...disinclined to fight me until spring, but—"

"But winter is the best time for war."

"On the plains it is, yes. Here it snows and the wells and lakes freeze over and people are too busy trying to keep warm and not starve."

I felt foolish and saluted. "Of course, I had not considered the difference."

"Understandable. You haven't been here long. But in any case, it looks like it won't change anything. You see, not all the northern Kisians have bowed to me or allied themselves with us, so even with the Chiltaens and the southerners keeping out of the way for now, it will take many Swords to hold what we have against uprising and malcontent."

"Your Swords are always ready to fight for you."

"So they might be, but if I send you all out into various parts of my empire to keep the peace, I will have none of you here. I also risk Levanti lives when there are already so few of us by comparison, and how would you communicate with the people you are protecting and being served by?"

Language, so many of the problems came back to language. The difference between Levanti and Tempachi was enough to make clear, nuanced discussion difficult, but close enough to allow for basic understanding if you added a few hand gestures. Kisian was nothing like either, and hearing it spoken all around me hadn't helped me learn it.

"And," he went on when I didn't answer, "if I let Grace Bahain and the rest of my Kisian allies deal with the problem as they have so very helpfully offered to do on my behalf, I risk having them keep the peace in their own names, not mine, and the people of Kisia will go on seeing us as conquerors to be ousted."

It was what we were, but still I did not speak.

"And if I send say ten or even twenty Levanti out with each group of Kisian soldiers, putting some sort of"—he waved a hand—"joint command in place, it's no better. Not only is that spreading my Swords thin and risking Kisians turning on them, but with only three Levanti able to translate fluently we run into the same issue as the first idea. Because they know the language, the Kisians would end up taking over. How much more encouragement would loyal Swords need to desert their herd?"

He had talked himself out and for a moment sat in silence.

"We ought to learn their language," I said at last, though I hated what the words meant. I was proud to be Levanti. I wanted to build a new home for us, but was it worth it if the only way to do so was to conform to another culture? Hadn't we fought the city states because that was exactly what we didn't want to do?

Gideon grimaced. "It would take a while, too long for the purposes of this mission. And... that wasn't how this was supposed to work, Dishiva. We did not suffer so much to lose ourselves completely." His sighs seemed to be getting heavier. "There is no good answer and yet I must find one."

I wanted to sit with him at the table, wanted to offer all the comfort I would have offered a fellow captain, a Levanti, a friend, but the crimson silk robe he wore acted like a protective shield I could not bring myself to penetrate. Whatever had been his intentions for this empire at the outset, he had chosen to don the trappings of a Kisian emperor, to wear their clothes and speak their language, to eat their food and drink their tea and sit upon their cushions, eschewing *herd master* for *His Majesty*.

So I stayed where I stood with my hands gripped tight behind my back, trying to keep the rest of my stance and my expression calm despite the turmoil his words had let loose inside my head. I had come to speak of Leo, to ask him not only about the holy book but also about what he planned to do with this Veld Reborn, to warn him of the extra danger the priest could pose, but with so troubled a look upon Gideon's face I could say none of it.

At last he looked up with a forced smile. "At least since I cannot put off marrying Lady Sichi any longer we will soon have an excuse for celebration. I feel we could all do with one."

"Putting it off? You said marrying her was important."

"It is, I just wished to choose when. Waiting gives me time to weave a safety net should I fall from so high a tree." His words brought back memories of climbing the rough trunks of the olive trees at Hophset Shrine, of the horsehair nets herd members would stretch beneath the children as they climbed to the thin, supple branches right at the top. Homesickness stabbed deep into my stomach.

"Grace Bahain is beginning to get…impatient to be sure of me," Gideon went on, the spill of his worries splitting my confidence like fruit oozing through an overripe skin. They had gotten like that sometimes, near the coast, when bursts of rain could drop whole rivers upon a grove. "Can I even trust Lady Sichi? I don't know."

"Nuru thinks we can."

He gave a tired, mirthless laugh. "Can I trust Nuru?"

"You have to," I said. "You have to trust us because you cannot do this alone."

The words vibrated with suppressed passion, but he gifted me only a wan smile and reached for his wine bowl. "That sounds like something Rah would have said." He looked away. "Go on, I think I would like to drink and be maudlin on my own for a while."

Uneasy, I left him to it, glad it had been me and no one else who had seen him in so troubled a state.

Lady Sichi had been out in the yard when I saw her last, but as I passed her door the sound of deep laughter came through the panes and I halted.

"Who is with Lady Sichi?" I asked of Esi and Shenyah, the two Jaroven women guarding her door.

"Dom Villius, Captain," Shenyah said, curling her long fingers to salute. "He met us in the entrance hall."

I bit back a frustrated growl and knocked two raps upon the door before sliding it open. Leo looked up from the table exactly as he had when I'd walked in on his meeting with Gideon, and pretending this wasn't the second time we had done this today, said,

"Ah, Captain e'Jaroven," saluting me in the Levanti way, which made me itch to chop off his hands.

"Dom Villius," I returned. A glance at the tray informed me he had been there longer than I would have liked, the tea almost gone from his bowl. A second, smaller bowl sat beside it, filled with what looked like rabbit droppings.

A smile twitched Dom Villius's lips and he popped a rabbit dropping into his mouth. While he crunched it, I realised everyone was staring at me, waiting for me to speak my purpose.

"My apologies, Lady Sichi," I said and, unable to think of another excuse, added, "I wished to speak to Nuru."

"If it's about the—"

She stopped at my intent stare, and mumbling something to Lady Sichi, Nuru ducked past me into the passage, the smell of dried flowers wafting with her. Conversation resumed. Lady Sichi was a quiet, serious young woman when she was alone, but in the same way she performed for the Levanti out in the courtyard, she performed for her visitors, Dom Villius no exception.

Nodding to the woman who would be empress, I slid her door closed, grateful for her Kisian ladies sewing in the corner. Leo Villius was the last person I felt comfortable leaving her alone with.

"I'm sorry I didn't meet you to talk to that soldier," Nuru began pettishly as I pulled her out of earshot of my Swords. "But—"

"That doesn't matter. He's dead."

Her jaw dropped. "Dead?"

"Yes. Did you tell anyone you were supposed to be meeting me there?"

Nuru shook her head, jaw still dropped, her mouth a circle of shock.

"Did you tell anyone I spoke to the man when he arrived?"

Again she shook her head.

"Did you tell anyone about him at all?"

"No! Why would I? He was just a soldier."

I bit back the urge to point out all Swords were soldiers and ought not to have jewelled pins stuck in their hair. But whatever recriminations I might have uttered were waylaid as running footsteps fought their way to my ears. "Captain!" Loklan was hurrying toward us. "Captain, I—"

"Can we make another time to discuss the horses?" I said. "I am—"

"It's not about the horses, it's... it's one of the pilgrims, Captain. She—"

"Livi."

Loklan stepped back, a glint of fear in his gaze. "Yes. How did you know?"

"A hunch. She was unwell. What happened?"

"She took an arrow to the throat, loosed from the north tower."

I tried to look surprised, tried to force shock to my face though I felt none, only a sick horror that tasted like bile. "An arrow... Did you catch the—?"

I broke off as Loklan held up a bow. "Keka found this on one of the upper floors. Nothing else."

I took the bow and ran my fingers along its worn length, but I didn't need to examine it. I knew whose it was because I had carried it with me every day since being Made a Sword of the Jaroven.

Loklan looked at a spot on the wall past my ear, neither he nor Nuru daring to say a word.

The door to Lady Sichi's room slid open and Dom Villius stepped out, he a curse I seemed unable to escape today. "Captain," he said, striding toward us. "I have an answer to your earlier query if you will give me a moment of your time."

Unsure what else to do, I thrust my bow back into Loklan's hand. "Yes, of course. I'll be with you in a moment, Loklan. To discuss... the issue. With the horses."

My horse master's eyes widened, but he nodded. "Yes, Captain."

Nuru took the opportunity to excuse herself, and having hovered for a few awkward seconds, Loklan followed, leaving me alone with the God's child.

I must have worn out my ability for diplomacy, for rather than wait for him to explain his meaning, I said, "Why are you here?"

His brows rose. "I am paying respects to my future empress."

"No, I don't mean why are you here. Why are you *here*? Gideon killed you. Why come back?"

"Because belief is more important than life. Resolve more important than fear."

"Well, I don't trust you. And if anything happens to Gideon, or to Lady Sichi, I will kill you. And if you come back, I'll just do it again. And again. As many times as it takes for your god to get the message."

He met this threat with a bland look. "And to think, I caught up with you to tell you where you could find a copy of our holy book."

"Where?"

"Locked in one of the storerooms downstairs. They are still in the travel boxes and shouldn't be too hard to find."

Refusing to thank him, I turned on my heel and was halfway to the stairs before he called after me. "You're very welcome, Captain."

While the upper half of the manor was all heavy wooden beams skinned in decorative panels, the lower portion was hewn from stone. The palace at Mei'lian had been the same, owning the same confusing collection of small storerooms with heavy doors. Despite Leo's confidence, it would have taken all day hunting room to room to find the books, but panicked Kisian voices met my ears at the bottom of the stairs. The acrid smell of smoke bit my nose and sent my steps thudding along the passage.

A group of Kisians had gathered outside a heavy storeroom door. Smoke spilled out and they were shouting at one another while a man tried key after key in the lock with shaking hands. Others held buckets of water and large blankets at the ready. Even as I approached, two soldiers ran toward them from the opposite end of the passage, water slopping from buckets in either hand.

"What's going on?" I demanded as I joined them, every breath of smoky air making my head throb.

The woman closest gestured at the door and rattled off a squeaky response between coughs, before pointing up at the roof.

"Emperor Gideon!"

"Wait," I said, gripping her shoulders. "Are you saying Gideon's room is up there? Shit!"

The man with the ring of keys flailed it in the air, turning to shout at those crowding behind him. I slammed my foot into the door. It did not open, but more smoke puffed through. I kicked it again, holding my breath against the onslaught of smoke, smoke that was beginning to fill the passage, stinging my eyes and shredding my throat. When a third kick did nothing, I wrenched one of my swords from my belt and thrust it into the gap above the lock. While I levered it, a Kisian soldier slammed the door with his shoulder, coughing all the while. He rammed it a second time, and the sound of splintering wood pushed back my rising panic.

"Again!" I shouted, and though he could not have understood the word, the meaning seemed to be enough, for as I tugged my sword hilt, bending the steel, he threw himself against the door. More cracking. The other soldier joined us, adding his might, and the door burst wide, slamming back against the wall as smoke poured forth in acrid black clouds. One of the soldiers grabbed a bucket and ran in while his companion hacked upon the floor, tears streaming. Tears wet my face too, but I snatched up the other buckets and fought my way in, lungs bursting. I threw the water blind, and dropped to the floor to suck lungfuls of slightly clearer air as more water splashed over me. More footsteps. More coughs. Blankets came in on a tide of short, sharp shouts. More water followed. And slowly, bit by bit, the panic waned into pained gasps.

When I dared to look up through watery, stinging eyes, it was to see the boxes full of Lord Nishi's books sitting in the centre of the room, charred and dripping, bundled blankets covering them like a lid. A servant was pointing at a pair of lanterns hanging above, seeming to suggest one had fallen and set the books alight. I had neither the energy nor the language to tell him he was wrong.

When I felt well enough to stand, I risked a look under the blankets. Only wet ashes and charred pieces of leather remained. Not a single book was left, even at the bottom of the box.

14. RAH

The little boat rocked more violently than an unbroken horse, churning the soup and wine in my gut. I felt better once I had thrown up into the dark waves, though not well enough to do more than grunt as the empress shouted into the wind. She was pointing at distant lights, wind and rain pelting her face and ripping loose her dark hair, the pale robe she wore more sail than the one furled above our heads. At one end of the boat the big white and gold dog lay as flat as it could, like a roll of fur to be traded at market.

The boat rocked still more, its timbers creaking as the empress strode its length and dropped onto one of the benches, gripping the oars.

Clouds passed back over the moon, leaving us in darkness. I hadn't realised how bright a few moments of moonlight caught in a gash between clouds could be until it was gone. Only my grip on the side of the boat allowed me to aim overboard when the next urge to vomit swept over me.

"Rah!" the empress called over the rhythmic slap of her oars hitting the water. "Rah!"

I patted my way across the small deck toward the rowing bench and pulled myself up with aching arms. It had been at least twelve years since I had last rowed anything, since the Torin had summered with the Sheth along the Uku River in the golden days of my youth. The Sheth boys had laughed at our lack of aptitude with their little river boats, but if the Empress of Kisia laughed now the sound was lost to the storm.

I grabbed the oars and thrust them into the sea. The sudden drag almost ripped them from my hands, but I lifted them and brought them around, hitting the empress's oars with a crack. Thrusting them back into the water, we managed a few more pulls, only for it to end with another clack that sent vibrations up my arms.

She kept rowing, and over the sounds of the sea and the rain, began to shout the same word over and over, a few seconds apart. She was giving me a beat. With my stomach lurching toward sickness, I once more pulled the oars around and dropped them into the sea, hauling them toward me.

It became easier to ignore my stomach's demands as my world narrowed to her voice. Squalls of rain pelted us from every side, and when brief snatches of moonlight cut through the clouds it illuminated nothing but the black, rolling sea and Empress Miko's back. Water dripped from her hair and her robe stuck across her shoulders, showing the bulge of her muscles with every pull.

Most of the time we were alone, in the middle of nowhere rowing to nowhere, surrounded by endless sea, but now and then a light would appear on the forward horizon, or the looming bulk of land would rise. Always on my left, the land, and though Kishava had often mocked my sense of direction, I knew that meant we were travelling south. I just didn't know what south meant. I needed to get to Kogahaera. To my people. To Gideon.

Losing myself completely to the empress's rhythmic shout, I didn't notice the growing calm until our oars once more collided. The wind had died to a gentle breeze and the rain to a drizzle. Even the sea had stopped pitching us up and down with quite so much ferocity.

I had not thought it possible for my arms to ache more once I stopped but they did, and I hissed a breath through gritted teeth. The empress hunched forward on her bench, heaving deep breaths. For a time neither of us had strength to do more than huddle upon ourselves and wonder how we had ended up in such a place. I was in a small boat, off the coast of Kisia, in a storm, with the Dragon Empress and her dog. The dog had not moved, and I envied its safe, dry hidey-hole.

Empress Miko stood suddenly, the movement rocking the boat more than the waves. She pointed at the sail and spoke, her voice hoarse from shouting our rhythm. She cleared her throat to try again, only to find it no better, and gestured instead. She was asking if she ought to unfurl the sail, but my knowledge of sailing was minimal and I could only shrug. She began working the knots loose with shaking fingers. At last the small sail unfurled and, catching the wind, lurched the boat toward the dark bulk of land still tracking alongside.

The empress squeaked and pointed along the coast then at the shore, and no matter how little I knew about sailing, it was more than she did. Oh, how the children of the Sheth would have laughed. But the empress didn't laugh when I grabbed the sail arm and turned it until we were heading the right direction; she sagged in relief. I pointed from the rope to a nearby iron bracket and she moved to tie it in place, but as soon as she let go the wet rope pulled loose. Snarling, she tried again, threading the rope around itself in a decorative mess.

A second snarl spurred me to motion, and keeping low for fear of falling into the dark sea, I crawled toward her over the slippery benches. I held out a hand rubbed raw upon the oars, and after a reluctant pause, she gave me the rope. The fickle moon once more dove behind its blanket of cloud, but I needed no light to tie saddle knots, even with rope so thick and sodden.

I crawled back to the other end of the boat and sat with my legs drawn up before my aching stomach. I couldn't tell what had hurt it more, all the rowing or all the vomiting.

Behind me, the empress's dog whimpered. Recognising a fellow sufferer, I held out my hand to let it sniff me before I ruffled its ears.

"Shishi."

Empress Miko had curled up at the other end of the boat, but her shadowed form gestured toward the whimpering dog.

"Shishi," the empress repeated. "Miko. Rah. Shishi."

"Shishi," I murmured, smiling at our first successful dialogue as I scruffed the dog's ears. "That probably means something to your mistress, but to me it's the rustle of wind in the trees. In summer, when their leaves are dry."

I kept my hand on Shishi's head for a long time, trying not to think about my empty stomach. I wished I could ask the empress where we were and where we were going, wished I could ask what had happened, wished I could be anywhere but caught in a boat with someone I couldn't understand, but as Matriarch Ama had always said, wishes were for sunny days of plenty. In hard times all you can do is laugh and keep walking.

"Lovely night," I said, gesturing at the clouds and the spray-swept darkness. "Very...atmospheric."

The empress tilted her head.

"You don't think so? I understand, sometimes it's hard to appreciate what you've got when you see it all the time."

Her eyes narrowed.

"Our weather is a lot better."

She rolled her eyes and gave up on me, lying down in the bottom of the boat. Shishi nudged my hand to keep me patting her. "I think I won that argument, don't you?"

She pressed her head into my hands and I lay down to rest, taking comfort in the dog's proximity.

When I woke from a doze sometime later, it was to the overwhelming need to purge the nothing in my stomach, and I lunged drunkenly for the edge of the boat. Weak predawn light had changed the sea from black to deepest blue, and as my bile peppered its surface I breathed the bite of salty water deep into my lungs.

I sat back, stomach cramping, and once more reached out my hand. The dog was gone. While I dozed, Shishi had slunk away and now lay with her head upon Empress Miko's leg. They were both asleep, a companionable sight that could not but make me think of Jinso. We had been through so much together, he the constant in every day since I had been Made. Travelling together, eating together, even sleeping side by side upon the dry grass. My *ilonga*, a friend I could never replace, left behind to the care and mercy of Kisians I could not trust.

I stared up at the sky. At least the rain had ceased, allowing the ever-brightening dawn through cracks in the clouds. And on the horizon the lights of a ship winked.

"Empress," I said. "Empress."

She started awake, causing Shishi to back away as the empress rubbed heavy-lidded eyes. I pointed to the ship. It was little more than a shadow on the horizon, but words exploded from her lips with the force of curses.

Pulling a dagger from her sash, she cut through the sail-rope, sending the boat lurching once more toward the dark land. Shishi leapt out of the way as water sloshed up over the side, soaking the empress's feet.

The boat rocked, but before I could help, a gust of wind caught the mangled sail, propelling us faster toward the dark shadow of land. A loud crack split the air and shuddered the boat. Thrown off my feet, I tumbled over the tortured sound of splitting timbers and hit water. Breath burst from my lungs. Something scraped my arm and my leg as I struggled toward air amid a curtain of bubbles, only to cut my hand on sharp rocks as I broke the surface.

The boat's keel loomed overhead at a drunken angle, its timbers juddering as waves crashed around its stricken hull. The waves swept on toward the beach, but in the roiling sea there was no sign of either empress or dog, only floating scraps of wood and sea foam.

I spun, legs pumping. "Empress!" I shouted to the rising wind. "Empress!"

A voice answered and I spun toward it. She was clinging to the back of the boat. Blood dripped down her cheek, and as our eyes met, she stuck out her arm, pointing. "Shishi!"

I had seen nothing but the pale crests of waves, but trusting the empress's higher vantage point, I struck out in search of the dog. The Sheth children had mocked my swimming as well as my rowing, but I clawed my way through waves that slopped at my face, again thinking of Jinso—my oldest, most loyal friend, left behind. I would not let that happen to Shishi. Could not. And though my arms and legs ached I kept on, spurred by pleas that transcended language.

My clothing weighed me down, but there was little I could shed barring my boots and my sword belt. The former I parted with, pushing each off with the other foot as I hunted signs of white and gold fur amid the waves, but even as I gripped my belt buckle, I knew I could not let it go. I had lost my home, my herd, my horse, and my honour. I would not lose my last sword too.

Still clinging to the wreckage, the empress shouted again, pointing now toward the land. I struck out toward the shore, stopping only to look around, but weighed low in the waves I could see nothing and feared every moment the empress's anguished cry. Some mad part of my mind insisted it was just a dog, but my heart replied that Jinso was not just a horse, and I swam on with cramping limbs.

A cry erupted behind me and I spun back. My sword bumped my leg as I turned, hunting Shishi to the tune of Empress Miko's cries. A nose peeked above the rolling waves. Shishi was struggling to stay afloat, her paws digging and her panicked eyes bulging through slicked-back fur.

A few kicks brought me to her side and I tried to haul her up, but the combined weight of water and fur and a dog large enough to be a wolf was too much to lift. She would have to stay in the water. I looked around for Empress Miko, but she had disappeared, leaving the boat just a timber skeleton being torn apart upon the rocks.

Fear jolted through me. I wasn't sure I could even save the dog, let alone the empress as well. Might I get Shishi to land only to find the empress had drowned? Ought I—No, that was the sort of dangerous thinking that got Swords killed. She had sent me for Shishi so I would save Shishi, trusting the empress could take care of herself.

Constantly changing the way I carried the dog—first under one arm, then the other, then trying to manoeuvre her onto my stomach—I struck out toward the shore chanting a mantra. I needed rest. I needed food. I needed never to have to swim again for the rest of my life.

As the shore grew steadily closer, I began stopping every few lengths to see if I could stand, but except for sharp, jutting rocks the water remained deep until we were close enough to see dawn light creeping up the sand. When my feet found solid ground I stood, exultant, and lifted Shishi from the waves. Water ran off us like a hundred tiny waterfalls, doing little to lessen her weight.

The dog made no attempt to break free, not then nor when we stood in shallows being sucked out to join the next crashing wave, and though I had been doing most of the work her chest was heaving.

I struggled clear of the clinging ocean and staggered up the beach, legs shaking. Once out of the water, I set Shishi down in a patch of sunlight and she collapsed into a trembling mess of sodden fur.

I did not want to swim back out, hated the thought so much that I did not immediately turn to discover the empress's fate. It was only a moment of hesitation, but it stung me with shame, as did my relief when I turned to see her swimming toward us through the gold-flecked sea, the supply satchel on her back.

Freed from further obligation, I sat on the damp sand beside Shishi to wait, my mind numb.

By the time the empress staggered up the beach, my breathing had calmed and my legs ached rather than cramped, but I did not move as she collapsed on Shishi's other side and pressed her face to the dog's damp fur. Somehow the three pins keeping her hair up had survived the swim, caught in the tangle of what had once been a neat bun. They stood proud now, the tines of a trident pinning her to the beach.

I don't know how long we stayed there, watching the clouds roll and the sea beat its eternal frustration against the land. It might have been mere minutes, or long hours, and we might never have moved again had not a ship appeared on the hazy horizon.

The empress stood and, muttering in Kisian, bent to pick up the still unmoving Shishi. I knelt to help, knowing too well how heavy the dog was, but the empress bared her teeth and hissed. Sand stuck to one side of her face and clumped in her hair, and I raised my hands in surrender. She lifted the dog on her own, and with her robe clinging about her legs like damp cobwebs, she made for the mass of trees as fast as she could, listing left to compensate for Shishi's weight.

I grabbed the satchel and followed.

At the treeline, twisty limbs reached out to gather us into a dense forest, and the sand encrusting my feet brushed off upon damp loam. Water dripped from the canopy and birds sang, fluttering from branch to branch, their wings indistinguishable from the dense foliage blocking out the sky. Unlike the bright, open beach, the forest world was dark and moist and full of insects that buzzed about my face.

Without looking back, the empress wended her way through the trees and on up the slope. I lingered only to cover our tracks as best I could without losing sight of her, a task that became easier as the steepening slope stole her determined pace.

At the top of a mossy ridge she set Shishi down and sat, head in hands, sucking great lungfuls of air. Down in the next gully a stream bubbled toward the sea, and leaving the empress to catch her breath I started toward it, planting my bare feet sideways to better keep my footing. Yet I caught slippery leaves and, unable to save myself, tumbled down the slope like an ungainly hedgehog. Everything spun and the supply satchel dug into my back, but at last I skidded to a halt at the bottom with leaves stuck all over me. If everything had ached before it throbbed now, and I sat stunned beside the rushing water, trying not to think about the sharp pain in my thigh. This was no place to need sewing up again.

The empress joined me a few minutes later. We drank our fill, and then she led the way back up the slope and on toward some mountains looming through breaks in the canopy. Having lapped at the stream, Shishi rediscovered the use of her legs and walked the rest of the way.

I knew not whether we were being followed or where we were going, just followed Empress Miko ever upwards, the pair of us having to lift Shishi up any steep climb or boulder. With the cloud cover it was impossible to tell when noon came and went, but after hours of walking slower and slower in the oppressive heat, Shishi gave up. The regal animal flopped onto the track, her white and gold fur draping the mud like a blanket.

"Empress," I said, when she kept walking. The woman turned, and upon seeing her dog lying with its tongue lolled into the rain, her face twisted into an agony I knew well and she jogged back.

"We must find somewhere to stop," I said.

Empress Miko replied before I had finished, holding her palm flat toward me.

"Stay?" I pointed at the exhausted Shishi and crouched beside her.

The empress nodded, and a brief smile flitted across her face. She made the same gesture again and set off at a half jog, soon disappearing into the rain.

"You are a very brave dog," I said to Shishi, glad of the chance to rest. "Your mistress is very brave too, I think. She would make a fine Levanti, fearless and determined."

Everything I had tried to be, burying my shame in righteousness and honour, only to end up here. The rain drummed its tip-tapping fingers upon my back. "I hope she won't be long," I went on, disliking the silence. "I should find you something to eat. I hope you haven't been fed on fine food like Korune house dogs, because we won't find any of that out here."

Talking to Shishi was even less useful than talking to the empress, but she soon stopped shaking and shifted her nose closer to my leg.

The empress was not gone long, and her reappearance, beckoning from a ledge farther along the rise, stirred Shishi to motion. The dog moved slowly, but move she did, suffering only to be lifted when there was no other way to reach higher ground. As I had talked to the dog, so the empress talked to me as we climbed higher and higher up the mountain. Trees gave way to shrubs and then to grasses as the slope steepened, and having risen above the canopy I risked a look back toward the sea. It was so far down, the smashed remains of our boat so small that for a dizzying moment I was sure

I would fall. The other ship was still out there being tossed up and down on the waves.

Empress Miko called out. She was pointing toward a dark, narrow opening in the rocks ahead—a cave all but hidden behind a thin waterfall. The water spewed from the ledge above to smack upon our stony plateau, running over her feet. Pointing again, she turned to encourage Shishi into the cave, only to give up and carry her around the falling water.

The cave was larger than it appeared from outside, and having ascertained it was safe and dry, I went back out in search of wood and food. I wanted to lie down and never move again, but there was no herd to help and I doubted the empress was used to collecting her own dinner.

Dry wood was hard to come by. Food was easier with mushrooms and berries aplenty, but not sure whether either were safe to consume, I left them to stalk mud crabs up the riverbank. Making messy kills of half a dozen, I carried them back as colour began to drain from the sodden forest.

The empress was hissing angry words when I returned. She knelt in the cave opening, leaning over a collection of her own sticks, trying to make the wood spark. She had collected the mushrooms and berries, along with a few things that looked like dirty roots and a crushed bunch of flowers. She sucked a flower stalk as she worked and had just discarded it to reach for another when I dropped the wood and crabs beside her.

"Try with these," I said, handing her the driest of my sticks and drawing my knife to peel the wet bark from the rest. With a mutter that might have been thanks, she returned to the task but was no more successful.

"You have to keep it going," I said, watching her start and stop with the two sticks she had chosen. "Keep an even pace. And this one"—I pointed to one by her foot—"would be better." I held out my hand and she gave me the sticks, but it was with such a scowl that I bit back all complaint about the mess she called a fire. Perhaps I could rebuild it when she wasn't looking.

Empress Miko watched me work with folded arms. It took longer to create a spark than usual—fatigue, I told myself, not because she was watching. At last a flame flickered, but even when it caught upon the leaves the empress's scowl did not soften. She picked up another flower and, having nipped the stem between her teeth, sucked as she brushed the mushrooms clean with her skirt. She had spread the contents of the supply bag out to dry as well, but none of the sodden items looked familiar.

Working in silence we soon had the beginnings of a good fire and a pair of crabs cooking. Night swept in outside, and Shishi curled up in the corner of the dry cave, only the gentle rise and fall of her back proving she had not yet given up on life.

"I hope these mushrooms aren't poisonous," I said as I bit into one. "There are a few varieties back home that are awful. One, it's called a redcap or redlobe because it looks like a red flower with five lobes, has killed more horses than I like to think about. They're attracted to it for some reason, and almost as soon as they eat it, they're twitching and frothing at the mouth. You have to purge it if you don't want to die, but horses can't vomit, so..." I shrugged, trying not to think of all the horses I'd watched die. Old and young. Sick and well. Even Gideon's *ilonga*. Did he ever think of her now?

I cleared my throat, but the lump stayed. "Our horse masters keep some with them for putting injured horses out of their misery. It's better than desecrating their flesh."

The empress stared into the flames, nibbling her own mushroom. Despite how hungry she must have been, she ate as though at a fine table rather than kneeling in a dirty cave.

"We don't often eat crab," I went on, unsure if I ought to be turning them as they cooked. "We Torin have never spent much time at the river mouths. We're steppe folk, used to hunting ante-lope." I splayed my hands and set them atop my head like antelope horns. "Antelope. There are boars in many of the forested areas as well, and fish"—I put a fin atop my head with a waving hand—"in the upper streams at the right season." A pang of homesickness twisted inside me and I stared out at the darkening sky. "We aren't used to this much rain either. Even in the deltas it doesn't get this wet at any season." Still the empress didn't respond. "And we have two moons." I held up two fingers and our symbol for *moon*. "The Goddess Moon sits upon the horizon like a shy sun. She waxes and wanes the same as the Watchful Father does, but only half is ever visible even in the northern plains. She is like a mother, watching over us."

The empress looked up at this, peering at me in an attempt to understand.

"My mother died when I was young," I said, talking now as much for myself as for her. "She got sick and there was nothing the healers could do. They tried. My father was gone before I was old enough to remember him, but there was always someone to care for me. Our herd is our family. We do everything for the herd."

I stared into the flames, watching them lick around the crabs' hard carapaces. "I think Gideon still believes it, he just chose a different path."

At the sound of his name, Empress Miko's gaze narrowed. "Emperor Gideon?" she said.

"How strange that sounds, but yes, I suppose he must be that now. He is a good man, at least he was. I can't forget that." I shifted my position and stared right at her. "Do you know?" I said, the intensity of my gaze catching her attention. "Do you know he is being manipulated by Grace Bahain? That *he* is the one who made all this happen?" I pointed in the direction that seemed right for where we had come from. "He used us. He used the Chiltaens.

Just to take the throne from you." My voice cracked on the words, barely able to imagine what sort of man would destroy so much, would end so many lives, for something so meaningless. It did not negate what the Chiltaens had done to us. Or what Gideon had done to Kisia. But in that moment, I needed to know she understood we had not been completely at fault, that her real enemies were in her own lands speaking her language.

Her brows lowered. She didn't understand the words, but perhaps she sensed some of their meaning or knew the truth already, for she looked away, her head weighed down with grief.

I stared into the fire and she at the rain, neither of us speaking again until the crabs were cooked. Cracking a shell, I peeled out a length of soft white meat and held it toward Shishi, still hiding in the back of the cave.

"Here," I said, waving it in her direction. "Come near the fire to dry off."

When she didn't move, I threw it halfway. The dog eyed it, tail beginning to wag, and then slowly, so slowly, she crept toward it, licking the air. The meat was inhaled the moment she reached it, and I dropped another piece closer. Less hesitation this time, and the meat was gone. I set a third in my palm, and after sniffing, she drew close and ate that too, her rough tongue tickling my fingers.

I ruffled her ears. "There, it's not so bad here by the fire." I set a chunk of crab down beside me and Shishi settled with it between her paws.

When I looked up the empress was watching me, her smile wan. She nodded at the dog and spoke, her smile trembling. My stomach fluttered at the trust in that look, the gratitude, and unable to meet her gaze I reached my hand out to pat Shishi's head. My fingers brushed hers amid the fur and she snatched her hand away, her cheeks reddening. It might have been an apology she uttered, cradling her hand and looking away, chin lifted proudly, but whatever lie she was trying to make me, or herself, believe, she succeeded only in looking vulnerable.

I took a crab from over the fire and held it out. "Crab." When she looked at it I pointed and repeated, "Crab."

She attempted the word, and though she didn't get it quite right, I smiled at the sound of my words on her lips. The only Chiltaens to have learned our language had done so for very different ends. She tried the word a second time and almost got it. Taking the crab, she pointed at the fire.

"Fire," I said, and she tried that word too. Once she had it to her satisfaction she pointed at a stick, a leaf, the ground, a puddle of rainwater and then at Shishi.

"Shishi?" I said, but the empress shook her head and pointed again. "Oh. Dog."

For the rest of the evening we ate our meagre food and shared our words, taking turns to name things and roll our tongues around new sounds. When we ran out of things to point at, we moved on to simple phrases, but slowly as the fire began to fade so too did our spirits, fatigue bleeding in with the cold.

We settled down to rest on either side of the dying fire. It was not the most comfortable of places, but exhaustion makes up for many things and I was on the verge of sleep when a sob broke the peace. So unexpected was it that I looked first at the dog, but it was Empress Miko's shoulders that shook. She buried her face in her knees, hugging them to her chest like a child.

"Empress?"

I set my hand upon her shoulder, offering my own strength as I would for any Sword in distress, but she pulled away, and lifting her head like a baying wolf, she wailed. With barely a break for breath, the wail became a stream of unintelligible Kisian laced with sobs. Most of it made no sense beyond conveying her misery, but I caught repeated names. Syan. Edo. Bahain. She gestured to me and spat Gideon's name in a spurt of anger, before hopelessness set in. She spread trembling hands, and tears tracked down her cheeks as she spoke of Mei'lian and repeated the names Jie and Manshin and Oyamada over and over. I had no idea who Jie and Oyamada were, but I knew Manshin. The old warrior who had sat on the throne in her armour and tricked us all. Who I had seen locked up in the palace. I wished I could tell her he lived, but all I could do was listen to her outpouring until she was spent. She curled up then, sobbing and repeating a single name over and over. Mama.

I let her be. There was nothing I could do to ease her suffering except call the eyes of the gods to her pain. And so, turning my back to give her privacy with her grief, I sang our lament, thinking of the time I had done so while chained to the ground in southern Chiltae. They had wanted to break our spirit, and they had failed. Levanti could be beaten, tortured, killed, but not broken. Never broken. I had to keep telling myself that.

———————◆———————

The next morning, I prepared to leave. We had only the one bag, my sword, and the clothes we stood in, so it didn't take long. I doused the fire, checked the hillside was clear, and watched the drifting grey clouds with hope the rain might hold off, yet throughout it all the empress didn't move. She just lay there, patting Shishi and staring at nothing.

"It's time to go," I said. And when she didn't move or reply or even seem to hear me, I pointed out the cave mouth. "I have to get back to my people."

Shishi lifted her head and wagged her tail, but the empress remained.

"What happened back there was awful," I said, stepping into her line of vision. "What has happened to your empire is enough to break anyone. But we cannot break. We cannot walk away. If we do not go back then that...*Bahain* will get everything he wants and destroy everything we care about. If I don't get back in time to stop him my people will die, having been nothing but pawns in a war not of our making. Gideon will die." Emotion cracked my voice and I swallowed hard, trying to bury the fear, but it was already too late. "I cannot stay here and let it happen, whatever our part in this has been. And you cannot lie there and let them take your throne." I didn't understand her world any more than she understood my words, but once I had started I could not stop. "You are the Dragon Empress. You rode fearlessly into a battle you couldn't win. You escaped when you ought to have been captured and here you are still free and strong and capable."

She replied in a forlorn tone, and lying there with her cheek squashed to her arm she looked younger than I had ever seen her. Younger and more vulnerable. Yet like a Levanti I knew this fiery woman's spirit could not truly be broken. Hopelessness smothered her like a blanket and I knew the feeling of loneliness it brought so well that it tore at my heart.

I crouched down beside her. "You are not alone," I said. "Your Manshin is alive." And having indicated her, I attempted to convey the dragon mask he had worn by baring my teeth and curling my fingers into horns. "Minister Manshin."

"Manshin?" she said, the strange name bringing life back to her eyes if no smile to her lips. Empress Miko rose from the stone floor. Not to her feet, but it was a start.

"I will go get some berries. And water. We will eat and then go, all right?"

However little she understood, she nodded, wiping wet eyes with a determined swipe of her hand.

Leaving everything behind, I ventured down the mountain as I had the day before. I itched to get moving, but an hour delay for a full belly was not a bad trade.

The forest was loud with birdsong and chirruping insects, their noise stealing the crash of the nearby waves despite every breath being laced with salt. I had never seen anywhere like this on the plains, something I was grateful for as I slid on bare feet down steep inclines toward the river, landing in ever more piles of mud and sodden leaves.

"I should have kept my boots," I said to no one as I scraped mud off my feet. "Better on my feet than sitting at the bottom of the sea scaring fish."

A clump of wild berry bushes tangled along the upper riverbank, and stretching the bottom of my damp tunic, I formed a little pouch and began dropping them in. Most of them. I ate every fifth—all right, every fourth—for although they weren't sweet, my stomach was rumbling.

A small suck of a breath made me turn, already drawing my blade with berry-stained fingers. A soldier halted bare paces from me, grinning, the sword he wielded owning far greater reach than my knife. He greeted me with a Kisian *hello*, before adding, "Levanti dog," his smile stretching all the broader.

I backed up, holding my knife in front of me and still cradling my pouch of berries. He followed, his outstretched sword a promise he could and would kill me if I made him do it. At least he probably thought so. It had been a long time since I'd seen anyone hold a blade like they were asking to be killed.

"Having a bigger blade doesn't help much if you're going to hold it stupid," I said.

The Kisian twitched his head to the side, still smiling. I let my tunic go and, as the berries tumbled out, caught a handful and threw them at his face. The moment of shock was all I needed to get close, negating his advantage. Hand to sword blade, fist to face. The man reeled back a step and I plunged my knife into his neck.

Blood spurted as I yanked the blade free, leaving him gasping as he fell amid my abandoned berries.

"Down!"

I dropped, training kicking in before I realised the word had been spoken in Levanti. Something whooshed overhead, followed by a crack of wood hitting skull, and I found the empress standing behind me like an avenging demon, a thick branch in her hands. Another soldier dropped between us, stunned or dead; it didn't matter. Either way his head leaked blood into the undergrowth, further ruining the berries.

"Thank you," I said. "I guess they sent men to find us after all."

There was no sign of others, but the forest that had felt welcoming and safe was now alive with all too many sounds that could have been footsteps or hushed voices, every shadow owning a figure about to leap.

I got to my feet, abandoning the berries. "We should go."

Empress Miko hadn't dropped the branch. "Manshin. Mei'lian? Kogahaera?"

It took me a moment to realise she was asking where he was. Where she ought to go. "Mei'lian," I said, though Kogahaera was where I needed to be.

"Mei'lian," she repeated, the word determined, and in a sudden flurry of activity, she pulled off both the soldiers' sandals and handed a pair to me. "Mei'lian. Manshin."

I nodded, but I was not crossing an empire for her minister. In truth I was not even crossing an empire for my people, but for a man who had accepted me at my worst, only to push me away rather than let me see him at his. Gideon had always been there for me and I could not fail him now.

15. CASSANDRA

I woke to pain and heaviness and the sure knowledge I needed to sleep forever. Rain pelted the roof. Brazier coals clinked. I wanted to pull the covers over my ears and go back to sleep but could not move. The scent of incense crept through my sleepy haze. Then a rustle of movement. A whisper. Footsteps cracking reeds. I ought to roll over, to open my eyes and prepare to defend myself, but I couldn't bring my heavy body to move at all.

I urged it back toward sleep, but a swirl of anxious thoughts rose on a tide, nagging for attention. More than ever I wished I still had all those quarts of Stiff I'd lost in the ambush.

More footsteps trod past, and with a lick of dry lips I made a demand for the most wondrous of drinks. "Tea."

What? No, Stiff. I meant—

"She's awake!" Kocho's voice, but it was not his feet that appeared before my swimming gaze. Simple blue linen filled my vision as Saki knelt.

"Tea," I repeated. My lips but not my voice.

"Tea, Lechati," Kocho said, his voice a little distant as though he had stuck his head out the door to shout. "Her Majesty wants tea!"

"Her Majesty? I'm no fucking Majesty, old man," I said, forcing myself to roll over in search of him. From the open door Kocho stared, jaw dropped, before his gaze darted to Saki. She shifted her weight, rustling fabric by my ear.

Slowly, Kocho slid the door closed. "You were right," he said to the young woman at my back. "But... how?"

No answer came.

"How what?" I said, some of the heaviness sloughing off me like excess skin. I sat up, though muscles I had never known existed ached in ways I had never thought possible. Everything felt wrong, hands, legs, even my lips. "You're staring."

Pain sheared through my knees and the gentle spinning of the room made me want to lie back down, but I clenched different hands into different fists and glared at Kocho, the only one who could answer. But he didn't have to answer. Realisation dawned like a wildfire sunrise, and I looked at the legs I had tried to bend, at the hands I had clenched and the body that felt all wrong. Not my legs. Not my hands. Not my body. Without thinking I pressed the hands that were not mine to my chest, only to rip them away from breasts far too small and—"Fuck!" I had just touched the Dragon Empress's tits.

They aren't magical, she said. The empress. The God-be-damned empress in my head as She had always been. *Although I would appreciate it, Miss Marius, if you refrained from touching them again in future. Or any other part of me. Even better, you could leave.*

"I... I don't know if I can. Shit, where's She?"

"She?" said Kocho. "Oh, Kaysa? She's been in her room since the exchange. I thought maybe we'd lost you because I couldn't hear you anywhere, but Saki said you were here. She tried moving you while you were asleep, but though she could take you out of there she couldn't root you back in your own body again. The master is fascinated."

"Well, he can be fascinated about someone else's bloody problem," I snapped, every word sounding like a snippy Empress Hana. "Get me back into my body."

Kocho looked to Saki, and for a silent moment they seemed to communicate without the words the rest of us needed. Then Kocho grimaced. "Saki doesn't think she can."

"What do you mean she doesn't think she can? She put me here, she can get me back out."

"No, she didn't. She didn't touch you at all. The master thinks a transfer must have happened at the moment of death, like you shifted into the corpse but because he brought Her Majesty back to life her soul didn't leave, or maybe did only to come back, or... who knows. This is all very strange and I don't know what to say. I'll go get Kaysa. She might be able to pull you back like she would from a corpse."

He hurried out, leaving me to sit in silence with Empress Hana. The empress had far more presence within me than She had ever had—her voice louder, her thoughts stronger, her body stretched tight as though we sat shoulder to shoulder within a single skin.

I wanted to get up and follow Kocho, but the effort of standing seemed beyond me. Everything ached. Not the ache of an injury that would heal, not the daily aches a hot bath could mend, the sort of aches that cut deep into every joint and made me feel older than my years.

Don't forget, this body is younger than yours, Miss Marius.

I couldn't tell if she reminded me so I would not be rude, or so I might know I had been lucky, for I could discern no intention above the jumble of thought-noise. And a jumble it was, strands of thoughts and words seeming to tangle in amongst mine, far more distracting than Hers had ever been. She had just been an annoying presence, a taunting voice that never left me alone.

Saki's clear purple eyes watched me—watched *us* as I navigated the new sensations. She owned the same fire the Witchdoctor had imbued into Kocho, needing answers to questions that brought only more questions, the seeking of knowledge as keen a drug as any amount of Stiff.

What is this Stiff you keep thinking about?

The thought of trying to explain the drink to the Dragon Empress left me as speechless as the staring girl. Yet saliva dampened my tongue at the thought of it, and I clenched and unclenched hands that were not mine only to find every joint ached, even in her fingers, the knuckles stiff like they had been broken in a punch.

The more Saki stared the more aware I became of time passing. Kocho had not returned. My room was not far. Even had Kaysa been with the Witchdoctor, surely Kocho would have run and—

I stood, shocked by how weak my legs felt. They shook like those of a newborn animal standing for the first time, and I would have fallen but for Saki's grip upon my wheat-coloured sleeve. The empress had retreated from the blinding bolts of pain ripping through her knees, but I forced them to stand, to straighten, and at last deeming me able to hold my own weight, Saki let go.

The pain ebbed but did not dissipate, and my first step off the sleeping mat made me question the wisdom of a second. But Kocho still had not returned. Panic quickened my breath far more surely than the pain settling in my joints.

"Why does it hurt so much just to walk?" I said through gritted teeth.

From the swirling thoughts in my head Empress Hana said, *It has never been this bad before, even at its worst. Normally I can function through it and the worst bouts have only ever laid me up for an afternoon.*

"But what is it?"

I don't know. People call it the Imperial Disease, but Torvash says that no human medical condition can be attributed to a distant, angry god and that sometimes things just go wrong on their own. And sometimes those malfunctions cannot be fixed. My body is attacking itself, he says, and his knowledge is not sufficient to change that, only to postpone the day I inevitably destroy myself.

She spoke with matter-of-fact resignation as I forced our legs toward the door, Saki hovering. It hurt like walking through fire, but at least I had found my balance. Empress Hana was shorter, her legs thinner, her feet smaller, and her body less top-heavy without the weighty breasts I was used to, but so long as I concentrated on each step I could account for the changes without wobbling. Much.

We reached the door at a slow shuffle. Kocho had shut it tight to keep the heat from escaping, and as the hand that wasn't mine slid it open, cool air from the passage hit me like a fist to the face.

"This is ridiculous," I snarled as I reeled back, joints stiffening. "There must be something the god-man can do."

He has a very good sedative. And some things to dull the pain.

"Then let's bloody well go get some."

Don't you want to look for your body first?

There was no sign of Kocho in the dark passage. When had it become night?

Miss Marius, I am not as stupid as you seem to think me. You cannot put me off by thinking about the time. Your body. Go find it so you can leave me to die in peace.

Fear simmered, but hoping she would not see it, I said, "You aren't allowed to die yet, Your Majesty."

That, Miss Marius, is not your decision to make.

Saki joined me in the passage, holding a lantern aloft and walking alongside as I shuffled toward answers.

My room was dark and cold and empty. No Kaysa. No Kocho. No Lechati. And despite her silence I was grateful for Saki's presence. She stood solid and sure, her lantern beating back a night made all the more strange by the body in which I walked.

Trying not to panic, I doubled back, gaining speed as our joints warmed up. In the central hall where the great tree held court, rain snuck in around its canopy, looking like drops of molten gold in the arc of Saki's lantern. I had not thought it possible, but the clinging stink of its rotting blossoms reeked worse than ever, and even more iridescent purple blooms were turning to brown sludge upon the steps. I started down carefully, clutching the stair rail with fingers that felt swollen.

"Is there any part of your body that isn't broken?" I began loud but ended in a whisper as the first words echoed around the tree-choked space. "Does your hair hurt too?"

Is your mind always this sarcastic and unnecessarily cruel?

"Cruel?"

The empress didn't answer, but her thoughts filled with displeasure and...hurt? Frustration? They were vague shapes of feelings rather than clear outlines, but I'd never felt either from Her.

At the bottom of the stairs Saki went ahead across the stepping stones to light the way. All around us the shallow pool plinked and rippled with the falling rain, drowning the blossoms that had made this their grave.

As we reached the far side, echoing voices rose to mingle with the rain. I sped toward the workroom.

"He is doing what?" came the Witchdoctor's voice, pouring through the door on a tide of lantern light. "How does he know where we are?"

"Someone must have followed us," returned Kocho. He sounded more agitated than I had ever heard him and I hurried on, step after aching step, straining to catch the sound of Kaysa's—of my own voice. "I don't know what he wants," Kocho went on. "But he has more people with swords than we do."

"Where is Saki?"

"Upstairs with the empress and the Deathwalker. I should get back to them, I said I would—"

I stepped into their light. "Where's Kaysa?"

"Saki," the Witchdoctor said, and in the brightness I could only hear his tread approach. "Lechati is searching for a way through their blockade so you can reach the Door. It seems the hieromonk is not satisfied with his trade and has come to renegotiate it."

"At night," Kocho said. "With torches. And men with swords."

"If Lechati finds a way out then take Deathwalker Three with you," the Witchdoctor went on, and as I adjusted to the bright light I found three pairs of eyes watching me. Kocho bit his lip and did not meet my gaze. I didn't need to be able to read his mind to know what troubled him.

"She's gone, isn't She?"

The old man nodded. Silence followed, filled with nothing but the endless rain. The lingering hope that had powered me here drowned in panic, and crushed beneath the weight of all Empress Hana's pains, I slid to the floor and stared, numb, at the play of dust in the lantern light. She was gone. I was gone. My body, the only one I had ever known, strong, healthy, capable—gone. I had known since the moment Kocho left the room in search of Her, had known and yet been unwilling to admit, unwilling to accept that after all these years She had won, had stolen my flesh, leaving me nothing but a passenger in this broken shell.

Footsteps melded with the storm and Lechati returned at a run. "They appear to have us completely surrounded," the young man said, out of breath. "But there might be a way to sneak out through the moon gate and into the garden, though if Her Majesty isn't capable of walking it might be—"

"I'm not leaving without my body," I said. "She cannot have gone far. I can feel it."

And I could, like a rock of certainty that no amount of panic or pain could wear away.

As though I had not spoken, Lechati went on: "It will add significantly to the difficulty of escape and the length of our journey if she must be carried."

"No one is carrying me because I am not going," I said, slamming my fist into his foot for emphasis.

The young man hissed and gripped his toes, hopping to keep his balance as he spilled swear words in his native tongue.

Miss Marius! You are in my body now and as it seems I may be stuck with you for some time, do remember that people do not see an uncouth whore when they look at me, but an Empress of Kisia. You must behave accordingly.

"Bullshit!" I snapped. "I'll do whatever I like while I'm in charge."

A thrust of anger blindsided me and I could not stop her saying aloud, "Miss Marius would like to apologise for her disrespectful behaviour, but as her *issues* leave her unable to apologise, I shall voice her contrition on her behalf. However, though I do not condone her way of speaking, I must second the insistence that we are not going anywhere until we find Miss Marius's body. To continue like this much longer would make me wish for death more than my illness has ever done. Get her out of my head."

This last she addressed to the Witchdoctor. As impassive as ever, he replied, "I have attempted to restore Deathwalker Three to her body by all means open to me, without success. Saki is unable to help. There is a possibility that even Deathwalker Three's second soul would not be able to revert the shift that occurred when you died."

"So I need to almost die again to get rid of her?" the empress said, wincing as she got us to our feet.

"No," the Witchdoctor said. "You did not almost die. You did die. But if my hypothesis regarding the mechanics of a Deathwalker is correct then it is another person who would have to be near death for the transfer to be repeated, and it would not be Miss Marius who was moved on, rather yourself."

"Me?"

"Yes, because *she* is the Deathwalker. She can move the second soul in and out of your body, you cannot. It is merely my current theory, however, and something I look forward to testing further. To that end I request that you go with Lechati and Saki to the Door."

"No."

His sculpted brows rose. "No?"

"No. You are speaking in possibilities and suppositions. You are also speaking of an eventuality where I am forced from my body into the skin of yet another unsuspecting person. This is not a desirable outcome. We will find Miss Marius's body."

"You seem to think this is up for discussion," he said, his tone almost bored despite Lechati hopping foot to foot, turning all the time to look along the shadowy passage. He kept parting his lips only to say nothing as his master took on the force of Empress Hana in full imperial manner. "You cannot stay."

"You're right, it is not up for discussion," she agreed, and I revelled in the triumph that lit her soul. "I cannot stay. I am leaving in search of Miss Marius's body and no one is going to stop me."

More running steps split the silence and the Witchdoctor looked to the newcomers—a pair of Kisian servants I had seen about the house. "They are in the Wisteria Court, Master," one said.

"There's another group in the garden," the other added.

Their words dredged up memories—a stone courtyard thick with rain and fallen petals. Beneath the steepled roof of twisting vines I ran, every splashing step so loud someone was sure to hear me, to shout, to give chase.

The crutches are a pain, but if Cassandra can use them, so can I.

"She went out through the Wisteria Court!" I cried. "Kaysa."

One of the servants had been speaking. She paused to glare at me, before going on, "He is asking for you, Master."

"Then I will go," the Witchdoctor said. "Lechati, take Saki and—"

"But, Master, they have us surrounded. There's no way out."

Anyone else might have sworn, but Torvash merely narrowed his eyes and said, "Very well. Lechati, Kocho, stay here with Saki and Deathwalker Three. I shall speak to the hieromonk and return, although if this house has been compromised, we ought to move on regardless of the outcome. I will not have my studies interrupted by the importuning of men bloated by their own ill-perceived sense of power."

Before anyone could object, the Witchdoctor strode away along the passage with no diminution of assurance. Did he really think talking to the hieromonk would be enough? If the man had lost half—more than half—his army at Mei'lian he would be in no mood to be refused anything.

"What does the bastard want?" I said, turning on the two servants.

"We don't know," one said, lifting her chin. "We did not stop to ask him. Kocho, I am worried. You said nothing of this sort of thing. I could be cooking for a lord or a merchant and—"

"And have been burned alive by conquering Levanti," the old man said. "The master knows what he's doing. Now stay here with Saki and Lechati." He too set off along the passage, his gait nowhere near as even and confident as the Witchdoctor's had been.

"If he knows what he is doing then why do you need to run off?" the woman called after him, but Kocho just waved his hand irritably as he vanished into the deep shadows.

I snatched the lantern from Saki's slackened grip and, ignoring Lechati's outcry, followed Kocho. If Kaysa had gone out through the court, I would too, and no foul slug of a hieromonk was going to stop me.

What are you doing? You don't even have a weapon.

"So? You wanted to die, didn't you? Stop complaining and let me get on with it."

Her aching knees and tired muscles stole all hope of speed, but though every step hurt I forced myself on. She was right, I needed a weapon. Something. Anything. I had walked around and around this house and found nothing but the foreign-looking things in that gallery. I would have preferred something simpler with a sharp point, but clearly the world had stopped caring what I wanted.

"Nearly there, nearly there," I chanted through every stiff step, switching the lantern from aching hand to aching hand to better bear its weight. "Nearly there."

The gallery looked out upon the Wisteria Court, yet by slipping in from the workroom I could avoid its open doors—open doors through which Kaysa had run with my body.

"We already made a deal," the Witchdoctor said outside as I shuffled into the empty gallery.

Rain stole the reply, but leaving the lantern in the middle of the floor, I crept to the shuttered windows. Out in the courtyard stood a forest of men. They grew from the flooded stones, each holding a spitting pitch torch. Except for the hieromonk. The surrounding firelight flickered upon his linen mask, making his face appear more alive than usual, but it was no improvement.

"I will take them both back," he said with the confidence of a dozen armed soldiers at his back.

"And return what? Your son?"

"No. You give me the empress and the whore and I don't burn down this house and kill everyone inside, yourself included."

The Witchdoctor managed to look even more bored. "I am a god," he said. "I do not die."

"Perhaps not, but all your...friends will. And all your papers, all your books and your notes. Very flammable."

The rain fell unheeded around them and everyone held their breath. Here were two men who would not back down, who were used to getting their way.

"Shit," I hissed, stepping back from the window. "Time to go." I turned to the wall of old weapons, but the two sickle blades were gone. And just as I could remember striding out through the Wisteria Court in my own skin, I could remember taking them from the wall, and the joyous feeling of their weight in my hands.

"She took them."

How do you know?

"I . . . remember doing it, even though I wasn't there. I remember leaving too, and . . ." I tried to look further but felt only the sensation of rain and wind biting my face as I exulted in my new-found freedom. "She's riding. North, I think, but I can't be sure. Fuck, she could be going anywhere, could already be miles away."

Then we had better get out of here.

I grabbed a finely etched club from the sad remnants of a once fine collection. It hadn't looked heavy, but it dropped straight to the floor, dragging my hand with it. It took two hands to lift, and cradling it like a child, I returned to the window.

Remarkably, the two men were still talking, though the hieromonk's guards had edged closer, their weapons glinting menace in the torchlight.

"What do you mean you don't have them anymore?" the hieromonk snarled over the plink and plop of heavy drops falling around him.

"I refer to the escape of Deathwalker Three. Miss Marius left us earlier this evening and we have as yet been unable to recover her."

The hieromonk laughed. "Outwitted by a whore, some brain you have. I will take the empress then and search the house to be sure."

"Very well," the Witchdoctor said, and I gaped as he stood aside to invite them in. Why give in to this man who had gone back on his deal? This man who had threatened him—he a god who could not be killed and had nothing to fear.

You are not very observant.

"Shut up," I hissed, as out in the court the soldiers moved forward. "I need to think. We have to get out of here."

It's Saki.

"What?"

It's Saki. He would give up anything to protect Saki.

"Oh, don't give me that romantic shit," I said. "He's a god and she's a girl who can't even talk, she—"

Can remove a soul from a body with her hand. Without apparent effort. Working for a man who studies how the soul works. He might have been directing each and every one of those tests he put you through, but could he have achieved any of them without her?

I stared at the figures in the Wisteria Court. The first soldiers were passing Torvash, entering the house, and he just stood there letting them by. No sneaky attack, no attempt to stop them, nothing but that impassive, beautiful face owning neither heart nor soul nor trace of empathy. He was not going to fight for us.

Kocho told me Saki is the first of her kind that Torvash has ever found. He can find more of you. He can find more of me. We are just numbers on a scroll.

Footsteps thundered through the house. They drowned out the rain, drowned out the voices, drowned everything but a creeping dread I could not shake. Why run? They would only give chase. Why fight? I could kill a hundred and there would still be another left to take me down.

Really? That's it? You're just going to give up?

"You wanted to die."

To die, yes, not to be taken hostage, not to be used, to be made into a weapon against my people. If this is really it, if there is no way out, then kill us both now before it's too late.

She was right. Better to die than be in the hieromonk's power, but even as I accepted that thought a fresh flood of anger spilled through me. How dare he make me so afraid? How dare he leave me with so little choice? I would rather die than let him take me, but I would die cracking his skull not my own.

There was no time to run. They were coming, shouts and footsteps filling the house. Any moment someone would see the lantern, would come through the door, and when they did, I would be ready. I gripped the club in both hands, determination all that kept me standing. "Come on," I muttered under my breath. "Come on. Come and get me."

A soldier entered, his pace the quick step of someone expecting to glance around and hurry back out. But he kicked the lantern, sending it skidding across the wooden floor. In the wake of the noise, his expression rolled from shock to confusion, to something all too like amusement. He smiled, as one might smile at a child attempting to look big walking in their father's shoes. "Going to swing that at me, are you?" he said, and I realised without the robe and the headdress and the throne, Empress Hana was a small, unthreatening woman with blonde curls like a child's doll.

I shuffled a step back.

Grinning broadly, the man strode in, glancing over his shoulder only once as though he might call others to join the fun, but why share a woman if you didn't have to? He sauntered closer. "You may as well drop that now, Your Majesty," he said. "You might hurt yourself and His Holiness wouldn't want you injured. Much."

I hated to agree. It probably would hurt, but as long as he died it didn't matter. The club was not the weapon we needed.

The man stopped just out of reach and spread his arms. "Well?"

His knees were bent, ready to step or swing or duck and catch me off balance, but he thought he was facing a frightened empress, not a killer.

I stepped, signalling every intention to swing, only to thrust the club hard into his gut like a punch. Air burst from his lungs, and as he doubled over, I wrenched the weapon up into his face. The crunch of his nose breaking was blissful, bested only by the crack of his skull as I smashed the side of his head. Even before he hit the ground the yearning call of death sang.

Dropping both club and knees to the floor, I touched the man's bloodied forehead. His temple had been smashed in, his skull fractured. He was dead and calling to me and yet... I could not use him. No matter where I pressed my hand I stayed resolutely inside the empress's body.

What's wrong?

I stared at the mangled skull, oozing blood in the light of the toppled lantern. All around us footsteps milled through the house. "He's calling to me but I can't... The Witchdoctor was right. You can't move me into the dead. I can't move me. I can only move you. You have to do it."

What? No! I don't know what to do.

"And you think I do?" I said. "Just get us the hells out of here."

Wait, how do I—

I touched the body again, and though Empress Hana did not flow with the same ease as Her, she did flow. Slow and sticky like treacle, like she was holding on, clawing not to leave. But leave she did, passing out through my hand as She had done back in Koi, and upon the hillside when we had separated for the first time.

Footsteps approached. "Casius!" someone shouted, but when a figure darkened the doorway it was not alone. Two men looked at the body, then at me, kneeling at its side, but before either could move, the dead soldier stirred. His arms twitched. His legs shifted. Then the empress got unsteadily to her feet inside the dead man's skin and looked down at her hands. Big, strong hands attached to big, strong arms. It didn't matter that blood still leaked down the side of her head.

"This is amazing," she said in the man's deep tone, and

hearing the sound she laughed and looked at me, one eye wide, the other a popped mess. "Now where's that club? We're getting out of here."

She found it before I could answer, and still laughing, strode toward the two men. The club smashed the shock from the first soldier's face, cracking his jawbone like an eggshell. He fell in a spurt of blood.

"What the fuck, Casius?" The second soldier's voice shook as he looked from the empress to the man she had just killed, blood and brain ooze mixing on the gallery floor. "We're your friends."

"Are you?" she said in the man's deep voice. "That's a shame. Which one of us decided attacking a peaceful house of learning was a good thing to do?"

"What? We...We just do what we're told."

She lowered the club and grunted. "Then we chose the wrong master." Her blood dripped from ear to shoulder. "Get out of here, but if I see you again, I won't spare you a second time."

"Hey!" I said. "You can't let him go, he'll run for others. Do you want to get out of here or not?"

The soldier stepped backward, glancing from me in my empress skin to the empress in her Casius skin. "Of course I want to get out of here," the empress snapped in her deep voice. "But I am a better judge of character than you, and I will thank you not to interrupt me." To the trembling soldier, she added, "Your friends are dead. Go before you're dead too."

The man turned and ran.

"We're going to pay for that," I said as the empress strode toward the door. I shuffled after her, detesting the stabbing pains in every joint. "He's going to tell everyone what he saw and the hieromonk won't believe for a second that I've already escaped."

Empress Hana shot a scornful glance over her shoulder, Casius's burst eye making the expression all the more horrible. "He's just going to run," she said. "I know the sort. Forget him, we have to find another way out."

"But there isn't another way," I said, snapping along at her heels amid the echoing din of searching soldiers. "Lechati said the place was surrounded."

"It's a big place," she rumbled back. "So unless the hieromonk has a lot more soldiers at his command than he used to, that's a damn thin line. I know this place. The last Laroth was the man who kept me hidden from Kin"—she hacked an odd, constricted laugh—"while also serving as his military commander. I hated him in the end, but I have wished for his guidance more times than I would like to admit." She stopped and I almost walked into her sweaty back. "That way," she said, pointing down a narrow passage full of shafts of lantern light. "There's a door into the garden near the long gallery."

"But there are sol—"

Empress Hana lifted her hand, and though I bared my teeth I stopped and listened. Distant voices filled the narrow passage, carrying from rooms being torn apart in the search. An exultant cry erupted ahead, followed by the metallic clink of jewellery.

"Look at this!"

"That doesn't look like either of the bitches we're looking for."

"Oh, fuck off."

A man dashed into the passage, his lantern flaring. "Casius!" He almost dropped it. "Your face!"

"Just a bit of blood," the empress said. "But I found me an empress."

A second soldier appeared in the doorway, followed by a third. "Good job," one of them said. "Better get her to His Holiness before he starts shouting again."

"Fuck yes, let's go," another agreed, eyeing me around Casius's shoulder. "Why ain't she running? Happy to be saved from these freaks, eh, Your Majesty?"

I scowled as the man stepped toward me saying, "I'll hold her so she doesn't make a break for it."

"Hands off," the empress said through Casius's lips. "You think you can weasel in on my prize? Go find the other one."

The three men looked at one another in the shifting lantern light. "Right then." One stepped back into the doorway. "You better get going."

Murmured assent came from the others and I screamed into the silence of my head. She had given herself away and now strode on, carrying her Casius skin with the pride of an empress unable to hear my warnings.

I followed, but as I drew level with them fingers closed around my arm. Spinning back, I gripped the man's wrist, twisting it in the way I had perfected on many a drunk and leering lord. His wrist snapped. Or rather it ought to have. The empress's hands were not as strong as mine and the man merely cried out and backed away, cradling his hand. A snarl tore along the passage. Two knives had been buried in Casius's back, but rather than fall, the empress swung around and caught both attacking soldiers with a great sweep of her club. They fell in a crash of wood and bones and paper screens, leaving only the one with the injured wrist cowering. Unwilling to leave another witness, I pulled one of the knives from Casius's broad back and stuck it unceremoniously into the man's throat before he could even begin to babble pleas for mercy.

"Fine, you're right," the empress said, checking all three were dead with a nudge of her boot. "Of course they know what a Deathwalker is." She jabbed a finger at me. "No 'I told you so' either, you hear?" She laughed. "It feels strange telling myself off. I hope I don't usually look quite so much like a stunned hare."

"Not the time to wonder," I said in a low whisper. "We're not going to make it to the garden without running into more of them. I've got a better idea."

"Then by all means lead the way, Miss Marius."

I shook my head. "I don't know where we are in this maze of a fucking ugly house. Where's the tree room? We need to get upstairs."

"There's a narrow servants' stair nearer the west courtyard, would that work?"

"Servants' stair. Really?"

"Can't have them walking around where people might see them," she said, and it was impossible to tell with Casius's s broken face if she was joking or not. Either way she led me on, stopping now at the end of each passage as she hadn't before. Knives to the back seemed to have reminded her that even dead bodies could be broken.

With her knowledge of the house, we reached the servants' stair without running into anyone else who wanted us dead. All sounds faded as we left the Wisteria Court behind.

The servants' stairway spat us out in the upper passage, light from the central hall tracing shapes upon the floor. It lit a trio of figures from behind—one slightly hunched and shuffling, one seeming to glide, and the third like a shadow following in their wake.

"Kocho! Lechati!" I called, hurrying toward them with tired, aching steps. "Saki!"

They must have heard me but they did not stop, just rushed on down the other passage and out of sight.

"Hey!" The empress dashed after them in her Casius skin. "Wait! What—?"

As she reached the corner a distant door slammed. "I told you so," she scoffed, turning to walk back. "We've been sold for Saki's safety. What's this brilliant escape plan of yours?"

"So you're allowed to 'I told you so,' but I can't?"

"Yes, Miss Marius, because whatever bodies we currently walk in, I am an empress and you are not."

"You mean you *were* an empress."

She stopped before me and folded Casius's arms. "You think we have time for this?"

I held her gaze in challenge for longer than I ought, precious seconds slipping away. She didn't budge, might have stood there until morning without backing down had I not rolled her very own eyes at her and turned away toward my room. It was as dark and empty as it had been when I came in search of Her less than an hour earlier.

"If we can smash the frame, the hole should be big enough for me to climb through," I said, pointing up at the shuttered slit of a window. "This body is quite a lot smaller than mine was, and you've got a very handy club."

She grinned, a stiff, lopsided smile with a broken man's face.

The crack and smash of wood was loud enough to give us away, but with the dead body's strength she made short work of the frame. "Once I'm up there, I'll reach back for you," I said, stepping into her cupped hands to be boosted. "A touch was always enough to pull Her back."

"But I could just walk out in this body," she said. "He's one of the hieromonk's soldiers."

"With a great big hole in the side of his skull and blood dripping everywhere."

"I don't care! This body is amazing. It doesn't tire and it's stronger than I ever was and—"

"It's dead," I snapped, turning to glare at her. "It's dead and it will only get more dead. Bodies don't stay all warm and limber, Your Majesty, if you haven't noticed. They go stiff and cold and lose their ability to move. Remember that man you thought was Leo Villius? My second soul, my...Kaysa was in there. And all she could do with it by the time I arrived was open her eyes and stare, trapped inside and frightened."

Casius's one good eye widened. I pressed my point. "So if you want to get a few more good hours out of it only to be trapped in it forever, fine, stay, but there's no guarantee I'll be able to find you again. Just lift me up to the damn window so I can get out of here."

She did so without apparent effort, and reaching through to grip the outer sill, I wriggled my way out. The chill wind whipped at my face as I emerged into the night like a moth birthed from its cocoon, and balanced on my stomach, I reached back a shaking hand.

The empress didn't take it. "But can I jump myself from body to body?"

"Fuck, I don't know!" I said through gritted teeth. The windowsill was cutting into my stomach. "But Kaysa couldn't and you're not even a Deathwalker. Just take my fucking hand and let's get out of here."

Still she hesitated, gnawing the dead man's lip with the dead man's teeth, before at last she sighed. "Fine, but we have to do this again."

"No problem. Anytime. Now let's go!"

Empress Hana reached Casius's hand up to mine and the moment our fingers touched her soul poured back into my flesh like air into lungs, stretching them to bursting. The soldier finally fell, crumpling into a bleeding heap on the reeds. Freedom called from beyond the window, blown on the cold, stormy breeze, and feeling heavy now I wriggled on through the narrow gap toward it, already considering the best way to navigate the turn and drop and wishing I had a body better able to hold its own weight.

It's a long way down. Perhaps we ought to have thought twice about this.

"It's nothing if you know how," I grunted, hoping she wouldn't sense my fear of the looming drop.

Hoping I won't notice only makes me notice, Miss Marius. Perhaps you should put me back inside—

A hand closed around my ankle. I squawked a strangled cry and tried to turn, to kick, but the window was too narrow. The fingers tightened and pulled. My hold on the outer sill slipped as I was tugged back, but I managed to hook my elbows outside of the window and wedge myself in the aperture.

"It is not my intention to break your arms, Deathwalker Three," spoke the impassive Witchdoctor. "But if you continue to hold on like that then it is the inevitable outcome."

"Shit!" I tried to turn and pull free, but he gripped my other ankle. Pressure mounted in my shoulders and every attempt to lever myself out merely infused my body with a pain like it was stretching, ready to snap.

"I believe it is the accustomed practice to count to three in order to warn recalcitrant children of impending consequences," he said. "We can employ such a method here if you would find it useful."

"Fuck you, god-man," I said, and kicked with both feet, catching him on the chin with the tip of one wooden sandal.

He didn't even grunt. "One," he said, the implacable voice sending panic fizzing through me. "Two. Thr—"

I drew my elbows in and we slid back through the window to land ignobly in his waiting arms. "I see Her Majesty's good sense prevails again," he said. "Well done."

"Hey!" I snapped, about to point out I had been able to make that decision all on my own, thank you very much, but he had already started walking toward the door without putting us down. "We can walk."

"So I have surmised."

He strode out, his long-legged gait eating up the passage. Beneath the thud of his steps the house was eerily quiet.

"Put me down," I said, and when he didn't, I rolled, only to find no freedom. Every vain kick and squirm hurt, but still I wriggled all the way to the stairs. On the top step I bucked, because even breaking an arm getting thrown down the stairs would be better than going back to the hieromonk, but the fucking god-man didn't let go. He didn't lose his balance or loosen his grip, just carried me down the stairs and out through the mire of rotting flowers and rain.

"Please don't do this," I said when words were all I had left. "Don't give us back to *him.*"

"At first you spat and fought not to be given to me and now you wish not to be given back," the Witchdoctor said. "I do not like interruptions to my experiments, but there are occasions when one must choose the lesser of two evils, as you humans would say."

He splashed his way toward the workroom, the house still hanging quiet around us. "Is she that important?" I said. "Saki?"

He slowed his pace but didn't stop. "Yes."

The sort of answer with which there is no arguing. So I dug my teeth into his arm. His sleeve tasted of ink and smoke, but even when I tried to tear it, the god-man didn't flinch. What ought to have made him howl and drop me had no effect at all, and by the time I gave up voices had sprouted in the distance. Not shouts and bangs and running steps, but the desultory conversation of people waiting.

Rain fell into my face as the Witchdoctor stepped out into the Wisteria Court, hushing all with his presence. "One Empress of Kisia," he said, finally setting me on my feet. "You will no doubt find the Deathwalker upon one of the surrounding roads, making good her escape."

The hieromonk's expressionless mask could not smile, but the man beneath it undoubtedly did. "How lovely to see you again, Your Majesty," he said.

"Lord Villius," the empress replied, lifting her chin to better look down her nose at him despite his superior height.

It wasn't the way one ought to address the hieromonk, but he smiled all the same. "It'll take more than disrespect to upset me. Captain Aeneas?"

It was as well the empress had taken over, for I would have flinched at the captain's sudden appearance, his scarred face unchanged since our first meeting north of Koi. "Yes, Your Holiness," he said, sparing me nothing but a glance.

"See *Her Majesty* to the carriage. If we leave now, we might still catch up with the Deathwalker." His eyes seemed to twinkle through the mask's slits as he spoke, but a moment later he had turned away, already calling orders to his men. Captain Aeneas remained, a frown marring his face as he looked from his master to me and back.

"Come, Your Majesty," he said as the soldiers began filing out. "There's no point fighting now."

Empress Hana lifted her chin again, and pride winning over pain, she walked regally toward the gate.

16. MIKO

I t took days to climb down out of the mountains, snatches of sea view replaced with the occasional glimpse of the Tzitzi River, snaking its way across the land to the north. Were Grace Bahain's men watching it? Waiting for me? Or were they still behind us somewhere, chasing us across the landscape?

The first town we stumbled upon sat nestled at the foot of the mountains, its bustling market and well-kept roads proof one of the area's well-known fur routes ran through it. That made it a more dangerous place to stop than a smaller village, but we had been walking for days in the rain and the very thought of an inn made my cold, clammy skin yearn for the touch of dry clothes and warm sheets.

"We should find somewhere to sleep the night," I said, slowing my pace as buildings rose around us. "And get some proper food." My stomach squelched along with the mud beneath my stolen sandals.

With his long-legged gait, Rah caught up and replied in a rumble of Levanti.

"I don't think anyone will be looking for us here," I returned, guessing what he had said. "Although you stand out a bit."

I glanced at my stoic companion. He was taller than most Kisians, and although many days without shaving his head had left a nap of wavy dark hair that hid his branding, even Kisian clothes could not hide the dark colour of his skin. Shishi too was sopping wet, her underside no longer the colour of gold but of mud.

The promise of a dry sleeping mat, warmth, and food drained slowly away, leaving a bitter taste on my tongue. Any innkeeper would take one of the jewelled pins in my hair in return for food and mats for the night, but not with a dog leaving muddy prints everywhere.

An inn lantern came into view—a bright, hopeful sun piercing the grey evening with its promises. Not the sort of inn catering to the nobility, but what was a little noise and dirt when hot food and anonymity were on offer?

I gnawed my lip, aware of Rah's tilted head in the corner of my vision.

"New plan." I walked on, my resolve stiffening at the smell of food. Rah followed, he and Shishi turning with me from the main road into a narrow street beside the inn's yard. A wooden gate sat open. Inside, a long stable house abutted the main building, sluicing water from its own slanted roof onto the yard stones, obscuring the stable hands sitting within. Only their laughter teased through, along with a twinkle of lantern light.

"All right, stay here," I said, gesturing *stay* as much to Rah as to Shishi. "I'll be right back."

With a nod, Rah dropped into a crouch, his hand upon Shishi's sodden coat. Leaving them, I returned along the alley, glancing back only once to be sure they hadn't followed. Neither had, at least not with their feet. Their eyes seemed to track me even after I took the corner and knew myself out of sight.

Alone, I hurried the short distance to the inn door. With every step the sounds from within grew louder and the smells stronger, but neither prepared me for the onslaught that hit the moment I ducked beneath the low lintel. The inn was full of people—a few well-dressed merchants, but mostly commoners in woollen robes of blue and brown and green, plain and unadorned by anything but the occasional embroidered sash. Some still wore their storm cloaks, though most had hung them on hooks along the front wall—hooks so full that cloaks occasionally slipped unheeded to the floor.

Groups, large and small, knelt around square tables so close together that the back of one man was all but pressed against another, but no one seemed to care. Bottles of wine far outnumbered the smattering of teapots and bowls, while serving girls carried long trays of steaming food through the mass like floating dancers. One walked past, wafting a divine smell in her wake, only for it to be swallowed by the soupy stink of damp wool and mud and an unsavoury tang I couldn't place. It seemed at one with the constant, overloud babble and bursts of laughter that rolled across the room. At the closest table a group of men were dicing, little bronze coins gathered between them, while in the corner two played Errant amid a large, voluble crowd of onlookers.

"Out of the way, girlie," someone grunted as they pushed past me in the doorway, not stopping to stare as I had done. Hoping no one noticed my confusion, I followed the new arrival toward the bar. Without speaking, he dropped a trio of coins on the bench top and leaned there, watching a young woman pour him a bowl of wine, her cheeks reddening under his scrutiny. She must have felt the weight of my gaze too, for she glanced up only to look away again, doubly confused.

An aproned man behind the bar lifted his brows. "What can I do for you, girl? You looking for someone?"

"No," I said, more hastily than I had meant. "No. Well, yes, but..." My cheeks reddened as his brows rose still higher into a nest of oily hair. "I am looking for my brother but I do not expect him for a while. I would like a room for the night. And food."

The man looked me up and down. It was not done to walk around in just an under-robe, but until that moment I had not cared that my outer robe and sash had been lost to the cliffs at Syan. I drew myself up, refusing to be so belittled by a commoner.

"By yourself?" the man said, proving there was no limit to the height his eyebrows could rise.

Having received his bowl of wine the other patron moved off into the noisy crowd, leaving the young woman trying to cool her burning cheeks with the backs of her hands.

"Yes. I trust there is no problem with that? I can pay you well." I pulled one of my hairpins from that morning's sodden attempt at a bun, and dropped it on the bar. In the lantern light the gold horse shimmered, its sapphire eye gleaming.

The barman snatched it up, turning it over in calloused hands. "Where'd you get this?"

"That's my business. Will you take it?"

The young woman had stopped trying to cool her cheeks and was staring at me now, open-mouthed, while the barman's brows dropped into a scowl. He chewed his thoughts, jaw working, then closed his fingers over the jewel. "I'll take it. A room for the night? And food?"

"Yes, a room overlooking the stable yard so I can watch for my brother's arrival."

"Very well, though might I suggest you take your meal upstairs, my lady; there are plenty of watching eyes and wandering hands here. The storms make everyone tetchy."

As if to corroborate his words, shouts rose from the Errant game in the corner. One onlooker had grabbed the front of another's robe and together the pair stumbled into a table, sending wine bowls flying.

Swear words hissed from between the man's lips. "Take this one upstairs, Gi. Make sure she has everything she needs." He dashed away on the words, the rumble of his angry voice charging before him.

"This way please, my lady," the young woman said, ducking out from behind the bar and gesturing toward the stairs. I followed her up the narrow stairway to an equally narrow hallway on the second floor, lined with doors. The noise from the main floor was muffled, yet the barman's shouts still rang clear. "Papa does not like it when people break wine bowls," the girl said with a grimace. "He says they are worth more than most of our patrons." A little smile quickly became a comical look of horror and she covered her mouth and bowed. "Present company excluded, of course, my lady. I meant no disrespect."

I assured her I had not taken it so and followed her to the end of the passage where she slid open a door with plain paper panels. A small room with clean matting awaited me and I sighed. Dry. Warm. Comfortable. "I shall have food brought up at once," she said. "Will there be anything else?"

"Do make it a *lot* of food; I am very hungry. And another pillow for the sleeping mat." An explanation about liking to spread out as I slept began only to get tangled before it reached my tongue, leaving the young woman to a knowing, pursed-lipped smile.

"Of course," she said. "Wine?"

"Tea."

Surprise lifted her brows almost as high as her father's. "As you wish. Oh, and if you would be wanting a bath…" She very deliberately looked me in the eye rather than risking offence by staring at my muddy clothes. "The back stairs will take you down to our small bathhouse. It's nothing special, but the water is warm and it's only used by people taking a room for the night so you shouldn't be disturbed."

"Thank you."

She bowed and stepped back into the passage, sliding the door closed behind her. To the retreating beat of her footsteps, I dashed to the window. Its shutters had been firmly closed against the rain, but I threw them open. Night had closed in fast, and hoping I had not left them waiting too long, I climbed through the open window and down onto the stable roof. Its slant was not as steep as I had feared, and I made its length without slipping and dropped to the ground at the far end. No one shouted after me, and with darkness for cover, I slipped out through the open yard gates and back into the alley.

Rah and Shishi were still waiting. Both sat in the lee of a house, its overhanging eaves shielding them from the worst of the rain and the rising wind, but at sight of me Rah rose, Shishi at his heels.

It was harder climbing back up, made all the worse by slippery sandals, but with the prize being a dry room and real food, I swallowed my pride and let Rah hoist me. I scrambled the rest of the way, latching on to the eave and hauling myself over the edge onto the tiles. Shishi had always been heavier than she looked, but even with so much water in her fur he lifted her up to me. Disliking the height, she panicked, her claws scratching burning lines across my arms, and it was all I could do to hold her tight and carry her across the sloping tiles.

Rah joined me beneath my window as little more than a dim, rainswept shadow. I pointed to the window, which earned a quick nod and a smile before he jumped to grab the sill. Muscles bunching, he lifted his whole weight toward the promise of food and rest, sliding headfirst inside, his wiggling sandals the last thing I saw before he disappeared.

I held my breath, fearing I had sent him through the wrong window, but his head soon reappeared, followed by his arms, reaching down to receive the shaking mess of wet fur. I lifted Shishi as far as I could, hoping it would be high enough, and my heart sang as she was lifted free.

Shishi disappeared inside, before Rah stretched his hands down to me. At one time, pride would have had me refuse his assistance, but in the last few days I had come to rely on him in a way I had never thought possible and I took his hands without thinking, his strong fingers closing around mine.

I slid in over the sill as he had done, but neither he nor Shishi got out of the way in time and I half squashed them both. Shishi let out a sharp yelp and leapt away, trailing damp fur over Rah's face. I laughed at his mud-streaked grimace. "Very pretty."

He grinned and I recognised a few words of his reply, which made me proud beyond reason.

Having checked the room was safe, I spread my arms in triumph. "See? Dry." I patted the reeds, while Shishi curled up in the corner, eyeing us indignantly. "I paid about a hundred times more than it was worth, but I think—"

A knock shook the door, dropping the smile from my face. Rah made to move, but I held up my hand, pressing the other to my lips. Shishi's tail stirred. "Yes?" I said.

"I have brought your tea, my lady," came the young woman's voice. "And your...second pillow."

My cheeks reddened as I wondered how much she had heard. The deep rumble of Rah's voice carried surprisingly far. "Just, ah... just set it down out there. I am...changing my robe." I grimaced at the unnecessary detail, but the girl seemed to find nothing amiss.

"Oh, I'm sorry to disturb you, my lady, I'll just leave the tea here. Your meal will be another half hour or so, I'm afraid. The kitchens have been busy tonight."

"Thank you."

A tray clattered, and a pair of footsteps made their way back along the passage. As they faded into the din below, I let go a long breath. Once more gesturing for Rah to stay, I went to the door and slid it just enough to peer through. The hallway was empty but for a tea tray, a pillow, two thin towels, and a pair of worn woollen robes. I pressed my hand to my mouth, muting the strangled little cry that broke from my lips. I had not thought to meet with kindness as a dishevelled nobody at a common inn, and I had to wipe away tears as I gathered everything up.

"Towel," I said, setting it all down just inside the door. "And a robe. We could go wash." I motioned cleaning my arms and face. Almost I asked if that was something Levanti did and immediately felt ashamed. Of course they did. They might do things differently, but if I had learned anything since meeting Rah and Tor it was that Levanti were not the barbarians they had been painted. They were just warriors who did not look the same as us.

"Towel," Rah said, repeating my words in the way we had grown used to. "Robe." He picked one of them up and examined it while I poured out tea. "Tea," he added, looking at the steaming bowl I set before him.

I had not taught him that one, and I felt a warm glow of pleasure that he had been paying enough attention to pick it up. "Yes, tea. Hot." I feigned burning myself. "Steam."

He repeated those words too, then took up the bowl and held it cupped as I did. His hands were bigger than mine, making it unnecessary to hold it so, but nothing could have made me tell him.

I blew the steam off the top of my tea in three long gusts of breath, the repetition of an old routine seeming to knit closed some of the cracks in my soul. We drank in silence, but I wished I could ask him what he thought of the taste, whether it warmed him to the bone as it did me, wished I could tell him that the smell of it made me think of my mother and of lazy days sitting with Tanaka and Edo dreaming about the world we would build. That world was all but destroyed now, lost with Tanaka's life, and its broken pieces were so scattered I doubted I could pick them up at all.

Perhaps it was just as well I couldn't say any of that, so close did fury and sorrow live beneath my skin.

Once we had finished, we gathered towels and robes and went down to the bathhouse. I checked the hallway was clear before Rah stepped out and had to command Shishi to stay behind, but we made it down the narrow steps without running into anyone.

Used to the neatly carved bathhouses in the Chiltaen style, I was not prepared for the rough stone that bit at my feet. It was a shapeless cave full of steam and the scent of damp moss and earth, and Rah drew a deep breath and let it out on a string of blissful words. He pointed at the jagged pool, and with his brows lifted in question I knew I would have to lead the way.

I set down my towel and robe and stared at the wall. I had gotten used to avoiding the need to share a bath by rising early, but it was too late now to hurry back upstairs and pretend I wasn't desperately in need of a wash.

When I turned back, Rah had already started stripping off the mud-stained vestiges of his clothes, his dark skin shiny with rain or sweat or both. I looked away, something in the rippling muscles of his shoulders indecent to the eye.

Before I could even untie my sash, a splash and a gasp heralded Rah's entrance into the pool. He spoke, his words coming to me through a haze of steam that seemed to have filled my head with wool. "Hot," he said when I didn't answer, Kisian words ever a delight on his lips. "Steam." Then, with a laugh he added, "Tea!"

"Yes," I said, the voice mine and yet not mine. "There are hot springs in these mountains. I didn't know they ran so close beneath the town like in Giana, but..." I trailed off, knowing he couldn't understand my words and feeling foolish. As foolish as I felt still standing fully clothed beside the bath.

Whether because he was genuinely curious or because he had noticed my embarrassment, Rah strode through the waist-high water to peer at the crack through which it trickled. And it was little more than a crack, allowing the ingress of a small amount of water, a delicate balance that seemed as lucky as it was fragile. Rah stepped in front of it, all broad back tapering to a waist adorned with a pair of dimples pressed into the skin, and again I pulled my gaze from so complete an expanse of bare flesh. While he was occupied, I stripped off my robe as fast as the damp, clinging material would allow, and gracelessly hopped in, dropping low so the stinging hot water lapped at my chin. I had to sit on the rough stone base of the bath to achieve it, but I would rather be completely uncomfortable in every way than risk ever moving again.

Turning from the wall, Rah dunked his head beneath the water and emerged viciously rubbing the short pelt of his hair as though trying to get rid of it. Despite never having watched a Kisian man wash his hair I was immediately struck both by the conviction that this was not how they would do it, and yet it was exactly how they should.

Leaning my head back I dropped my own hair into the water in a far more reserved manner, removing the other two golden hairpins and shaking it out. By the time I lifted it again, weighed heavy with water, Rah had retreated to the other side of the bath. It wasn't a big bath, a few long strides all it would take to traverse, but the thick steam made him seem farther away, a mere memory in the haze.

In all our days travelling together there had always been silence, but never before had it felt strained, a silence so desperate to be broken it lodged shards of glass in my throat. I tried to swallow them and think of something to say, but our easy exchange of single words seemed childish now, to point at the water and call it water the act of a fool. I chided myself that Rah was the same man whether dressed in mud-stained leathers or naked and lustrous in the lantern light, but I couldn't convince myself it was true.

Having finished with his hair, Rah leant his head back on the edge of the bath, baring the rigid line of his throat. He had closed his eyes, and knowing he could not see me I let myself stare a moment, revelling enough in the joy of discovery to outweigh my discomfort. Sparse stubble covered his jaw and the bulge of his throat was sharp, but an eye travelling down his neck to the place between his collarbones would find softness yearning for touch.

I had never wanted to touch anyone before, my adoration for Edo having always been a passive thing as an observer enjoys a fine piece of art. I had yearned more for him to care for me as he had for Tanaka as their ever-strengthening connection shut me out, but though I had to look away again the moment Rah opened his eyes, I was honest enough to admit I wanted to keep looking, wanted to touch his skin, to know how it felt, how radiantly warm he was and a million other nebulous ideas I could not fully grasp.

As though he knew my thoughts, he looked my way, his gaze heavy. He spoke in the quiet way he had, and although he had probably made some remark about the bath or being hungry or tired or bored, my heart pounded like a war drum. I wanted to escape. Escape the intensity of his dark eyes, escape the physicality of his presence, escape the uncomfortable feeling the bathwater had lit me on fire.

"Miko?"

He spoke my name with a drawn-out emphasis on the first syllable, at once both completely wrong and the nicest I'd ever heard my name sound. I looked up and he lifted his hands from the water, but before he could achieve more than pointing at me, a new voice broke upon our silence.

"Who says *he's* the one making the decisions?" someone said, the echo of their voice drawing closer down the stairs. "That's what regents are for, isn't it?"

The words left me cold to the bone despite the water's warmth.

"He already lost one of those," came a reply.

"Ha! You believe that nonsense? No general is going to take orders from a girl, whoever she is. More likely Grace Bachita fell in battle and they're using his death to make sure no one will support the bastard princess. I don't want an Otako on the throne, but to say she killed him is ridiculous and doesn't do the young emperor any good."

Hope had begun to take root in my mind since Rah had spoken of Minister Manshin, hope there might be a way through this political mire, but...those names, spoken here, my story so dismissed. I was but a foolish girl again with ridiculous dreams.

One of the speakers stepped through the narrow doorway, surprise halting him in place. "Oh, looks like we have company."

I had not cleaned myself as completely as I would have liked, but I would rather leave the task half done than remain. "We were just finishing up, if you would give us a moment," I said.

The man shrugged, glancing back at his companion stuck behind him on the stairs. "We'll wait."

They stayed standing in the stairway, continuing their conversation in lowered voices. I knew not whether I was most trying to hear what they said or trying not to, and climbed out of the bath with my heart racing. I had my towel around me before I thought to see if Rah was looking, and glanced over my shoulder to see him drying his hair, the rest of his body bare from head to foot.

"Ah, if she's sensible we won't see her again," came the voice from the stairwell. "Surely even a stubborn Otako can see when they're not needed anymore."

A laugh met this and I needed to get out of there now. Yet even as I gathered my robe around me, I thought that a sensible woman would stay to glean what information she could, not allow herself to be frightened away by a few sneers and a total lack of respect.

But today I was not a sensible woman.

We made our way up the stairs to find two overflowing food trays sitting outside our door. It all looked delicious, but right in the centre sat a large dish of cabbage leaves stuffed with crab, a speciality of the eastern highlands that my nurse had always ordered when I felt poorly as a child.

Tears leaked unchecked from my eyes. Another life lost to a war that seemed infinite in cost yet scarce in triumph. If Rah noticed my tears he said nothing. He must have been as starving as I, but still he waited until at last I wiped my cheeks, and dragged the trays inside.

———————◆———————

We ate. We drank. And perhaps to keep from our own thoughts, we spoke, each on our own subject and to our own purpose, though I liked to think that there in that warm, dry space surrounded by the hum of the inn, we knew each other's meaning. Rah sat across the fast-emptying trays, one leg beneath him, the other bent before him in a way no Kisian would ever have dared sit, picking at the broken remains of the last crab roll with one hand and patting Shishi's head with the other.

As the evening wore on the noise from the main room got louder and more rowdy until at last people began to depart, the bang of the front door punctuating almost every thought. Footsteps started coming up the stairs too, some alone, others accompanied by slurred and giggling voices. People thudded around in their own rooms and murmured conversation spread through every wall, stealing our comfort. Silence fell between us then, because if we could hear them, they could hear us, but after I slid the empty trays back into the hallway and closed the door, I could not but feel there was more to our silence than caution.

Still with his hand upon Shishi's head, Rah did not look up when I returned. Yet seeing him sitting at ease beside the guttering lantern I thought of his gleaming skin and realised with a start more pronounced than the revelation deserved that we were alone. We had been alone since the disaster at Syan, yet somehow, out in the wilds, sleeping in caves and haylofts, it had been all right. Here, surrounded by civilisation, with an actual feather pillow and the sounds of people enjoying each other's company all around, *alone* meant something more.

The muddied feelings from the bathhouse returned, and to busy myself, I rolled out the sleeping mat. There was only one—the overlarge sort inns always provided, even to travelling emperors and their families. I had wondered why when our palace mats were narrow, and now that I understood I felt ashamed of my younger, naive self. Of course the serving girl hadn't blinked upon being asked for a second pillow.

By the time I had the mat unrolled, Rah still hadn't moved. His attention was caught to Shishi, yet I became increasingly aware of his every tiny movement and the rhythmic intake of his breath. Was he thinking the same thoughts as I? Probably not, I told myself, tugging a wrinkle out of the mat. After all, what attractions did I have apart from my name? A name that meant nothing to a Levanti used to a very different sort of woman.

I dumped both pillows on the sleeping mat and said defiantly, "I am going to sleep," pointing at the mat and miming sleep in such a way that stole all decisiveness from my words. "Goodnight."

He replied. Calm. Gentle. Unchanged. No sign of the consternation I felt at being alone with a man whose handsome features and lithe, powerful body were suddenly all too present. Almost I wished we had snuck into a barn and slept on straw so I need not have thought about it at all, about him. But we hadn't and I was.

Despite the robe having been fresh, I'd donned it in such haste in the bathhouse that it was damp from my skin and the long, sodden skein of my hair. Had I been alone I would have taken it off to dry, but what would he think of me if I did? What would he think of me if I didn't? If I lay on dry sheets in a damp robe? The thought made my skin crawl.

Still patting Shishi, Rah sat with glazed eyes, staring at nothing but the play of lantern light on the matting. Not the actions of a man interested in the woman with whom he shared the room, so, unsure whether I felt more anger, disappointment, or relief, I turned down the lantern and undressed as fast as I could. I kept my back turned so I couldn't see his face, then having hung my robe I dashed to the mat in just my skin, defying him to find me attractive enough to move.

The pillow was soft and the duvet warm—a real sleeping mat like I had not used since leaving Mei'lian. Yet still I scowled as I snuggled into it, keeping to the very edge so he would not think I sought his touch. It wasn't long before I heard him move, heard the sound of one sandal hitting the floor, followed by another. Fabric rustled. Then, as I had done, he padded barefoot across the matting to wrestle his robe onto a hook. I glanced up, wondering if I ought to help, but one glimpse of his dark, bare skin and I closed my eyes again, intent on being asleep no matter how fast my heart was beating.

A few minutes later he had either given up on the hooks or succeeded, for he padded back across the room, spoke a few soft words to Shishi, and slipped in beside me. The sheets moved, cool air teased my warm skin, then stillness settled. I was all too aware of his warmth beside me then, of the sound of his breathing and even his smell, but he shifted no nearer to the central line than I had done, leaving my inner turmoil complete.

It took me a long time to get to sleep. Sounds of revelry and sleep and pleasure surrounded us, but I could only hear the even rise and fall of his breath and wonder if he too was lying awake.

———◆———

I awoke feeling less rested than when I had lain down. Busy sounds made their way through the floor, but by the darkness creeping between the shutters it was not yet dawn. Rah was asleep with one arm up over his head, his dark skin and even darker chest hair making the inn's off-colour sheets appear white by comparison. I dressed, and though I was glad he wasn't looking, the heat of the night seemed to have dissipated, leaving me feeling like a foolish, gangly girl. But as I thought of everything I had overheard the men say the night before, my dashed pride hardened into resolve. Of course they doubted me. Of course they underestimated me. But I would show them, as I would show them all, that the empire was mine.

My robe was not quite dry, but I slipped it on, wriggled my feet into my stolen sandals, and crept into the hallway, gesturing for Shishi to stay when she lifted her head, tail wagging.

An older woman stood behind the bar downstairs, tending those patrons sitting silent in the predawn light. She looked me up and down with even more distaste than the man had shown the night before, but she forced a smile and asked what I wanted. Breakfast and passage to Mei'lian, I said. I didn't care if we went sitting in a wet hay cart or on stolen horses, one way or another I had to get back.

17. DISHIVA

I sat beneath the jutting eaves and watched dark clouds piss upon the yard. It had been three days of relentless rain. Three days that had brought more and more pilgrims, two deaths having done nothing to stem their enthusiasm for Leo Villius.

"And then you nail it on and these nails, see..." Loklan said. "They're shaped like that so they bend outward and can't hurt the hoof."

And Leo had smiled at me. Had blessed me. Had assured everyone I had been with him and could not have loosed the arrow.

"Bo says it will make the difference between them splitting and not. It'll take a while to make all the shoes, of course, but—"

He broke off, and after a few moments his silence drew me from my scowling stupor. I turned. My young horse master raised his brows toward his freshly shaved scalp. "Everything all right, Captain?"

"Yes." I brought my attention from the rain-soaked yard to the dimly lit warmth of the stables. "This could mean the difference between being able to ride in this climate and not, and if we're making this our home then nothing could be more important."

"Why then do I get the feeling you weren't listening, Captain?"

A faint smile traced his hurt features. His skin needed thickening, but he was a good horse master, so I stood and clapped my hand upon his shoulder. "Because I wasn't," I said. "My thoughts were elsewhere, but that doesn't make what you're doing any less important. It just makes me a terrible captain for not listening to my horse master's counsel."

His smile stretched to a grim line. "For what little it means, Captain, I believe you didn't have anything to do with that pilgrim's death. Or the attempt on Emperor Gideon's life. It's not like you were near either."

And yet somehow, despite these facts, despite my loyalty, whispers were getting around.

I pointed to the horseshoe in his hand. "If you're sure these will work then have them put on all our horses. You're excused from guard duty to get it done."

Loklan saluted. "Yes, Captain. Thank you."

"If it saves our horses from going lame then thank *you*."

His cheeks darkened and he looked away, shuffling his boots in the dust.

Out across the yard the gate gong sounded for the third time that morning, and sheltered in their storm cloaks, four soldiers dashed through the pelting rain to open them. I had been about to walk, or rather run like a wild rabbit across the sodden yard to the manor, but leaned against the wall to wait until the new arrivals cleared the area. The gates would open. A handful of pilgrims would shuffle through. One of the Kisian soldiers would take them to see Leo and then I could get on with my work.

The gates creaked open. Figures appeared in the widening aperture. Not just a gaggle of pilgrims. A crowd. With flags. And horses. My hand leapt for my sword, but there had been no warning called and I stayed, rooted to the ground and squinting through the rain. Movement around me stilled as others stopped to stare at the newcomers.

"Kisians?" Loklan said. "Is that the duke's flag?"

Others spoke Bahain's name and I had to agree it looked like the horse galloping from the waves he had blazoned on his banner, but his soldiers had all arrived with him days ago. "Not pilgrims?" I said.

"It doesn't look like it, Captain."

"Good." And yanking up the hood of my hated storm cloak, I strode into the rain.

But Grace Bahain was ahead of me and I stopped halfway to the gates to watch him speed across the yard, a tail of retainers and guards flying behind him. Matsimelar was there too, the sole Levanti in a very Kisian scene.

As the lead rider slid from the saddle, Grace Bahain met him with a bone-crushing hug. The stiff, proud duke let the newcomer go as quickly as he had embraced him and stepped back, the heavy rain stealing their words from my ears. Foot soldiers spilled into the camp, blocking my view of the scene—a scene that seemed to be devolving into an argument. Or more accurately, a rant. The new arrival bowed his hooded head before a whole new storm.

While the shouting continued, our Kisian allies met the newly arrived soldiers in a dance of whispers. News spread around me, and in the centre I stood caught like a fly in a silk web. Something was wrong. Trouble rumbled as loud as the thunder overhead.

I pulled my feet from the sucking mud and continued on toward the hovering Matsimelar. "What's going on?" I said as I approached, turning my head so I could hear his answer rather than just the patter of rain on my hood.

He didn't look my way. "Grace Bahain's son has arrived."

That made sense of both the embrace and the berating. "He doesn't seem pleased."

Matsimelar sighed. "What do you want, Captain?"

"I want to know why the Kisians are all so worried. It's—"

"Part of your job to know, yes," he finished for me. "Just like it's part of your job to question pilgrims who end up dead."

"Oh yes, just like that. Really that's at the top of my list. Questioning people who don't end up dead is just a waste of time."

The saddleboy snorted. "It's hard to follow since Grace Bahain is hissing a lot, but I'm guessing his son was meant to capture Empress Miko and failed, and His Grace seems to believe it's a deliberate betrayal and isn't pleased."

"Empress Miko? So she's definitely not dead." I looked around at the Kisian soldiers milling in the rain. "That's what's upsetting them?"

He shrugged. "I guess so. They might have already known, but if so I'm not sure why they would be so tense. Either way, it's probably not a good time to tell them we knew she didn't die at Mei'lian. Although it won't take long for the soldiers to realise the Bahains already knew too."

"Shit."

"I don't think it will matter. Most of them are as loyal to the duke as we are to our herd masters." We shared a look. "All right, as loyal to him as we *were* to our herd masters."

We watched the scene a few moments in silence, before Matsimelar added, "Although even if none of these lords and soldiers want to support her as their empress, the fact she's out there still fighting for her empire is bad news for all of us."

I couldn't disagree and wondered what Gideon would say. We'd had more deserters disappear in the last few days and he hadn't yet sent any Swords to quell the uprisings in the north. The indecision was unlike him and this was the last thing he needed on top of that problem. And there was still Leo. The threat Gideon couldn't even see.

I glanced up at Matsimelar, all youthful features marred by sleeplessness. I didn't want to ask anything more of him, hated that he had already been put in such a position, and yet there was no one else. "That woman, Livi."

"What about her?"

His response was chilly, but I forced more words out. "She had a copy of the holy book."

Silence.

"People are always coming and going from the pilgrims' residence now," I went on. "You could go. Just to check on them. Ask for the book. Steal it if you must."

"Steal it!"

"Shhh," I hissed. "Matsi, you know I didn't kill her. You know I didn't set fire to those books. But both times I've asked questions about the faith, pilgrims have been killed."

"Perhaps you shouldn't defy our gods to ask about theirs."

I scoffed. "Oh, come on, if our gods were striking them down, they wouldn't have been killed by people. Tell me this doesn't seem very strange to you."

Grace Bahain had finished berating his son and was looking around, taking stock of his small audience. I turned, hiding my face with the stiff side of my hood. "I won't ask another thing of you."

"Well, that would be nice. Everyone is always 'Hey Matsi, what is this soldier trying to say?' 'Hey Matsi, can you tell that girl she can ride me?' 'Hey Matsi, did he just call me a dog?'"

"What you do for your herd is more valuable than anything the rest of us do. I will speak to Gideon about giving you the chance to be Made, and if he refuses, I will have you Made as a Jaroven and will be honoured to have you as a herd brother."

A few silent moments stretched their tension between us before he said, "But only if I steal a book for you."

I ought to say no, but the need for the holy book, to know what Dom Villius didn't want me to know, burned too hot. I said nothing, knowing my silence was answer enough.

Voices drew close as Bahain's son and his entourage passed us on their way to the stables. Matsimelar's dark eyes flitted from me to the duke and back. His jaw set. "Fine. I'll do it."

Despite the difference in our rank, I pressed my fists together to salute him. "Thank you."

The young man just grunted.

———————◆———————

Gideon was sitting with an unknown Kisian when I went up to his room, and despite having come straight from the courtyard the news had arrived before me.

"You've come to tell me about Empress Miko, Captain," he said as I entered. "There is no need." He added something in Kisian to the end of this, and the man who had been kneeling beside him at the table, brush in hand, got to his feet. Bowing respectfully to first Gideon then me, he let himself out.

"Who was that?"

"A local scribe. He has been helping me with my Kisian, though as you see, writing it is very hard. I think I will employ scribes forever." He had gestured at the page before him, a mess of lines and blotches, ink covering the side of his hand. "There was something else you wanted to say, Captain?"

So much, but something in his expression ambushed the first blurt about Leo Villius and instead I said, "Have you decided what to do about the northern unrest? Your Swords are ready to serve whenever you need."

"Nothing needs to be done about it."

"Nothing... Do you mean there is no unrest after all?"

He folded his arms. "I am quite capable of making these decisions without your input."

"Yes, but—"

"Captain Dishiva, if you have nothing more useful to say then do—"

Clacking sandals stormed along the passage. I braced myself as the door slid. "Grace Bahain to see you, Your Majesty," Kehta en'Oht said, sticking her head into the room. "Shall I . . . ?"

He was right there hovering behind her, his face a calm mask. "Send him in," Gideon said, and while Kehta slid the door all the way, I shifted to a place against the wall, not ready to leave yet not wanting to be in the way.

Grace Bahain strode in and bowed to his emperor. That at least seemed a good sign and the tone with which he addressed Gideon sounded respectful. I could tell little from his stance and his restrained body language, but watching Gideon I slowly tensed. The Kisian duke was backing Gideon into a corner. Pride stiffened him, but his expression held the hunted look of a bristling dog. I could not begin to imagine what they were speaking about, what concessions were being forced from him, until Gideon looked past Grace Bahain to me.

"Gather half your Swords, Captain," he said. "We travel to a nearby shrine within the hour."

"A shrine?"

"Yes, Captain. Kuroshima Shrine. Apparently it is where Emperor Kin was married to his empress and now where I will be married to mine. We will travel with an equal number of Levanti Swords and mounted Kisian soldiers and make the journey as quickly as possible."

A dozen objections leapt to my mind but the one that found its way out first was: "If you make Lady Sichi's box carriers run they might fall down dead."

"She will ride too," he said. "Bahain assures me she knows how."

I glanced at the duke, not sure if the gleam of triumph in his gaze was real or imagined.

"Are you . . . sure this is wise, Your Majesty?"

"Yes." A snap of frustration. "Organise your Swords. Leave

the other half behind to keep the peace here. If we leave soon we should be back in time for a celebratory feast. Apparently, it is not the Kisian way, but it is ours and we will honour it. We all need something cheerful."

I wanted to ask if the rush to marry was because Empress Miko was known to be alive, if it was to protect his own interests or Grace Bahain's, or whether the duke was concerned Gideon might change his mind and not marry his niece after all. Was that it? Had Gideon been stalling in the hope of finding Empress Miko? In the hope of marrying her instead? Grace Bahain might have an army, but marrying their empress was a much stronger message to the Kisians that we were here to stay.

Under Grace Bahain's eye I could voice none of it, could only bow and hurry out, my surcoat snapping like a flag behind me.

With a sharp rap upon the door I strode into Lady Sichi's room like a whirlwind, interrupting a round of giggling. Nuru was standing before the long mirror, attired not in her usual armour but in a pale silk robe that glowed against the dark hue of her skin. Her hair had been done up too, and Lady Sichi and two of her Kisian companions were moving around her, clucking at creases and tucking up stray hairs.

They all froze at my entrance. Lady Sichi gave me a look of cool enquiry, while her ladies stared at the ground. Nuru, at least, had the sense to look embarrassed. The urge to rip all such finery off her and yell that she was Levanti not Kisian was hastily swallowed. Weren't we all adopting Kisian ways? Kisian food? Kisian language? Again I buried my fears about how much we would need to conform for this empire to succeed.

"We are leaving for Kuroshima Shrine within the hour," I said, addressing myself to Nuru. "Gideon and Lady Sichi are to be married at once. Do whatever you need to get ready. You'll both be riding."

Lady Sichi's eyes widened as I spoke, and not for the first time I wondered how much of our language she really knew. How many Kisians were learning in secret for the sole purpose of being able to spy on us? Leo had.

No, not the time to worry about him. Leo Villius would have to wait.

———————◆———————

It was easy to choose the fifty Swords who would accompany the emperor, for only half our horses were fit to travel, Itaghai fortunately amongst them.

The fifty riding with us donned storm cloaks over their crimson, while the rest remained behind under Keka's command. Lady Sichi and her two companions were dressed and cloaked and mounted on Kisian horses, small beside Nuru e'Torin riding a Levanti steed. She had knotted her long hair tight at the nape of her neck and donned her armour and swords, looking now like the fierce, strong Levanti she had been born.

When we left Kogahaera, fifty Kisian soldiers rode with us, along with Grace Bahain, his son, and half a dozen other lords whose names I could never get right.

Side by side, Grace Bahain and Gideon led the way while I followed like the good guard dog I was. Despite the rain, which fluctuated from pelting to misting and back, my spirit soared to be riding once more. Itaghai had been cooped up in his stable for days, let out for short runs when the weather permitted and left to fret the rest of the time. I had been too caught up in my new duties to do more than leave him in Loklan's care, but as the wind whipped by my ears it swept my guilt away with it. Whatever we were giving up for the safety of a new home, we would never give up this. Could never. Horses were in our blood.

We rode through the rain-soaked afternoon, alternating between a canter and a walk. Steam rose from our horses but it left them barely winded compared to the Kisians' lathered and drooping nags.

"Captain."

I snapped my head around so fast it hurt my neck. "What?"

Jass had drawn his horse up alongside, his face shadowed beneath the jutting peak of his hood. Rain dripped from it and ran in rivulets down the waxed fabric like fine cracks in stone.

"Nothing in particular, Captain, just thought I'd make conversation."

Around us chatter mingled with the ever-present percussion of hoofbeats and rain. Jass stepped his horse closer as we took a bend in the winding road. He looked capable out of the saddle, but in it I had to admit he was quite a sight. On horseback one couldn't even tell he was half a head shorter than most Levanti.

"Then by all means start one," I said.

"What do you think of this sudden marriage?"

I threw him a look. "I thought you meant a light, entertaining conversation."

"We could do that too. Actually, I've been thinking we need to organise a Hoya pitch. A lot of Swords would be glad of the opportunity to play, even in the rain."

I nodded but said, "I think Gideon's hand is being forced," taking care to keep my voice low enough it was for his ears alone. "I'm not sure he wanted to marry Lady Sichi at all despite saying the alliance was important."

"You think he meant to marry Empress Miko?"

Once again surprised to find he'd had similar thoughts, I nodded. "Yes. He hasn't said anything, but…"

He edged his horse close enough that our knees touched. "I've heard there are about twenty-five Oht Swords who have been missing since we took Mei'lian, yet Captain Yiss doesn't seem worried and none of the Oht have deserted."

I stared at him. "You think...searching for her?"

Jass shrugged. "When I heard, I wondered what mission they had been sent on but couldn't come up with anything. Until now."

It made sense. Even Grace Bahain could not deny that marriage to Empress Miko would be best for the empire. And if he tried...Maybe Gideon had planned to keep her somewhere safe and marry her when he had gained a little freedom from the duke. I didn't know enough about politics to see how it could have worked, but that Gideon's hurried marriage had come hard on the heels of the empress slipping through Bahain's fingers was no coincidence.

"Makes me wonder what concessions he has to make in marrying a member of Bahain's family," Jass went on. "I know fuck all about the way Kisian families work but it must give Bahain some extra power or assurance, or why push for it?"

Sensible words, but the whispered way he spoke made me uneasy. "Why are you telling me this?" I said, shooting him a searching look around the edge of my hood.

"Because you are my captain and I care what happens to our emperor, but if you've changed your mind and don't wish to be burdened with my unconsidered opinions I'll keep them to myself."

Every moment I gave him no reassurance I expected him to drop back, but he didn't. "And honestly," he added after a long silence, "my old friends are boring these days. I am no longer content with reliving old hunts and talking over old times. I want to create new memories. Here."

I could not miss the meaningful look but I had no response. Sometimes he seemed so young and awkward, while at others he was serious, and I found I could not pin him down, could get no sense of his age or his intentions or his character, nothing beyond my traitorous body's interest in having him again.

Fortunately, before my lack of response could be deemed rude,

Gideon sped once more into a canter and Itaghai followed, stealing away any further chance at conversation.

———————————◆———————————

There were *so many steps*. I had thought to find the shrine beside a road, not to have to climb a mountain on foot to reach it, but Kuroshima, it seemed, was special. My Swords grumbled as they dismounted at the edge of a quiet village. Its people eyed us warily.

In the drizzly afternoon Kuroshima village was a hidden hollow of a place surrounded by dense forest on two sides, a river to the east, and the mountain to the south. It had the quiet, untouched look of a holy place, and despite their grumbling, my Swords kept their voices low as though fearing to wake the dead.

Nuru marched toward me as I slid from Itaghai's saddle. "There are two sets of stairs," she said without preamble. "Both go to the shrine at the top, and there are no other paths. His Majesty must go up one side and Lady Sichi the other. Send half your Swords on each side and leave five or six here with the horses."

I blinked at her short, competent orders and stared her down. For a long moment Nuru stared back, far too much assurance in that youthful face. But she was a saddlegirl, no Made Sword yet, and eventually she looked away, murmuring "Captain" and saluting. "They are His Majesty's orders."

When I didn't reply she pouted and turned away, a flash there of the young girl I had gotten used to seeing flounce around in her increasing amounts of Kisian finery.

"That was...interesting," spoke Jass, reining in beside me. He had ridden the rest of the way at my side even when further conversation had been impossible.

"Yes," I agreed, looking around as the last of the travelling party arrived in the clearing. Unlike Nuru, Loklan hadn't given up any of our ways and had ridden at the back, the better to keep an eye on all the horses currently in his care. He had even pushed back his hood to ensure his vision was not impeded. "You're staying with the horses," I said as he approached. "We have to walk the rest of the way, so choose five or six others to stay with you while we're gone. I assume the Kisians will do the same."

"Yes, Captain."

"Keep an eye on their horses anyway, if you can," I added. "I don't want to get stuck out here all night because Lady Sichi's horse went wandering."

"Yes, Captain. With your permission I'll keep Massama and Yafeu with me as I don't think they're fit for a long walk."

"Senet too," Jass said. "Her knees have been giving her trouble since our march south."

I nodded. "See if there are any others who would struggle with the stairs and keep them with you to guard the horses. We'll split the rest. I'll take half up one side of the stairs." Jass nodded, and reading in his face a determination to remain with me, I added, "And you can take the other half up the other side."

"Me?"

"Yes. Why not?"

"I'm not a Jaroven."

"No, but you're a Sword of the Emperor, so you're no higher or lower ranked than any of my other Swords, Jaroven or not. With Keka back at Kogahaera and Loklan staying behind, I have no Hand to draw from. So you're it. Go pick half. You're with Lady Sichi. I'll walk with Gideon."

Leaving him no time to complain, I walked into the crowd of Swords already shouting orders and gathering half as I went. Gideon stood at the base of the stairs, conferring with a man in a long, pale robe, not unlike the one Leo wore but belted in the Kisian style. He had no storm cloak and the fabric was wet through.

Still in her storm cloak, Lady Sichi was recognisable only by the number of people crowding around her at the base of the other stairs. Jass joined them with his half of my Swords, and although Grace Bahain was there with a bunch of his own men, Jass did not hang back. He strode right in, and despite being short and stocky for a Levanti, he stood tall above the duke, a hand upon his swords.

I squashed a smile and waited for Gideon.

"How high are these stairs, Captain?" Tafa en'Oht asked, appearing at my side.

"I have no idea, but if Kisian priests can climb them so can we."

"You can be sure of that, Captain."

In truth I wasn't sure, only determined, and I needed all that determination for the climb ahead. The beginning was easy enough, but I soon realised that for once we were at a disadvantage against our Kisian allies. Their houses were full of stairs and their empire an ever-undulating spread of hills and valleys, of jutting mountains and terraces. They were used to climbing. We were used to flat terrain and sleeping on the ground, and we suffered for it. I knew not how high the stairs would take us, but I was soon regretting my very existence as my thighs cramped and burned. With every step I was convinced I would die if I took another, but the Kisians took another and so I forced my leg up, following the crimson hem of Gideon's robe.

It took forever to reach the top, yet when the stairs finally levelled onto a blessedly flat path the sun still rode high. It could not have taken more than an hour, probably less, yet it had felt like a lifetime of torture. Many of my Swords gasped for breath and hissed at cramps—even Gideon slowed his pace—but the Kisian priest leading the way was not even out of breath. At least the Kisian soldiers and two of their lords had the grace to look pained.

I had expected grandeur, but it was a small bird's hollow of a shrine that welcomed us atop the mountain—a nest of interwoven metalwork hung with tiny paper lanterns. A small altar sat at one end where another pale-robed priest stood waiting. Jass stood just inside the opposite arch with his half of my Swords, but of Lady Sichi there was no sign.

"She's tidying herself up," Jass said when I approached. "She has her people with her, and Nuru, but I left Anouke and Esi as well since she seems to prefer female Levanti."

I nodded, but not daring to stop lest my legs turned to stone, I strode a circle of the shrine. Gideon had removed his storm cloak to reveal a glorious crimson robe, and when Grace Bahain, his son, and the other lords did the same the space filled with bright, shining silk. Yet when Lady Sichi swept in dressed in a pale pink robe laced with gleaming silver threads, I held my breath. History would not remember my name, but it would remember this moment. For here in the hollow of Kuroshima Shrine the first Levanti emperor would take a Kisian bride with the blessing of her countrymen.

Lady Sichi knelt across the altar from Gideon, each speaking what sounded like a prayer. The priest spoke prayers too, filling the space with his musical tones. Despite the number of Levanti crammed into the shrine his confidence did not waver, not then nor when he tied a white sash about Lady Sichi's waist. The knot was more complex than any I'd seen a Kisian wear, yet he formed it with well-practised fingers while looking to the heavens.

When at last Gideon rose from the altar the Kisians hailed him, their acceptance clear. He had married one of their own, had solidified their allegiance, yet it was a grim man who drew me aside as we prepared to descend the mountain. "When we get back to the horses send someone to Mei'lian with a message for Sett," Gideon said.

"One of my Swords?"

"Yes, it cannot wait until we return to Kogahaera. This ceremony will not be complete for seven days, but..." His nostrils flared as he sucked a deep, calming breath. "I need Sett and fast. I fear I am running out of time."

"Seven days?" Jass lay naked on my sleeping mat. "Seven days? You mean after we walked up all those fucking stairs and walked back down and had a whole feast to the gods, he still has to wait seven days before they are married?"

"Apparently. They wait seven days to ensure the blessing of the gods and only *then* is he allowed to untie the knot and bed her. At which point they are married."

He shook his head, the short stubble of his hair rasping against the pillow. "Kisians are very strange." He went on absently stroking my bare arm, but his expression grew serious. "So that means anyone who doesn't want this to go ahead still has seven days to kill one of them. Who's on duty?"

"Every single Sword who didn't come with us."

I'd had the same thought after Gideon's anxious demand for his brother, unable to quite bury my fear no matter how much I tried.

Jass sighed. "It's going to be a long seven days. Does it include today?"

"I don't know. I'll ask Nuru in the morning."

He kept stroking my arm, his warmth a comfort against my aching body. Whether it had been the exhaustion of the day, the wine, or the constancy of his companionship that had led us here, I had no intention of moving again until I had to and he seemed similarly inclined. He had sat with me at the feast, and through a series of unspoken looks we had both known we would arrive here, a fact clinched when he had asked where I was in my cycle. "That's what made me realise I'd been an ass to you that first time, you know," he had said. "That I'd let years of respectful habit slide without a thought. My herd ought to be ashamed to own me."

Someone knocked upon the door, stilling Jass's fingers.

"Who is it?" I called, poised to leap like an arrow loosed from the curve of his arm.

"Matsimelar," came the translator's voice, muffled by the door. "I've got that thing you asked for."

I jumped up from the mat, already grabbing my clothes. "Hold on a moment," I said, thrusting one leg after the other into my worn breeches, fingers trembling upon the ties.

There was an annoyed grunt from the vague outline outside the door, and in a low voice Jass whispered, "Do you need me to hide?"

I shook my head as I yanked on my tunic and strode to the door, the old reed matting as sharp as a thousand pins beneath my sore feet. The door slid easily, and having leaned out to be sure Matsimelar was alone, I waved him in and closed it behind him.

A low-burning lamp lit the interior of my all but bare room, leaving the saddleboy nothing to look at but Jass lying propped upon his elbows. The two young men acknowledged each other with a nod, and Matsimelar, shaking back the long strands of hair escaping his ponytail, withdrew a book from beneath his tunic. It was the worn volume Livi had kept her hand upon while we talked, but the saddleboy didn't immediately hold it out. "What do you plan to do with this?" he said, sitting the spine on his palm. It fell open. "It's all in Chiltaen," he added, licking his finger to turn a few pages. "Even I can only understand half of it. Maybe less. They were far more interested in teaching us the spoken language than the written language, and when they did it was all straightforward words. This stuff looks...poetic. Like this, it's something about a door upon a coast that you walk through and find yourself exiting through a door in a desert, like someone wrote down their dreams and now people worship it."

"I don't know," I said. "But I have to try. I'll find a way."

Matsimelar sighed. "If you can't find anyone else to help, I'll translate it." He licked his finger again and turned another page. "If you'll have me Made."

"I gave you my word."

He snapped the book closed and held it out. "Thank you, Captain. I have…been afraid of meeting the gods without any sign of the sacrifice I made for my people. Careful," he added, wiping his hands upon his tunic. "It's all sticky from those herbs she was burning."

It *was* sticky. It had also brought Livi's scent with it, like her spirit clung to the beloved book even in death. Matsimelar lifted a hand to his nose and sniffed, making a face. "Gross. I had better get back now before someone wonders where I've gone."

He coughed as he turned, thumping his chest with a balled fist. Jass sat up. "Are you all right, Matsi?" he said as another wet hack burst from Matsimelar's mouth. The saddleboy spun back, his eyes wide. He closed a hand around his throat, foam spilling from the corners of his mouth as he opened and closed it like a fish.

"Fuck!" Jass was up in a billow of sheets, but even as he rose, Matsimelar fell, crumpling to his knees as more foam poured forth. His panicked eyes bulged, and he scratched at his neck, tearing trails of blood into the flesh.

"No no no!" I said, dropping the book to kneel before Matsimelar. "Shit, what do we do?"

"Stick your fingers down his throat! We've got to make him bring it back up."

I pushed my fingers into his gaping mouth, digging through foam and mucous, but everything had swollen to a ridiculous size and I couldn't make him gag.

"I can't! Something is blocking the way!"

The saddleboy's face turned purple and his eyes rolled. Foam poured down his chin as Jass stumbled about the room throwing things as though in search of something, anything that might help, but he must have known as I did that there was nothing we could do. Before I could speak, Matsimelar toppled face first onto the reed matting like a falling tree. There he lay unmoving, his eyes wide. He stared at Mona's scales now.

Jass froze in the sudden silence. "Don't put your hands anywhere near your mouth," he said, his gaze caught to the book upon the floor. "The redcap is on the cover."

I stared at him, grief constricting my throat. Jass stared back. "You haven't, have you?"

"I...I don't think so," I said, grateful I could form words.

He let out a shaky breath and looked again at the still form of Matsimelar. "That's...that's not an accident, is it?"

I shook my head.

"Do you think someone tried to kill you but got him instead?"

I nodded. "It's Leo. I'm sure of it," I whispered. "I talked to a pilgrim and she died. I asked for a book and they were all destroyed. There is something in that thing"—I pointed to the book on the floor—"that he doesn't want me to know. Doesn't want *us* to know."

Without the presence of a dead Levanti he might have scoffed, have argued, but he did neither. "What do we do?"

"We have to hide the book somewhere until I can figure out what to do with it," I said, holding my foam-slick hands at arm's length. "He might know Matsimelar was bringing it to me, but if the book just disappears and we drag Matsi out into the passage then there's no proof he got here with it. Leo might suspect but he won't know where it's gone."

"I can take it," Jass said. "I know somewhere I can hide it. It'll take a while, but I can be back by morning."

"No."

"No?"

"Don't come back."

Jass stared at me, opening and closing his mouth in a way all too reminiscent of Matsimelar struggling for breath. "What do you mean don't come back?"

"I mean stay with the book. Hide. I...I don't know how Leo knows what he does but I'm sure you aren't safe here anymore."

"And you are?"

"No, but I'm your captain and I can give you a direct order."

Jass's incredulous look darkened to a scowl. "Dishiva—"

"We don't have time to argue. Take the book and go. Please, Jass. That's an order."

For a moment he glared stubbornly at me, before he lifted his fists to a stiff salute. "As you wish, Captain."

I couldn't thank him with words, only a grim smile. He returned it as he dressed but said no more until he had picked up the book using a spare tunic from my pack. "Wash your hands," he said then, glancing at Matsimelar on his way to the door. "And don't die, Captain. You can consider that an order too."

He disappeared without another word. Left alone, I dragged Matsi's body out along the passage, trying not to think of his fear that he would die unmade, trying not to think of his frightened face, trying not to think at all.

 ## 18. RAH

The cart stank. I didn't want to know what it stank of; it was too great a relief not to be walking anymore, to be moving faster. Unlike the Levanti Plain, Kisia was full of rolling hills and jagged mountains, of curly trees, dense groves, and raging rivers. It had more flowers and animals than I had ever seen in one place, but step after step across its endless landscape I had only come to hate it. At first for what had happened here, and then for its rain.

Rain had once been a welcome respite to be greeted with an open mouth. Now it was a curse. It even dripped through the cover of today's cart, no doubt adding to the foul smell clogging my nostrils. Shishi's damp coat and my own unbathed musk weren't helping.

But at least we weren't walking.

Empress Miko sat cross-legged just out of the rain, as far from me as it was possible to get without braving the weather or the cart's suspicious contents. She had been quiet since we left the inn a few days back, and I had found myself disinclined to fill the silence. I'd finally experienced something of everyday Kisian life, and while its food and drink were strange, sleeping upon the floor had been familiar enough to make me wish for home. To remind me what I was fighting for.

"I wonder how you would do on the plains," I said to Shishi, curled up beside me rather than risk the rain by her mistress.

"I'd have to cut your fur short or you'd overheat. You could be shorn like a true Sword of the Levanti." I ran my hand over my overlong hair. "All right, a true Sword of the Levanti who has a scalp blade."

I had sawed off a few tufts with my knife the night before, but by the empress's fleeting grin it must have looked ridiculous.

"The Torin don't have a lot of dogs, but the Oht use them for hunting."

The empress looked around, eyes wide in question.

"Your mistress looks shocked," I said, still talking to the dog. "Perhaps I said something rude. Was it *hunting*? Or *Oht*?"

She narrowed her eyes and looked back out at the rain.

"Definitely *Oht*. I wonder what it means. Whatever it is, I love that I can sit here and say *fuck shit horse dick* and get no reaction at all, but *Oht*"—she glared over her shoulder at me—"is a problem."

Gideon would have laughed. Hell, even Tor would have laughed. Shishi just wagged her tail. "I'll take that as high praise for my sense of humour."

The empress glanced back at us again, but whatever her opinion, I'd take talking nonsense to a dog over having to think.

Our slow progress had become my daily struggle. It was so hard to keep walking at a pace I could maintain, to keep doing all I could without collapsing and no more, because my thoughts had only to wander and I was back with my people, imagining their new Kisian allies slaughtering them once they were no longer useful, just as we had slaughtered the Chiltaens. I thought of Yitti and Himi and Istet, of Dishiva and Sett, and of Gideon, always of Gideon, standing proud and betraying our tenets with such belief in a future that might never exist. And in the darkest moments I imagined them all dead because I could not get there in time. In those waking dreams I was alone again, that shame-filled child sitting at the edge of the herd knowing he had failed his people, only now there was no herd, no plains, and no Gideon, the weight of his arm around me nothing but a bitter memory.

You cannot win a battle you killed yourself reaching.

It was not an old Levanti saying, for all too often battles had come to us, but it had become a recent adaptation of the old adage "If you expend all your energy in the hunt you have none left for the kill."

Evening was coming on fast and I hoped we would not stop. Better to doze against the juddering side of the cart and get closer to our destination than try to find somewhere dry to sleep.

Unfortunately the carter showed no interest in continuing through the night. When the cart stopped, the empress immediately began what sounded like negotiations, returning after a few minutes with a triumphant smile. Shishi leapt down to greet her, and speaking to me for what felt like the first time that day, the empress pointed to the middle of a clearing where the driver had dumped a rolled-up tent.

"Fire," she said in Levanti, and though she didn't need to tell me it was always nice to hear her use my language, that one single word a testament of value and respect.

I repeated it in Kisian before falling into our routine. Find the driest spot. Collect wood for a fire. Scavenge for food and water. All before checking Shishi was well, and settling down to a cold and uncomfortable half sleep shivering beneath the stars. It had been warm when we first arrived in Chiltae, but the farther south we travelled and the closer winter crept the more I yearned for the dry heat of the plains.

The empress had bought food back in the town, and while we ate we huddled close to the flames, sheltered by an angled half tent the driver erected over the fire. When we had finished, Empress Miko checked my wound, giving me something between a nod and a grimace, before settling down to sleep. Shishi lay with her, pressed against her back, and the driver was soon snoring.

Despite the tired ache in every part of my body, I could not sleep. As we didn't travel much in winter, it was a time for giving back to the gods and the earth and remembering our dead. With such chill breezes blowing, I ought to have been carving a stone for each of my lost Swords. Eska. Orun. Kishava. Gam. Fessel. Hamatet. Amun. Asim. Ubaid. Hehet. Maat. Ren. Dhamara. Juta. My Swords had removed me from my captaincy, but I was still bound to them, my every failure linking me more strongly to a responsibility I could not run away from this time.

The names of the lost circled my thoughts until I fell into an uneasy doze, afraid I was forgetting someone, there had been so many.

Some hours later the rumble of cart wheels filled my dreams only to live on into wakefulness. They were approaching along the road, bolts of lantern light shearing through the drizzle to light the road ahead.

"Empress," I said, rolling to find her already awake, propped on an elbow with her breath held. Perhaps sensing her mistress's tension, Shishi had also lifted her head, the approaching light shining on her watery eyes.

In a flurry of movement, the empress was up, dashing toward the road with her arms waving. She hailed the driver, and caught in a beam of lantern light, she made a bedraggled figure.

The pair of horses slowed. Heavy with fatigue, I propped myself up to catch the tone of their conversation. The driver seemed disinclined at first, answering in gruff, short snatches, but she wore him down with poetic strings of words, his light falling upon her like she was a performer in a shadow play. I had once put one on with Eska, the pair of us caught in the silent world between campfire and woven screen, nothing but darkness above and the low-voiced murmur of our audience.

Eska. Orun. Kishava. Gam. Fessel. Hamatet. Amun. Asim.

Ubaid. Hehet. Maat. Ren. Dhamara. Juta. A whole other life to which I could never fully return in spirit even if I could in body.

"Rah!"

The empress's call dragged me from the sleepy morass of my thoughts and I gathered our mediocre supplies, hurried on by the snap of the driver's voice. As I shoved the last blanket into the satchel, the driver gave a shout and wheels ground upon stone. The cart started forward.

"Rah!" the empress shouted again, beckoning from the back of the cart, and hating everything that had become of my life, I lumbered after it. Shishi leapt up to join her mistress, and as the cart slowly picked up speed, I threw first the new sack and then the satchel up to her. The empress caught them before leaning out, urging me to jump. With one last burst of effort I leapt onto the back rail only to snatch at empty darkness. I would have fallen back but she gripped my hands and pulled me in, sending us both toppling onto lumpy sacks and a startled Shishi. The dog yelped and the empress laughed, bursting forth with a chattering wealth of Kisian disembodied by the darkness. I could feel the warmth of her body through the damp, clinging fabric of her robe and thought back to that evening in the hot pool beneath the inn. The way she had looked at me, and even more the way she had so purposefully *not* looked at me, had been enough to heat my skin to a fever.

Now we had fallen together, and only as her chatter faded did she seem to realise, as I did, that neither of us had moved. My heart thumped. I could kiss her here in the darkness, could tell her how much I admired her spirit and her pride and her honour, but I could not let myself be distracted from my purpose. I drew back even as she sat up, gently moving out from beneath me.

In silence, Empress Miko patted Shishi's head and went to sit on the back rail, her legs dangling toward the road. Snatches of moonlight caught her dark hair, and while she stared out at the night, I stared at her, adding still more thoughts to the mess of my mind, no sleep to be found.

————————◆————————

The city of Mei'lian came into view the following morning, a mere smudge so like every other that we might have missed it had not the cart stopped with an abrupt jolt, almost sending me into the road. Holding on to the back of the rain cover, Empress Miko leaned out to see why we had stopped. The wind whipped at her robe, pulling it tight about her body, and determined not to think about the warmth of her lying naked beside me, I climbed up the other side to see the road ahead.

The sight of the city filled me with an excited flurry. Mei'lian on the horizon meant that after all these days travelling, on foot and then in a succession of carts, with nothing to do but stare at the rain and fret, I was almost there. Beyond Mei'lian, Kogahaera waited.

Shouting ahead, Empress Miko exchanged words with the cart driver, then pointing at the city, turned an aggrieved expression my way. I looked again at the distant smudge upon the plain. From our distorted perspective, the river we had been following seemed to run directly behind it, owning its own city-smudge, but the distance we still had to go hardly seemed worthy of such distress. Then I saw the third smudge to the south owning tiny banners and flags that waved in the wind.

An approaching army.

Kisians taking back their city? That seemed the only possibility, a possibility that at first sight was of little interest but soon spawned a dozen fearful thoughts. That the city being under attack would make it difficult for Empress Miko to reach her minister was the first and least worrying of them all, for it was soon followed by the fear that Sett and all my Swords were still in the city, maintaining its token defence. Would they fight to defend it? Would Gideon ask it of them? Expect it of them? Or was this a triumphant army camped beyond the walls and I had come too late?

I could utter none of it. The language barrier we had slowly been eroding was back, more present than ever. Whatever friendship we had managed to grow between us out in the Kisian wilds meant nothing here. I was still a Levanti sworn to my people.

Empress Miko leapt from the back of the cart and strode up to the driver, leaving Shishi to sit up and swish her tail. I crouched next to the dog, losing my hands in her fur as much for my own comfort as hers. "I'm worried," I said, glad to be able to speak and know I would not be judged or questioned. "I think your mistress and I are going to disagree soon and we won't even be able to explain why. In truth I should never have gotten on that boat."

I had thought so a hundred times. But I had and the gods themselves only knew what might have happened to the empress without me. She was capable and strong and probably she would have been all right, but I thought of her lying still in the cave and that *probably* became laced with enough fear to sicken my stomach and make me hate the wish I had never come. She deserved better than that. Better than me.

Shishi tilted her head back to lick my face.

"You only do that because you don't know what I said."

My hand stilled in Shishi's fur as the carter raised his voice, his tone clear. He was disagreeing with his empress, if only he knew it.

Within a few minutes, the empress returned, her face flushed and triumphant. She began speaking only to stop the moment she met my gaze. Unlike back in the hot pool she did not look away, did not flush, just lifted her chin, and I wondered if in that moment she had all the same thoughts I had and it was Empress Miko standing before me in a way it had never been before.

Only the carter's warning call broke the challenge of her gaze, and she climbed into the back of the cart without another word.

Wheels grinding on stone, the cart started forward, once again travelling toward Mei'lian. At least whatever her plans were, we were still heading in the right direction.

Despite the presence of Shishi between us, tension remained and I could not look at the empress. Instead I watched the road pull away behind us, its wildflower border hammered flat by the rain. It had stopped with the dawn, but still the worn stones gleamed and a myriad of small puddles dotted its breadth like the pockmarked surface of an almond shell.

"I'm going to have to leave soon," I said. "I'm sorry."

She didn't answer. The cart rocked gently on.

Hours passed, and I was trapped with my own thoughts. I had peered out time and time again to see how far we were from the city, fretting at a pace that seemed to be drawing us no nearer, yet in the middle of the afternoon the cart once more began to slow. There was no obvious reason for it, and suffering from the same impatience as I, the empress stuck her head out to see why. I gripped her arm, but even as she spun a scowl on me, understanding widened her eyes. For as the rumble of wheels on stone quietened so the thud of hoofbeats rose to overwhelm it.

With a hand to her dagger, Empress Miko dropped into a crouch, hissing angry words between her teeth. Her other hand closed around Shishi's collar, and very carefully, she peered around the side of the cart. Wind tugged at her hair, leaving it stuck to her damp forehead when she turned back, her eyes wide with a fear that chilled my veins. The hoofbeats grew louder, yet still the empress stared at me, seemingly frozen by indecision.

"Levanti?" I asked in a low voice.

She shook her head. "Kisian."

I wasn't sure if that was better or worse. Levanti I could at least speak to. Kisians were complicated and after the events at Syan seemed more likely to be enemies than friends.

The cart jerked to a halt, snapping her into action. Gripping Shishi's collar, the empress crawled deeper into the cart, dragging the dog with her. With a frantic gesture, she bade me follow, crawling to her side over lumpy sacks that made a dry, grating sound beneath my shifting weight. Their smell was odd and musty, managing to overwhelm even the stink of wet dog.

The hoofbeats slowed and voices pierced the air. Empress Miko's whole body tensed as she pressed her ear to the canvas, her lips parted and her eyes glazed. Shishi scuffed around, trying to get comfortable, causing the empress to tighten her grip on her collar until Shishi's paws scrabbled, her eyes popping from her head.

The driver was speaking with the newcomers—at least four riders, going by the clink of bridles and the clop of hooves. Whatever was under discussion the driver's responses were meek. Fawning. Empress Miko's name was spoken and she squeezed my arm—that all the warning she was able to give.

Outside someone slid from their saddle, landing on the road with a thud. Footsteps approached. My hand crept to my sword hilt, but before I could draw it, the empress passed Shishi's collar into my hand. Our fingers met in the tangle of wet fur as we both clutched the leather band, and she looked up to meet my gaze.

"Stay," she said, pointing at a sack beside Shishi. "Goodbye, Rah."

Before I could gather words or even thoughts to argue, she let go and shuffled toward the cart entrance. Even as I parted my lips to hiss a warning, she turned back, little more than a dark shape against the brightness outside as she held up a staying hand. No words, just a gesture and a wry smile before she crawled to the backboard and stood, her skirt fluttering as she proclaimed her presence.

A shout of surprise rent the air and the empress responded—stiff, icy, imperial, more empress now than I had ever seen her. And while she faced her enemies, I crouched in the darkness and waited.

Empress Miko stepped from the end of the cart, but her voice was soon raised in argument nearby, the response that of a man amused by a tantrumming child. I picked at the knot on one of the carter's sacks until the rope came loose, and slid it between Shishi's collar and her fur. "Sorry," I whispered as I tied her to one of the cart poles. "But we can't have anyone seeing you."

I nuzzled her fur as I tugged the knot tight. Then, lifting my hand to her as the empress always did, I crept away across the sacks toward the light. Hunkered down at the end of the cart, I peered carefully out to see what was happening.

The snap glance I allowed myself revealed a dozen soldiers, half on horseback, half on foot, two of them holding the empress's arms like a prisoner as she shouted at their apparent leader. I leaned against the side of the cart and listened to them moving around. Knowing nothing of Kisian politics, I could only guess who they were and what they wanted, and I gripped my hands into tight fists, hating my own indecision. There were too many to fight them all. Even had I not been exhausted and been in possession of both my swords, even had Jinso been with me, there were still too many. And yet the call of what was right and good and honourable sang to me, and I knew I ought to do something. Ought to try.

That's the sort of thinking that gets you killed for nothing, Eska would have drawled. *How very you.*

The cart driver's voice cut through my thoughts, indignant, but orders were snapped and footsteps approached the cart. It looked like the choice was about to be taken out of my hands. I gripped my sword hilt and watched the bright aperture, waiting for a figure to appear.

Someone cried out. Grunted. Footsteps scuffled. I kept my eyes on the open end of the cart, but my heart raced as running steps sped past. The cart driver shouted. Shishi whined. I glanced back at her just as a sharp slap of horseflesh cracked like lightning and the cart lurched. Not having been holding on, I slid toward the opening, scrabbling to grip something, anything to keep from falling. Even as my fingers found purchase on the cover's metal pole, I hit the back of the cart, breaking the wooden lip and sending sacks tumbling into the road amid shouts and clattering wheels. But for all the cries and lost cargo, the cart plunged on. Shishi whined again, but it didn't matter, the Kisian soldiers were shrinking away behind us. They were wrestling with the proud figure of the empress, and I realised then that she must have broken free to scare the horses, whether to save me or Shishi it didn't seem to matter.

I watched from safety as they chained her hands and marched her toward another cart waiting at a distance. Their leader pointed here and there, giving orders as he shrank to the size of a child and then an ant.

I crawled toward Shishi over the jolting, bounding sacks as finally the driver got the horses under control and the cart began to slow. I glanced back along the road, and the sound of labouring horses able to go no farther was not the comfort it had been a moment before.

"Shit," I said, eyeing the three Kisians on horseback approaching fast. I had no bow, no javelins, nothing I could throw but lumpy sacks, but if I could take one down before they caught up then maybe, just maybe I could take the other two in a fight.

Scrambling to Shishi, I pulled open the sack I had untied earlier, spilling red-skinned fruits around my knees. They were about the size of my palm and evenly weighted, and while Shishi licked my cheek in search of reassurance, I chose the two biggest before shuffling back down the cart.

The driver had slowed his struggling horses to a walk, but the soldiers were still coming. I hefted one of the fruits. At this distance, Gideon would have been able to put a javelin through each of their throats within seconds, but I had nothing like his skill, and licked my lips, heart racing.

They began to slow a dozen or so lengths back, fanning out to overtake the cart. I threw the first fruit at the closest rider's head and, sure it would miss, followed it with the second. One hit him in the chest, shocking him enough to duck—only for the other to hit his head. Whatever the fruit, it was hard enough to send him reeling, and he tumbled sideways out of the saddle.

His companions shouted. The cart halted with a rough jerk. And once again, I gripped the hilt of my sword and blew out a hard breath, waiting for them to come to me. Behind me the driver called out and the soldiers shouted back. Feet hit the road. Wary footsteps approached. A figure appeared in the bright aperture, and I launched myself feet first at his head.

I had detested the hard Kisian sandals, but they smacked into the man's face with a satisfying crack. He fell back, smothering a cry as I landed on the road, tearing my sword from its scabbard. That first upswing sliced the length of a second man's sword arm. He dropped the blade, hissing, and I slammed into him shoulder first, knocking him off his feet.

Footsteps thudded behind me and I spun, catching the first soldier a deep slash across his face just as a jab came at my torso. It caught the fabric of my robe as I dodged, but the man fell, his blade clattering onto the stones. Before there was even time to consider if it was necessary, I had slit his throat, sending blood pouring onto the road. The other soldier had smacked his head and was dead or unconscious, it hardly seemed to matter which in the sudden stillness, the day silent but for my ragged breathing.

A step scuffed behind me and I spun, sword raised, to find the driver with his hands held before him in surrender. He trembled and his gaze kept shying to the man bleeding out on the road.

I lowered my blade. "Get out of here," I said, shooing him. "No, wait. Let me get my dog first." I pointed at the back of the cart and held up my own hands to show I meant no harm, bloodstained as they were, before climbing in to free Shishi. I could have just taken a horse and ridden hard for Kogahaera, have thought of nothing but my own goals and my own plans, but the empress had done everything she could to save me and I could not abandon her now. In the palace in Mei'lian was a man who had worn her armour and sat in her place when enemies came for her throne, a man unflinching in his loyalty. All I could do was trust he was still there. And that Gideon would be all right for just a few extra hours.

19. DISHIVA

I paced the five strides from one wall to the other and back, cracking reeds with my heel as I spun. One, two, three, four, five, and turn with a sound like beetles being crushed beneath the sole of my boot. One, two, three, four, five, back the other way, staring at each of the walls as though my troubles were carved upon them.

Three days. Three days out of the seven required for the emperor's marriage ceremony and the best I could say was that Gideon and his not-yet-wife were still alive. Matsimelar was dead. We'd lost more deserters. And everywhere I went Leo was there before me. He visited Lady Sichi. He walked about the stables. Whenever I went to see Gideon he was there. In fact every time I left my room I was sure to see him and had taken to leaving it less and less, unable to face his mild smile, his little nod, and his blessings.

Five strides and turn. Five strides and turn. I paced it fast and I paced it slow, but it never ceased being five strides. No more. No less. This five-by-five square had become my world, a world full of fretful memories and self-recrimination.

And fear.

At any moment Matsimelar's killer could return for me. And there was no one to stop them.

Someone cleared their throat outside my door. "Di?"

I had tensed, but it was only Lashak. I called for her to come in and she slid the door, an apologetic smile turning up one corner of her lips. "Well, hello there, stranger," she said, leaning on the door frame. "I was wondering if I'd not been seeing you because of that sweet, young bit of meat that had been giving you the eye, but I see you're all alone. What was his name again?"

I made to shape his name, but as I glanced up at Lashak the word faltered, falling from my lips. Her expression was all concern and friendliness, yet the overwhelming feeling that I could not trust her, could not trust anyone, had grown steadily. "Jass," I said, forcing it out rather than letting the fear rule me. "But he's gone."

"Deserted?"

"Probably. I don't know."

Lashak stepped into the room, closing the door behind her. "Are you all right, Dishiva? You don't look well."

Whenever I ate, I examined every tiny bit of food, smelling it and squashing it between my fingers, just in case, but I was increasingly sure I could smell that awful sticky smell on everything, even my hands.

"I'm fine."

I paced back, counting my strides through the weak sunlight. The rain had been patchy today, deep blue storm clouds alternating with bouts of drizzle.

One, two, three, four, five, and turn. Lashak just watched me from inside the door. One, two, three—Out at the gate the gong bellowed, halting my steps. No warning followed and through the window I watched the closest soldiers run to open the gate. More pilgrims, no doubt, their number increasing every day to the point where more than one of the little residences had to be made over to their use while most of the Levanti went on camping in the mud.

As the gates were pulled wide, a figure hurried down the manor steps. A white-clad figure with fair hair left to catch in the breeze. Leo. Not heading toward the new arrivals, but crossing the yard in the direction of Lord Nishi's residence. Halfway he stopped and turned, lifting a hand to protect his eyes from the sun as he peered up at me.

"Shit!" I hissed and dropped beneath the windowsill, slumping against the wall with my heart racing. How had he known I was watching?

"What the fuck is wrong, Di?" Lashak stood before me, leaning to see out the window. "Dom Villius? Is he what's bothering you?"

"You mean he doesn't bother you? The man was dead, Lash, dead. We killed him and then we made damn sure he was dead and then he just walked right in again like nothing was wrong. Why didn't anyone find that worrying?"

She shrugged. "It wasn't the first time he'd done it. Remember all that talk about how he had his own head in a box when we were travelling with the Chiltaens? I might not have believed it, but both Tor and Oshar snuck in and said it was true, and Rah saw it. The world is full of weird things and maybe his god really does bring him back—who am I to say that's wrong?"

A soft tap sounded on the door, and sure it was somehow him, I bit my tongue and scrabbled back in panic. As though my five-by-five room owned anywhere to hide. "Di, it's all right." Lashak went to open the door.

Jass stood on the threshold, breathing hard. A glance at Lashak and he slid past her, closing the door hurriedly in his wake. "I thought you said he was gone," she said.

"He's meant to be. What are you doing here?"

"I'm not here," he said. "I told Loklan to put it about that I was sick and you know how bad he is at lying. By now I imagine everyone thinks I died of redcap poisoning too."

"That is *not* a good thing."

Jass shrugged. "Better than being thought a deserter and unable to come back."

"No. Better you couldn't come back. What have you done with the—" I looked up at Lashak. "Just tell me it's safe."

"That what is safe?" Lashak said.

Jass ignored her. "It's safe. Shit, you look awful."

I stared up at him from my place on the floor. "You expected different? Someone tried to kill me and here you are walking in like nothing is wrong. Get. Out!"

"Kill you? Di, you had better tell me what the fuck is going on now."

"Are we trusting her?" Jass said, pointing up at the Namalaka captain.

"Are we—Excuse you, young blood, but if you're insinuating I cannot be trusted then—"

I hushed them both, pressing a shaking finger to my lips. "Someone will hear you, please stop. Yes, we're trusting Lashak because I'd rather die than live in a world where I couldn't. So you can get out of here knowing I'm fine and she's with me."

"Slow your pace, Captain, no one is going to think it strange to see me around," Jass said. "And there's no use me sitting out in a cave waiting for something to happen. I've had an idea about translating... the book."

"You've—what? How? Wait, cave?"

"Book?" Lashak said. "What book? One of you had better start explaining soon or I am going to scream."

I looked up at Lashak. "I will explain everything, I promise. Why don't you step out while we deal with this and I'll come find you as soon as I can."

She gave me a long look, but nodded. "You better be taking care of my Di, young blood," she said to Jass, and got up to let herself out.

Silence hung a few moments after she left, but where he ought to have continued with his reason for coming, he said, "I didn't volunteer to be one of your Swords because I wanted to protect Gideon. Nor because of you, though after that night in the—"

Another knock sounded on the door. "Shit," I hissed. "He knows you're here. Hide!"

"Where?" Jass mouthed, his eyes darting from the messy sleeping mat to my saddlebags and around the torn matting.

The knock sounded again. "Captain Dishiva?"

Not Leo's voice, and both Jass and I froze in place like statues. "That you, Tafa?" I said.

"Yes, Captain. Emperor Gideon wants to see you."

I let my breath out in one long sigh. "All right, I'm coming," I said, then jabbed my finger at Jass and hissed, "You stay here. Lock the door behind me and don't go anywhere."

"Lock it?" he whispered back as I picked up my crimson surcoat from the floor. "It's half made of paper."

"So? If someone tries to punch through it just stab them."

"Everything all right, Captain?" came Tafa en'Oht's concerned voice out in the passage. "His Majesty wanted me to bring you as quickly as I could."

I glared at Jass. "Everything is fine. I'm ready," I said before turning toward the door, mouthing *lock it* one more time as Jass hid in the corner. Without waiting for an answer, I slid the door and stepped out into the passage, closing it behind me. Tafa looked me up and down, and whatever Jass and Lashak had seen she saw too and grimaced.

"You don't look well, Captain." Her gaze lingered on the scratches covering my hands and arms from where I'd rubbed torn handfuls of reed matting to scrub myself red and raw and clean.

"Just tired," I snapped. "Now let's not keep His Majesty waiting while we gossip in the hallway."

"No, of course, Captain," she said, and commented no more.

I entered the emperor's room to find he wasn't alone, but at least

Leo wasn't present. Sett was with him, the pair locked in a low-voiced conversation from which even the click of the closing door could not rouse them. Heedless of my presence, Gideon went on talking, his voice a rumble like distant thunder. Sett's forehead was bent to Gideon's shoulder, his pose all too reminiscent of a reprimanded child.

"—relying on you because you were the only one I trusted," Gideon said, holding his brother to him. "It was...important to me, you know that. He was important to me." His voice caught and for a moment Gideon looked away, before going on, "And Manshin?"

"He was too stubborn to listen," Sett said, lifting his head from Gideon's shoulder and meeting his gaze squarely. "I could have offered him everything and he would have refused. I told you that marrying Empress Miko was the only way you could—"

"They have stolen that chance from me. *You* stole that chance from me when you let Rah run around playing saviour." Gideon patted Sett's shoulder while his stare lingered. The man squirmed. For a long moment they stood like that before Gideon spun upon his heel and smiled at me, a bright, brittle smile like the painted face of a doll. "Dishiva, exactly the Sword I wanted to see."

I didn't know whether he preferred a bow or a salute anymore, but he had called me a Sword, not a guard, so I pressed my fists together in respect and uttered the words still foreign to my tongue. "Your Majesty."

Leaving Sett by the window, he strode toward me, making no comment about the change in my appearance three days' worry had wrought. "I have a mission for you. Two, in fact. It seems those Kisians south of the river have decided to march on Mei'lian and retake the city."

Sett's head snapped up. "They're what? How do you know?"

"It doesn't matter how I know, though you ought to have been able to tell me since you've been sitting in the capital all this time doing nothing."

Sett parted his lips only to snap them closed again. The weak sunlight paling one side of his face did little to lighten a heavy scowl.

"We cannot hold Mei'lian," Gideon went on. "And even if we could there's no point. The river is our border for now and it's a waste of time to protect anything south of it. We will build a new capital and burn the old one."

After a beat of silence that seemed to stretch taut between Sett and me, I said, "Burn it?"

"Yes. There's no other choice. We cannot hold it, but if we let them have it back, they claim a great victory over the Levanti. If you leave tomorrow there should be time to evacuate the people, saving them from the cowardly Kisian prince who would rather burn his own city than face Levanti in the field."

It took me a moment to catch up. "Wait, we pretend Kisians are burning their own city and go in to rescue the people?"

"It won't be pretend. Two Kisian battalions will go with you. They'll set the fires in an organised fashion, starting in the farthest quarters to allow maximum time for the people to escape. They'll wear Ts'ai sashes and burn it in the name of their boy emperor while the Levanti and Kisians bearing...Bahain's symbol help the citizens in the name of their *new* emperor."

I had been a captain of the Levanti long enough to admire the pragmatism, had fought the Tempachi long enough to hate cities and those who dwelled in them, but to dislocate so many...So many children and elders, some unable to escape without help.

"That—" I closed my fists but could not close off my voice. "Many people will suffer for that. Die. Have their homes destroyed. Their way of life."

Gideon lifted his brows, and as I met his gaze I knew he

understood. People would die. History would be destroyed. Thousands upon thousands of people would be left without a home. But it didn't matter. Not to him.

I saluted. "With respect, Herd Master—"

"With respect, do I have to find myself another captain, Captain?"

I could not shift my gaze from his without capitulating, but trying to outstare Gideon was like trying to outstare a snake. He stood firm, his piercing gaze seeming to press me back though he did not move, and all too aware my refusal would just end in my replacement, I shied to look at Sett. His expression was unreadable.

"I hope I can trust you and Sett to organise this," Gideon said. "Although you, Dishiva, won't be going to the city. I have another task for you."

I lifted my chin. "Yes, Your Majesty?"

"The recent deserters," he said. "They haven't been going north. Not going home. They are camping in some swampland between here and Mei'lian, half a day's ride off the road, and they're planning to attack us."

"Attack us?"

"Yes. I do not know what has twisted their minds. Perhaps something of the sickness that plagued the plains has followed us here after all, but I refuse to let all of this fail under the blade of a few honourless Levanti."

I swallowed, but fear blocked my throat like a squeezing fist.

"You must put down this rebellion before it happens. Take a dozen of your Swords, find their camp, and put an end to this."

Stalling for time while I gathered my thoughts, I said, "Somewhere between here and the capital is a big area. They could be anywhere."

"That's true, but I trust you haven't forgotten your tracking skills in so short a time."

He said it almost sweetly, but it was anger that set his jaw and hardened the lines around his eyes. Gideon's gaze lingered a moment before he began pacing, every ray of weak light tracing the golden threads in his robe. "I know this is not a pleasant task I have given you, Dishiva, but it has to be done by someone I trust and I am fast running out of such people, it would seem. I do not know what has turned our people's minds, but I know you well enough to be confident it could never infect you."

"I am ever a loyal Sword of the Levanti."

"I know you are," he said, halting his pacing to stand before me again. "I know you'll do whatever it takes to discover the location of the deserter camp and root this out before it turns ugly. You leave first thing in the morning."

"And the three days left until you're married?"

"The Swords you leave behind will protect me. And by doing this for me you give no reason for anyone to want me dead."

I wasn't sure what he meant, but my thoughts were already reeling. He was asking me to kill my own people. Levanti had fought wars before, herd against herd when transgressions had not been able to be overlooked, but they were rare things born from years of hurt. That some had chosen to desert and head home I could understand, but that they had chosen to remain here, to plot against us, made no sense.

"There must be an explanation," I said. "A misunderstanding. I will find them and speak to them as an envoy, but—"

"Dishiva." Gideon stepped closer. "You do not appear to be listening to the words I am saying. I am your Herd Master and this is the task I am giving you. If you do not wish to do it you may step down or challenge me, but understand what it will mean to have to step into my place."

Again his stare had pressure. Weight. It pressed me back and pinned me and I could not speak. How many times had I watched him and known he was the only way, that no one else could tread this balance as he could? What had changed?

"Is this Leo's plan?"

My question rang out into the deepest silence I had known. Both Gideon and Sett stared at me and it took all the steel my bones possessed not to buckle. I stood, hands clenched, tense from head to foot. It was one thing to trust in Gideon, quite another to trust in Dom Villius.

"Leo told me you don't like him," Gideon said. "That you believe he is responsible for the deaths of his pilgrims."

Oh, how pitying his smile. I had rarely seen a thing that enraged me more. Until he kept speaking.

"I know the Chiltaens hurt you, Dishiva. But you cannot pit your hate against them all for the actions of a few. Dom Villius is—"

"Not your friend."

I took a step in this time, anger trembling through my limbs. "You cared about Rah. He was important to you. And yet you let yourself be manipulated by the very man who turned him from us. Why?"

He flinched, but stood his ground. "Manipulated? You have no faith in your Herd Master?" Gideon spread his arms wide. "Then why don't you challenge me?"

They would not follow me. Not the Kisians, not even all the Levanti. To challenge him would be the end of this, the end of everything we had tried to build here, everything we had hoped for, or...the end of me.

For as many breaths as I dared, I gave him back stare for stare, but at the point it was break or be broken, I looked away. And that was it. I could voice no more objections, leaving me nothing to do but bow and wait to be dismissed. Sett had stiffened to a statue by the window.

"Good. You may go, Dishiva," Gideon said. "You do not have a lot of time to prepare."

I turned to leave, but he gripped my arm, his other hand closing over my branding. Held prisoner as much by shock as by his strong grip, I tensed as he lowered his lips to my ear. "I want their heads, Dishiva," he said, and I shivered at the warm tickle of his breath. "Not to honour but to... discourage others from leaving."

Gideon let me go as suddenly as he had taken hold, his gaze oddly far away, and a second shiver chilled my skin. How close did we stand to the brink of destruction that he would speak so? That he would demand such things of me?

But I could not ask or challenge again, could only mumble a "Yes, Your Majesty," and walk to the door assuring myself that in a few days when his temper had cooled he would not want such a thing. Sliding it open I walked blindly out into the passage. Even when I heard it close behind me, the weight of Gideon's gaze did not lift.

Tafa was there on guard with Baln and I put my hand on the Oht woman's shoulder. "Tafa, I need you to gather some Swords for me. Quietly. We will need Loklan with us for the horses, but otherwise just make sure you pick Swords whose loyalty to Gideon is absolute. A mix of herds too," I added, thinking through the look of the thing. "And keep it quiet."

"You said that part already, Captain. Trust me, I can do it. What do you want me to tell them?"

"For now, just that we have a mission and will be leaving first thing in the morning. They need to be prepared, but—"

"Keep it quiet."

"Yes, that."

"Got it, Captain."

She nodded at Baln. "I'll send someone to cover me. You in?"

"You know I am," he said as I walked away along the passage

in a daze, my hands clenched to keep them from shaking. I had walked the path between my own rooms and Gideon's too many times to get lost, even with my thoughts tugging every direction, but a small, persistent piece of my mind kept shouting at me that deserters were not our biggest concern. Someone had killed Nods. Someone had killed Livi. Someone had killed Matsimelar and burned all the holy books, and that enemy could take advantage of my absence. But what did they want?

As I passed Lady Sichi's room the door slid. Expecting Nuru, I sped my pace to avoid her, only to almost collide with Leo. I fell back as he emerged at his slow, decorous walk, his mask hanging around his throat like an unwanted scarf. Massama and Esi were on duty outside Lady Sichi's room. Both grimaced when I scowled, but it wasn't their place to refuse him entrance to the lady's room.

"Ah, Captain Dishiva," he said, his brows lifted in pleasant surprise. "How nice to see you. I do hope," he added, lowering his voice to a conspiratorial whisper despite the continued presence of my Swords, "that you will soon find the person responsible for the poisonings. And the burning of the holy books. Lord Nishi has been quite upset."

"So, I imagine, are the dead," I said.

"There is nothing to fear in death so long as your body is cared for and given back to God. I requested of Emperor Gideon that the young Levanti be buried and his body blessed and he was wise enough to agree."

I gasped. "Buried? And what of his soul?"

"If you mean his head," Leo said with a tolerant smile. "It was removed first, though I did my best to educate His Majesty that such brutality was not required. The soul can be freed back to God if the body is placed in the ground."

I had no words. Fury had been filling me up bit by bit, in a trickle at first and now in a flood. If Matsimelar's soul had been trapped thanks to the cajoling of a Chiltaen priest my outrage would have known no bounds. Even allowing his body to be buried without its head was not our way. We burned bodies, letting the smoke rise to the Watchful Father.

"I am very sorry for your loss, Captain," he said. "I understand the young man was a good friend of yours as well as being a very capable translator. Useful when there is something you wish to understand."

Though he looked solemn and spoke pious words, I could not rid myself of the feeling he was laughing at me. "Yes," I said. "Very useful. But I have just this moment left His Majesty and he is in agreement that all Levanti must learn Kisian. We cannot build a new empire without being able to understand one another, after all. I look forward to learning all the...stories of your people as well as theirs."

He smiled, and without hesitation exclaimed, "Oh, that is good news!"

"I thought so. Lord Nishi will be pleased to be able to share copies of your holy book once we barbarians can read them." I forced a bright smile. I could feel Massama and Esi staring at me as I went on: "Would it not be the perfect book to learn your written language from? He could read aloud to any interested in hearing it."

Leo met my bright smile with one even sunnier. "Why did I not have that idea myself? Understanding is the first step on the road to tolerance. Shall I organise it while you are away?"

"I..."

I had not told him I was leaving. That meant he was even deeper in Gideon's confidence than I had thought. There was no other logical explanation, yet his eternal smile renewed that nagging itch of doubt, and a truly mad idea blinded me. Even as I thought it, I smothered it with a smile vapid enough to challenge his.

"A brief scout of the area hardly counts as being *away*, Dom Villius," I said, waving an airy hand though my heart thudded like a galloping herd. "But by all means you may organise a reading of the holy book. Both Nuru and Oshar are capable of translating the spoken word for any Levanti interested in attending."

As I spoke I concentrated upon a very different mission, the maddest and most foolish mission I could imagine—being sent north to Koi, taking Leo's head to the Chiltaen forces entrenched there, a warning from Emperor Gideon that should they refuse to surrender the city we—

Leo's smile hardened to a fixed grimace. I tried to hold his unblinking gaze as it flicked from one of my eyes to the other, side to side like a man reading.

"Of course you would do best to seek His Majesty's approval first," I said. I sounded weak and breathless, but he didn't seem to be listening to my voice anymore.

If I can just keep him standing here talking until the others arrive, I thought, fixing my smile in place though it hurt my cheeks. *He's gotten so complacent thinking he has us all under his thumb, he'll never see it coming. But Gideon is too smart for him. Are those footsteps? Come on, Esi, grab him. The others are here. Grab—*

Leo spun on Esi in a flutter of white linen. She leapt back, but Massama stepped in and rapped her knuckles on the back of Leo's hand, making him spill the dagger into her waiting palm. And all the while I stood caught to the floor, too shocked to move.

He could hear my thoughts. There was no other explanation. The gods-be-damned little shit could hear everything, could read my mind like a book, and now he knew that I knew.

Leo raised his hands in surrender. "My apologies," he said with a little laugh, turning first to Esi, then to Massama, who still held his blade. "I thought I heard someone behind me and after all the attacks on my people I cannot be too careful."

Massama accepted his apology with a murmur but slid his knife into her belt, daring him to ask for it back.

I needed to leave. I needed to get out of there. He could read my mind and he knew and—

"Captain," he said before I had taken more than three steps along the passage. "A blessing before you go."

I turned back, grateful for the protection of our unwitting audience as Leo caught up, that hard, brittle smile back. "May God follow you wherever you go," he said, standing before me. "May he keep you from making costly mistakes. May he have mercy upon your fallen soul."

A murmur of thanks parted my dry lips and I had no choice but to turn my back to him and walk away—to walk, not run, though I wanted to give in to panic and flee. I tried to stay calm, to think, but the moment I considered doubling back to see Gideon, or telling my Swords, my panic rose afresh. Leo might still be listening, still be reading me. How close did he have to be? Did he have to be looking into my eyes?

No footsteps followed, though my heart hammered so loud I couldn't be sure. *Don't turn. Don't check. Keep looking ahead. Keep moving.*

The passage had never seemed so long.

I sped up as I reached the corner, and as soon as I was out of sight, I ran. Pelting along the next passage in a storm of footsteps and panic, I almost crashed into a maid, almost shouted at her to run, but she was safe as long as she didn't know. Anyone I told was dead.

I ran into my door, but it wouldn't slide. "Jass!" I hissed, thumping upon the wooden frame with the flat of my hand. "Jass, it's Dishiva. Quick, unlock the door!"

Nothing.

"Jass? Jass!" I pounded again and looked around, sure I'd heard footsteps. No one. "Jass!"

A distant voice spoke a greeting. The maid. I turned, pressing my back to the locked door that hid my only ally as Leo replied. A blessing upon her. Slow steps followed, solemn and pious and frighteningly inevitable. "Fuck!" I spun back, pounding the door again. "Jass! This isn't funny, I need you to open this door."

The footsteps drew closer, slow and steady.

"Jass!"

Getting no answer, I punched through the pane closest to the bolt and reached inside, the thick paper scratching my arm. The approaching footsteps filled my mind as I drew back the bolt and threw the door wide, only to catch sight of Jass lying on the floor. "Shit!" I slammed the door closed and bolted it. "Shit!"

Breath wheezed between Jass's swollen lips. Dry foam flecked his chin and the whites of his eyes were mere flickering slits, but though his arms and legs were stiff and trembling he was not dead. Not yet.

A knock shook the door. "Captain Dishiva?" Leo's voice filled the room as he peered through the hole in the paper. "Ah, were you too late to save another friend? How sad."

I hauled Jass's head onto my lap, and as the paper screen crackled, I prised open his jaw and thrust my fingers down his throat. It was swollen and choked with foam, but not caring if I hurt him as long as he lived, I pressed deep, digging until at last he gagged and retched. His body took over and I rolled him from my legs as foam burst from his lips, followed by the entire putrid contents of his stomach.

A sash snaked around my throat, yanking my head back against Leo's leg. "You just had to be too clever, didn't you, Dishiva," he said, the words an ugly growl. "Too suspicious. All because you blamed me for Rah's dissent. But I can assure you, he was quite able to be a traitor all on his own."

The sash tightened and I gasped breaths through an ever-shrinking hole. In front of me Jass retched over and over, lying in a spreading pool of vomit, but even if he survived, I would be dead before he could move.

Leo tightened the sash as I scrabbled to get fingers under it. "You're right and he will get the blame whether he survives or not," he said, gleeful. "Because being found beside a corpse never looks good."

This was not the way I was going to die. If I could edge a foot out and spring up...

Leo laughed and pressed his weight onto my shoulders to keep me down.

"What's your next bright plan, Capt—"

I rolled, the tight sash about my throat dragging Leo with me. He cried out amid a confused flurry of linen and sick-soaked reeds, and the sash around my throat loosened. I staggered up gasping and gripping my neck, every breath full of knives. Leo had landed on Jass, his back arched over the groaning Levanti, but though the God's child had cried out in pain he rolled clear, one sleeve soaked in sick and clinging to his arm.

I drew my dagger and faced Leo across the small room. He had lost his weapon to Massama, yet he owned no fear as he stood ready to fight, unarmed and smiling. He spread his arms, inviting attack. "Come on, Dishiva, why hesitate? Strike down the unarmed priest and suffer the weight of such dishonour."

"You are no priest," I snarled, and snarl it was, the words coming hoarse and broken from my throat. And the fool just stood there and smiled, giving me the perfect opening to stick my blade in his gut.

I stepped in, thrusting for his unprotected stomach and ready to slit his throat in the aftershock. But Leo moved fast as a river snake. His fingers closed around my wrist, forcing the dagger down before twisting it from my hand. Instinct dropped me beneath his thrust, but when I kicked at his knee he leapt back with a triumphant, boyish laugh.

I stood, clenching and unclenching my empty hands. He had known what I would do and been waiting to perform an almost perfect disarm. If I hadn't dropped I would be dead on the floor beside Jass. Only instinct had saved me.

"Going to try again with your sword?" he jeered, his eyes flashing with excitement. "You know it would be easier if you gave up and died."

Out beyond the window the yard buzzed with activity. There were Levanti everywhere, enough Swords to beat Leo a hundred times over, but even if I called them they would not be here in time, and who would believe Leo could read my mind? Even Jass was no help, but he groaned and rolled when my gaze darted to him, the last of the vomit having been purged from his stomach.

I was on my own. Me against Leo, and he had my knife.

The God's child lifted his brows. "You've finally figured that out. You have been on your own since you arrived. This camp is mine. Gideon is mine. The empire is mine."

"Horseshit. You are all lies and trickery, and if you want me dead then come and kill me."

Mimicking his action, I spread my arms, inviting him to strike. I feared death, and I forced that fear to the front of my mind, focusing on it in the hope it would choke his thoughts.

Leo licked dry lips. "That isn't going to work."

"Then kill me. Now, before there are two against one and you're done for."

Jass had rolled clear of his mess. If Leo tried to attack him, I could strike. If he went for the door, he'd be dead before he slid the bolt. Leo's only option was to kill me and fast.

A smile solidified on the young priest's face. "You think I can't? I was trained by the best teachers in Chiltae."

"Then stop talking and do it."

He leapt, stabbing at my neck, but I threw up a deflecting arm and twisted it around his. With his elbow locked I forced him face first toward the floor. I dodged away as he slashed at me with the other hand, and he rose with blood leaking from his nose and an ugly sneer. His gaze flicked to the door.

"Why did you kill them?" I said.

Leo wiped the blood from his nose with his clean sleeve. "Why ask questions you already know the answer to?"

"Why don't you want me to read your holy book?"

"Again with the stupid questions." He stepped as he spoke, a slow sidestep toward Jass. The start of an attack or a feint? If he took another then—

No, don't think about it, don't think about it, don't let him win.

Leo leered. "You kill me and I'll just come back and return the favour."

He lunged, switching the blade to his off hand as he came at me. I fell back a step, and giving myself to the calm that lay beyond the rising panic, I moved without thought. I stepped as I had done thousands of times in practice, blocked as I had been taught, and twisted his arm. This time I slammed my palm into the back of his locked elbow, exulting at the snap of bone.

The God's child howled and hissed, but he caught his dropped dagger in his other hand. His left arm hung useless, but still he faced me, spitting fury. "I am Veld Reborn," he said, spittle bursting from his lips. Pain seemed to have melted away his calm facade, leaving something more animal than human beneath. "This will be my empire, and the more you enrage God the more pain he will pile upon you until you beg for a quick, dignified death."

"Do you even believe any of this stuff?" I said. "Or do you just use it for your own ends?"

Jass hauled himself onto his knees, trembling like a branch of storm-blown leaves. A glance was all I could spare him for Leo lumbered forward, his broken arm swinging and his smile fixed.

Like the inevitability of his steps in the passage, here stood a man who would not quit, who would return the moment he was dead and come after me again. And next time I might not be so lucky.

Grinning, he took a second lumbering step. Then he lashed out, whip fast, and all I could do was fall back, dodging the tip of the blade as it slashed the air before my eyes. He pressed his advantage and thrust again, nicking my arm. Hot blood stung as I backed up, almost stepping on Jass's leg. He seemed to be speaking, but his hoarse whisper was nothing over the thundering blood in my ears.

"I only need to get you once," Leo said, teeth gritted against the pain of his broken elbow. "You have to be lucky every time."

No, I thought, *just long enough for Jass to recover.*

Leo's gaze snapped to Jass, increasingly dangerous despite his weak state. I didn't need to read his mind to know his intention, and leaving no time for doubt I darted in low, catching the God's child as he lunged. My shoulder met Leo's gut, and carrying him back, I slammed him against the wall in a crack of wood. His fists pummelled my back. His sandal struck my shin. In a tangle of limbs and linen we fell, and however well the best Chiltaen masters had taught him to fight with a blade, they'd never taught him to scrap on the ground. I pinned him easily and smashed my fist into his pretty face. Blood spurted from his nose, then from a split lip as I hit him again and again, pounding him into the matting floor.

He tried to buck and bite and fend me off with his one good arm, but I caught it as he reached for my throat and broke his wrist. Never had the snap of bones been so joyous. Leo howled and my soul sang. I had dreamed night after night of getting free of my chains and beating Commander Legus to death while he slept. Such dreams had sustained me through our forced march south, through the memories I could not escape, but now, faced with the chance to see them through, I lowered my fist. The sight of Leo's broken, bloody face sapped my fury to a simmer. If he died now, he would just come back.

Jass watched me, still trembling, his bloodshot eyes owning more life than I had thought to see.

"Are you all right?" I said, keeping my weight on Leo. "I mean, as all right as..."

I trailed off, but Jass nodded, seemingly unable to speak.

"I'm sorry."

As I spoke he looked over my shoulder, and my heart leapt into my throat as I turned to find Nuru and Lady Sichi standing in the doorway. Before I could manage a word, the lady strode in and kicked the prostrate Dom Villius in the side of the head with her sandalled foot.

"Hey! We don't want him dead!" I threw out my hands as his head lolled into unconsciousness.

Unabashed, Lady Sichi spoke and Nuru said, "In fact we do, Captain, but I take your point that we do not want him to come back again if that's something he truly does. I have not been sure who I could trust, but it has been increasingly clear Dom Villius has a dangerous level of control and needs to be stopped."

"But you've been having tea with him almost every day."

Nuru didn't bother translating this, just gave me a look.

"We have to get him out of here," Lady Sichi went on. "But I'm not sure—"

"Caves," Jass croaked, and we all stared at him.

"There's somewhere we can hide him where no one will find him?"

Another nod followed by a convulsive swallow and a gasp for air. A second nod as he regained control of himself. "Through the cellar," he whispered. "There are caves. They lead into the mountains."

I leapt up. Someone could come by at any moment. Gideon could send for me or a servant might peer through the hole in my screen and Leo couldn't be here if they did. He had used his own sash to strangle me, and I snatched it up to tie his broken arms.

Lady Sichi began to speak again.

"The lady says I will keep watch to be sure you get out unseen," Nuru said. "And she will stay behind to clean the mess so no one suspects."

"I have to be back by morning," I said. "I have a . . . mission, and it will be noted if I am late in setting off."

Jass shot me a searching look, but said nothing.

"Then hurry back, Captain," Lady Sichi said through Nuru's lips. "And when you return from that mission I think you and I need to finally have a proper talk. If we cannot trust one another after this, when could we?"

Weak though he was, Jass helped me truss up the unconscious priest and stuff a ball of fabric in his blood-filled mouth. Then, when Jass found enough strength to walk, I slung Leo over my shoulder. It was time for Veld Reborn to disappear.

"Where are you going?" Jass asked in his rasping voice after we had left Lady Sichi behind, Nuru striding ahead to be sure the way was clear. "This mission."

Perhaps I ought not to tell him, but I rebelled against the idea I had to live in a world without trust and said, "Gideon wants me to deal with the deserters."

He turned and looked at me, and in the seriousness of that gaze I recalled that he had begun to tell me he hadn't joined my Swords to protect Gideon. Or for me. What better way to walk around the manor unquestioned than to be an Imperial Guard?

"You have connections to the deserters, don't you?" I said to him. "That's what you wanted to tell me. You joined my Swords so you could smuggle supplies and people in and out. That's how you know about the caves."

Jass nodded.

"I could call that treason."

He met my gaze, his half-lidded eyes unblinking.

"But then," I went on, "you are helping me get this shit out of here."

"I don't know what your mission is," he rasped, every word an enormous effort. "I don't know what he told you, but they aren't dangerous. They just want to go home. And since Tor disappeared from Mei'lian, likely to join them, they may also be the only hope you have of finding a translator for that book."

And I was being sent for their heads.

20. CASSANDRA

I had been a city girl all my life. I had been born in Genava, had worked in Genava, killed in Genava, and I had fully expected to one day die in Genava. It hadn't only been my home, it had lived in my soul with its broken gutters and dark laneways, its broad squares and its columns and its ever-present shuffle of merchant traders along the docks. Confined once more in a carriage, I could not but yearn to be back there in my old life instead of cooped up with only the hieromonk for company. We stopped to sleep and we stopped to change horses, but otherwise we stopped only for news.

It was all really boring news gleaned from terrified or wary Kisians, little more than gossip about where Levanti had been spotted in the surrounding area, until one day the carriage began to slow with nothing but open fields visible beyond the window. I settled back into the corner and tried to recapture my doze, but the hieromonk scowled and slid open the hatch that separated us from the driver up front. "Why are we slowing?" he called.

"There's a pair of scouts ahead, Your Holiness. Captain Aeneas has ridden on to see if they have news from Koi."

The hieromonk grunted. "Very well."

The carriage stopped with a jolt. The hieromonk sat taut in his seat, radiating impatience and tapping his foot until at last Captain Aeneas opened the door. As ever he did not smile.

"News, Captain?" the hieromonk snapped.

"Yes, Your Holiness. The scouts have just come from Koi."

"And what did they have to say?"

The captain cleared his throat, glanced at me, then back at his master. "They are just on a routine scouting mission, but they did mention... back in the city... the presence of"—another glance at me—"Leo Villius."

"What?" The hieromonk jumped up, hit his head on the low roof of the carriage, and sank back onto his seat hissing. "Leo? Are you sure?"

"Yes, Your Holiness."

"Can there be a mistake?"

"No, Holiness. I checked. It's Leo." A third glance at me, wary and unfriendly.

Leo, whose life had been my commission. Leo, whose head I had taken, ready to hand to his father in a sack, only for Leo himself to retrieve it.

"How did the damn boy get there so fast?" the hieromonk said. "He ought to have still been days away."

"I couldn't say, Holiness."

He gnawed at his lower lip, scowling like a thwarted child. The captain remained unmoving in the doorway, sunlight gleaming on his damp hair. I must have stared too hard for he turned, a small notch appearing between slanting brows. Our eyes held and the scowl deepened, puckering some of his scars.

Don't give yourself away, the empress said.

How can I? He can only see you.

Always assume people are smarter and more astute than you think. There is nothing more dangerous than underestimating an enemy.

It was a basic precept and I felt stupid. *You sound more like an assassin than me.*

You're used to being the one with power. I'm used to protecting myself on fear of death; it gives one a very ingrained perspective on such things.

"Where are we?" the hieromonk said, returning suddenly from his place of deep thought.

"The scouts said we're about five miles from the Rice Road, though they suggested we go the long way up the Willow Road to avoid—" Captain Aeneas broke off as the hieromonk shooed him out of the way and, leaning out, looked around. Not just ahead and behind but all around at the hazy trees and fields. "We must hide it."

Captain Aeneas left a beat of silence. "Hide it, Holiness?"

"Yes. It will not be safe in Koi now."

Another pause. Tension hung between the two men, while outside sunlight sparkled upon the damp landscape. "Someone will have to stay to look after it."

"Yes, someone will have to stay to look after it. Someone I trust."

That silence again, heavy and fraught with unspoken words. Then, with the smallest of sighs, the captain said, "I will stay. I will need supplies. And someone to help carry it."

A smile broke the hieromonk's deadpan expression. "And you shall have both, Captain, along with my gratitude. I shall send someone back for you when it's safe."

"I could take Swiff," he said. "He is quiet. Discreet."

Again a beat of silence. Outside, birds were singing, making the close space of the carriage feel all the more unreal. "Very well," the hieromonk said at last. "Do so. Tell all the others to sit in the cart to wait, and ensure you make no sound that might give away your direction."

"Yes, Holiness." Captain Aeneas nodded, military promptness returning as he stepped back into the sunlit day, leaving the hieromonk to close the carriage door himself like a commoner. He made no complaint, just drew a curtain across the window and sat back.

Outside muffled voices moved around the carriage. Thuds emanated from the cart. Slowly the sounds began to fade, until Captain Aeneas's clipped words dropped into silence.

"Where is he going?"

Don't! Just keep your mouth shut.

The hieromonk lifted his brows. "Where is who going, Majesty?"

His mild smile was punch-worthy. "The captain," I said, ignoring Empress Hana inside her own head. "This seems a very odd place to leave someone."

"Does it? Good."

Leave it there. We don't need to know what he's doing. We just need him unsuspecting.

What was it you said about underestimating people? I said. *Being wilfully ignorant is just as stupid. Knowledge is power, which you damn well know. Now shut up and let me do what I do best.*

Seducing people? Or killing them?

"I saw your son's body," I said, ignoring her. "When your army took Koi. I saw him, lying in his own blood upon the floor without a head—"

I didn't.

"—and now you say he is alive and in command of my city?" I was proud of having thought to say *my city*, and of the haughty way I lifted my chin. Perhaps I was getting the hang of the imperial thing after all. "Either someone lied and your son was not my prisoner, or someone is lying now. Which is it?"

"Neither." He no longer looked over my shoulder. "We are the chosen of God. We serve him and in return he looks after us." He touched the silver mask pendant hanging about his neck, but despite the smile his fingers trembled.

I had grown up in the shadow of the One True God, had been told that to serve him would be my salvation, but never in all those lessons, in all those lectures at the hospice, had God's miracles been more than stories. Arguments bit at the inside of my lips, but I could voice none of them without giving myself away, could only rant to the disinterested empress, who watched me like a cat sleeping with one eye open.

If I could trust you, I wouldn't need to.

When I made no answer, the hieromonk stared unseeing at the drawn curtain, his fingers still touching the necklace. But what had started as a mere acknowledgement of his faith was now a fevered thumbing of the metal, as though rubbing it hard might bring God himself into our presence.

The silence stretched. Every part of the empress's body peppered me with pains and complaints, but she folded its hands and I kept it upright, watching every twitch of the man's expression, every movement of his hands, and understanding none of it. Why trade us for the box? Why steal us back? Why fear Leo finding it? So many questions whose answers lay within the box even now being hidden by Captain Aeneas.

Noise eventually returned, every footstep and voice louder and stranger than before, as if my ears had forgotten what they sounded like. An awkward laugh. A shout to the driver. Then at long last the carriage door was pulled open. Sunlight bright like fire streamed in, pricking my eyes, and upon the glinting road stood Swiff, Captain Aeneas's man.

"Is it done?"

"Yes, Your Holiness, we—"

"Say nothing! You know the rules. Nothing. You have told no one?" The hieromonk's gaze flicked one way along the road and then the other.

Swiff shook his head. "No one, Holiness."

"Good."

The hieromonk held out his left hand, and awkwardly wedged in the doorway, the soldier bent to kiss it. Unseen by Swiff, the hieromonk's other hand crept beneath the carriage seat. Before a warning cry could escape my lips, he had buried a knife in the back of the soldier's neck. Swiff jolted and thrashed, half attempts at words spilling from his lips. The hieromonk yanked the knife out and struck again, cutting only the meat of the man's neck. The carriage shook all the more as the narrow doorway impeded his death throes.

Hating the messiness of the kill, I snatched the bucking dagger hilt from the hieromonk's slippery hand and jammed the blade into Swiff's throat. A few final twitches and the man slumped, half in and half out of the carriage like a limp set of steps.

"Give me that." The hieromonk snatched back the blade. Almost I tightened my hold and kept it, but we had drawn a crowd and every soldier left in the priest's entourage watched on, staring with slack jaws at the fate of their comrade. "You know the rules," the hieromonk said, addressing them with his usual haughty assurance. "No one can know. No one."

As he stared defiantly at the watching soldiers, he tensed and untensed his jaw, causing a muscle to bulge in his cheek. "Well? What are you staring at? Remove the body and continue on to Koi."

Touch it.

"What?" I said aloud, too shocked to think before speaking.

The hieromonk glared at me, his jaw still working.

Touch the body. Quick. Put me into it. We can't save ourselves from in here.

Two soldiers had already stepped up to remove the dead man from the narrow doorway. They half pulled, half lifted the body, and with no time to make it look subtle, I flung out my hand, brushing his forehead. The empress escaped like the letting go of a deep breath and my whole body relaxed, growing lighter. From the opposite seat the hieromonk's gaze narrowed. My cheeks had hardly ever reddened, but the empress's did now, and in an attempt to mask my odd behaviour I muttered a few words of prayer as the soldiers dragged the body out of reach. Some grunts of effort, the scraping of boots on the road, then once again the carriage door closed, shutting me in with the hieromonk.

Having expected exclamations of shock and horror, the silence from outside was deafening. It stretched on, endless and empty. Footsteps shuffled. The carriage shook. Then it started forward, the thud of hooves muted by the mud.

Minutes passed that felt like hours and still there was nothing.

Clever of her to play dead and be dropped upon the side of the road, but if she waited too long to attack, she would lose her chance.

Despite the pervasive stink of blood coming from the crimson-washed floor and the hems of our robes, the hieromonk began to relax. A mile or so farther on he leaned back against the cushions and let out a sigh, fixing his smile upon me.

"Well, Miss Marius, it seems you and I are alone at last."

I stared at him, unable to find the clever words I needed.

"You ought not to be surprised, you know," he said, resting one pale, blood-flecked hand upon my knee. "You are a very unique personality with a very unique turn of phrase. I don't know what that madman did, but I ought to thank him. You may not be so alluring in this body but you are far more useful."

And still there was no sound outside but the occasional laugh and the grind of carriage wheels.

"Hoping she'll save you? Even if the body survives long enough to find us, she's no assassin and my guards will catch her." He laughed. "Maybe I'll lock her up like that. I've always wondered what would happen if the body totally disintegrated. I'm sure it'll be quite the experience for her."

No shouts outside. No cries of pain. The empress was gone.

The hieromonk smiled triumphantly at the spoon like it was the finest thing he had ever seen. "Ah," he said, holding it like a chalice before him. "It is not until you leave civilisation behind that you realise how much you miss these simple things. A spoon, able to hold all sorts of food within the curve of its bowl, whether it is liquid or solid. Easily held, easily cleaned, easily used. Even the Levanti use them, you know? But the Kisians, who claim to be the pinnacle of culture and knowledge, slurp their soup from the edge of the bowl like animals bending their heads to the stream."

My own soup bowl stood before me, and while my Chiltaen soul had been about to pick up the spoon, it was a Kisian heart that sustained my life. So I picked up the bowl and, flashing him a smile, set my lips to the rim and began to slurp—a long, drawn-out sucking noise like his aforementioned animal was struggling to get the last dregs from the bottom of its trough. Empress Hana would have been horrified, but Empress Hana wasn't here.

The hieromonk scowled into his bowl. I slurped on.

We had travelled well into the night after leaving the empress behind in her dead Swiff-skin. Taking advantage of a brief break in the rains, the hieromonk had ordered we press on toward the Willow Road and lodgings more befitting his position, yet inn after inn had been abandoned or burned to the ground, and it had been midnight before we stopped.

The Kisian innkeeper had greeted the hieromonk and his entourage with popping eyes, and for a horrible moment I had been sure he would turn us away. How could a Chiltaen holy man and his Chiltaen soldiers be welcome when Chiltaens were responsible for so much death and destruction in the north? Yet though the innkeeper drew himself up and refused to bow, his courage had failed at the sight of the armed guards and he had welcomed us in. I had considered begging them for help, but in Empress Hana's body I looked even more Chiltaen than I had in my own. Golden ringlets!

It was a miracle she had been accepted as an empress of Kisia for so long, Otako or no.

While I slurped my soup, leaving behind all the tough shreds of cabbage floating in it, the innkeeper's wife slid the door and bowed, tea tray in hand. I stopped slurping while she served, swirling the pot and pouring the pale golden liquid into first one bowl then the other, in the opposite order to how she had removed them from the tray. The urge to catch her eye and signal for help rose again only to be suppressed. No one would believe me an empress without finery.

"You must be well placed for news here," the hieromonk said.

Whether he interrupted her task deliberately or accidentally, the woman swallowed the insult and said, "Yes, your lordship. Many come this way."

"What news from Koi?"

"Your people still hold the city."

He seemed to want more and waited, but when nothing else was forthcoming the hieromonk said, "And from the capital?"

The woman finished pouring and placed the teapot in the centre of the table. "Nothing from the capital since it was lost, though we will hear fast enough when it is retaken."

"Retaken by whom?"

"By the empress. Our living god."

"Empress Hana?"

The woman had completed her task but stayed kneeling beside the table, the tray upon her lap. She shook her head without looking up. "No, may Qi bless her passing. Empress Miko."

I still held the soup bowl an inch from my lips, and though my arms trembled I kept it there, determined not to draw attention to myself. The hieromonk's bland smile faded. "The last I heard, Empress Miko was dead."

"Oh no," the woman said, and despite her bowed head and humble demeanour, there was strength in her words as she went on: "They may want us to believe that, but the Otakos are gods and our gods will not fail us."

His smile was amused. Pitying. "That is belief, my good woman, not truth."

The woman looked up, her gaze fierce enough to make the hieromonk flinch. "The truth is that she lives. That she is gathering her forces to retake the capital. She will crush those who did this to us and make every Chiltaen and every Levanti sorry they ever stepped across our border."

She lowered her gaze to the tray again, and in the heart-thudding silence that followed I could believe I had imagined the whole, so quietly and humbly did the woman go on kneeling beside our table. No longer able to hold my bowl aloft, I set it down. If only I could make them understand who I was. *Who I wasn't,* She would have said, and berated me for even thinking of putting commonfolk in danger fighting for a fake empress.

The hieromonk's brittle laugh broke the silence. "Ah, the hopeful stories of the downtrodden," he said. "The more hopeless their situation the more grand and embellished the stories become. She will be hailed as an immortal goddess next and defeat her enemies in battle with a spear of sunlight." His mocking gaze rested on the greying hairs atop the woman's bowed head. "If you have no real news to share you may take your stories elsewhere."

The woman's knuckles whitened upon the edge of the tray as she rose. "Your Lordship," she murmured from the doorway, bowing first to the hieromonk and then to me. The door had closed before the hieromonk could do more than work his jaw in anger. And while he glared at the closed door, I slid my dinner knife from the table into my lap.

When he turned back, I picked up my soup bowl, lacking the grace Empress Hana would have achieved with the very same hands. "Are you sure that's wise, Your Holiness?" I said when he lifted a spoonful of soup to his own lips. "I don't think the cook likes you very much."

"If it comes to that, I don't think she likes you very much either," he said, and drank it defiantly. *"May the gods bless your passing."*

———————◆———————

The innkeeper's wife led me to my room, but under the watchful gaze of one of the hieromonk's guards I could say nothing. She pointed out the house's amenities in clipped tones and disappeared before I could be rid of the man, leaving me to help myself out of this mess. As usual.

It took a long time for the inn to grow silent. I had tried propping myself against the wall to keep from sleeping, but this body felt fatigue like I had never known and even sitting I managed to doze off and on, in and out of strange, twisted dreams, until the innkeeper and his wife eventually went to bed. Then the soldiers downstairs stopped talking and moving, stilling to the occasional creak of a floorboard. And then even that stopped.

I slid from the warm covers into the chill of the shabby room, its reeds too damp to crackle beneath my feet. Pausing in the doorway I listened for any sounds before very slowly sliding open the screen. It was dark in the passage, but I had counted the number of steps between my door and the hieromonk's on the way up. I counted it now as I took each carefully, one steadying hand upon the wall, the weight of the dinner knife in the other.

Thirteen and a half steps. I reached out and found one of the door's smooth paper panes pulled taut like the surface of a drum. Spider-like, my hand crept along the frame to the handle, and with even more care than I had taken with my own door, I slid it slowly back. Just far enough to slip through.

Faint trails of lantern light snuck between the shutters to fall upon his sleeping figure, outlined in the gloom. Having waited to be sure he lay still, I crept in, glad of the soundless matting. Easier and easier, though having to end the hieromonk's life with a dinner knife would be as messy as it was memorable.

Marking the rhythm of his breath, I eased out one of my own as I bent an aching knee to the floor and adjusted my grip on the knife. It was far from sharp, so I lifted it to plunge from a height.

The hieromonk's eyes snapped open. His hand leapt, closing around mine so tightly I thought the empress's fragile bones would snap. "Thought you could trick me?" he said, the words like velvet against my ear as he pulled me close. "You thought if you lulled me with your compliance and your illness I would be stupid enough to let you creep in here and kill me. Well, Miss Marius, you're playing with the wrong man if that's a game you want to win. I have survived the political dance too long to be such a fool." He drew out the last word almost lovingly, his lips to my ear and his hot breath sending a shiver through my skin.

"Is this all you've got?" he mocked. "Where's my spitfire?"

His tongue touched my ear and I turned, snapping my teeth in search of something to bite. The hieromonk laughed. "You disappoint me," he said, and rolled, pulling me with him. My shoulder hit the floor and then all his weight was on me, hot and heavy and pressing me into his mat. "I thought you'd fight me. I thought you'd want to kill me more than you wanted to fuck me, but I see the whore wins out every time."

The words sounded crude upon his pious tongue and I tried to buck him off only for him to slam my tailbone into the floor and tear open my robe. His warm hand gripped my breast. Not my breast, Empress Hana's breast. That ought to have made it easier to bear, but it only made it worse. This body was not mine to treat as I wished, not mine to shame. She might have abandoned me, but the thought of him defiling her flesh made me grip his ear and yank it hard, sinking my fingernails deep.

The hieromonk yelped and rolled, dragging me with him. It ought to have been easy. I knew how to snap a man's neck and where to bite for maximum pain, but no matter what I did he swatted me away like an annoying fly, laughing all the time as though enjoying our silent struggle in the darkness, crashing from one side of the floor to the other. I wanted him dead and he ought to be dead, and had I been inside my own body he would have been, but this stupid, weak, broken thing couldn't do what I needed, couldn't maintain pressure without cramping, could not lift his weight without trembling, could neither escape nor finish the task, and the longer we wrangled the more sure I became of how it would end.

A feeble cry of frustration escaped my compressed lips and the hieromonk laughed. "You sound as if you are not enjoying this, my dear," he said, breathless with exertion or excitement or both. "Surely you cannot be sick of your illustrious profession?"

I tried to spit in his face but had barely enough saliva to wet my tongue. "Fuck you," I snarled instead. "Get off me."

"Oh, you're worried about Empress Hana? Don't be, she wasn't called the whore of Koi for nothing." He sat back and, gripping my hips, pulled me to him. "You should know well enough that a woman's only power is between her legs."

"These legs?" Making use of the breathing room he had given me, I hooked one leg then the other over his shoulders, squeezing his neck. Like all men who had never had to fight for their lives, he tried to pull back, but with my feet linked at the ankles, I drew him down with every ounce of strength I could find in these weak limbs. He flailed, hitting me wherever he could and hissing like a snake, but I gripped my shin and pulled it to me, crushing his throat. The hieromonk thrashed. He twisted. He tried to pull free. If I could just hold on, if my fingers had more strength, if their knuckles didn't scream with agony as I tightened my hold... But no matter what I did pain flickered its darkness across my vision and I trembled and cramped, and wrenching back hard he slipped red-faced from my grip, sucking rattling breaths.

A blade appeared at his throat. It did not threaten, did not pause, just dug hard into his flesh and in one graceful movement slid across his neck. Blood poured in its wake. The hieromonk's struggling breaths grew wet and he clawed uselessly at his throat, hands slick. For a few horrible moments he loomed over me, gasping for a breath that would never come, swallowing convulsively to stem blood that would never stop, and then like a falling tree he gave in to a force greater than his own and fell. Unable to roll out of the way I braced for his weight, but the body was lowered gently onto the reeds beside me. And there, blade in hand and a disgusted sneer upon his lips, stood Swiff.

"Where the fuck have you been?" I said.

"Trying to catch up," the empress snapped with the dead man's lips. "These dead bodies don't tire, but it still takes a long time to run the same distance as a carriage. I had to stop and ask after you at every inn too, and dissuade everyone from sending for a physician. And the guards were looking for me. Idiots."

The gashes in Swiff's neck had dried but did not look any better for it. His face was pale too, and when the empress crossed the room to light a lantern his gait was stiff. The fingers must have worked though, for light soon flared and its sudden brightness brought horrors forth from the night. The hieromonk lay face down in a pool of blood, soaking into the matting as it spread, staining one side of his face and swallowing his silver pendant. His dead body didn't call to me, and without the song's tugging insistence I found something even more terrible. Swiff's feet. Empress Hana had removed his boots, but his ankles were so swollen and dark that he looked to still be wearing them.

"Oh yes. Running with these slabs of meat was no easy thing," the empress said in the dead guard's low voice. "I wasn't worried. I thought if there's someone who can handle herself it's the famous Miss Marius." She looked meaningfully from the dead hieromonk to my open robe. "It looks like I was wrong."

"I can take care of myself just fine," I said, pulling the robe to cover a revealed breast.

"You didn't appear to have the situation well in hand. And those are my breasts you're covering, so don't bother. I've seen them before."

I could have done without her body's propensity for flushing red in angry embarrassment. It did so now, causing a smirk to twist Swiff's lips—a smirk I could have borne better had I not known it was the empress making it. "I could have killed him a dozen times if your body hadn't been so weak."

A heavy silence fell, and I stared at the fallen hieromonk. I ought to have been glad he was dead, glad of the revenge and the freedom that were now ours, and yet the sight of his body upon the floor sank an anxious stone in my stomach. He had taken too many secrets with him. Had left too much unknown.

"If we leave now, we can put a lot of distance between us and here before anyone finds him," I said at last, though the prospect of travelling again so soon made my already aching body protest. "Kaysa has kept going north. She'll have to stop sometime and if we keep going, we can catch up and—"

"No."

"No?"

Swiff crossed his arms, and with the empress's scowl upon his face he looked more ferocious in death than he ever had in life. She pointed his finger at the dead hieromonk. "We have an opportunity. That's not just any dead body, that's the hieromonk of Chiltae. Think of all the things we could do with that."

"What happened to just wanting to be rid of me so you could die in peace?"

The empress didn't answer, but she didn't need to. For a dead man there was fire in Swiff's eyes.

"You heard about Miko."

Still no answer.

"Even if the stories are true and she's still alive, what can masquerading as the hieromonk for a day achieve? Don't fool yourself it can be longer. You're starting to look stiff in that body already."

"We are less than a day's hasty journey from Koi."

"That still doesn't answer my question."

I wanted to lie down upon my mat and let sleep carry me away, but the empress stepped forward in her Swiff-skin and pointed at the hieromonk. "This man is all that's left of the Chiltaen command this side of the border. Koi is his city now. The Chiltaen soldiers left there are his to command. There are hundreds of ways we could make use of them, of him, and there will never be an easier way to get inside the castle."

I closed my eyes. "Getting inside is one thing, how about getting out again? This is the only body we have and once you have to abandon his, how does Empress Hana of Kisia just walk back out?"

"Why walk out at all? I have made many deals with the Chiltaens in my time and now we have a common enemy. If there was ever a time to forge an alliance it is now."

When I didn't answer she began to pace across the matting with her blood-swollen feet. "I have many allies in the north, people who will fight when an Otako calls, and with them and my knowledge of Kisia, a combined Kisian and Chiltaen army could destroy the Levanti before they take root. Especially with winter on the way. I doubt they're used to snow as we are."

"After the Chiltaens conquered half your empire you want to be friends?"

"I will do whatever it takes, Miss Marius, to help my daughter. I made a promise and I don't intend to break it now."

I was too tired to argue. In my own body I might have shouted her down, but all I wanted to do was sleep. Perhaps in the morning I would be able to make her see reason. "Why would the Chilt-aens even want to fight with you?" I said, making one last attempt at carrying my point. "They have their own borders to defend. They've lost too many soldiers to waste more clearing Levanti from your lands."

"Kisia today, Chiltae tomorrow. Having seen what they are capable of, what makes you think this Levanti emperor will stop at ruling half of Kisia? The south is still whole and strong so why push that way when it's much easier to head north and take a weak-ened Chiltae? All he needs are some strong allies desirous of seeing Chiltae destroyed and he could be done within the year, and then take his time squeezing the south when it suits him."

"Perhaps you should go and make a deal with the Levanti emperor instead; you seem to have his plans all worked out for him."

Silence reigned for a few long minutes, nothing but gentle night sounds to invade our lantern-lit sanctuary. Servants would come with the sun, but until then we were alone with the dead.

"Have you ever felt loyalty, Miss Marius?" Empress Hana asked eventually. "Do you feel it toward your country? Your people? Your family? Your...sister whores?"

"You may call it loyalty, but it sounds like another form of ser-vitude to me," I said. "To be loyal to Chiltae is to give my life for it and get nothing in return. You can persuade fools into think-ing that's honourable, that their sacrifice means something for the greater good, but what are they really dying for? Chiltae isn't a per-son. It's not a thing. It's just the name of a place."

"It's an idea."

"That's even worse. Die for an idea?"

She folded her arms, bulging Swiff's muscles to look intimi-dating. Weak little Empress Hana was enjoying the strength and freedom of a dead skin all too much. "What is justice if not an idea?" she said. "What is freedom if not an idea? What is culture if not an idea? If you do not fight for it then someone can take it from you. Can take your way of life. Your freedom. Are those things not worth fighting for?"

"Worth fighting for? Perhaps. Not worth dying for. If you want to travel to Koi in the hieromonk's body then you can go on your own. I don't want any more part in this. I just want to get my body back and get out of here. But right now, I'm going back to my room to sleep." I gestured at the hieromonk's body and staggered to my feet, almost falling. "You can explain all this to his guards."

She was there, the arm of the dead guard held out to catch me. His skin was cold. "Let me help you to your mat," she said, the deep rasp of his disintegrating voice oddly kind.

I let her help me back to my room and the blessed comfort of my sleeping mat, and I lay down while she moved about the space on those swollen feet. I listened until fatigue drowned even the wracking pains and I fell asleep. But it was not an easy sleep; too often was I roused by little sounds like the swish of fabric, the clink of buckles, and a deep, musical humming. Lantern light flickered around me whenever I stirred. One time I rolled over to find Swiff sitting over a chamber pot, knife in hand, letting the blood from his swollen feet run into the bowl.

"Just testing," he said. "Didn't dare to on the way in case they stopped working."

The dead guard went on humming as his blood trickled out like thick, clumpy soup.

Later the touch of his skin was cold and Empress Hana pressed close, her soul a flitting presence full of determination and shame and grief. Always grief.

Touch him, quick—we're running out of time.

More voices joined the myriad of waking dreams as the night

wore on. More footsteps. I opened my eyes a second time to see the innkeeper and another man, both in their night robes, struggling to carry out the now limp and lifeless form of Swiff. But even as I parted my lips to call them back, to beg they not take him away, the hieromonk appeared and set a heavy hand upon my forehead. "Back to sleep," he said with a grim smile. "Everything is all right, they are taking the assassin away."

Voices whispered on. Water sloshed. Silence did not come until dawn when at last I found something deeper than a doze, though dreams continued to trouble me. I dreamed of walking through the pale dawn, of a wind that whipped rain into my face and bit deep into my bones, chilling them until I felt they would never be warm again. I dreamed of aching legs and doubt. Of freedom and loneliness. But more than anything I dreamed of walking. Always walking. Pressing on toward a horizon yet often looking back like a leaf caught in a current that tugged in both directions, forming an eddy from which I could never escape.

Kaysa?

I was sitting huddled beneath a blanket that stank of horse and damp, watching the sun rise. A cold wind battered my face, blowing loose strands of hair. I kept pushing them back behind my ear only for them to be swept forward again, forcing me to peel them off my lips. It was frustrating, but somehow...glorious, even the dullest sensation something to be revelled in for its novelty. Its richness.

So much to see. So much to do. I would forget Cassandra soon enough, I thought, but anger tore through me at the very sound of my name, the feeling bitter and sharp and twisting. So much she had stolen from me. So much time. So much hope. So much life.

Kaysa?

I woke to the sound of still more rain. Rain and the thunder of horses' hooves and carriage wheels flying fast along a road. A real road, not the pitted dirt tracks we had travelled of late. Every limb ached and memories filled my mind like a half-formed nightmare, yet I forced open heavy, itchy eyes.

The hieromonk of Chiltae stared at me from the opposite seat, something like his usual mild smile dawning in response to my confusion.

"Good morning, Miss Marius," he said, and it was his voice, even down to the mocking drawl. Had I imagined it all? Surely Empress Hana could not manage so fine an impersonation of him, even using his skin. A cloak covered his throat, but his eyes were bright and there was colour in his cheeks—neither normal for a corpse.

I didn't answer, but when I tried to push myself up to face him, a chain clanked between my wrists and I could not part them. "What—?"

"Sorry about that," he said. "But you made it very clear last night you wouldn't come with me, and as I need my body, I can't let you walk away with it. You really left me no choice." The hieromonk set a finger to his chin in mock contemplation. "I never thought I would live to be grateful for my debilitating disease. How pleasant it is to be wrong."

"You fucking bitch," I said. "After all that grand talk about loyalty and freedom you tie me up and drag me along just so you can be revenged on the people who took your city?"

"*You* took my city from me," the empress said, her words peeling the hieromonk's lips back from his teeth in an ugly look. "*You* are the reason Koi fell. *You* are the reason I no longer have my body. So you're damn right I'm going to drag you along, but not for vengeance—for duty. For my daughter. Because if I'm going to die, I want to die knowing I did everything I could to protect Kisia, to protect our way of life, to protect her." She made a gesture that was all too like flicking hair out of her face, though the hieromonk's was too short to get in the way. "Really, I'm only taking my own body by force; the fact that you're squatting in it is none of my concern."

"I can kill someone with my hands tied, you know."

"No doubt you can, Miss Marius, but can you kill a body that's already dead? It seems unlikely. We have a few hours until we arrive, however, so you're welcome to try it to pass the time." She pointed to the colour on her cheeks. "Just don't mess up my paint."

21. MIKO

The young man stared at me from the corner of the cart. A roughly erected awning protected us from the storm, but the wind still blew rain beneath it, and from its drooping centre a steady stream of drips thudded onto the wooden boards. He didn't seem to notice. I had considered shuffling out into the rain to put more distance between us, an option that was still open.

Everything from his fair hair to the straight lines of his features marked the young man as Chiltaen, but what was a Chiltaen priest even doing this side of the Tzitzi River? Chains linked his hands as they linked mine, but he looked too well treated to be a common prisoner picked up by the same patrol.

Despite his unblinking stare, he didn't seem to know I was present. It was the stare of someone whose thoughts were elsewhere, only the clenching and unclenching of his jaw proving he was even alive.

The cart bumped on along the rutted track, flanked by soldiers. I had tried asking where we were going, had tried asking them to loosen the chains cutting into my wrists, had even tried asking who the unresponsive young man was. They had ignored me and on we rolled toward a meeting I couldn't but dread. Wherever they were taking me, I knew to whom.

Jie.

"He is calling himself Emperor Kin Ts'ai, second of his name."

It took me a moment to realise the young man had spoken, so little had his expression changed. "Pardon?"

"I said he is now calling himself Emperor Kin Ts'ai, second of his name, not Jie. It was his grandfather's idea"—I scoffed, but the young man went on—"because what general wants to fight for an unknown and untested boy?"

He winced at the end of his own words and clenched his jaw tight.

Had it really been so obvious I'd been worried about where they were taking me? Had I said Jie's name aloud?

I narrowed my eyes, taking in his pretty features and tousled hair. "Who are you?"

Still seeming to focus through me rather than on me, he said, "Miko Ts'ai, daughter of Empress Hana and Katashi Otako, born in the spring of—"

"I know who *I* am," I snapped, though my heart thudded at the sound of my true father's name. "I asked who you are."

Another wince. He blinked rapidly, trying to focus. "Miko? Oh!" He laughed, a chuckle that ended in a gasp of pain despite no sign of injury. "How amusingly does God play his pieces upon the board. Miko Ts'ai. Well, well, you sure have shown up at just the right time."

"Shown up?" I jangled my chains. "I was captured on the road, I didn't just wander in."

"Yes, sorry about that, but I really had no choice. Events are moving much faster than I expected."

I stared at his distant yet increasingly euphoric smile. "No choice? What in all the hells are you talking about? Who are you?"

"Leo. Leo Villius."

Dom Leo Villius. The man my mother had planned for me to marry, I the price for a Chiltaen army to support Tanaka's claim. I parted my lips only to close them again, my heart beating uncomfortably fast. Tanaka had brought Leo Villius's body back as a trophy. It had lain beside his in the shrine, but it had looked nothing like the young man now staring at me from the other side of the cart.

Silence stretched away before us, broken only by the endless thud of rain dripping from the saggy awning. A wheel splashed into a pothole, jolting the cart roughly side to side. "It was my bodyguard your brother caught and killed," he said at last, making no attempt to hold on though the cart rocked dangerously. "Even so I was sorry to hear what happened to him. Your brother. Such an awful loss for your family."

I could only swallow the lump that rose in my throat and acknowledge his kind words with a nod. Leo Villius seemed to have lost his strange abstraction, but went on clenching and unclenching his jaw and hands with rhythmic precision.

"And sadly," he said when I didn't speak, "by the time I reached Koi on foot it was too late. We might still have salvaged things, at least I like to hope we could have, but—" He shrugged and made a hopeless little gesture with his bound hands. "I think we have come too far for political marriage to make any difference now, don't you?"

I had to agree, but no words could find their way past the lump solidifying in my throat, formed as much by anger as sadness and guilt. Whatever his kind professions of peace, Dom Leo Villius had been on the battlefield at Risian—not the act of a repentant priest.

He flicked his straw-coloured hair out of his face with a toss of his head and peered out at the rain.

"I cannot imagine worse weather to fight in," he said after a time as the cart bumped us along the increasingly muddy road. "But Emperor Jie—I mean Emperor Kin, second of his name, hasn't got a choice. If he cannot prove to his generals he can retake the city they will find a new leader." He looked at me as though pleasantly surprised to find me there. "Oh, look! A new leader. What good timing you have, showing up in our hour of need."

"I am no threat to anyone's leadership in the south."

"No? Morale has been low since the city fell. The generals argue amongst themselves. Some want to retake Kisia, others think they should just hold the border. Some want to follow Jie, others scoff at him for a child. Lord Oyamada is not well enough liked and neither are the boy's attempts to make a leader of himself, to play the emperor when all the generals really want is a puppet that does what he's told."

"How do you know this? And why are you telling me?"

"Knowledge is important. How can you do what is right in the eyes of God without it?"

"What do I care what your God wants? And even if I did, is there really a right and wrong anymore?"

The Chiltaen priest shrugged a shoulder clad in the pale linen of his calling. "That depends what you want. There is nothing like war for turning people on one another."

I did not want to agree. I wanted to tell him that in the face of adversity the Kisian people would come together, would fight together for our land and our freedom, but no sooner had the anger leapt to my tongue than it was ambushed by the memory of Grace Bahain's defection. Of how I had barely escaped Koi alive in the wake of my mother's rage. Of how I had turned on Jie, had tricked him, pushed him aside and stolen the throne from under him because I believed it was mine, believed I could do a better job of fighting for Kisia than he ever could.

"Don't worry," Leo said, once more turning his beatific smile upon me. "Whatever happens, in the end there is always God."

———————◆———————

The tent stood alone upon the hilltop, its crimson flag snapping in the ferocious wind. Soldiers marked the edge of the small clearing, sunlight glimmering upon their damp storm cloaks. I could not see their faces, yet I stood proud beneath their stares despite my dirty, sodden robe, and counted them out of habit. Twenty I could see, which probably meant thirty in total. Hardly an army. A secret meeting in the last of the daylight, these few men the only ones who could tell this story to the pages of history. If there was anything worth the telling.

I climbed down from the cart, my bound hands stealing even the semblance of grace. Dom Leo Villius followed, seemingly at ease, yet this was Kisian land surrounded by Kisian soldiers, and the Kisian tent flew the flag of the Ts'ai dragon. Fear crept its chill into my bones. We had parted well, Jie and I; it was what had come after that changed everything.

I made no move toward the tent until a soldier gripped my arm. Without him I might never have approached, preferring the unknown. I had been wrong about the Bahains, and without Manshin, without Rah, without even Shishi at my side, I was utterly alone. The Chiltaen at my back did not count as a comfort. He had spent the remainder of the journey alternately wincing and humming a dirge.

Golden light spilled through the fluttering gap in the tent as we approached, along with the murmur of voices. My guard cleared his throat. "Your Majesty, we have—"

"Bring her in."

The guard snapped his mouth shut with a clack of teeth and, still gripping my arm, pushed me before him. I wanted to dig my feet in like a child, to lean back against him and shout that I would not go and he could not make me, but such a show would have been beneath me. Wear the mask. Live the mask. Be the mask. If mother had taught me nothing else she had taught me how to hide my thoughts and my fears behind cold pride.

With no one to hold the curtain aside I was pushed through it, able only to sense a dry, empty space before my captor shifted his hand to my shoulder, buckling my unsuspecting knees. They dropped hard onto worn, spiky matting.

"We found her on the river road near Mei'lian. Exactly where the priest said she would be," my captor said, ignoring what sounded like a satisfied little grunt from Leo behind us to add, "In the company of a Levanti."

"Just one?" came a familiar voice though its tone was harsher. Surer. I looked up and my gaze climbed the length of Jie's fine imperial robes all the way to a face as youthful as I remembered. Jie had not had time to age greatly since our last meeting, but it was a different boy who stared back now. Perhaps he would think the same of me. Perhaps he wouldn't care.

"Just one, Your Majesty," the soldier said. "A runaway by the look of him. He didn't even have a horse."

Jie huffed out a little burst of air. "Anything else?"

"No, Your Majesty."

"Then you may let Dom Villius go," Jie said. "He upheld his end of our bargain."

A moment of silence followed, not long enough to be an objection but just long enough for the soldier at my back to register disapproval. Long enough that Emperor Jie Ts'ai inclined his head regally, challenging him to utter a complaint. The soldier did not and chains clinked behind me, followed by a shuffle of steps and Dom Villius's voice. "It was a pleasure to be of assistance to you, Your Majesty. May God guide your steps."

And with a brief flurry of footsteps and silk curtains, the young priest and the soldier were gone.

"I told you not to let him go," said Lord Oyamada. The boy's grandfather and regent hovered behind him, the closest thing the tent owned to a piece of furniture. It seemed they had come in a hurry, bringing nothing but themselves and a silk cage with which to hide this meeting from the world. "Now they will all think you're weak."

"Better weak than someone who lies and cheats and reneges on their agreements."

Silence followed. Silence and the unblinking stare of Kin's bastard heir. I stared back, determined not to look away, not to admit the shame his rebuke wrought.

"Princess Miko," the boy said at last.

"Prince Jie," I countered, watching for a flicker of a smile that never came. If anything he pressed his lips into an even thinner line, and for the first time I could see Emperor Kin's blood come to the fore. His stubborn chin jutted the same way, and while he didn't have the same flare of anger in his eyes yet, there was time enough for him to discover what a driving force hatred could be, like his father before him and my father before me.

Lord Oyamada stepped forward. "That's Emperor Kin, second of his name," he snapped. "And you will bow and grant the proper obeisance."

"No," I said. "I will not." The man began to bluster his outrage but I spoke over him. "I will not besmirch my honour by professing a loyalty I do not feel nor offer obeisance to an emperor I cannot fight for."

My words might have been fists, so stunned they left both men. Jie recovered first. Throwing away the mantle of the adult, he glared sullenly at me like the child I remembered. "You did not seem to mind lying to me before. It was very clever of you to trick me into leaving so you could steal my throne. How long had my father been dead? Did you never think I might want to see him before—"

"He was dead before you arrived, and if I had not taken your throne Grace Bachita would have. In your name he would have abandoned half the empire without a fight."

"Instead of abandoning it after a fight that lost us how many soldiers?"

"At least I *tried*. He would have had us run like children."

"So you put an arrow through his head?"

"Yes! And I would do it again."

I had intended calm. If Jie had too, then we had both failed. He no longer stood straight but bent over to spit his anger in my face, while I bared teeth used to being tucked away behind a false smile. Wear the mask. Live the mask. Be the mask.

I let go a held breath. "This is not helpful," I said. "Kisia is in danger of being crushed altogether and we are fighting like—"

"Like children?" The boy bristled. "I do not deem it childish to be angry at the murder of my uncle and regent at your hand."

I prepared to throw his father's crimes in his face, to paint for him the scene in Koi's throne room where Emperor Kin had ordered my brother's immediate execution, but though anger shivered through my skin I said none of it. Tanaka and I had always said that Emperor Kin and our mother had weakened Kisia with their hateful division, however earned that hate had been. We had shaken our heads over it and vowed we would be better, that under our rule Kisia would not be so weakened, so divided. And now here I was reading from the same script that had seen the empire break.

Leo Villius had been right.

A slow, deep breath calmed an anger fast turning to disgust. "We have to be better than this, Jie," I said, and would have reached out placating hands had they not been tied so tightly. "If we do not unite Kisia to fight as one then we may as well hand the whole thing to the Levanti emperor right now."

"Unite Kisia?" Lord Oyamada said, lifting his voice to join the conversation with a bold step forward. "The north is gone and the south is already united behind their emperor. You stole the throne and lost it. You will never be allowed to do so again."

"The north is only lost if we let it be lost! Grace Bahain has seen value in using the Levanti for his own ends, but those who support him in fighting for the Levanti emperor only do so because they have no other choice. Or because when offered the choice between fighting for a foreign emperor or a Ts'ai they chose the barbarians."

"Then they are traitors."

"No, they do what they think is best for their families and the people who work and live on their lands. Emperor Kin crippled anyone openly supportive of the Otako claim. What reason have they to think you will be different?"

The boy's jaw dropped. "The Levanti attacked us!"

"No, the Chiltaens attacked us. Bahain and the Levanti just took advantage of us both."

Jie turned away to pace a few steps back and forth, clearly troubled, but Lord Oyamada stayed where he was and curled his thin lip. "Defending traitors and barbarian invaders now?"

"Merely pointing out the truth, Lord Oyamada."

The man leaned in to growl, "The truth is that you are a manipulative Otako bitch who will say anything to get her way. We underestimated you once, but not again. Jie is lord of Kisia now, and—"

"Half of Kisia."

"—he doesn't need a snake like you—"

"The half that freezes over in winter and is cut off from almost all trade routes."

"—hissing in his ear, waiting for your moment to kill him as you killed—"

"How long do you think the food stores will last?" I said, speaking to the pacing Jie while his regent kept railing.

"—Grace Bachita. The best Otako is a dead Otako; Emperor Kin—"

"And should you survive the winter, you will have to choose

what is more important to protect, your rice fields or your fishing villages, your people or your capital, all the while knowing you will go down in history as the emperor who let the Levanti keep half your empire."

"—knew what he was doing when—"

Jie rounded on us both. "And what would you have me do? I can defend this border, I cannot beat the Levanti in open battle, especially not with all of Grace Bahain's military might behind them. You proved that at Risian and I am in no hurry to repeat your mistake."

"I would have you *fight!* I would have you make peace not with your conquerors but with me. Together we could—"

"Together?" Oyamada scoffed. "Together indeed. Are you proposing an alliance?"

"There is no other way."

The older man sneered, once more stepping in front of his grandson, emperor or no. "No doubt you understand it is traditional in such cases for each party to bring something to the negotiating table. We have soldiers and land and coin and food and an emperor with the loyalty of his people. What do you bring but a tarnished name that has no value here?"

It was like listening to my mother. So many years of hearing her speak ill of the Ts'ai, of Emperor Kin's birth and his allies. The Usurper, they had called him, the general who would be emperor. Yet the common people had loved him. Had fought for him. Had believed until the last moment he would defend them from the conquering Chiltaens. How different things might have been had Kisia's emperor and empress been able to set aside their differences and work together. I did not want to marry, did not want to walk the road of sacrificial duty my mother had fallen from, but we could still do this together. As brother and sister, as Tanaka and I had once planned. We had to. We had run out of other choices.

Hands still bound, I got to my feet. "You forget that I am both Otako and Ts'ai," I said, glad for once for my extra height. "That I am descended from the true line going back as far as our history recalls, and even to your southern generals that means something. Emperor Kin Ts'ai, first of his name. Emperor Tianto Otako, fourth of his name. Emperor Lan Otako, third of his name. Emperor Yamato Otako. Emperor Tsubasa Otako. Remember? How many of those are Ts'ai? You want to take Kisia back, you need me. I failed at Risian and you might fail here, but we can do it *together*."

"We need no overgrown bastard girl born of a traitor," Lord Oyamada spat. "If Jie announced you his bride he would—"

"I did not offer myself as a bride," I said, anger flaring again as the man looked at me like I was a bug. "I offer an alliance."

Jie turned away, cheeks reddening. Lord Oyamada started to laugh. "An alliance," he said. "Not marriage, just an alliance, as nebulous as it is dangerous. What is it you propose? Two emperors? Rule half the empire each? And when you marry another, we hand the throne to someone else again? No. I cannot believe we are even having this conversation. Emperor Kin was emperor of Kisia for over thirty years. His people loved him. His chosen heir is before you, and you stand there speaking of alliances when you should be bowing at his feet, pleading for your life and offering to serve him in whatever way is required of you."

"I will not dishonour myself with pleas. My life is nothing to the empire's survival. If my death could save Kisia then I would go to the headsman with pride."

Lord Oyamada snorted. "A fine speech. Your death would end the division of loyalty once and for all and if that is not enough reason then it is not really Kisia you care about."

"I have already explained my death would not achieve that. If the Levanti emperor treats them well the northern families will go on following him and Bahain before another Ts'ai. Especially a Ts'ai *child*. I will not die for that when from a position of greater power I could lure back their allegiance."

"You will go to the headsman whether you like it or not, you manipulative shrew."

"Jie," I said, looking past the fuming lord to the young boy in a grown man's clothes. "You are listening to the wrong people. You have lived out of the world too long, learning from books. Take guidance not from those who would burn Kisia to see the Otakos die, nor from those who would cheat you for their own power, but from—"

"Someone who has already betrayed me once?" Jie said, turning a look of hurt upon me. "Someone I chose to trust against the better judgement of my guardians?"

His words left me momentarily speechless. So long ago it all seemed. For me, perhaps. Not for him. "I had no choice, Jie," I said. "I would not abandon half of the empire then and I will not do it now. No child can—"

"*No child can lead Kisia in battle. No child can rule in a time of war.* Yes, so I have been told. My councillors may not say so to my face, but I am not stupid. But tell me, *sister*, how many times have you been told you cannot rule because you were born a girl?"

My mouth opened and there it stayed, devoid of words, my heart aching with the truth his question conjured. Fierce anger blazed in his eyes. "You did not even let me *try!*" he went on, brushing away an angry tear. "You did not seek to help me. You did not offer support. You just got rid of me like the annoying little boy I am and stole my throne, my title, my empire, all so you could ride out to a glorious battle. All so you could prove a woman could do it too."

Jie turned away, crimson robes sweeping upon the old matting. "I am finished here."

"I will send for Moto," Oyamada began. "He can perform the exe—"

"No," Jie said, and the triumphant glee slid from Lord Oyamada's face. "No, we will take her back to camp. Whatever else they might say of my reign it will not be that I was dishonourable. Whatever my feelings on the matter, Princess Miko is owed a proper execution. One that everyone can see, putting all rumours to rest."

A shadow of the triumphant smile returned to Lord Oyamada's face. "Wise, Your Majesty."

"Jie," I began. "I—"

"That's Emperor Kin, or Your Majesty," the boy snapped, rage seeming to have overwhelmed his hurt. "And I said we were finished here. You have nothing to say I wish to hear. We will return to the main camp tonight and in the morning you will be executed properly as befits your rank and birth. And then I will have achieved something even my father was not able to—the ultimate destruction of the Otako line, once and for all."

22. DISHIVA

Tafa had chosen well. Too well, perhaps, considering my growing doubts about the deserters. Apart from herself she had chosen Baln and Kehta en'Oht, two of the longest serving of Yiss's Swords that had become mine to serve their emperor; Yafeu en'Injit and Jakan e'Qara, both men who had also left their herds to join mine; and four Jarovens—Moshe, Esi, Shenyah, and Loklan.

Unsure of our mission, I watched them all now, watched who they rode with and who they spoke to, sketching alliances in my mind.

Once we had reached the caves, Jass had told me everything he knew about the deserters, yet I felt vulnerable armed with his knowledge but not his presence. He had suffered for me. He had helped me haul a broken and bound Leo through miles of cellars and caves and storm-lashed mountainside. Then he had stayed behind because someone had to keep Leo alive.

By the time I had returned through the underground caves that connected the manor to the mountains it had been almost dawn. Lady Sichi had cleaned my room as best she could but the smell of blood and vomit lingered everywhere. I'd been desperately in need of sleep but there had only been time to wash before meeting my Swords at the dawn meal.

Itaghai had done all the work that first day, leaving me to doze in the saddle.

Our camp had been tense and quiet that night, a feeling that carried into the second day and hadn't abated by the time I led my nine Swords off the road at a shrine with chains hanging from its eaves, exactly as Jass had described, trusting me without demanding to know the specifics of the mission. As I had been determined to trust Lashak, so had he been determined to trust me. Trust, the ultimate resistance to fear, and all we had left.

Jass had given me very precise directions and had made me repeat the landmarks to look out for over and over. *Shrine. Fork. Carved tree. Large boulder in a pool of swamp water.* The deserters hadn't been able to go too deep into the swamp, he had said, what with the rains swelling every puddle to a lake, but half a day's ride from the road kept them safe from travellers and soldiers alike. When I had asked him why there and what they were doing, he had merely flicked a glance at the trussed-up Leo and shrugged, weary. "Being Levanti."

We followed the track, and the deeper into the sodden forest we rode the darker it became, the trees seeming to close in around us like wary enemies. No one spoke above a mutter, but every word was a complaint about the sticky, close air, the smell, or the incessant swarms of mosquitoes that followed us everywhere.

Shrine. Fork. Carved tree. Large boulder in a pool of swamp water. We turned right at the fork and headed downhill at the carved tree. Fixated on our destination, I didn't notice Loklan edge his horse alongside mine on the muddy track. "We ought to make camp soon, Captain," he whispered, making me jump. "It's heavy going in this muck and the horses need resting." He pointed at the crack of sky visible through the drooping canopy. "It'll be dark soon."

Glad to put off deciding the fate of the deserters until morning, I called a halt over my shoulder. There was none of the grumbling I expected. My nine Swords just went quietly about their tasks, the silent acquiescence oddly troubling. Baln and Kehta hunted out an open space between two large trees, and while they yanked out small shrubs and cleared the area of rocks, Moshe began a circuit to check the surrounds. Shenyah, the only Jaroven to have been Made in exile, helped Loklan check the horses, Jakan went for firewood, and Esi and Tafa searched for fresh water, chatting together in a way that threw doubt on my assessment of their loyalties. Only Yafeu hung back, staring belligerently at me. Having already dismounted, there was only so long I could avoid him.

"Yes, Yafeu?" I said, summoning fortitude with a deep breath.

"We should...scout out the deserter camp, Captain."

It was nice to be proved right about one of them at least. "And risk warning them of our presence?" I said to be sure, an utterance he met with a heavier scowl. "No, I don't think that is wise, but if it eases your fears, I plan to talk to them before making any...rash decisions."

His glare softened. "It does, Captain. I do not...I do not think we should..." He let the words trail away and glanced around in an all too suspicious manner. "Some of the others are talking of setting up an ambush. Or attacking them in the night."

"Do others here share your...disinclination for this?"

"Esi, I think," he said, lowering his voice. "She told me about how the God's child drew his blade on her. She thinks he has too much influence with Gideon and that it's he who wants this, not our herd master."

I left my own story about Leo untold. "He does," I agreed. "Loklan will stand with me regardless; Shenyah too, I believe."

"Yes, but Baln is the emperor's man. And Moshe. The Oht are very loyal to Gideon and I fear they will—"

"No," I interrupted loudly as Baln and Kehta returned across the clearing. "I think we'll need the Kisian tents tonight, as much as I detest them. Just set them up in the standard formation so the horses aren't confused."

To his credit, Yafeu pressed his fists into a salute with a "Yes, Captain," and took the tightly rolled tent from the back of Itaghai's saddle.

"I'll help you," Baln said as he approached. "Kehta says she doesn't want my company out hunting because I make too much noise."

"Well, you do," the young woman said, throwing him a dirty look. "What good hunter can't stop singing?"

"The best hunter."

She scoffed and, with a nod to me, took her bow from her saddle and strode back across the clearing.

"She's very good, Captain," Baln said, perhaps misinterpreting my scowl. "Best hunter the Oht have seen in a long time, at least since we got so keen on sticking around the coast and fishing." He laughed. "If there's any game to eat around here she'll find it."

I forced a smile. I had asked Tafa to choose Swords who would not blink at anything I asked them to do in Gideon's name, but the more I doubted our mission the more I doubted them. And now knowing I wasn't alone in my doubt only made it harder still.

———◆———

The fragile peace lasted until morning. Or rather until I announced I would first go alone to talk to the deserters.

"But—" Baln en'Oht spluttered, seeming at a momentary loss for words. "But there are only ten of us to the gods only know how many of them, Captain. This was only ever going to work because we are better supplied and can catch them unawares. If you go down there, you'll give our presence away and we'll be outnumbered."

"My orders were to deal with the deserter threat," I said. "And if there's a way to do that without killing them, I'll take it. Right now, we need as many capable Swords as we can get. Gi—His Majesty won't thank us for leaving him less Levanti, but if any of you think otherwise then now is the time to challenge me."

I glared at them. They all wore different degrees of scowl, but none met my gaze over the cold coals. Except for Baln. Our eyes held for a long, tense moment, before I lifted my brows. "Well? Anyone?"

"No, Captain," Yafeu said, followed quickly by Shenyah, no sign of her youth in her face as she stared around at her fellow Swords in a challenge of her own.

Loklan hastily shook his head, and though all the Oht hesitated, when Baln didn't challenge, Tafa and Kehta both muttered their refusal. Moshe was an old Jaroven I'd inherited with the Third Swords, but he had never been the most respectful of warriors and I held my breath awaiting his decision—an eventual refusal. The rest followed in short succession. The captaincy was still mine, but by the hammering of my heart I knew how close it had come.

"All right," I said. "It will take most of the morning to get there and back, but with luck and some quick talking they may surrender to Gideon without anyone having to die. If they believe I am a lone envoy we can still mount a surprise attack if all does not go well."

"And if they kill you?" Jakan asked, crushing an errant coal beneath her boot.

"If I am not back by nightfall, then in the absence of Keka, Loklan takes charge." I caught his look of wide-eyed horror and wished I could have spared him the responsibility. He was a good horse master, good enough to one day be a herd master, if Baln didn't slit his throat in a challenge first. Had I been able to name another tracker then Loklan would have been spared, but Khem still Resided, his soul trapped with his body, and could not be set aside without a horse whisperer's intervention. "Loklan is also in charge until I get back."

They all saluted, even Moshe and Baln once I glared at them. It seemed I had to be quick and successful or this mission would go to the hells faster than a Sword caught dozing on their watch.

Having left instructions to hunt in case I returned with many more mouths to feed, I checked Itaghai's bridle, double-checked his saddle, and triple-checked the holy book was still in my saddlebag before setting off deeper into the fen. *Shrine. Fork. Carved tree. Large boulder in a pool of swamp water.* We had passed all but the large boulder the day before, beyond which Jass had said I would find the deserter camp backed into a steep ridge. *Follow the track,* he had said, *even though it seems to lead you in circles.* It did, but I trusted him and urged Itaghai on through the mud and the drizzle, making him nervous with how often I twisted in the saddle to peer back the way I had come. But only Baln's gaze seemed to follow, his almost-challenge nipping at the heels of my confidence. He hadn't been wrong in all he said. Neither had Gideon. Yet neither had Yafeu or Jass. There was truth all around, yet I could see no path through the mire.

"Stop!"

Gripping a sword hilt, I searched for the source of the voice. It wasn't hard to find, for the young man perched upon a branch above the path was making no effort to disguise himself. Everything about him was Levanti from the colour of his skin to the shape of his features, yet his clothing had the cut of a Kisian soldier and his hair hung long and loose. Despite his aggressive shout, he made no move toward a weapon, instead tilting his head in a way that reminded me all too much of Rah in moments of confusion.

"Who are you?" he called down. "You look familiar."

"My name is Captain Dishiva e'Jaroven, commander of Emperor Gideon's Imperial Guard."

It might have been wiser to leave the last part unsaid, for the boy's face went from a dawning smile of recognition to a hateful scowl, and he pulled a bow from his back. "Then unless you can talk very fast, I will loose this arrow into your eye."

"I am here to talk. Jass sent me."

He had nocked an arrow, but even had he the skill to put it through my eye he lowered it enough that it would have hit the mud at Itaghai's feet instead. "Jass?"

"Jass en'Occha. He took a position as one of my Swords so he could smuggle supplies for you."

The bow lowered a little farther. "That isn't a lot to go on."

"Why don't you just let me come in and talk to whoever is in charge. You can always loose that arrow into my back if I turn out to be a traitor."

The saddleboy seemed to consider this a moment, then keeping hold of the bow, leapt down from the branch. "That's true," he said. "But I know Rah trusted you so you'll get at least five minutes to explain yourself before I do. It's him I was waiting for."

"Rah?"

"Yes. I'm Tor e'Torin. You probably don't remember, but I was Commander Brutus's translator."

Memories of those Chiltaen commanders hit hard, catching me unprepared. The fatigue and the illness, the shame and degradation. A lump of grief rose in my throat and I could not swallow it in time to answer, but the saddleboy went on without seeming to notice the stiffening of every muscle in my body.

"Rah was one of the few Levanti who was kind to me," the boy went on, something of belligerence in his expression. "At least he was."

He pressed his lips closed and scowled at nothing, or perhaps at all the words he had left unsaid. Words whose unspoken meaning clawed at my heart.

"Was?"

Rah had been kind to me too.

"He's not the man I thought he was," Tor said with a disgusted snort. "Following that Kisian empress around instead of fighting for his people." He spat on the ground. "I left them at Syan and sped back here to fight for the cause he abandoned. But...I thought he wouldn't be far behind me."

His brows lowered and he ran his gaze over Itaghai and my saddlebags, then back up at my swords. The bow trembled in his tight grip.

After a long pause he snorted. "Come on, I'll take you to Ezma."

The name meant nothing, but we'd been exiled in such great numbers that was hardly surprising. "Ezma?" I said. "Is she in charge around here? What herd is she from?"

"No, no one is really in charge," he said, ignoring the second part of my question. "But Ezma likes to greet all the newcomers and, you know, check them over."

I did not like the sound of that, but with little choice I followed Tor along the track between crowding trees, each dripping the night's downpour upon us. He said nothing more as he walked ahead of Itaghai, glancing back every now and then as though expecting me to run.

"Here we are," he said at sight of the large boulder Jass had mentioned. "Welcome to the last of the true Levanti." Tor sped up the short slope, his Kisian sandals cutting into the mud.

Unorganised, Baln had called them. Undersupplied. Ill-prepared for a fight. A gaggle of lost and desperate Levanti hiding in a swamp and dying of foreign sicknesses. I had known they were supplied, but even I had not expected a camp more than a hundred Swords strong and as neatly organised as the most meticulous herd. Protected on one side by the steep ridge and on another by a river running fast enough to bring fresh water, it was a haven amid the mire. Levanti were busy tending horses, skinning recent kills, gutting fish, and even sawing wood—a thing I had so rarely seen Levanti do that my eyes widened. They were building. Not just camping but *building*.

Many of them stopped what they were doing to stare at me and I realised too late I ought to have removed my imperial surcoat. To do so would have meant coming as myself rather than Gideon's representative, and again I found myself torn between two ideas of myself. The Dishiva who served a Levanti future whatever the cost. And the Dishiva that Rah would have smiled at.

With many Levanti stopping to stare, it took all my pride to stand tall as I followed Tor to a small hut not far inside the camp. A Kisian child stood waiting and held out his hand for Itaghai's reins with a sunny smile. I glanced at Tor, but when he said nothing, I handed the reins over, too glad to escape the whispering and the scrutiny. And the sight of Levanti of all herds living together. Building together.

"Who's the child?" I whispered as we stepped inside. "Is Itaghai safe with him?"

"Ichiro? Just a boy some Bedjuti found on their way here. His family were gone and he had no one to look after him, so they brought him with them. Until I arrived they had no translator either, so he's been picking up our language just by listening. It's amazing."

Someone in the shadows cleared their throat and I squinted.

"Oh, sorry, Ezma," Tor said, and saluted to a figure little more than an outline in my still sparking vision. "This is Captain Dishiva e'Jaroven, Gideon's head guard, but she says she just wants to talk."

"Does she indeed." Not a welcoming tone. The woman stepped forward, and her unusual outline slowly coalesced into something I had not expected to meet this side of the Eye Sea. Like Tor she was Levanti through and through, owning a strong jaw and high, delicate brows that expressed every emotion, yet unlike the saddleboy she wore no Kisian attire, dressed instead in traditional

Levanti armour mended with strips of local wool, new leather, and even silk as though she had used whatever she could find. The pair of swords hanging upon her left hip were Levanti, but the knife upon her right was not—another replacement for something lost perhaps. Yet it was her head I could not stop staring at. Unlike a Made warrior her hair was long and loose from crown to belt, and crown it was for atop her head she wore a horse's jawbone, cut and hollowed and strapped in leather to form a circlet, one-half of the curved joint rearing like horns on either side of her head.

My knees acted on their own, dropping to the dry rush floor as I saluted. "Whisperer."

The woman didn't smile, but her scowl softened at my proper show of respect. "At least you have not forgotten your heritage as easily as some," she said, steel in her voice despite the softness of her appearance. "What do you want, thrall of Gideon?"

I got warily to my feet, parting my lips only to close them again. What *did* I want? I had told the others I had come to persuade the deserters to return with us and kneel before Gideon, and that if they did not, we would attack. Looking around now I could see how laughable either mission was. These people had no intention of recognising Gideon, and no wonder when they had a whisperer to guide them. And to attack...There were just too many of them and their camp was too well established. And they had a whisperer.

"Where did you come from?" I blurted rather than answer.

"The same place as you I imagine."

"I mean...you weren't with the Chiltaen army like the rest of us, were you? I think I would remember seeing a whisperer."

"No, I wasn't. The good thing about being exiled all but alone is that you attract less attention."

My hand flew to my mouth. "An exiled horse whisperer? How? Why?" It took a unanimous vote from a full conclave of horse whisperers to exile one of their own, and I had never heard of it happening in my lifetime. Yet here she stood.

"You did not come to speak of me," she said. "Perhaps you bring a message from your emperor? Is he offering us gifts? Or death?"

I did not wish to answer but my hesitation was enough.

"Ah, death then."

Tor snorted from beside the door. "I would like to see you try."

I did not wish to try and yet I could not find words to explain it all. Leo. The book. The city about to be burned. The empire Gideon was trying to build for us, the home—a home challenged by their very existence living here in this swamp and not saluting him. Had I been a horse, the whisperer would have understood it all at a glance, but despite my lack of equine features she lifted her hand to Tor and said, "Not so bloodthirsty, Tor. You are a fool if you think this Jaroven came here to declare war upon us, despite Gideon's orders."

"He thinks you're dangerous," I said.

Ezma smiled and shrugged, her hair falling from her shoulders. "He's right. I've been collecting your deserters since you crossed the border with the Chiltaen army. Only a few at first, Swords who didn't want to fight for Gideon but were too afraid to speak up. One here, another there, sneaking away into the night. Not enough that anyone would notice amongst the dead. The tide has grown steadier, which is why we have built a temporary camp here safe from him and yet close enough to take in any who leave and protect them."

"He believes you're preparing to attack him."

Her brows went up. "Does he? But what business is it of mine what the First Sword of Torin chooses to do with his exile?"

"He isn't exiled," Tor said. The boy met our questioning stares with a slight lift of his chin. "We were one of the first to come here. We were exiled for a cycle, but when that cycle was up Gideon did not take us back. He already had allies then. Plans. And I had already been sold off to the Chiltaens as a translator."

I had known Gideon had been here for at least three full cycles, but that he had chosen not to go back rather than having been captured surprised me. But it was the word *translator* that spilt words from my mouth.

"Translator. Yes! Of course, you're Tor."

"I did say that."

"Yes, but Jass said you might be here."

"Jass?" the whisperer said. "You have heard from Jass?"

"Yes," I said, keeping my gaze pinned to Tor. "He said if you were here you might be able to help me with the book."

Tor looked over my shoulder to Ezma, and both bewildered, they said, "What book?"

"The Chiltaen holy book. Oh, where is—" I darted back out into the sunlight to find little smiling Ichiro still holding Itaghai's reins, seeming to be tilting his head side to side trying to get the horse to copy. The boy offered the reins to me, but I waved him away and dug my hand into the saddlebag until I found the linen-wrapped book. In a moment I was back inside the hut, sunlight flashing white in my vision. "This book."

I held it out to Tor, but he did not immediately take it. Once again he looked to the whisperer. Her face was an expressionless mask. "What is so important about the Chiltaen holy book?"

"I think it holds the secret to what Dom Villius is doing. I think he is trying to use us to build a holy empire, and the truth is in this book." I held it out to him again. "Please look at it. Please help me."

"I..." He took the linen-wrapped book from my hand. "I... suppose I could try, but I don't see what good it will do."

"It might make the difference between losing only a few more Levanti lives and hundreds. Please try to translate the parts relating to a man called Veld. Oh, and wash your hands after you look at it. The cover was painted in boiled-down redcap. I've cleaned it as best I can."

The book fell from its linen wrapping to land, pages splayed, upon the rushes. "Redcap poison? What—?"

"Dom Villius knew I was onto him. It was meant to kill me, but it killed Matsimelar instead."

"Matsi?"

I paused in the act of picking up the book. "You knew him? Oh, of course, I'm sorry. You would have been saddleboys together. When I asked him to steal the book for me, I never imagined this would happen."

I didn't hold the book out a second time, but Tor took it from my hands. "Leo killed him?"

"Yes. If not with his own hands he certainly ordered it done."

"Then if you promise to end him, I will translate your book." He gave a humourless little bark of laughter and added, "I'll add protecting Leo to Rah's list of poor decisions."

"I understand your anger, young Tor," Ezma said. "But Rah e'Torin is the only Levanti who stood up to Gideon. If for no other reason he deserves more respect."

The young man bowed his head. Anger suffused his features and for a moment I thought he might retort, but he just gripped the book and said, "With your permission, Whisperer, I will leave you to talk."

"By all means. And, Tor?" she added as he turned to leave. "Do be careful. While it would be important for Derk's training to experience purging someone of redcap poison, let's not risk it, all right?"

"Yes, Whisperer."

He walked out, throwing us into darkness as he blocked the entrance, only for the light to return at his passing. "The boy had quite a falling out with Rah, I believe. He does not tell me so but I see. He seems to be watching the track in the hope his captain will return."

The whole time she spoke Ezma did not take her eyes off me, and unnerved by her scrutiny, I changed the subject. "Who's Derk?"

"Derkka en'Injit, my apprentice. I was not exiled entirely alone. His soul was deemed corrupted by mine so he was not allowed to stay and take my place. But enough pleasantries, I think; you did not come here to discuss what has come before. Come, sit with me, Dishiva e'Jaroven."

What has come before. The phrase twanged thoughts of Leo and his rebirths in my mind, but I shook them away. The whisperer settled upon the loose rushes, and it was nice not to have to consider the order in which courtiers were allowed to sit as in Gideon's presence. I didn't have to think about who might be watching, or where Leo was at this moment, I just sat, rushes sticking to my damp boots. Ezma smiled encouragingly. It ought to have been patronising but it wasn't. There was comfort in her presence. To a Kisian she might have looked fearsome with her heavy jawbone headpiece, but to any Levanti she was the epitome of our people, the perfect mix of warrior and priest with an affinity for horses few could best.

"Now I want you to listen very carefully, Dishiva e'Jaroven," she said, leaning forward, elbows on her knees.

I braced for a threat, but when Ezma spoke again it was to utter something far worse. "Zesiro en'Injit," she said, leaving a brief pause before going on. "Nefer e'Sheth. Amun e'Torin. Lok e'Bedjuti. Kamas en'Occha. Ptapha e'Jaroven. Isi e'Bedjuti. Tor e'Torin..."

She was gifting me the names of every deserter in the camp and putting their souls in my hands.

They offered me food and they offered me sanctuary, but my first responsibility was to my Swords so I refused both. In the mid-afternoon drizzle I travelled back the way I had come, lighter by a book yet weighed down with souls. To attack them would end so many lives, but even if they were not an active threat, if word got out a horse whisperer stood against Gideon, his support would fracture. Loyalty to Ezma had kept her secret so far, but all it took was one slip of the tongue. Or one man capable of reading minds.

The camp we had made the previous night looked small and inhospitable after the deserter camp, and the faces of my Swords even less welcoming. They looked to have fractured into the comfort of their herd groups: Tafa, Baln, and Kehta stripping meat by the fire; Loklan, Shenyah, and Esi by the horses, while Moshe, Jakan, and Yafeu kept to themselves, separate and silent as though they did not feel welcome in either group.

It was Kehta who saw me first, and setting aside the carcass she was cleaning, she rose. "Captain," she said, the bloodied blade still in her hand. "Did you find them?"

"I did," I said. And before she could challenge me further, I added, "And we're not going to attack."

They all stilled about their tasks, but no one joined Kehta on her feet. "Not going to attack? Do you mean they've agreed to bow to Gideon?"

It would look too aggressive to remain mounted, so I slid from Itaghai's back into the mud, buying a few moments to think.

"Well, Captain? Have they?"

"No." I met her stare. "They don't want any part of this war. They are no threat and not worth our time."

Tafa slowly got to her feet, leaving Baln the only Oht still kneeling. No one else had so much as blinked. "No threat?" Tafa said. "You said they had plans to attack us. So they have said they will not? How can we be sure? And even if we can be sure, leaving honourless deserters unchallenged is a threat to everything Emperor Gideon is trying to build. How many Swords could we lose to this foolish idealism over what it means to be Levanti? Show me a single herd that is the same as another. That has the same code and the same ways and lives off the same land. Some herds stay in the mountains, others on the plains or near the rivers or the sea. What is so wrong about a herd that conquers? That rules? How does that make us any less Levanti than those down there who prefer to stick to the old ways? I am still Levanti here"—she put her fist to her chest—"and I will fight to protect my herd as would any Levanti."

"And the preservation of our herd relies on rooting out those deserters," Baln said, finally joining his herd sisters in their stand before the carcasses. "Who threaten our new way of life."

"But they are Levanti!" Shenyah cried, stepping forward. "And while we are all different there is one thing we share and that is we don't kill other Levanti without challenge, not for food or horses. That is the very purpose of the Meeting."

"How dare you lecture me about my own people, little girl," Tafa snarled. "I have been a Sword of the Oht longer than you have even been alive."

"Clearly long enough to forget what all children learn at the feet of their elders. That there is only one thing more precious than water or horses—*Levanti*."

Kehta laughed. "Your naivety would be amusing if it wasn't so poorly timed. Those are stories. Ideals. As impossible to reach as the stars themselves. You're a Sword of the Jaroven, you cannot tell me you've never seen someone die in a challenge. Never seen someone struck down by their own blood, their own herd, their brothers and sisters in the saddle."

Anyone else might have shrunk back. Almost I wished the girl would, but Shenyah drew herself all the taller and gave the Oht women back glare for glare. "Better the death of one to settle a disagreement than allowing a fight that could kill hundreds or fracture a herd. Ideals are only out of reach so long as we let them be." She folded her arms. "If those Levanti have no intention of attacking us then I refuse to attack them. I will not forget where I came from."

Kehta snarled and might have lunged at the girl, had Moshe not risen from his perch upon a fallen trunk. Everyone stilled as he started toward me, seeming to choose a side. "Whatever we might argue makes us Levanti," he said, ambling at his ease, "the one thing that never changes, herd to herd, is that we obey our captain's orders whether we like them or not. We choose the best person for the job, then follow their instructions. Yes?" He swung his gaze around my Swords as he stopped a step away. "Captain Dishiva has given orders. It is our job to obey them." Moshe paused, perhaps expecting an outcry that never came. "But then you were given orders too, weren't you, Captain?"

In one smooth movement, he drew his knife and slashed at me, and had I not already doubted his loyalty he might have slit my throat then and there. Instead I dodged back, tripping as the tip of his blade sliced my arm. I landed in the mud as overhead Shenyah cried, "Hey! You can't do that, you made no challenge!"

Kehta laughed. "Let it be, little girl."

Kicking up mud, I scrambled to my feet as Moshe drew his swords.

"There was no formal challenge!" Loklan said.

"Stay out of this, Horse Master."

"The gods must see!"

They were all just voices whirling around me, trying to pluck my attention from Moshe, who leered now as he hefted his blades. "I knew you wouldn't do it," he said. "Keka always said you were weak." He slashed at my torso and almost slit my skin, so stunned had his words left me.

"Keka?"

Moshe laughed and slashed again, forcing me to give ground as he advanced. Behind me Shenyah's furious tirade grew louder. "Oh yes," Moshe said. "Good, quiet Keka. Can't talk so he's worthless now, right? Give him guard duty. Leave him behind to look after the poor little Kisian woman, more like a matriarch than a Sword."

"Tradition is very clear. The gods cannot choose the most worthy—" Shenyah broke off in a pained cry as I backed toward the fire, conceding still more ground to Moshe while I tried to make sense of his words. Keka had been my second for a long time. We had fought together. Been exiled together. Suffered together. And I had thought we were building a new life together. When had I started walking my path alone?

My next backward step sank my boot into a pile of entrails discarded from the kills.

"Oh, look! Fresh meat!"

I spun at the creak of a bowstring. Baln stood behind me, an arrow nocked and drawn. Whether in defence or blind terror, my knees buckled. As I dropped, a sword spun toward Baln's back, hitting him hilt first and pitching him into the mud. Yafeu had his second sword drawn and stalked toward the stunned Oht, but Jakan leapt at him like a tiger and the pair went down in a burst of fists and mud and flailing steel.

Moshe lunged at me and I threw a handful of entrails into his face as I rolled, gaining my feet only to find both he and Baln facing me across the pile of muddied meat. Without a word, Baln began circling behind me, making it difficult to keep both men in sight. On the other side of the camp, Tafa had Loklan pushed back to the treeline, and nearby Esi danced around Kehta. Shenyah continued to berate the Oht hunter through the blood leaking from her nose. The girl hadn't even drawn her sword.

I lunged at Moshe. One of my blades caught his arm and the

other almost sliced open his gut, but the man growled and edged back and our wary dance spun on around the makeshift camp.

Someone crashed into a nearby tent in a stream of angry cursing, but I could not look around, could not help. Not as Baln advanced with a series of jabs at my face. I reeled back over the skittering woodpile only for Moshe to lunge into the corner of my vision. My foot caught a tent peg and almost I went over again, but someone caught my shoulder and Yafeu was there, blood oozing from a nasty cut on his face. No words of thanks. No time. He was gone again in an instant.

Needing this finished, I charged Baln, punting sticks into his shins only to turn and dart a slash at Moshe, but the man caught my blade on his own with a grating of steel. He dove in, only to meet my boot. Moshe gasped and tottered back, stunned, but when I lunged for the kill someone threw me sprawling sideways into a low tent. Damp canvas closed over me like wings, spiking my panic. I flailed with swords made useless, before dropping them and drawing my knife to slit the fabric like a thick skin.

Baln loomed through the opening, sword raised. I rolled, hissing as his blade pierced my arm. It burned as he ripped it out and slashed, catching the side of my face as I rolled back. My hand closed around the hilt of my abandoned sword, and with blood and pain leaking from my arm, I thrust it up. Its tip cut into his belly and I pushed to my knees, turning the steel within his gut and thrusting it deeper. Baln staggered, crashing back through the woodpile as the foul smell of his stomach contents seeped between his hands.

He spat at me as I got shakily to my feet. "I curse you in the sight of the gods, Dishiva e'Jaroven," he said, all but tripping over the still forms of Yafeu and Moshe, atop one another, each of their deaths the last act of the other. "I curse you never to rest and never to rise, and to be forever forsaken by the Goddess and . . . the

Watchful...Father. I—" His knees hit the mud. "I curse...you... Dishi...va..."

Baln slumped, but as though caught by dead hands, I could not move. On the other side of the camp Kehta had Esi around the throat. Esi scratched and tore at the arm choking air and life from her body, but Kehta only tightened her hold and dragged the Jaroven toward the fire. I made to move, but Shenyah finally drew her blade and sliced the length of Kehta's spine, tail bone to skull. The Oht hunter turned with a hiss, dragging Esi around. Like a righteous executioner, Shenyah swung at the exposed side of Kehta's neck and the woman howled, blood spraying from her throat. A second blow almost removed her head. Esi slid from her hold as Kehta crumpled dead at Shenyah's feet, hunched as though in prayer.

Silence buried the broken camp, drawing Tafa's attention from my horse master. At the sight of Baln and Kehta's bodies her eyes widened, and with a snarl she plunged her short knife into the rump of Loklan's horse. She wrenched it out again as the animal reared, and shoving Loklan out of the way she ran crashing off through the trees. With a furious roar he tore after her. Within moments their footsteps had faded away leaving nothing but Shenyah's croons as she caught the injured horse's reins and tried to calm its panic.

Esi got slowly to her feet and together we stared around at the carnage. Bodies. Blood. Broken tents and a mud-clogged fire pit. And all our horses scattered into the trees. I could not speak while we retrieved them. I could not speak while Shenyah tipped out the whole contents of Loklan's box and tended his horse's wound. I could not speak when, like the empty clay shell of a human, I knelt numbly in the mud to take the heads of our fallen. I started with Moshe. Blood poured free with my first incision, the escaping liquid seeming to drop with the weight of stones.

In lightening myself of the souls Whisperer Ezma had placed

upon my shoulders, I had taken on a heavier burden still. These had been my Swords, their safety my responsibility, my trust in them as required of our code as was their trust in me. I had failed at the most basic of our tenets, and worse. By failing to fulfil Gideon's orders, I had betrayed him at a time when he needed me most, when he and our fledgling empire were most vulnerable.

My chest tightened as I worked. Esi had her knees beneath Yafeu's head, focussing on each cut rather than stare into his lifeless eyes, and I wondered if she had the same thoughts I did. The same regrets. The same fear over what would come next. If she did, we didn't speak of it. Couldn't. My throat was as tight as my chest, every part of me blocked with grief and rage. Better to keep it locked within, where the only person it could harm was the person who deserved it most.

Me.

23. RAH

A sea of people poured from the city gates carrying armfuls of possessions. Some pushed handcarts or had children riding on their shoulders, the noise a symphony of footsteps, shouts, and squeaking wheels. The current ran strongest around the outer edges where individuals carrying less skirted the central, deep flow, which even included a few of those curtained carriers for the old and the sick. Or the rich. I knew which it would have been back home, but if I had learned anything in my exile it was that Kisia wasn't home.

That fact was reinforced over and again by people bunching up to get out of my way, one look at my face enough to frighten most of them into putting as much space between us as possible, my every attempt to ask why they were leaving the city met with fear.

I walked on against the current, Shishi at my heels. Despite people trying to avoid me, the closer we got to the gates the harder it became to push through.

A woman with a child on her hip brushed past, hitting me with a sack as she tried to turn out of my path. Another man ran over my foot with the front wheel of his handcart. As people pressed in, one shouted at me, pointing the way they were walking as though I were a fool. Others shook their heads. A young man with dye-stained hands stepped into my path and raised his fists, shouting, only to be yanked back into the moving current by an older woman. Another raised his hands in thanks.

Shishi yelped as someone trod on her paw. I bent to pick her up, buffeted on all sides. Despite the crush, she scrabbled to get down, eventually settling for putting her front paws on my shoulder and looking back the way we had come, panting so fast that her chest sucked in and out against mine. She drew more eyes than I had on my own, but at least they stopped slamming me with their shoulders—their respect for the dog greater than their respect for a Levanti.

I shuffled toward the open gate, my stride becoming shorter and shorter as we approached the bottleneck. Where the crowd was thickest some people were pushing and shoving, while others just hurried on, silent, intent, afraid. I felt their fear, but it was the crumbling wall I hunted, for the enemies who had wanted me dead. Enemies I had once called my kin.

Feeling safer in the centre of the crowd, I pushed through the middle of the gateway, shuffling around curtained carriers and carts and people in robes of all cloths and colours. No Levanti called to me. No one fought through the crowd to reach me. After all, what was one man to a whole army of Kisians?

The crowd was even thicker inside the gates. The square was packed edge to edge, people and vehicles squeezed out into the surrounding streets as far as I could see. Trails of seething life wound between buildings with caved-in roofs and broken shutters, and walls blackened by fire—all remnants of the Chiltaen conquest. A conquest these people had not fled until now.

A bite of fear tightened my arms around Shishi, but I could not turn back now.

I pushed on toward the palace. No doubt there were faster routes than along the main road crammed with people, but I knew only the way Leo had brought me in and Jinso had brought me out, so I wound my way through the press of people creeping, at the pace of snails, toward freedom.

By the time I could walk freely the sun had sunk halfway toward the horizon, and with a sigh of relief I set Shishi back upon her paws. Cramps pinched arms held too long in one position, so while she relieved herself upon the road I winced and stretched tired muscles. "You're a lot heavier than you look," I said as she returned, panting, to my feet. "Or perhaps I've gotten weaker."

She couldn't answer but trotted loyally at my heels like I was Empress Miko.

The imperial palace stood in the centre of the city, tall, old, and silent like the Hissing Tomb upon the plains. Its stones were not as worn nor its gardens as dead and tangled, yet it owned something of the same haunted look. The horse whisperers of old had been laid to rest there, but it had long since been abandoned, just as people were abandoning the palace now.

Two Levanti stood outside the palace gates. Both were dressed in the traditional style, neither wearing a silk coat nor an oiled cloak, and for the first time I felt ashamed of the sandals upon my feet. Their scalps were freshly shaved too, unlike my overgrown hair twisting into loose curls, and while I dragged exhausted limbs they stood strong, the spread-foot, loose-kneed Levanti stance designed to withstand even the fiercest gusts of the Eastbore. For a mad moment I wanted to run, but whatever my fears these were my people, my Swords, and I had to believe they would do me no harm.

I recognised the twins before they recognised me, but by the time I halted before them both Himi and Istet were staring at me like a ghost.

"Himi," I said, saluting first one then the other. "Istet."

"Captain?" Himi managed, finding her voice before her sister. But her words seemed to shatter Istet's dumbfounded silence and the older of the twins scowled at me.

"Except he isn't our captain anymore, remember?" She lifted her chin and her hand strayed to her sword. "Rah. You're meant to be a long way from here."

"I was but I came back. Gideon is in danger."

Istet's hand remained upon her sword. "Aren't we all, all the time?"

"His ally, Grace Bahain, intends to use us and then do away with us so he can take the throne for himself. I've come back to warn him."

Himi looked from her sister's sword hand to me and said in a low voice, "Gideon isn't here. You shouldn't be here either, Rah. We're burning the city at nightfall and if Sett finds out you're here…"

"Burning the city? Why?"

"So the Kisians can't have it back," Istet snapped, her grip tightening around her sword hilt. "Now are you going to leave, or am I going to have to draw this damn thing?"

Her hateful scowl hurt more than the threat. I had been her captain and she my Sword. "Did I lead you so badly, Istet? That you would strike me down defenceless?"

"You're not defenceless." She jabbed her free hand at my single surviving blade. "Just draw it."

"Against a Torin? Against my own Sword? Without challenge I would not."

Istet's face screwed up into an ugly snarl. "Damn your honour. You should have taken us home."

"Istet," Himi hissed. "Don't do this."

"Eska was right," Istet said, ignoring her. "You were just too afraid to challenge the herd master so we all had to suffer your exile. And see what has become of our honour now? My soul will be heavy when I am judged, but yours will break the scales."

"Eska challenged and lost, sister," Himi said. "The gods made their choice."

Except I knew the truth. No intervention from the gods had seen me beat Eska the night he challenged for my captaincy. Nor had I fought better. I had just been more afraid. And ever since, I had held tighter and tighter to the precepts of our code only for more and more of my Swords to slip through my fingers, leaving me with nothing but the heavy weight of my own soul.

Yours will break the scales.

So much to say, but every admission of guilt and apology that formed on my tongue clotted into a single mass and stuck my lips closed. What words could ever be enough? Words could not change the past. Could not bring back Eska and Amun, Kishava and Orun and Juta—bright, young Juta with his whole life before him.

It was all I could do to keep my wail of despair trapped behind my teeth, but when I made no answer Istet's lip curled and she gestured at Shishi. "Did you lose Jinso too? That's a lovely guilt-dog."

Unable to tell the truth and yet refusing to lie, I appealed to Himi. "That man I was locked in the cells with, the one we found sitting on the throne in the empress's armour."

"Minister Manshin?"

"Yes, him, is he still here?"

I braced for more of Istet's ire, but the twins shared an uneasy look. "Why do you ask about the Kisian man?" Istet said.

"Because I need him."

Again her lip curled, but before she could snap at me, Himi stepped between us, gripping my arm. "Rah, do you..." She dropped her voice to a whisper. "Do you want him alive?"

She would not meet my gaze, only stare at my feet. "Yes," I said. "I would free him."

Gnawing her lip, Himi shared another look with her sister, full of meaning. "The Minister has been...uncooperative." Himi glanced around at the smattering of servants hurrying through the palace gates. "He has refused every offer Sett has made him on

Gideon's behalf, but the man is Empress Sichi's father and is highly regarded amongst the Kisians, so he cannot just be killed. He—"

"Empress?"

I spoke loud enough that a man hurrying through the gates behind Himi looked around, only to speed up, clutching his stack of papers and scrolls as one might hold a child.

"Yes. Gideon married Lady Sichi to solidify his hold on the empire. I think it was the terms on which he had the support of... Grace Bahain."

How tightly the man had entangled Gideon hollowed me with fear. "I was at his castle. Grace Bahain has been hunting for Empress Miko so he can marry her and claim the throne when he kills Gideon. I need to free the minister and get to Kogahaera."

Himi shared another long glance with Istet, as though seeking permission. "Just take him inside before someone sees him, Himi," Istet snapped. "And on his own head be the consequences. For once."

"All right," Himi said, shifting foot to foot. "Sett has almost everyone out in the city with the Namalaka, so we're unlikely to be seen. He's inside, but..." She seemed to be trying to convince herself. "As long as he doesn't see you." She bit her lip before answering my unasked question. "He's angry, Rah. Angry at us, at you, at Gideon, at everything." She looked once more at her sister, and infinitesimal though it was, Istet nodded.

"I think I can protect the gate from attack on my own for a while," Istet said, waving a hand at the all but empty square. "But I won't lie for you, Rah. I won't add to the weight of my soul for you. I won't tell Sett you're here, but if he asks, I'll answer."

"I could not ask more." I saluted her. Istet merely nodded and turned to stare out at the square like an attentive guard, Himi and I ceasing to exist.

Himi's fingers tightened around my arm, a brief, nervous

squeeze, there and gone with a grimace. "Come," she said, hurrying in through the palace gates. "Leave the dog here."

"No, she has to come with me."

"Why?"

"Because I have a message for Manshin but I cannot speak much Kisian and neither can you."

"Neither can the dog."

"No, but the dog doesn't need to speak. The dog *is* the message."

Himi gave me an odd look, and a pair of men carrying a flat stringed instrument through the palace doors almost dropped it when they caught sight of Shishi, her tail up and wagging like a flag.

"Why are they staring at the dog like that?" she said, hurrying up the steps. "Is it a rare breed?"

She stepped inside and we passed from the weak afternoon sunlight to the cool, damp-smelling interior of the outer palace—a place I had first entered upon a very different pair of heels. "No," I said, pushing aside memories of Leo I still wasn't sure what to do with. "At least I don't think so. She belongs to Empress Miko."

Himi stopped. "Are you mad?" she hissed, spinning to stare at the dog like it had just sprouted a hundred hands. "Empress Miko? What are you doing with the empress's dog?"

"That's a long story for another time. If you want no further part in this I understand. I can find my own way."

Himi shifted her weight, looked at the dog, at me, and then back over her shoulder at the daylight pouring through the open doors. She let out a long, heavy breath. "Fuck it, let's go. If I do nothing, I will regret it forever. No one should have to die like that."

"Like what?" I said, hurrying to keep up as she pelted off along the passage.

Stopping as suddenly as she had started, Himi turned on me, her answer a half snarl. "Burned alive. In his cell. With no way of getting out."

She spun away on the words, the furious thunder of her booted footsteps matching the deep thud of my heart. Burned alive. No Levanti would give even their greatest enemy so dishonourable a death, yet Sett must have ordered it. Or Gideon. The fact that either could even contemplate it gnawed at my thoughts.

In silence Himi led the way through the outer palace, through narrow passages, empty rooms, and abandoned courtyards, stopping to peer around every corner until we reached the prison stairs. Without pause, Himi started down them on quick, nimble feet, but Shishi sat at the top and refused to move.

I called her, but though she half rose and wagged her tail, she stayed where she was.

"Shishi!" I said, patting my thigh. "Come on."

She didn't come.

"Maybe she's afraid of the dark?" Himi said. "There's a lantern farther down—should I get it?"

"I don't think it's that. It's probably the smell." I went back up the stairs and she lifted her paws onto my legs only to leap back and gambol around, tail wagging furiously. "Come on," I said, kneeling. "I know it smells bad down there, but I need you. Without you, he won't understand."

She didn't come to heel, but she did sit long enough for me to lift her. I didn't have to carry her far, but my arms soon burned with their earlier pain.

The darkness deepened as we descended into the bowels of the palace, and despite the many other rooms off many other passages, the stink of the cells at the bottom permeated it all. Even without the lantern Himi lit, we could have found our way by following our noses. As the stink thickened, Shishi scrambled to be free and once again ended up looking over my shoulder like an overlarge child. I couldn't blame her. The smell was becoming solid, the sort of smell from which you can't escape even if you hold your nose because it tastes just as bitter.

The sound changed as we descended too, our steps and the squeak of the lantern ceasing to echo as the palace above crushed all sound. All light. All life.

When my feet found the bottom, Shishi wriggled for freedom, digging her claws into my neck.

"Hey, stop it," I said.

"Let me close the door." Himi swung back with her lantern and a thud sounded behind me. "She might find some pretty disgusting things down here, but she can't get out now. There's no other entrance."

I set her on her paws and she ran for the door. She sniffed at the tiny gap beneath it and around the side, jumped up, and finally seeming to accept it would not open, sat before it with an air of protest.

"We must be quick," Himi said, grabbing the key from a hook on the wall and dashing, lantern swinging, toward the first cell.

I followed, glancing back at Shishi's whimper. "We'll get out of here soon," I assured her. "We—" I choked on my words. Minister Manshin stood at the bars, his pale, gaunt face a shadow of its former strength. Yet he still stared with bright, angry eyes.

With his hands clasped behind his back, he snapped a few words and I needed no translation to know this would be harder than I had hoped. Incandescent rage was keeping this man alive and it would burn the first person it touched and everyone thereafter.

"Give me the key, Himi," I said. She had backed off a step, clearly seeing what I had, but she passed me the key. I held it up to the bars, trying not for threat but for promise. He glared. Pointing to myself, I said, "Rah e'Torin."

Minister Manshin's eyes narrowed and he spat on the stones at my feet, replying with a word I recognised from Empress Miko's vocabulary.

"I don't think it was wise to tell him you were a Torin like Sett and Gideon," Himi said, still keeping her distance.

"I don't think so either. He just called me a dog." I cleared my throat to try again, pointing to the cell where I had spent time after Gideon's coup. "Rah," I said, and gestured with the key, pretending to lock a different cell. "Rah, prisoner."

He turned his head as though trying to hear me better.

"Rah...um..." I started to sing the Torin mourning song I had sung to the darkness of my cell. His eyes widened in something like recognition and I stopped, repeating my name and pointing at the cell again. "Rah. Rah free"—I gestured to the lock and key— "Minister Manshin. Empress Miko needs Minister Manshin."

"Empress Miko?" the man repeated, gripping the bars and pulling himself so close I could smell his stale breath.

"Empress Miko south," I said, gesturing in the general direction that felt like south. "Umm...with Kisian army. Soldiers?" I mimed marching soldiers and felt like an idiot. It was just as well Himi had come, not Istet, for all the words I had learned from Miko were little use in communicating such information. "Taken...caught..." This time I pretended to catch Himi. She let out a squeak of surprise but let me feign binding her hands and marching her away.

The minister asked a question, attempting to pull himself through the bars.

"Jie," I said, guessing at his meaning and answering with the only name I knew. "Jie."

The minister hissed, and I knew he understood. Yet he narrowed his eyes and suspicion poured in Kisian from his lips, *e'Torin* the only word I understood. It had been a mistake to tell him my name and never had I thought to be ashamed of it. But though he might not trust me, he would trust her.

Kneeling on the damp stones, I patted my thigh and whistled to Shishi, still sitting before the door. Her tail wagged but she owned her mistress's stubbornness. I went to pick her up and as I approached her tail wagged so fast it made her whole back half rock to and fro, but when she realised I wasn't coming to open the door she abased herself on the floor. I wrestled her into my arms nonetheless, a putrid hint now added to the whiff of damp and mud clinging to her coat.

I carried her back to Minister Manshin's cell, and the moment he saw her, his angry suspicion dropped away. "Shishi?" he said, joy choking his voice.

I gestured, offering him the dog, and set her down so I could unlock the cell.

"Minister Manshin," I said as I did so. "Take Shishi. Go help Empress Miko."

There was so much more I wanted to say, so much more he needed to know. About Syan and the empress's guard, about the army and the impending destruction of Mei'lian, but all I could do was turn the key and let him out.

The lock clicked. The minister wrenched open the door and strode out, his eyes alight with purpose. Himi flinched, but rather than go for our throats the man knelt to ruffle Shishi's fur. She gave his filthy face a lick.

My shoulders slumped as I let go a long breath. It had not been my duty to free him, not my duty to help the empress, but the guilt I had been carrying at all we had done to her empire lessened a little. I had tried not to worry about her, tried not to recall how she had looked at me, tried to think only of my people, but it had been impossible. In the end she had sacrificed herself to keep me safe and I hoped this would be thanks enough.

"Come on," Himi said, striding back toward the closed door. "We have lingered too long. The sooner you get out of here the better."

She reached for the pitted metal handle, and the door swung into her, slamming her back against the wall with a cry. Glass smashed and the lantern's oil-soaked wick fell onto the stones to eke out a poor light.

"You couldn't just heed my warning and leave," Sett snarled, striding into the dim, cell-lined room. "You couldn't listen for once, couldn't think of something other than your honour and your code and your gods-be-damned stubborn need to be the centre of everyone's world. I ought to have killed you rather than let you strut around the empire turning loyal Swords against Gideon and—"

"He didn't need my help to achieve that," I said, and as footsteps hurried away up the stairs I gripped a handful of Sett's surcoat. He tried to pull free, but I grabbed his arm, digging my fingers into his flesh. "He did it on his own by ordering the burning of cities and innocent men."

"And here I thought you couldn't betray him any more than you already had," Sett spat.

The injustice of his words stung me and I flung my arm in the direction Minister Manshin had escaped. "That man is the only one who can help Empress Miko, and helping Empress Miko stops Grace Bahain marrying her and getting rid of Gideon, because that's what he means to do, Sett. I came back because Gideon needs to know Grace Bahain is not his friend, that he intends to turn on him, that—"

"You think he doesn't know that? You think he hasn't always been aware of how dangerous this would be, holding his own in a political world he knows so little about? Every decision he has made has been with an eye to the power of the Kisian lords he had to court, and now—"

He snapped his jaw closed upon the rest of his words, gritting his teeth and staring into the corner of the room as though haunted by something he saw there.

"And now?" I prompted, fear speeding the thump of my heart. "And now what, Sett? Is Gideon... is Gideon all right? He is not... dead?"

Sett shook his head. "Oh no, not dead."

"Then what?"

He jabbed a finger hard into my chest. "I told you he would need you. I told you he would need your help, need you to be there for him, and you know what? Not for a moment did I doubt you would do it, not for a moment did I fear for him, knowing you would be there, but you chose honour over him. You chose to care more for the weight of your soul than for him. You chose to doubt him. To question. To make him afraid of every decision he made, fearing it was the wrong one even when there were no other choices. If not here then where? If not now then when?"

The barrage of his condemnation was not just like punches to the face or the gut, but like he had prised open my chest and squeezed my heart until I could not breathe for the pain of it. Because whatever my reasons had been, however I had tried to hold to our tenets, I had sacrificed Gideon to do so, unwilling to see his purpose beyond the wrongs he had committed in its name.

Gideon had cared nothing for honour and tenets and even the future of our people when I had needed him most. He ought to have told Herd Master Sassanji I had run away from my apprenticeship, but he hadn't. He ought to have encouraged me to go back, but he hadn't. Not then and not later, though our standing upon the plains had dropped in the aftermath of that day.

"I'm going to him," I said.

"Oh yes? And how far do you think you'll get?"

"I won't go alone. I will take my Swords with me."

His laughter was a humourless little snort. "They are hardly your Swords anymore."

No one had challenged me for the position of Captain, but neither had any of them fought to keep me as their leader. Perhaps they would rather go on being commanded by Sett, but if they really believed in Gideon and what he was building they would want to stop his Kisian allies ruining it all.

Steeling myself with clenched fists, I said, "Then I challenge you for the captaincy of the Second Swords of Torin."

Sett began to laugh. "I am not the captain of the Second Swords of Torin," he said. "But what can Yitti do but accept your challenge? Since you don't listen to me, I will have to hope you will listen to the end of his blade."

"I will not let Gideon down this time," I said, the words softly spoken though they cut at my very soul, at the crust of pride I wore over my shame. "You have my word."

I pressed my fists in salute, but Sett merely grunted, an ugly look flickering across his face before he turned toward the stairs.

24. CASSANDRA

I had hoped to have left the nightmare of Koi behind forever, yet as the sun set our carriage bowled toward the impenetrable city without slowing. Empress Hana had demanded speed over safety, but still her time was running out. The stink of decaying flesh had started as a faint trace only to grow as afternoon fled, concentrated by the lack of fresh air in our tight little box. At least the hieromonk's dead body still moved well, and the paint kept some colour on his pallid cheeks.

We had stopped talking. She because she had lines to rehearse and a corpse to tend; me because I was just too tired. And the weight of fatigue was all the worse for knowing what was coming. In the body of Empress Hana Ts'ai I was being carried into Chiltaen-held Koi as a prisoner, by none other than Empress Hana Ts'ai herself, in the body of the hieromonk of Chiltae. It was the sort of nonsense no one would believe.

I wheezed a laugh, while outside, the gates of Koi drew ever nearer.

The hieromonk stared out the window as we took the first of many turns winding down into the city. At the bottom of the hill it basked in the last of the daylight. Rain had just passed, leaving it sparkling like a bag of spilt gold, a shimmer that continued out beyond the walls. I shifted closer to the window.

"Fuck."

"What is it?" In a moment the empress was beside me in her hieromonk-skin, the pair of us staring at an expanse of military fortifications. Tents and pens and makeshift buildings, all caught within a palisade wall.

"That's a lot of Chiltaen soldiers."

"It is," she agreed. "More than I thought they had left. Reports of the army they had at Mei'lian must have been exaggerated."

"Or someone knew what was going to happen and made sure they weren't all there."

The hieromonk's curiously lifted brows were no less disdainful for knowing the empress was inside him. "Something you aren't telling me, Miss Marius?"

I had been thinking of Leo and the strange way he had of knowing my thoughts, but I shook my head.

The carriage began to slow.

"Still time to change your mind," I said. "Going in there will get us both killed." I gestured in the direction of the unexpected army. "If you needed further proof."

Outside, a guard shouted, and over the rattle of wheels came the sound of gates creaking open. The carriage's rumble quietened with the change to smoother stone, then evening-bathed Koi ambled by, a shadow of its former self. The walls and gates survived untouched, but inside the city, burn scars blackened whole streets, and smashed terracotta tiles clogged the gutters. Windows had been boarded and doorways left agape, and those few braving the streets kept their heads down and their hoods up despite the blessed break in the rain. A few ran at the sight of our carriage and guilt tugged at the heart I had been sure I did not possess.

I moved away from the window. The Kisians had killed many Chiltaens throughout history, had sacked our cities and burned our fields. Now was a poor time to feel sorry for them.

The road steepened as we raced through the darkening city, and despite the empress's continued urging for speed, the horses dropped from a trot to a walk, leaving her to tug fretfully at the linen mask hiding her slit throat.

When the carriage finally stopped, the empress had the hieromonk out of his seat and through the door before anyone could open it. I followed, bound hands making the task difficult to achieve with grace.

"Your Holiness," one of the castle guards said as she descended into the road. "We feared you lost when we heard what happened in the capital."

"I was fortunate to have been travelling behind the army at the time," she answered with the hieromonk's voice. "I must speak with the commander. Fetch a palanquin."

The word came out with the empress's accented Kisian, but although the guard's brows lifted in surprise it was a big step from "the hieromonk said a word strangely" to "the hieromonk is a dead man being worn by a Kisian empress." The guard's gaze flicked to me and his surprise was drowned beneath a wave of astonishment. "Empress Hana."

I froze, unsure what a deposed empress would do at such a time. She came to my rescue. "The palanquin, man, where is it?"

The guard saluted. "Sorry, Your Holiness, Commander Aulus hasn't been using it as he prefers to walk rather than be lazy."

Commander Aulus. I committed the name to memory and hoped the empress would do the same.

"Understandable," the hieromonk said, and I was impressed the empress inside him didn't bristle at the man's disdain. "Unfortunately, the empress is unwell and cannot walk the distance. So bring it. At once."

"Yes, Your Holiness. At once, Your Holiness."

By the time it arrived the pair of Chiltaen guards on duty had taken to staring fixedly at one another's helmets, while the remaining members of Captain Aeneas's men milled uncertainly behind the hieromonk's carriage. No one seemed to know what to do and I cringed inwardly. This was not a good start. All we needed now was for the hieromonk's body to start stiffening and there would be trouble.

Eventually four Kisian servants came hurrying down the slope with a palanquin rocking between them. I tried to catch the empress's eye, but she pointedly avoided my gaze as she invited me to enter. I all but tumbled in. She achieved a far more graceful entry despite wearing a corpse. Once we were both inside one of the carriers tried to stretch the curtains to hide the castle's defences from view, but a gate guard jabbed him with the butt of his spear and told them to hurry.

And hurry they did for the first part of the winding journey, but like the horses they soon slowed, puffing, as they made their way up the interminable slope to the castle proper.

"Do you know the way through this maze?" I said, keeping my voice low though I doubted the carriers could hear anything over their thudding steps and ragged breathing.

"Of course." The hieromonk's face owned wounded pride. "I am an Otako."

"No, you're Creos Villius, hieromonk of Chiltae, chosen of the One True God, and you'd better damn well remember it if you want to get through this alive."

She raised his mousy-coloured brows. "Oh, you care what I do now? I thought you wanted no part of this."

"I don't want any part of this, but now I'm here I'd like to get out again in one piece. The hieromonk didn't need the mask to look like he was wearing one. If you want to pass for him you need to stop using your face so much. Keep it blank. Keep your voice even. Act like—"

"An empress?"

"Something like that, yes."

She fixed the hieromonk's eyes upon me, the intent look enough to make me shudder at the memory of him. "You should remember the same thing, Miss Marius. People expect that body to act a certain way. I know it's hard when you have long since lost yourself to fury and hurt, but you must summon as much pride as you can, let it strengthen your every movement and stiffen your spine so it cannot, and will not, bend."

"Lost myself to fury?"

The hieromonk's brows went up. "You—"

"Eyebrows."

She let out a snort of air and relaxed the dead man's face. "You cannot be surprised," she went on, mimicking his monotone. "You and I are not so dissimilar. We were raised in the knowledge that our only value lay in what men could do with us, and we both found a way to turn it against them. I too have been an angry woman all my life, slowly drowning in what always felt like the sucking swamp of social expectation. But I am proud of my name. Of my family. Of my heritage and of my people. And that I have worn like a cloak, keeping me sane while I smile and simper and pretend to be the only version of me that's allowed to exist."

In the hieromonk's smooth tone her words tore through me, all the more painful for being unexpected. This woman, this Dragon Empress with her failing body and her disintegrating power, had lived a life torn by the same frustrations as I had. Had found ways to cope as I had, hiding the sharp edges of her soul behind a proud mask as I had hidden mine behind cold crassness.

"As hateful and hurtful as it is," she went on when I didn't answer, "there are a lot of reasons not to give up on the world, and especially not the part you can play in shaping it, because whatever everyone likes to tell you, you can. So gather that gods-damned pride of yours, whatever its rooted in, and be the empress I need you to be, all right?"

Once more into Koi Castle. I had thought myself dead the first time only to walk free. The second had been a suicide mission. Perhaps this third time my luck would run out.

If Empress Hana shared my fear, she showed no sign of it, nor any sign of interest in the castle that had once been hers. This castle where she had lived, where her son had died, where her life had crumbled around her.

The entrance hall possessed all its old, silent grandeur. The empress's mourning drapes had been torn from the windows along with all sign of the Ts'ai dragon, but though voices echoed from other parts of the castle, just here it was possible to believe time unwound, that beyond the great doors Empress Hana still sat upon the Crimson Throne. But it was I who moved the empress's feet now, following our escort into one of the castle's large arterial passages.

Away from the central chambers the castle buzzed with activity. Open doors allowed glimpses of off-duty soldiers eating and drinking and dicing amid Kisian finery, while other rooms were full of sleeping mats and murmuring voices. A few owned Kisian lilts, but most were the deep rumble of Chiltaen men.

We were led up some stairs and along another passage, whispers following in our wake. Knots of ambling soldiers stopped to stare, but the empress in her hieromonk-skin just acknowledged each of their pious bows with a nod and a tap of pale fingers to the mask around her neck.

Our destination was a room high in the castle, a spacious room with an adjoining balcony and all the trappings required for grand-scale entertainments. No such entertainment seemed to be planned, however, for although the remnants of a meal graced the long, low table, it had been pushed up against one wall to make space for a carpet of maps and papers. A tall man wearing a Chiltaen uniform bent over them, his brow furrowed. Behind him, a lattice screen shielded the papers from the worst of the rain, but it did nothing to keep out the breeze. Every gentle gust rustled the paper floor, lifting all corners not weighed down by a smattering of stones and bowls and vases.

The man looked up as we entered. "Ah! Your Holiness, we feared you lost at Mei'lian." His gaze flicked to me but his hard-lined face showed no surprise.

"Not lost, as you see, Commander," the empress said, drawing the hieromonk's body up tall. Her gaze swept to the other side of the room, and she added, "No joyous reunion, my son?"

I flinched. Sitting upon a cushion in the far corner, seemingly absorbed in prayer, was Leo—the exact same Leo I had first arrived here with weeks ago, whose head I had severed. The very Leo who had seemed able to look inside my head, lifting a hand to me now in silent acknowledgement.

The young man did not move from beside the brazier. A dozen of them encircled the room, their hot coals combating the chill of the insidious breeze.

"It is pleasant to see you, of course, Father," he said. "But I knew you were not dead so did not fear."

"We have had quite a number of pilgrims arrive to see Dom Villius since he joined us," the commander said, shooting something of a wary look at the hieromonk. "It seems word of his death in Mei'lian has spread and people wish to be blessed by the Reborn One. We hear the Levanti emperor is claiming he still has Leo, alive, so it is good to have him here setting those rumours to rest."

The commander's gaze flicked my way again. I was no empress, but even Cassandra Marius was not used to going so long without being the centre of attention in any room. I hoped Empress Hana was too deep in her appropriation of the hieromonk to notice how little interest her presence had garnered.

"Have you dined, Holiness?" the commander said, continuing to ignore my existence. "I can send for more food."

Empress Hana hesitated, no doubt wondering if dead bodies could eat.

"No, I ate on the road, Commander," she said. "We must talk without delay."

The empress walked her hieromonk-skin into the room, inviting me to join her. Commander Aulus lifted his brows. "Empress Hana," he said coolly. "I must admit I am surprised to see you back with us."

"Surprised and pleased, I hope, Commander," the hieromonk said. "Because if we don't do something about the rogue Levanti that Andrus let loose we are going to lose more than just a good chunk of our army."

"We are well defended here, Your Holiness. You did not see the army camped outside the gates?"

"I did see it. But the army appears well encamped and not in a hurry to go anywhere."

The commander's brows rose in true surprise. "Go anywhere? Why must it go anywhere? We are here for Chiltae's protection, although with Gideon encamped in Kogahaera it seems unlikely he'll come after us until the snows melt. And even then he has southern Kisia to quell first."

"That is very...wishful thinking, Commander. What does a barbarian care for borders? Tell me, if you were this Levanti leader, would you rather cross the Tzitzi River into southern Kisia and fight all their battalions for nothing but a rocky pass around the mountains, or take the ill-defined Chiltaen border in your easy stride and fight a severely reduced Chiltaen army for control of the

Ribbon and all its trade routes? A Chiltaen army, moreover, that treated your people cruelly." She lifted the dead man's brows and I had to bite back a reminder that the hieromonk didn't do such things. "Well, Commander? Which would you choose?"

"How are we to know what the barbarian wants or how he thinks, Holiness?"

"Because you are a smart man, and Gideon is a smart man. No mere barbarian tricks a whole Chiltaen army into getting itself slaughtered in the rabbit warren of a foreign city."

A rustle of movement came from the corner as Leo rose from his cushion. The others might have all but forgotten his presence, but I had been unable to keep my eyes from darting his way, wondering at his purpose. If he knew me for Cassandra, why had he not yet said so? Was this Leo different? Had he lost the ability to read my thoughts when I slid a blade between his ribs?

"My father is right, Commander," he said. "Gideon e'Torin may have appeared to be taking orders, but he was smart enough to deceive even Legate Andrus." The young man approached carefully across the papers. "And my father."

Once again the hieromonk lifted his brows. "And you, my son."

"No, Father, but there are some sacrifices that must be made." He stopped beside another brazier, standing as close to the smouldering coals as he could without burning his plain robe. Closer now I could see that his expression, if nothing else, was different to the Leo I remembered. My Leo had seemed younger, more carefree, but now his jaw was tense and sweat shone upon his brow. And though he smiled, his hands clenched to fists only to splay as far open as he could spread them and clench again as though in pain.

"I'm glad you are here to add your weight to mine, Father," he went on, his tone falsely bright like shattered glass. "I have been trying to persuade Commander Aulus that we must prepare to march upon Kogahaera at once. If we let the Levanti regroup we will suffer for it."

Commander Aulus stiffened. "The Nine think otherwise, that to engage the Levanti at this point would be dangerous. We are lucky to have even this many soldiers left."

"Luck never has anything to do with it," Leo said, and the empress looked from him to the commander, and I could imagine she was wondering, finally, if having come here was a bad idea.

Trying to regain some control over the conversation, Empress Hana said, "If we leave Gideon running loose, he will soon turn his eyes on Genava. From the Ribbon he could reforge ties with his homeland. We need to move now, Commander. Look at the gift I have brought you. Imagine the use Her Majesty can be. Just think," she went on, spreading the hieromonk's hand in a broad, sweeping gesture. "Empress Hana riding ahead of our army, ensuring safe passage and rallying the broken fragments of northern Kisia to our cause."

Leo looked down at the papers at his feet, and pointed at the large map held flat by four agate paperweights. "We could take the Willow Road while backup forces from Genava come through Tirin's Gap."

"Have you considered, Holiness," Commander Aulus said, "it may not be that simple with that boy calling himself Emperor Kin's son moving up from the south?"

"Emperor Kin's son?" The hollow words came from the hieromonk's lips and I willed my face not to move. The Dragon Empress would show no weakness.

"Yes," the commander answered. "Emperor Kin, second of his name, he calls himself. No one seems to know exactly who he is but he must have the backing of the generals since he is marching on Mei'lian."

"We have heard nothing of this."

Commander Aulus jerked his head at Leo. "Dom Villius brought the news, Holiness, though with Empress Miko still alive there is every chance they will rally behind her instead." He fixed his hard green eyes on me. "Really, Majesty, I find your imperial politics a little too complicated for my taste."

"Your corrupt oligarchy is much easier to understand, is it?" I said, enjoying the chance to voice my distaste in the empress's biting tone. "All those merchant houses and slippery bribes."

"Corrupt?"

The hieromonk lifted his hand, and I hoped no one else thought the movement looked jerky and stiff. "Let it go, Commander. We are attempting to save Chiltae from destruction, not start another war with Kisia."

The commander snorted. "And you really think the empress will help us with that?" He looked to me with a sneer. "Or are you hoping we will rid Kisia of the Levanti and then retreat back over our border, Your Majesty? Or perhaps..." He stepped closer. "You think that by the time we succeed in getting rid of the Levanti, we will be weak enough for your northern allies to wipe us out. Perhaps you have not heard that Grace Bahain and many others from the east have fully allied themselves with this Emperor Gideon."

In the corner of my vision the empress stiffened in her hieromonk-skin and I was glad the commander was looking at me. He smirked. "Ah, Your Majesty, I'm afraid you're just going to have to accept no one is going to fight for you. Your empire is broken beyond repair."

Finally moving from beside the brazier, Leo came forward. "It seems the Nine's belief in the power and strength of the church has waned substantially," he said, folding his arms tight across his chest as though to keep in the warmth.

"Losing almost the whole army will do that," Commander Aulus said. "I respect your positions, Your Holinesses, but I take my orders from the Nine and my orders are not to move from here and not to engage. You may, of course, travel back to Genava and discuss it with them yourselves. Take Empress Hana with you; she may be a valuable bargaining tool if her daughter decides to fight on."

The hieromonk sucked a deep breath as Empress Hana prepared to argue, but Leo moved first. "I'm afraid I don't have time for this, Commander," he said.

"Time for—?" Commander Aulus staggered back as Leo punched a knife into his gut. Once. Twice. A third time, his lip curled into an ugly sneer as the commander pressed his hands to the gushing wounds.

"Don't worry, Commander," Leo said, as the man slumped to his knees. "At least you weren't killed by a pair of whores."

Still attempting words, the man slid sideways and lay gasping at the edge of his paperwork floor. Leo stepped over him with a benign smile. "Give me your hands, Cassandra," he said, gesturing to my bound wrists with his bloody knife. "We can't go around tying up empresses. What will everyone think? Besides," he added, grabbing my arm and slitting the leather ties with which the empress had bound me, "I get the feeling you're about to have to pull Her Majesty out of my father's really quite revolting corpse."

The commander lay twitching upon the floor, his blood creeping toward his papers as he fought a slow death. Leo pulled aside the mask around the hieromonk's throat to better survey the damage. There was no mistaking the deep, bloodless slit. No matter how well Empress Hana had covered it with paint, the skin still curled out and away from the cut as the upper layer dried and tightened, and no one with an injury that deep should still be walking. Or talking. Or steadfastly refusing to bleed.

"Rough work," he said, and let the mask drop back into place. "Pull her back."

Neither of us moved. The words sounded calm, but something in the way Leo stood and spoke suggested the hulking threat of a wounded animal that could snap at any moment.

"I'm afraid you'll have to take the blame for his death," he said, pointing at the commander's body, his eyes now staring vacant and glassy. "But don't worry, it's all for a good cause. You want the Levanti out of Kisia? I am the only one who can do that and I will, but first, where is the box?"

"Box? What box?" the empress snarled through dead lips.

Leo laughed. "What box? Really?" He peered into the hiero-monk's face, perhaps hoping to read an answer in its painted features. Then he laughed again, the sound far more chilling. "Well, what do you know, it looks like Father finally learned. He peppered his idiocy with flashes of brilliance right to the very end."

Torvash's box. The hieromonk had heard Leo was in Koi and stopped to hide it, but—

Leo spun. "Ah, Cassandra. You know where the box is?" He gripped my throat. "Think of it as atonement for taking my life."

He flashed a smile as I scrabbled at his tightening fingers. "Come on, show me. Show me everything," he said, his eyes widening to mesmerising pools. "Where is the box?"

Before I could attempt a croaked answer, his grip loosened. A cry like a dying rock eagle tore up his throat and hot blood sprayed from his arm. Leo staggered back, gripping a blood-soaked sleeve, while Empress Hana stepped the hieromonk between us like a dead-meat shield.

"Fight all you want," the young man jeered. "But the only way you're getting out of here alive is by taking me to that box. Guards!" The empress lunged at him, but he darted away with a laugh, dripping a trail of blood over the paper floor. "Guards!"

The sliding doors slammed open.

Koi—impossible to get into, impossible to get out of, but I'd rather die trying than let him best me. So I kicked the nearest brazier and it fell, spilling smouldering coals over the matting and the commander's maps. Two steps brought me to a second brazier, which I tipped as the papers started to burn. A lantern sat on the table and I snatched it up too. Opening its glass hatch, I threw it—flame and oil and all—in front of the stunned guards in the doorway.

"Hana!" I shouted, tipping a third brazier into the blaze. "We're getting out of here! Come on!" She had pushed Leo back toward the balcony and I sped to open the lattice door, doubling the breeze darting in to swirl the growing smoke. "Come on, you idiot, let's go!"

She advanced on Leo, heedless of his knife stabbing her borrowed body—gut, arm, hand—slashing and cutting her anywhere he could reach.

"Your Holiness?" one of the guards called through the thickening smoke. "Commander?"

Flames chased me onto the narrow balcony where I sucked cool, fresh air. Far below, the courtyard sat like a dark pool encircled by walls. The gates stood open and freedom lay beyond, but Koi had not been built with escape in mind. Its overhanging roofs curved out like wings, making climbing up next to impossible, but down... My knees tingled at the very thought.

"Come on," I shouted as the empress burst onto the balcony, trailing smoke.

"You go first," she growled, the hieromonk's voice cracking. "I'll keep him busy." And she charged at Leo as he appeared, haloed in flames.

Working as fast as my stiff hands could manage, I untied the ornamental knot in my sash and passed its long tails between my legs, gathering the fabric into something close to pants. The cold breeze bit at my bare skin, but it was better than fire and sharp, pointy death, so I gripped the edge of the railing and pulled myself over. Arms already aching, I scrambled down the balcony's ornamental frame, dropping onto the jutting roof of the balcony below with a jolt of pain my knees wouldn't soon forget. Overhead, smoke poured from the castle like a raging dragon, while panicked cries filled the courtyard below. The great castle was on fire. Empress Hana was going to kill me.

I risked a look down and realised what I had taken for a third balcony beneath was just a collection of missing tiles on the curved roof below—*far* below. Too far for these knees. Even in my old body there would have been little chance of surviving without a broken ankle. Or worse.

"Shit," I hissed.

Something hit the balcony roof overhead and I tightened my grip, pain shooting through my knuckles. Another thud. A short rumble, then a stone launched from the curved roof, soaring out into the rain-flecked darkness.

"Cassandra?" the empress shouted from above, the hieromonk's voice drying out.

"I'm here!" I called as another bang hit the roof, this time shattering and spilling shards of tile. "What is that?"

"The mad little shit is throwing things at us! Where are you?"

Something else shattered on the roof, the sound reverberating with the buffeting of the wind. "I'm on the framework underneath. I'm not sure there's a way down, at least not without breaking a leg or two!"

"Have you tried the balcony door?"

I hadn't even thought of that, but rather than admit it, I just pulled myself back to the balcony level, shoulders aching.

"I'm coming down," Hana shouted.

"I'm checking it, all right?" I snapped back, but she joined me even as I spoke, lowering one stiff leg over the railing followed by the other. Leaving me clinging to the outside of the balcony, she made for the door, but Leo, singed and smoke-stained, appeared like a demon in the aperture. "How lovely to see you again, Father," he said, smiling as he stepped through the doorway. Hana lurched back, crushing my fingers against the railing. I let go without thinking, and as empty space yawned beneath me, I gripped the back of her robe. For a heart-stopping instant the flimsy fabric kept me from falling. Then my weight proved too much and with a rattling cry Hana overbalanced. In her hieromonk-skin she toppled over the railing, over me, and together we plummeted in a spinning flurry of white linen and rain.

Squeezing my eyes shut, I clung to her as I clung to life and she hit the curved roof first. The impact jolted through me, but lying atop her we slid together down the tiles, stopping at the eave where water gurgled in the gutter. The smell of the long-dead body was strong, but I didn't lift my head from its shoulder.

A crackle of gargled words broke by my ear, cutting over the myriad of distant voices. It came again when I didn't move, more insistent. Prising my fingers from the hieromonk's robe, I touched the cold, dead skin at his twisted neck, and like a rush of warmth and chaos the empress's soul reinflated our shell, panic giving way to peace for a single, glorious moment.

We were alive.

Hana turned our eyes up at the towering castle above. Smoke still poured from the meeting-room window, and from all around panicked shouts rent the night. The foundations might be stone, but from the main halls up, Koi Castle was built of wood and paper and it would all burn.

"I'm sorry," I said, my voice rasping like sand on skin.

The empress didn't answer. Didn't need to. Her grief, raw and bitter and all the more painful for being impotent, filled my eyes with tears.

We have to go was all she eventually said. *Leo Villius might think we're dead, but if he wants to be sure he'll have people out searching. We need to go before they shut the gates.*

The thought of moving another step that night made me wish we had died. Not the worst beating from the hospice boys had ever left me in such misery and pain.

"I'll take over," the empress said, and like warm water washing over me I let myself sink beneath her, my gratitude owning no words as she forced our body to its feet, arms and legs trembling.

Can we not make a habit of this? I said as she hobbled toward the adjoining parapet. *This escaping from Koi every few weeks thing.*

"Don't worry," she said. "I don't think either of us will ever come back."

25. RAH

Flames licked the edge of the grand doors. Smoke billowed from windows and balconies and crept in thin tendrils from gaps in the ancient woodwork. I had nothing but bad memories of the imperial palace, yet my heart ached. Burning the Motepheset Shrine would have brought a tear to every Levanti eye and weight to every Levanti soul.

"You're really going to burn it all?" I said, standing in uncomfortable truce with Sett in the palace garden.

"A broken and divided Kisia is easier to hold."

Sett turned from the inner palace, and together we walked out through the deserted outer palace, most of its furniture and art broken into piles of kindling to set the place alight. Istet smashed an oil lantern upon just such a pile as we passed, before moving to another, stuffing scrolls and papers into every hole.

"The other sites are ready," she called to Sett, her gaze fixing on him so hard she might have been trying to wipe me from existence. "Is..." Her stare intensified. "Is everyone out?"

"Light them," he said, without answering.

She saluted. "Yes, Captain."

Leaving me to trail him like an unwanted shadow, Sett strode toward the outer palace's once great doors. Smashed by the Chiltaens. Burned by the Levanti. We were securing ourselves a place in history that would not be kindly remembered.

Sett's stiff silence rebuffed all thought of argument. It was too late anyway. Plumes of smoke already filled the skyline, rising from the burning city to form a sooty, black cloud. Beneath it the palace square sat silent. No voices or footsteps, no murmur of life, not now nor ever again. The stone would not burn, but the buildings watching from all sides were built of wood and terracotta tiles, decorative shutters and reed matting and watercolour screens.

A familiar saddleboy stood in the centre of the square, holding Sett's horse. "Captain," Oshar said, his eyes widening at the sight of me.

Sett took the reins without thanks, without slowing his walk, without even looking at the translator. "General Bo?"

"He said to inform you that his men have finished with the... silk district? And were moving on to... I cannot recall its name, Captain, but the southwest quarter of the city. Captain Lashak has taken the southeast. General Korin the northeast and the northwest, either side of the main avenue, but he and the Second Swords are being held up by the number of people still trying to get out."

Sett sped his pace and his horse, not the *ilonga* he had been exiled with, had to break into a trot to keep up. Oshar's gaze slid my way as he jogged after Sett's long stride. Unsure I was the same man perhaps, with my hair growing and my branding difficult to discern. I had been itching to shave for days, weeks, fear always niggling that if I died now the gods would not see what I had sacrificed for the herd.

"Tell General Korin and Yitti to get a move on," Sett said as we reached the far side of the square. "Just keep working in. The fire will hurry people out better than we can."

A slight pause, then: "Yes, Captain, but if they have to make sure no one sees them then—"

"Just tell them to hurry."

"Yes, Captain." And with one last look at me, the saddleboy hurried away.

"You have Kisian soldiers with you?" I said as we left the square for the main street, its stones striped with shadows. "Burning their own city?"

"They are loyal to Gideon now. Or at least to the Kisian lords who are loyal to Gideon."

"So loyal they would burn their own homes? Their own history?"

He didn't answer, but whether because some of his fury had dissipated or because he realised his horse was struggling, he slowed his pace to a walk. Like the square, the top of the main street was deserted, its buildings owning only dark, staring windows and shutters that banged in the breeze.

"We needed the Kisians here with us for this," Sett said at last. "The people wouldn't understand us if we told them to hurry and get out. And they needed to see us all working together against the cowardly southerners burning their city."

"Cowardly southerners?"

He lifted his brows as though challenging me to call him a liar, but it would have been like calling the night dark. Burn the city and blame your enemy, sowing hatred for them as surely as gratitude for yourself. The plan was clever and brutal and I tried to tell myself Gideon could never have thought of it, but the order not to take the heads of the dead had been his, as had the order to massacre children, a fact I had allowed myself to forget during these weeks of trying to get back to him and save his life. Recalling it now made my insides twist.

It was eerie walking through the quiet city, but I was equally oppressed by Sett's silent stiffness as Mei'lian's empty buildings. This man had always been there, a tall, hulking figure in the corners of my life, yet without Gideon, Sett would have been no more to me than any other Torin, just one in a sea of faces, his horse's hooves part of the great rumble as the Torin made their way across the plains. Now its hooves walked alone.

"I miss the thunder," I said. "Our thunder. Not this…" I gestured at the sky. "But the thunder in the earth. The sort of thunder you feel in your bones, made of hooves and feet and cart wheels all working as one. The barrel wagons creaking and the children running with the foals. The constellation of fires at night, the smell of roasting nuts in the summer, and Masud breaking into song to praise the Goddess." A lump formed in my throat at the thought of the Goddess. Of all the things to cry over, I had never thought it would be a moon.

While I worked to swallow the lump, Sett continued on in silence. Then, like the words were being drawn from him, he said, "I always liked coming back last from the hunt so I could watch the herd cross the plain like an army of ants. And when the herd master called it a day the procession would bunch then break apart, spreading as people trickled off about their tasks. Horses. Water. Food. Wood. Fires. Tents. Each group its own little army talking and laughing as they worked."

The city had stank of mud and damp wool and fur, but now the acrid bite of the smoke outweighed it all as the wind flurried ash to our noses. We went a few more steps in silence, more and more smoke buffeting into our faces as the wind whipped around.

"But those days are gone, Rah," Sett said, returning to the present with a growl. "Be grateful the city states cannot take our memories as they can our land and our horses. Be grateful you don't have to be there to see it end."

"I still believe it can be saved. That we can fight for it as we have always done. Together."

He looked at me, a sardonic lilt to his smile. "That would require centralising the leadership. And what herd would ever accept a leader from another in peacetime? Gideon gets away with it because no one knows what to do, but at least he's doing something. He gives them purpose and hope and they forget he's Torin."

I had said something much the same to Tor when he had told me what I needed to do, where I needed to be, but I shrugged now. "They would unite to save themselves from complete destruction."

"Perhaps, but you would only prolong the inevitable. There is only one way to stop the city states and that is to destroy them, but then where would we get our grain and our metalwork, and where would we sell our horses? Your heart may lie upon the plains, but the world needs its cities now, needs its centres of learning. They say there's a room in the palace in Shimai where every wall is covered with scrolls, of wisdom and poetry and philosophy. Cities are like that—places where such ideas congregate like animals to waterholes."

"Then why burn one?"

"Because to feed the ground sometimes the trees must die."

It was an old Levanti saying, for those times when we cut down old groves to give their nutrients back to the soil, allowing future generations to grow olives and almonds and the wild rock pumpkins whose tangled vines covered the ground. Yet to think of people that way turned my stomach sick. And once again we walked in silence through the city, flames rising in our wake.

From the main road it was hard to tell how much of the city was on fire, but by the sheer amount of smoke it had to be a lot. To send soldiers in. To burn it section by section, house by house...Gideon didn't just want it uninhabitable for a short time; he wanted it gone. No symbolic place of power south of the river. And Kisian soldiers were helping him do it instead of joining the army gathered to the south.

A babble of panicked voices grew from the haze ahead, yet we saw no one until the thud of hoofbeats heralded the arrival of Himi and Istet. Both lifted their reins to salute as they emerged from the grey smoke. "It is done, Captain," Istet said. "We did a last check of the barracks and the stables to make sure everyone was out."

"And Manshin?"

"No sign, Captain."

Sett grunted and a grim smile twitched his lips, or perhaps I just hoped it did. "All right," he said. "Ride on. Tell Yitti to gather the Second Swords outside the city when they finish. Rah has challenged and it cannot go unanswered."

The twins had kept their nervous horses moving, walking in circles around us as Sett spoke his orders, but at this they both rode away, only Istet renewing her salute and saying, "Yes, Captain," before both disappeared into the smoke and babble.

Sett's words made my heart beat hard. In all the strangeness of being back with my people, of walking through a burning city and reminiscing about the plains, I had almost forgotten why I had come, why I had challenged him at all. Foolish not to have considered that Yitti would be captain of my Swords, but in truth it didn't matter who I challenged for the right so long as I won, because I couldn't fix this alone.

Fear solidified like a lump of iron in my stomach. I had not eaten properly for weeks. I had not slept. I had not trained. I had done nothing but walk and hope my injury was healing itself even as it ached. But worse still, I had not shaved my head. I could die unseen by the gods, or I could take Yitti's life. Two terrible endings to a war we should never have been part of in a place we should never have come to. Perhaps it would not come to that. Yitti was no fool, and surely he would want what I wanted, however much Sett might seek to stop me.

Despite the clouds of smoke, Sett ambled at his ease through the dying city, his horse at his side. Now and then Oshar joined him, giving a breathless report before running off again, leaving us to our silent procession through Mei'lian's last day.

When next running steps approached it was not the saddleboy, rather a pair of Kisian soldiers accompanied by a young woman. Her robe and sash were askew and dark hair tumbled from a once neat knot as she stopped outside a house, pointing at it and speaking so fast that every sound ran together. The soldiers seemed to understand her though, for both nodded and, one after the other, pushed their way into the building. Thuds and bangs reverberated through the small house, then the soldiers emerged carrying an old man between them. The woman darted forward full of scolding, and followed like a screeching tail as they hurried back toward the gates.

"Some of them are being very stubborn," Sett said. "They prefer to die than leave."

I sympathised but didn't say so.

"Gideon doesn't want them to die," he added in answer to my silence. "These are his people now."

"Except for Minister Manshin?"

It was Sett's turn to press his lips together and say nothing.

"You didn't know I was there," I said. "You came to let him go, didn't you?"

Still nothing.

"Even though Gideon gave you an order."

"You would have preferred I saw it through?" Sett snapped, only to look away, perhaps wishing the words unsaid.

Figures began to appear from the smoke. The square before the gates was still crammed edge to edge, while Levanti Swords and Kisian soldiers hurried the evacuation along. The fires had not yet spread this far, but fear spilled from the people as they fought to escape into a world where they had no homes, no food, and no future.

And there, shepherding people toward the gates, was Yitti. On foot rather than on horseback, speaking softly rather than shouting, helping Levanti and Kisian alike. This the man I had to challenge.

As though feeling the weight of my gaze upon him, Yitti looked up and our eyes met over the heads of the panicking citizens. A wry smile twisted his lips, expressing something of the sorrow in my heart. "Hello again, Rah," he called over the noise. "Such a surprise to see you."

Because of course he had known, as I had, it would come to this one day.

"Rah wishes to challenge you for the leadership of the Second Swords of Torin," Sett said before I could press through the crowd to speak to Yitti alone. "What say you, Yitti?"

Thinking to shout out my truths to him, to talk rather than fight, I looked around at the gathered crowd. None of the fleeing Kisians understood our words, but every single Levanti—Torin and Namalaka—stilled to watch like stones in the fast-flowing river of refugees. And even as I opened my mouth to explain and beg his help, I closed it again, unsure who I could trust.

"Why don't we take this outside the city," I said. "Somewhere more private and safe from getting burned alive."

The Kisians kept pushing toward the gates, crying and holding one another in a panic that had been lacking earlier in the day. Unlike us they did not know the city was being lit in an orderly fashion to give them the most amount of time to escape.

"No," Sett said. "You challenged here. Yitti must answer here."

"The city is on fire, Sett, it—"

"I accept the challenge," Yitti said, ignoring my complaint. He reached both hands to the swords at his hip but, nodding at the single blade on mine, drew only one. Gasps and whispers whipped through the Levanti as, refugees forgotten, they hurried to form a hissing circle. Citizens of Mei'lian were bustled aside and Sett's Kisian allies shouted, only to be ignored.

I licked dry lips as the circle swelled around us. Namalaka I had never seen before jostled amongst the First and Second Swords of Torin, every second face in the crowd one I recognised. Lok and Himi and Istet, Totoun and Bah and Tefnut, even Tep, Gideon's long-suffering healer, knelt in front of the other onlookers. Once it had been Yitti's job to hover ready to heal the injured, but now he faced me across the shadowy road, his expression showing none of the turmoil I felt. It ought not to have come to this.

Eyes turned toward me, granting me the challenger's right to speak first. "Gods stand on my side," I said, drawing my sword and trying to think of a way to make Yitti understand my reason. "I have failed a lot of people and now I..." Everyone was watching and I could not say any of what I wished to say, leaving me stumbling on. "I...am here to ensure that does not happen again. That we...that all Levanti...are kept safe."

Murmurs met this, surely murmurs of confusion rather than agreement, a flash of bewilderment crossing Yitti's face before he stepped in to speak. "Gods stand on my side," he called over the buzz of noise. "Too many times wrong, Rah. Too many souls lost. Eska, Kishava, Orun, Juta, Amun, Gam, Fessel, Hamatet, Ubaid, Ren, Asim, Dhamara, Hehet, Maat...Every mistake has a name, the name of someone you failed."

He listed them calmly, but every one was like a punch, dragging from me a reply I was not meant to make. "That's why I need to fight now!"

The circle hissed and shifted. Sett joined us, leaving the remaining crowd of Kisians to drain slowly through the gates of their doomed city.

Yitti stepped through shadows into a lonely patch of evening sunlight. I joined him in its bright arena and he shrugged, challenging me to strike first. Another step forward. Another lick of dry lips. Another jab of fear that I was going to die with my head unshorn like a saddleboy, that Yitti was angry enough to want me dead on the stones.

I am a captain of the Torin. The gods are on my side. I am a captain of the Torin. The gods are—

A laugh burst from my lips, sending a frown flitting across Yitti's face. "Like the gods give a fuck what we do," I said, and a surge of anger roared from the depths of my soul. I lunged, no graceful slash but a swing full of rage that caught Yitti off guard. He had just time enough to duck and lift his blade and they clanged together, reverberating in the streets of the dying city. Yitti staggered back off balance, but though I swung again, pressing my advantage, he slid beneath my blade and kicked my knee.

Stones rushed to meet me, battering head and shoulder as I rolled, all sense of where he was stolen by the stampede of refugees shaking the ground. The watching faces spun around me as I leapt to unsteady feet, feeling naked without a second sword to hold protectively before me.

Sunlight flashed into my eyes, the bright shock of it there and gone as I ducked and slashed at the incoming Yitti. He twisted away and brought his blade around, nicking my arm, but it was my thigh that bled. So much for Empress Miko's careful stitching. Whether Yitti saw the blood or not he pressed me hard on the right side, forcing me to defend with it, to step with it, to lead with it, every one of his methodical strikes only adding to my unseen suffering.

Eska's jeering anger was absent from Yitti's calm face, as again and again he struck at me only to be repelled. At any other time I might have laughed at how reluctant he seemed to strike a killing blow, but he kept coming, kept blocking and stepping, and if I did not finish this soon, I would dash myself to death against him like a wave against a rocky cliff.

I darted in, ready to feign a strike, but again light stabbed into my eyes like a blade and I flinched back. A line of fire cut the length of my arm, leaking blood as all around me voices rose in fury. Aftershocks of light stole all detail from the scene, so I held my ground, my sword raised protectively as I listened for the sound of close footsteps amid the shouting.

"Grab him!"

"That's not allowed!"

"Take that blade!"

"Quiet!" snapped the unmistakable voice of Captain Lashak e'Namalaka. "You will all stand your ground. This challenge is still in progress and until it is concluded we must show the proper respect. Bes, Ishaq, hold him down. In accordance with our code we will deal with foul play once this is settled."

Foul play. The light. I peered into the evening shadows as my vision cleared, hunting the scuffle. A group of Namalaka forced someone to their knees and kept them there, hands heavy upon their shoulders. And when the Sword looked up with a snarl it was Sett who glared at me, Sett who winced as the Namalaka pinned his legs to the stones with their boots.

Since you don't listen to me, I will have to hope you will listen to the end of his blade.

"All quiet!" Captain Lashak repeated. "The challenge must continue."

With an effort I dragged my gaze back to Yitti standing a few paces away, his blade lowered. He lifted his brows, asking a silent question, a question he gave voice to when I did not move. "Blood has been drawn, do you yield?"

"Dishonourable blood," I said, every fear for Gideon, for the future of my people, having turned to steel inside me. "I do not yield."

His gaze flicked to the wound on my thigh, but his flash of concern was squeezed aside by a nod and he lifted his sword. Dregs of evening light glinted off the blade. Had that been how Sett blinded me?

Yitti came at me, and as though the lump of anger in my gut weighed me down, I did not move. I thrust out, but he caught my blade in a wide slash that opened both our guards, yet without a second sword I could not strike. Yitti didn't have a second blade either, but he did have a boot, which he slammed down hard upon my injured thigh, sending such an eruption of pain through me that I fell back, seeing black patches as the world spun. Still more blood leaked from the empress's stitching.

"Yield!"

I had demanded the same of Eska, had warned him it was his last chance, but anger and pride had forced him on and now I understood. To yield would mean giving up and I could not do that, not again.

"Yield, Rah!" Yitti spat. "You're injured."

Deep shuddering breaths kept the darkness from drowning me and I scowled at him across the shadow-soaked road. "Not a wound of your making," I said, glancing my hatred at Sett, who glared back. "I do not yield."

Yitti growled in annoyance and once more lifted his blade. He closed the space with a few slow strides and thrust first, forcing me back. But I managed to nick his hand, and with a hiss he slashed low, ripping flesh and blood from my other thigh. I staggered a step as heat seeped out to soak my torn clothing.

"Yield," Yitti said again, and this time the hint of pity in his voice fanned my fury.

"I will not abandon him to die!"

Once again he had lowered his blade and this time I moved before I had finished speaking, feigning a jab at his face with my absent off-hand weapon and slashing in low. But he did not even flinch, just caught my blade on his and, stepping in to cramp the space, punched hard into my elbow. My sword slid through my hand and there was Yitti before me, the edge of his blade touching my throat like a caress. My sweaty fingers opened and closed upon air.

"This is your last chance, Rah," he said, the words whispered over the sword between us. "Please, yield. I give you my word I will take the Second Swords home."

I looked into his eyes and found no lie in them, no anger, only sorrow and the implacable promise of a man whose honour had never been questioned. This the man who had performed his role as healer despite his distaste for the job, a man who had never courted dissent, a man whose head it would have broken my heart to take no matter the reason, and I had to trust him.

"I came here for your help," I said, my words low and vibrant and for his ears only. "Gideon is in danger. The Kisians are not the friends you think them, just as we were not the allies the Chiltaens thought us."

Yitti stared back, his expression unshifting. Still the blade touched my throat, and there, an instant from death, all I could do was hope I had not been wrong about him. "If I yield will you help me?" I whispered, my lips sticking as though they hadn't been used for a long time. "Please?"

"No."

Anger had hardened his expression, making a mockery of my doubt. "No?"

"How many chances does a man get, Rah? How many mistakes and failures before enough is enough? Gideon is done. You are done. We are going home, which is what you ought to have been challenging me to do."

It was a deeper cut than he could have achieved with any weapon.

"You cannot doubt either that I mean it or that I will kill you," he said. "Yield, Rah. Yield. You cannot help him if you're dead."

The blade burned cold against my neck and there was no lie in Yitti's face. I had no choice.

"I yield."

The words rang into the silence, clanging like the heavy weights they were. To yield was to be exiled, to be banished alone, but no one seemed sure what to do or what to say. Had there ever been an exiled exile before?

Sounds from the dying city eked through the deep silence, but no Levanti spoke or moved. Captain Lashak unfroze first and strode into the circle. "Rah e'Torin, you are hereby exiled from the Torin herd and from the empire of Levanti Kisia. You cannot return to our lands, on pain of death, before the completion of one cycle spent atoning for your dishonour before the gods. But since we are already exiled, I'm not sure—"

"You fucking little shit!" In a flurry of limbs, Sett threw himself at me, sending us both crashing to the ground. My shoulder and hip slammed onto stone, but the stunning pain was nothing to the shock of his fist in my face. Lightning flared before my eyes and through the back of my skull as he hit me again and again, the pains melding into a continuous agony of existence. I could feel nothing of the rest of my body, could barely think or move or even hear, snippets of his rage all that got through to me.

"This is all your fault! You could have—You selfish shit, you— Just die!"

He must have been pulled off me, but the dizzy sense that I was no longer in my body remained and I could not move, could only lie still while fuzzy shapes shifted around me.

"Rah, here." Someone gripped my arms and my shoulders or maybe more than one someone because I wasn't helping much, yet they managed to get me on my feet, my legs trembling sticks beneath me.

"Rah e'Torin," Lashak said, her voice an anchor amid the slowly focussing blur. "It is your place to decide the fate of Sett e'Torin before you depart. His actions are a stain upon all Levanti honour, the action of flashing light into the eyes of a challenger alone worthy of death."

The silence broke in a wave of whispers and only then did I

realise how many Swords were watching and how many Kisian soldiers had stayed. They were all vague shapes in the haze of the burning city, my returning sight caught to Sett and Sett alone. I limped toward him, a buzz of fury beneath my skin all that moved me.

I parted my lips to speak, but my mouth was full of blood and I spat it at his feet. "You..." I began, swaying. "You attack me for having abandoned Gideon, you rail about how I should have been there for him, about how much he needed me, but where were you, Sett? Where were you? You're his blood brother, born of the same womb. He has many close supporters, people who have been here far longer than I, yet always it is me you spit and shout at, me you expect the world of, my shoulders upon which you drop the weight of responsibility."

"Because he loves you!"

"That's not how love works!"

A seething silence followed. I could not even think for the rage and hurt swirling through my head, every throb of my skull making me more and more convinced it had been split open.

"Well?" Captain Lashak prompted. "What is your pronouncement?"

Sett glared at me. "Go on, Rah, spill your incorruptible honour on me, your perfect virtue. You who shamed yourself and your people. *Whisperer.*"

"Go to the hells, Sett."

The First Sword of the Namalaka nodded without emotion, and in the breath of silence before the great outcry she stepped toward the Swords holding Sett captive. They forced him forward onto hands and knees and he did not fight, did not plead, just laughed. A low, rumbling laugh that cut beneath the uproar as, heedless of both, Captain Lashak lifted her drawn sword and brought it down point first upon the back of Sett's neck. His laugh died with a gurgle and his body fell flat upon the road, splayed like a gutted rabbit.

"The dishonoured one has been dealt with according to our code!" Captain Lashak shouted over the thunderous uproar. "If anyone so much as touches Rah e'Torin in retaliation for his decision they will answer to me. Let him walk!"

I stared at Sett's fallen body and told myself I had not meant the words so, that my curse had been taken too literally, but the fury still seething in my blood was bitterly satisfied at the outcome and I knew it to be false comfort.

Anger seethed in the circle around me. Sett had been their captain. Blood brother of their emperor. And I had just willed his death.

"Go on," hissed Yitti, still beside me. "Go."

I picked up my fallen sword and limped toward the city gates, increasingly sure I could not see out of one of my eyes but unable to quite grasp why. My mind seemed to have room for Sett's body, Sett's spitting fury, and nothing else. Every step I expected someone to stand in my way, to strike me, to trip me, to gut me where I stood, but every Sword stepped aside with a mutter or a jeer. I didn't want to see their faces, but I refused to look at my feet so I met their stares with all the pride I had left.

Once the Levanti had let me pass the Kisians did too, their curious, pitying looks harder to bear than the anger of my own people. I wanted to run but forced myself to walk all the way to the gate. And then I ran.

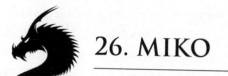

26. MIKO

A covered cart smuggled me into Jie's camp, proof that whatever his failings, he was not a fool. It would have been an easy win to carry me through the camp like a trophy, to let the southern soldiers vent their frustrations throwing rotten rations at me, but not all loyalties were split so clearly by geography. To execute me respectfully for treason was one thing, to publicly humiliate me might only fan the flames of dissent. It would have been the vengeful act of a child, and therefore one he would not allow.

I saw no one upon my arrival, not even Jie. A pair of guards quickly hustled me out of sight to a repurposed storeroom with a solid, swinging door and no windows. A small grating in the roof allowed a faint chink of moonlight to spill from a light well, illuminating nothing but a hastily laid sleeping mat.

For a converted storeroom it made a good cell. It took mere minutes to exhaust all hope of escape, leaving me hours of sitting with my thoughts, alternately angry and despondent, determined and hopeless. And in the darkest moments it was not my mother's words that returned to me, not Emperor Kin's, not even my brother's, but Jie's. *You did not even let me try! You just got rid of me like the annoying little boy I am.*

Every remembrance of it made me rise from the floor and pace, recalling all the times I had been told the same. That I ought to have been born a boy. That no woman could rule the empire. It was not the same though, not really. A child had not the experience, the knowledge or appearance. What soldier would feel confident riding into battle with a little boy leading the way?

You are not so very far removed from childhood yourself, my inner voice would say when I tried to defend myself to the darkness. *And what soldier feels better with an unseasoned woman leading the charge?*

"But I have proved myself!" I snapped at the empty room. "It is not the same."

It wasn't, but neither was it so very different.

You did not even let me try.

The words turned my determination to guilt and my anger to dross. But if age was no reason to remove him from power, then neither could it excuse poor decisions. An emperor ought to die before they let Kisia be so shamefully diminished. An emperor ought to fight. To fight and fight and never give up, not roll over like a beaten dog before ever riding into battle no matter how fearsome the Levanti were.

The memory of Rah joined me in the darkness. Silent, watchful Rah, always confident and sure and unflinching in his honour. I had wanted to hate him, had tried so hard to hold on to that anger, but in the end, I could only hate him for making it impossible to hate his people.

Footsteps sounded outside and I stilled my pacing, ears pricked to the clack of heavy wooden sandals. Not a guard then. Not a servant. Yet the quick approach slowed, the hesitant steps accompanied by the faint, mournful tinkle of ceramic bowls. The steps stopped some distance from the door, but my guard did not speak. I held my breath. I dared not hope and yet... Perhaps, were it just Jie and me, we might reach an understanding.

"My lord," rumbled the guard outside my door, his tone wary. "I am under strict orders not to let anyone see the... prisoner."

"Yes, *my* orders," spoke a voice that sank my heart. "Now I am giving you a new order. I will see her."

I looked around in the hope an escape route had suddenly appeared, but one had not.

A key grated in the lock, and with a squeaky click the storeroom door opened just far enough to admit Lord Oyamada and his tray before closing again. "Ah, I have brought you tea," the man said, a lantern swinging from his hand. "I hoped you would not yet be asleep."

He looked about as though expecting to find a table. Finding none, he set the tray down with an overemphasised groan of aching joints.

"Why are you here?" I said, remaining by the wall when he invited me to join him.

"To talk. To drink," he said, settling himself upon his knees with a wince. "This is our last opportunity, after all, and whatever I think of your family and your intentions, your knowledge is invaluable."

"You'll not execute me if I give you information?"

The man laughed, a tinkle of ceramic joining in as he moved the teapot. "Oh no, you're going to be executed either way, but as you professed your duty to the empire, I knew you would want to share your information in service of it."

"Only if you could be trusted not to use my information for your own gain. You want to know who the biggest contributors of soldiers to the military districts are, perhaps. You want to know who fought for Katashi Otako in the rebellion so you know which families to fight for and which ones to let die, but oh no, all those records are in Mei'lian and you can't get to them, can't even be sure the Levanti have left them untouched."

An unpleasant smile curved his lips while he served the tea. "You think you're very clever, don't you? I am not worried about the Levanti. What do they know about defending a city?"

"Then what do you want to know?"

"What you were planning to do. I understand pushing Jie away and stealing his throne when you had an army at your disposal, but what are you now? Just a single young woman with no soldiers, no family, and no money, and yet rather than running for safety, you came back. Why?"

"Because Kisia is all I know. All I care for."

"And so?" He slid a bowl across the tray, his shrewd eyes looking up through bushy brows.

What *had* I been planning? I had been travelling to Mei'lian to find Minister Manshin, sure he would not abandon me, that he would have a plan. I had been clinging to that goal with the obsession of one who had nothing else.

I lifted my chin, still not joining Lord Oyamada upon the floor. "My plans are my own business."

"So you had one? That does surprise me. You are very like your mother, and if Empress Hana was renowned for anything other than her affairs, it was for darting through the court like a fiery arrow without stopping to consider her direction. I imagine that is how she burned as many allies as she did enemies. Are you sure you will not join me for tea? It is very good. And it's the last cup you will ever have." He sipped his own, his top lip becoming pointed like a turtle's upon the rim. "I'm afraid Jie isn't coming," he went on when still I didn't move. "Were you hoping for him? Yes, I imagine you were. Sweet, impressionable little Jie. Given the chance you might have talked him around. It's too bad he isn't old enough to be swayed by his cock, hmm?" He nodded at the tea he'd poured, before lifting his own steaming bowl once more to his lips.

His visit wasn't going how I had expected. Proud, sneering Lord Oyamada was a different man without his puppet grandson to impress. Grace Bachita had been the same, and I couldn't but think poorly of Emperor Kin's foresight in choosing two such men to guide his son's footsteps. No doubt he hadn't planned to die.

The smell of the tea tickled my nose and dampened my tongue, and making a show of reluctant politeness, I knelt, joining Lord Oyamada in the circle of lantern light he had brought with him. Lazy swirls of steam still rose from the surface of the tea, and for a moment I was back in my mother's rooms as a child, bade to sit still and silent while she dressed. I had watched the steam curl from her teapot, been mesmerised by the glint of sunlight on gold silk threads, and the musical crack of reeds as maids came and went, whispering.

I cupped the tea bowl in both hands and lifted it, thrusting away the thought it might truly be my last. I was to die in the morning and right now only the man kneeling across from me could change that. A man who would give his whole fortune to see me dead.

Steam billowed into my face as I looked down at the sunken dregs in the bottom of the bowl, and almost I swallowed my own tongue. Not just dregs, but small, clear crystals mixed in with the leaves. Helio salt. Someone had slipped it into Mama's tea once, perhaps the same someone, but with his eyes fixed upon me I could not even take the time to wonder, could not show by look or tremble that I had seen it.

"May I ask you something, Lord Oyamada?" I said, jerking the bowl back from my face like one struck by a sudden thought. Hot liquid slopped over my hand and I did not need to feign my yelp. I set the bowl down and mopped the hot spill inelegantly with the skirt of my robe. I took my time about the task, enough to slow my rapid heartbeat before looking up. Lord Oyamada had frozen with his own bowl inches from his lips.

"You wanted to ask me something," he said when I returned his quizzical look. "Something of enough consequence to make you spill your tea." He set down his bowl. "Here, let me pour you some more while you recall your question."

"Oh yes, please do," I said. "I only wished to know how you intend to keep Jie under your control when he is of age. Shall you play the dedicated adviser and hope for the best? Or perhaps you have some more ingenious method in mind."

The man's bushy eyebrows lifted even higher. "Under my control?" he said, barely glancing up as he refilled my bowl. "What a strange notion. You speak as though I dislike my grandson and wish to take his place. For what it is worth, Highness, you could not be farther from the truth." Here none of the grandiose railing he had subjected me to back in the tent. This Lord Oyamada was quietly spoken and watchful. "It is you I do not like, and not only for your name but for the danger you represent to an idealistic young emperor. It truly is a blessing that you possess neither beauty nor a conciliatory personality, else getting Jie to agree to your execution might have been impossible. As it was, you made it much easier by so kindly pointing out that you had no interest in being his bride." He laughed. "Is there anything as fragile as a boy's pride?"

Lord Oyamada gestured to the renewed tea bowl with a smile. "Your tea, Your Highness."

My lips had not touched the poison, I knew they had not, and yet the room seemed to spin and shrink in upon me. This was it. If I didn't drink it, he would have another plan. A weapon, perhaps, hidden in his sash. This man didn't only want me dead, he wanted me dead without the fanfare, without the watching crowd, and without the final opportunity to appeal to Jie because there was a chance, however small, I might find the right words to reach him. I had feared not making it past the morning, now it seemed unlikely I would even survive the night.

There was no way out.

I took the bowl, all too aware of Lord Oyamada's gaze upon me. Watching. Waiting. I did not meet it, but I could imagine his tongue tracing his lower lip, dry with anticipation. His moment had come. Drinking the tea would make an easy end of this hell, but beneath that thought anger boiled. So often had assassins come for me because of my name, so often had I been told I was not good enough, that it was a pity I had been born a girl, and that I could not rule, should not. Would not. And I would not let them win.

Steam rose from the bowl, its ceramic warm in my hands. He had poured it with his right hand, so I hunted his left hip for signs of a hidden blade. I had to be smart. There might not be time to make a second guess.

"Something the matter, Highness?"

"Not at all," I said. "I am just musing on what a fine night it is to die."

I threw the bowl at his head. Lord Oyamada flung up his hand, but though it stopped the bowl from hitting his face it didn't stop the hot tea. He yowled with shock or pain or both and I crashed over the tray to pluck at reams of folded silk only to find no blade.

He pulled it from the other side of his sash and swiped blindly, eyes still half closed from the scalding water. I leapt back, kicking shattered bowls and sending the tray sliding into the lantern.

Lantern.

I snatched it up and swung it into Oyamada's head. The man dropped amid a dying flash of light and a tinkle of broken glass. Cooling oil hissed.

A key scratched at the lock and the door opened a sliver, the body of the guard blocking the light from the passage. "My lord?"

Slinking through shadows, I tugged free one of my remaining hairpins.

"My lord?" The door opened a little wider, enough to spill light over the dazed Oyamada.

"My lord!" The man lifted a blade, eyes darting in search of me. "Your—"

I plunged my hairpin into the side of his throat, the resistance of so much muscle turning my stomach. The man scrabbled at it, gurgling and trying to speak, his eyes wide and imploring.

"I'm sorry." I darted through the door. "I'm sorry."

I slammed the storeroom closed and turned the key with a shaking, bloodstained hand. The passage was empty. I was free, but what did it matter? I still had no allies. No army. I was completely and utterly alone, making a mockery of all those who had died to help me come this far. No matter how hard I fought I just kept losing, the empire crumbling beneath my touch.

Something hit the inside of the locked door. Muffled, Lord Oyamada shouted, "Let me out! You foul, traitorous whore!"

He hammered his fists upon the door, making enough noise to wake a household. I hurried toward the stairs. In the distance someone shouted. Another voice followed and I halted to listen. More voices, growing muffled, then nothing.

I crept up the stairs through alternate pools of light and dark, tensing whenever the house creaked. Every moment I expected guards to appear, but the house remained quiet, even when I reached the dim shadows of the main floor. Yet the house did not feel asleep, more like an animal hunkered amid the grass to watch and wait, the only sign of life its slowly swishing tail.

Upon reaching a long gallery I allowed hope to flare. Golden moonlight streamed in through tall, narrow windows, and moonlight meant outside and outside meant freedom. And there, thrown on a table in haste, sat my dagger, its unsheathed blade glinting orange.

Some luck at last.

I picked it up, feeling so much better with it in my hand. Now I just had to get past the guards that would surely be standing outside and then...

My toes dipped into the stream of golden light spilling through the window, and I looked up. Not a lantern as I had supposed. Not even a golden moon.

I hurried to the window, my breath held. Mei'lian was ablaze, smoke and flames reaching to a cloudless night sky. I had rejoiced in our first truly fine day since the beginning of the storm season, but now I willed the clouds to return, to drench the city and save it from becoming nothing but ash and memory. But I was no god and the clouds remained parted, allowing the stars the finest view.

I could not move. My heart ached and tears pricked my eyes. Mei'lian had been my home. I had tried to fight for it and failed, had promised the people I would return only to fail again. And now I could imagine their screams as fire licked from window to window and danced along tiled roofs. Everywhere the choking stink of burning flesh and smoke and—

"They must have known they couldn't hold it."

I all but swallowed my tongue as Jie appeared in the shadows beside the open shutter. Had he been there the whole time? Waiting? The boy did not look around. "So they chose to burn it rather than let us take it back."

Did he think I was Lord Oyamada returned from downstairs? I stepped away slowly.

"I wish I could just reach out and—" He stretched a hand toward the window and pinched thumb and forefinger together as though squashing the city, a hiss like dying coals spitting between his teeth. "After all, I'm meant to be a god, am I not?"

I took another step back, preparing to sprint for the doors. They were closed, the blazing city staining them gold.

"They're locked," the boy said, still not looking around. "I'm hiding from the generals." He barked a bitter laugh. "Isn't that a brave thing to do? I guess you were right about me being a stupid little boy."

"I never said that."

He looked around, his expression registering no surprise at the sight of me as his gaze travelled from my bloodstained robe to the knife clutched in my hand. "You didn't have to. Going to kill me? Is that your plan?"

"No."

"Then what?"

"You don't move and I walk out."

Jie shook his head, glancing back at the burning city, its flickering flames turning night to day. "I can't do that."

"Yes you can. You're the emperor. You can do anything you want."

"Not if I want to stay emperor. I have just lost Mei'lian on the eve of battle. If I lose our traitorous prisoner too, I may as well hack off my own head to save my generals the trouble."

"But you are Emperor Kin's heir."

Jie laughed, but the sound owned no humour. "You're so caught up on the importance of your name and your family that you can't see beyond it. Names don't matter anymore. They haven't mattered since my father took the throne. He broke the divinity of the Otakos. He set a new precedent. And having seen it done once *everyone* knows it can be done again. Kisia doesn't need an Otako or a Ts'ai, it needs a strong and capable leader, and as soon as they stop believing I can be that, as soon as they realise how much easier it is to rule without me, I'll be as dead as you and a new name will rise to the throne. General Moto perhaps. Or General Rushin. Someone who commands the loyalty of the soldiers like Emperor Kin once did. That is the only sort of leader Kisia needs now."

His words were wise beyond his age. He had been sheltered from life and raised upon lessons and war diaries, on politics and history and family lineages, and from outside the court had understood Kisia better than I had from within. An icy fear trickled through me. Was I outdated and unnecessary?

"Either way," he said, still watching the city burn, "I'm probably dead now."

"Then let me go."

Jie turned from the window, firelight caressing the side of his youthful face. "No." Once again his gaze slid to the knife in my hand. "How many assassination attempts did my father survive?"

The answer was sixty-four, but before I could speak, he drew his own dagger—not a common soldier's knife but an ornate blade made for an emperor.

"He told me once it had become a sort of game in the end," he said. "A test. People didn't want him dead so much as they wanted to prove he could die. But he rose from the ashes of the rebellion stronger than ever and renewed his legend every time they failed to finish him." Jie spun the dagger in his soft, fine-boned hands, the movement far more skilful than I had expected. "Only one of us is going to live to see the dawn, so tonight I start my own legend."

He shed his imperial outer robe as I backed away across the gallery floor. "No," I said, cold sweat sticking my feet to the wood at every step. "We can think of something else. I admit I wanted to hurt you when we first met, I wanted you to suffer because I could not make Kin suffer for what he did to my brother. To my mother. To me." He stepped toward me, a head shorter and yet menacing like a wolf. "I wanted to kill Bachita too, wanted to be rid of him before he could force me into marriage, before he could..." I let the words hang, unspoken. What did I know of a man's lusts? The memory of Rah in the bathhouse flashed into my mind only to be pushed away along with its uncomfortable desires.

Jie stalked toward me, his step a soft clack. "Uncle Bachi didn't want to marry you," he scoffed with the confidence of a child. "He always said the only good Otako was a dead Otako. If you're going to lie to me at least make it convincing."

"You want to hear the truth?" I said, retreating another step.

"The truth is I am taller than you. I am stronger than you. And I have been training longer than you. You can't win this fight."

"I can because I must."

Tanaka had owned such assurance, and the hole my dead twin had left in my heart widened like a wailing maw. Grief I had not let myself feel lumped in my throat and I took another step back, my grip on the knife shaking.

My back hit the wall, heralding my last chance to change his mind. "Jie, you are the only family I have left," I said. "Don't make me do this." Tears stung my eyes. Too many dead or lost to me. Tanaka. Mother. Ryoji. Edo. Manshin. Kitado.

The boy stopped advancing, but the bright, fevered light didn't leave his eyes. "I'm not making you do anything."

He jabbed at my gut only to pull up short and thrust savagely for my heart. Had I stepped left instead of right he might have killed me in a single move; instead his blade plunged into the meat of my upper arm. Pain sheared through my tired body like the bitter winter wind, but there was no pause, no time to think or feel or fear as he withdrew it with a frustrated growl and sliced at my throat. I dropped, and jammed the point of my own knife through his left foot.

Jie howled amid a symphony of tiny toe bones cracking, and lifting his foot to cradle it, he kicked me in the face. I fell back, pain thudding through the bridge of my nose and into my head. "We don't need to do this," I said, pressing a hand to my nose. "We can be smarter than our fathers, we can put our past aside and—"

"It's too late!" He leapt, the tip of his blade rushing toward my eye. My knife dropped as I caught his arm with both of my hands, the force of his charge throwing me back. My head hit the floor and darkness flared, but I locked my elbows to keep the blade at bay. Firelight gilded the side of his hair, but the rest of him was a snarling shadow as he sought to bury the tip of that ornate dagger in my throat.

Though blood poured from my wound, I held him off. Until Jie bit my wrist. Shock buckled my arms then and he fell onto me. I tried to roll clear only to get caught between his knees, but before he could stab me, I slammed my forehead into his. It hurt more than I had imagined, bone hitting bone, but he jolted back with a cry and his blade leapt from his hand, landing out of reach with a heavy thunk.

We paused, both stunned and bladeless and catching our breath, but before I could beg for a truce, his hands lunged for my throat. Firelit, his eyes gleamed with triumph. I tried to speak, to plead, but the words got lost in a string of strangled sounds and I squirmed instead, refusing to believe that after all this I would still not see the dawn.

A loud knock sounded on the door, cutting across the fevered huff of Jie's breath. "Your Majesty?"

That voice...

I tightened my hold on Jie's wrists, trying to pry his hands from my throat. He had the advantage of his whole weight, but—

"Emperor Jie? It's Lord Manshin, your father's minister of the left."

The boy dug his fingertips into my neck. With all my strength I tried to loosen his grip, enough that maybe, just maybe, I could breathe. Could move.

From the other side of the door came the clipped, efficient tone I had come to admire. "I have just this day come from Mei'lian, Your Majesty, and whatever our past grievances, I must speak with you immediately."

Rah had done it. Somehow. He had found me the ally I needed. I was no longer alone. And fighting through the pain in throat and arm and head, I prised Jie's hands just loose enough to gasp a stinging breath and roll. To the left, then to the right as fast as I could, throwing him off balance. His hands ripped from my throat.

"Emperor Jie?" came the concerned voice from outside. "Are you all right?"

"I'm here!" I tried to shout, but a baby bird croak was all that issued from my lips. "I'm—"

Jie leapt at me again. I wanted to beg and plead for him to stop, but could only roll clear and crawl toward the doors as Manshin knocked again. "Majesty? Majesty!"

I reached the matting beneath the table before Jie landed on my back, slamming my chin into the reeds. Knee cushions scattered as I flailed and bucked him off, spinning around with hoarse words spitting from my lips. "Stop this! We can talk. We can—"

He pounced like a wild animal, and in a tangle of arms and legs and scratching claws we rolled, slamming into the legs of the table and scattering the remaining cushions. If Manshin knocked again I didn't hear him, couldn't hear anything beyond the thud of my own desperate heartbeat and Jie's grunts and snarls as he scrabbled for my throat. I tried to shout for help, to scream, to shake Jie and stop this madness, but the boy dug his nails into my neck like burning needles tearing flesh.

"Stop! Jie, we don't have to—"

I cried out as he slashed my throat with his sharp nails, and through the thundering of my pulse came a banging upon the door. "Emperor Jie? Empress Miko?" The doors rattled in their tracks, and eyes alight, Jie gripped my shoulders and slammed me into the floor. My head hit the matting.

"Stop...fighting...me," he hissed, spit spraying my face. "Just die already!"

Something hit the doors.

"Just...*die!*"

He jabbed a finger at my eye and I rolled him onto the matting, pinning him with my knees. He tried to buck me off, creeping his hand toward the hilt of his fallen dagger. Blood poured from the wound in my arm and my throat burned, but the boy was not done, would never be done until one of us lay dead upon the floor. It was him or me, and I did not want to die.

Jie was so focussed on reclaiming his dagger he didn't see the cushion until I wrestled it onto his face. There I held it with all my strength, pinning it down with locked elbows while he fought to throw me off, wriggling and squirming and kicking.

A muffled cry wailed into the feathers, then there was nothing but the drumming of his heels hard and fast upon the wooden floor.

"I'm sorry," I whispered in my broken voice. "I'm sorry. I'm sorry."

The drumming sound changed as his sandals fell off, leaving his heels bruising upon the floor. His shoulders twitched. His head jolted. His grip upon my arms opened and closed and his fingers straightened, bending back even as they reached for me in the darkness.

"In the hands of the gods may you find true peace, in the hands of—" His tense, twitching body went limp. His heels stopped drumming.

I pulled the cushion away and there lay Jie, his face slack and discoloured. "Shit." My bare feet scuffed the floor as I scrambled back from his lifeless body, small and pitiful now without its rage. "No. No. No!" I pressed trembling hands to my cheeks, but I could not drag my eyes from the boy's broken body.

He had been just a child.

"Your Majesty?"

Manshin stood a few steps inside the doors shattered in their tracks. His face was thinner than I remembered, its harsh lines gilded by Mei'lian's rising flames. We had once tried to save that city. Together.

Without a word his gaze darted from me to the still form of Jie and back, and his expression hardened. I had no words, no plea, no explanation, nothing until he turned to leave.

I breathed a wheezy plea then. Lacking all intelligible words, the sound nevertheless confessed the depths of my fear. But he didn't leave. He called no guards. He just slid the doors closed as best as he could.

"Get up," he said, striding back toward Jie. "Your people need you."

"My..."

He crouched at the dead boy's side. "You're the Empress of Kisia, are you not, Your Majesty?"

"Yes," I wheezed. "But no one will follow me, not after..." I looked at Jie, his head lolling as Manshin lifted him off the floor. Minister Manshin was a tall man, and in his arms the boy looked a boy indeed, a child who ought to be playing with toys instead of lying dead upon the floor. I reminded myself he had wanted me dead, had fought with the ferocity of a much larger, older man, yet still shame poisoned every thought. It ought not to have come to this.

The minister crossed the floor and set the boy down upon a silk-covered window seat. Bathed in orange firelight, Jie's body sat propped against the stiff cushions like he had fallen asleep.

"Do you think people followed Emperor Kin because they chose him to be their emperor?" Manshin said, returning to the table. "Do you think they would have chosen a commoner had they been asked? No. Emperor Kin took the throne and held the throne because he knew the power of a good story."

Bending down, he poured tea into the only bowl on the table. No curls of steam issued from the spout, the liquid as lifeless as Jie.

"Emperor Lan was dead," he went on, carrying the tea back to the boy. "And whether or not it was Grace Tianto who did it, it made a fine tale. Lan and Tianto were well known for their heated arguments, and Emperor Lan had just sent Grace Tianto back to Koi in disgrace—how easy to believe that had been a final straw. Did it matter that Tianto hadn't been in Mei'lian at the time? No, it only made the story all the easier to manipulate. And before anyone could wonder how it had happened, a new emperor sat upon the throne."

Manshin put the tea bowl into Jie's slack hand, closed the boy's fingers around it as best he could, then let it go. The limp arm dropped, sending the bowl to smash upon the wooden boards, spilling tea and shards of ceramic.

"Now we have a story," he said, turning back to me. "An emperor too ashamed to see the dawn. It's time to get up now. You have to make these soldiers follow you and we don't have much time."

He walked to the door and there he waited—patient, loyal Manshin. He had come, the ally I needed, yet I could not drag my eyes from the lifeless boy basking in the light of his burning city. I was still alive. I could fight on. But at what cost?

27. DISHIVA

No one spoke as we left the campsite, Loklan, Esi, and Shenyah as dead-eyed as the heads in the sacks tied to the back of Itaghai's saddle. My mistakes. My responsibility to free their spirits or present them to Gideon, come what may.

Levanti watched us from the trees as we approached the deserter camp, and the sentry who greeted us took in our brandings and our stained clothing before his gaze came to rest on the sacks dripping blood and swarming with flies.

"We have a shrine and a burning pit," he said at last.

"Thank you, but I will take them back with me." I grimaced at the wrongness of the words, but the man made no judgement, only shrugged, leaving me to my dishonour.

A small crowd had gathered to stare and they all bowed their heads as Whisperer Ezma emerged from her hut, the prongs of her jawbone headpiece reaching for the trees. Behind me Loklan gasped.

"A Whisperer," Shenyah said, breathless with awe.

Ezma waved her hands. "Clear a path. Nefer, show these Swords where to go while I have a word with Captain Dishiva." She looked to Loklan, hovering around his horse. "Let them bring the injured horse through. Safer you leave the poor thing to be taken care of here than risk walking her all the way back to Kogahaera. If you must leave us, you may ride one of your fallen brethren's."

A moment of indecision, then with a grim smile, Loklan said, "Yes, Whisperer."

While they walked into the camp, Ezma smiled at the remaining crowd until they dispersed through the drizzle, whispering all the way. Once they were out of earshot she turned that smile on me, hard-lined and dangerous. "I want your word on peace, Dishiva e'Jaroven."

"Peace? I have no control—"

"I do not mean peace for this land. What Gideon does concerns me little beyond how it affects those Levanti who choose not to be a part of it. Give me your word you will not tell him where we are, or that I exist. We will not interfere in your plans or his if you leave my people alone."

My people. There was a possessiveness to her words that rubbed like sand upon my thoughts. Horse whisperers were not herd masters, not Sword captains; they were separate, individuals who were part of a conclave of horse whisperers but had no followers. Not like Dom Villius. Yet when I didn't speak she went on: "My people have done nothing to earn your emperor's ire and you must know that with a horse whisperer as their leader, we could. I could. If he makes me."

Behind her the camp was full of Swords who had come to lick their wounds and their honour, to beg forgiveness and to grieve, and to bask in the protective aura of a whisperer. Now that same whisperer—tall, graceful, and sure—stood before me speaking threats while a light dusting of rain sparkled in her hair like stars.

"I will tell him that rumours of a deserter camp are much exaggerated."

"Good," Ezma said. No smile, no grimace, nothing but a perfunctory nod. "I ought to have killed you last time rather than let you walk free but had you not returned, Gideon would merely have sent more people after us. This way is better for everyone."

I did not doubt for a moment she meant it, or that she could have done it. She had the poise of a skilled fighter while I had been named Third Sword of the Jaroven for my resourcefulness and my stubborn refusal to give up.

Soon Loklan and Esi and Shenyah returned, and still crushed beneath the weight of our collective silence, we prepared to leave. Ezma pressed rations and fresh water upon us and I climbed into Itaghai's saddle.

"Captain Dishiva!" Tor shouted, striding toward us. "Captain!"

I turned in the saddle, the translator's expression launching my heart into my throat. "What is it?"

"That book you gave me," he said, and I clenched Itaghai's reins as Tor went on. "I haven't been able to translate much yet, but I flipped through looking for all the references to Veld I could find, like you asked. He seems to have been a sort of early believer in a time when he was scorned for following the One True God. 'He who saw that which was and that which is—'"

"That which has been and that which will be," Ezma corrected. "There is an important difference."

"You know the book?"

She returned my stare with a challenging lift of her chin. "Missionaries reach almost everywhere on the plains, and there are certain phrases that stick in the mind. Do continue, Tor; it was rude of me to interrupt you."

Ezma folded her hands behind her back, but went on staring at me while the young man spoke. "Well, Captain, given he was so scorned for wanting to believe in something no one else believed in, it took me a while to see why someone would say Leo Villius is like him, but…"

Tor trailed off, biting his lip and looking from Loklan to Shenyah and back to me.

"But what?" I said when he didn't continue.

"Well, he dies, you see. Three times, so far that I am up to and I don't think I'm reading it wrong. I don't think it's a title, I think it's his name. Veld dies and he comes back and—"

"Dies how?"

"The first time he is killed on the orders of his leader. The second time he dies in a throne room when he stands up for his people."

I had been there for that one. I had seen it. "And the third?"

"The third time he is trapped in a cave."

I sucked in a shuddering breath and let it out slowly. It did nothing to calm my racing heart. "In a cave?"

"That's what the book says."

"And you're sure?"

"Yes, but it's a complicated book and Chiltaen doesn't come naturally so..."

"And after the cave...he lives again?"

Tor frowned. "Yes, it says he is reborn, but I haven't gotten any further."

"Try to get a message to me when you do, all right? I need to know what happens next."

"Yes, Captain."

I had not killed him, and when Leo had seen where we'd taken him, he'd laughed. He had not struggled or cried out for help, not tried to fight, and when Jass and I had set him down in the small cave he had merely wriggled, getting comfortable for the long wait.

He had known.

Beside Tor, Ezma still stood watching me with narrowed eyes and the sort of intensity Leo Villius himself possessed. I could not meet her look, sure on some level she knew what was going through my mind.

"Are you all right, Captain?" Loklan said as I stared at each of my Swords in turn.

"No. Yes. I don't know," I said. "But I have to go. I'll meet you back at Kogahaera. I...there's something I need to do."

"Before you go, Dishiva." Ezma stepped forward, her hands clasped behind her back. "Where were you born? Where was your herd?"

"I...uh, on the Essaph Plain, why?"

The whisperer nodded. "Then I need you to be very *very* careful indeed. We will meet again. Of that I am sure."

I rode through the day and into the night until I could push Itaghai no farther. We stopped far from the road where no one would see us, but I could not rest and could not eat, could only think of the laughing priest waiting to die in his cave.

The next day we broke clear of the fen and rode across rain-drenched fields to the mountains west of Kogahaera. By evening Itaghai was struggling with the seemingly endless climb. Everything looked the same in the blustering rain, every track edged in jagged rocks and caves and trees dropping their sick yellow leaves. Even when the rain eased back to a drizzle, thin waterfalls maintained the sound of furious water crashing upon the world, masking all other sounds.

A sensible person would stop for the night and make camp, would tend their horse and eat and rest and plan how to find the right cave in the morning. I kept going.

"Jass!" I shouted to the darkening sky, and cupping my hands to my mouth I called again. "Jass! Where are you?"

Itaghai flicked his ears in disapproval, but afraid of being too late, I urged him on along the dusky trail. "Jass!"

No answer came and I kept searching as night birds swooped from their hollows to hunt. More than once I leapt from the saddle, sure I had the right place, only to find the cave too small, too narrow, or entirely uninhabited. Yet this looked like the right place, I was sure of it, and went on calling for Jass long after I ought to have stopped. Just one more cave. Just one more.

I walked Itaghai on into the gathering shadows. For all I knew I was going around in circles or had wandered too close to the city and would be seen, but I went on shouting into the whipping wind all the same. It stole the words from my mouth while heavy rain hit my shaved scalp. Perhaps if I looked for the crack that led to the caverns beneath the manor, I could—

"Dishiva!"

I spun yet saw nothing but rain and rocks slick with moss, nothing but trees and ferns and flowers flattened by the storm. "Jass?"

No reply. I peered into the night as it closed its hand upon the world. "Jass!"

"Dishiva!" He appeared, a smoky figure in the haze.

"Jass! Is he alive?"

I leapt from my saddle as he jogged toward me through the dusk, and though he must have been burning to ask what had happened with the deserters, he said nothing, just lifted his arms and let me walk into them to be held. That he gave comfort unconditionally, that he gave it even though he had trusted me with the lives of many he cared about, brought forth tears I had been unable to shed. But I swallowed them because comfort was not why I had come.

"Is Leo still alive? Please, Jass, tell me he's still alive."

I could have pleaded. I could have shouted. I could have cursed him with every curse known to the Levanti tongue, but it would have made no difference to the slow shake of the head I received in answer. Without waiting for an explanation, I hurried toward the cave now so obvious upon the rocky mountainside.

Smouldering coals lit a shadowy space no more than a dozen paces deep. We had carried Leo out wrapped in my bedding, which

Jass had made into something like a nest in the centre of the cave. The remnants of a meal remained, along with a collection of small bowls woven from flaxen grasses. Jass had made it as cosy as he could, yet I strode through the light and the warmth to where Leo sat propped against the back wall, his bound hands in his lap. His head lolled and there was no trace of life in his glassy eyes.

"Leo?" I shouted into the young man's face, gripping his shoulder and trying to shake him. But the body was stiff and slid slowly sideways to lie like the broken collection of limbs he was. "Leo," I repeated, my voice breathless at the edge of panic. He was dead. But how? I hadn't been gone many days and I had left them with food and water and—

Still crouched, I spun back to Jass, standing in the doorway with Itaghai's discarded reins in his hand. "I told you to keep him alive."

"I tried," Jass said, and though in the light of the fire I could see how tired and worn he looked, how much the ravages of the poison still haunted his face, it did nothing to stem my fury.

"What do you mean you tried? He's dead!"

"You can't force a man to eat or drink, Dishiva," he said. "And trust me, I tried. Every time I poured water down his throat he would breathe it in and start choking. Any food I tried to give him he spat back out."

"Surely it takes longer than...How many days have I been gone?"

"Three? Four? Five? To be honest, I have lost all sense of time up here, but I think he might have been bleeding more than we thought too. There's certainly a large pool of blood drying beneath him, see?"

Jass pointed, and the hint of its scent coalesced into a stink.

"However it happened, he wanted to die and there was nothing I could do to stop him."

I got to my feet, hands clenched into fists. "Yes, he wanted to die so he could come back again. Come back and finish the job of killing us and destroying everything we have fought for."

"He might not. He—"

"He will. I took the holy book to Tor at the deserter camp like you suggested. That man, Veld, who they all venerate, he first died on the orders of his leader. Then he died being cut down in a throne room. And then he died in a cave. And then he came back."

Jass's eyes widened. "That's in their book?"

"Yes."

"No wonder the pilgrims think he is a reborn hero. What if he is, Dishiva? What if he really has been sent by their God to remake their holy empire?"

"Then we had better hope Tor finds out a way to kill him before he kills us."

For a moment we just stared at one another over the smouldering remains of the fire. Then Jass said, "Until then, what are you going to do?"

What *was* I going to do? I had been so focussed on getting here in time to stop Leo dying that I had given little thought to what I would do after. Yet there really was only one option. "I have to tell Gideon everything," I said, clenching my hands to keep them from shaking. "I have to make him see Leo isn't his friend. That Leo is only using him and—"

"And risk being executed for treason if Dom Villius has as much control over him as you fear."

"I..." I wanted to spill all that had happened, to tell him how I had failed my Swords and betrayed Gideon, how he needed support more than anything, how dangerous Ezma's presence felt, but when I opened my mouth to speak none of it came out. In the end all I could say was, "I have to try, Jass."

The words were a plea. I needed no agreement, needed no

permission or understanding, yet I wanted him to tell me it was the right thing to do.

He gave me what I needed with a solemn nod, and I covered the distance between us with four quick strides. "I'm sorry," I said, bending my forehead to his. "About all of this."

Jass snorted a little laugh. "Whatever for, Captain? Who doesn't like almost dying and—"

I pressed my lips to his, the gentle gesture better able to convey my gratitude than any words I could speak, and we stayed that way long after we should have parted, long after the kiss was complete, unwilling to let go.

———————◆———————

I stayed until morning, a morning I had hoped would never come. Curled upon each other's warmth, I told Jass what I could of the events at the deserter camp, and he pushed me for no more, content to know the Levanti who had chosen not to follow Gideon were safe for now. Tears had followed and for a long time he just held me close.

We had fallen into silence after that, and then from silence to gasping together upon the mat and at last to an unsettled sleep. I had dreamed of what awaited me back at Kogahaera, and come morning he only asked me once not to go.

"You'll have to travel to the fen camp on foot, I'm afraid," I had said. "I'll try to find a way to get your horse out there when I can."

"A Levanti? Walking?" He made a look of mock horror, but though he meant to make me laugh, ill-ease wormed into my mind. I had apologised because it was beneath him to walk, yet most members of our herd walked the plains, only the Swords allowed horses to scout and hunt and defend. Because we were better? More important? When had I started thinking so?

Jass's smile faded. "Don't go back," he said. "There is nothing you can do to stop Dom Villius if he returns; he'll know you for his enemy and…"

He left the rest unsaid and I was grateful for it. "I'm a captain, Jass, I cannot abandon my Swords. You know I can't. And surely Leo will not be back already. This is the only chance I'll have to convince Gideon."

"I understand."

Whether he did or not he made no further attempt to change my mind, and in silence we each prepared to leave, abandoning Leo's corpse to the dark recess of a cave in a mountain full of caves. Perhaps animals would eat him. It seemed a fitting end.

No goodbye would have been adequate, no wish for good fortune sufficient. All we could manage, facing one another that blustery morning on the hillside, was a mutual salute, a lingering touch, and a shared mumble of "May Nassus watch over you." Then I was in the saddle while Jass began his journey on foot.

It took most of the morning to reach Gideon's stronghold at the edge of Kogahaera, its two towers striving toward the clouds. The clang of the gong heralded my arrival, and while the sentries shouted greetings, the gates to the imperial compound were dragged open just wide enough to allow Itaghai through.

"Captain!" Massama strode toward me, gathering eyes as she crossed the yard. "You are alone. What news? Where are the others?"

"I have much to tell, but I must see Gideon first," I said, and dismounted before Itaghai could carry me straight on to the stables without stopping.

"His Majesty is in his room, Captain, but…" The Sword lowered her eyes and said, "Is…Esi…?"

I had sucked a breath, waiting for her to deliver some horrible pronouncement, that Gideon was injured or dead or mourning the loss of his empress to assassination, but the yard was calm and the manor quiet. "Esi is fine," I said, surprised by Massama's awkward stance. "At least she was when I last saw her a few days ago. They ought to be back soon."

Massama let out a sigh, nodded, smiled, and gestured rather vaguely toward the manor. "His Majesty is inside."

"And Keka?"

"Keka was in the barracks last I saw him, Captain. I can run and find him if you wish."

"No, I will find him when I am finished with Gideon."

"As you say, Captain."

I handed her Itaghai's reins, stopping only to untie the stinking sacks of heads. With one weighing down each arm I strode across the yard, daring anyone to accost me, but whether because of the dripping sacks or the ferocity of my expression, no one did. Yet eyes followed, turning to whispers as I passed.

I shivered as I stepped through the manor doors and into the cool, dry hall crossed with its heavy black beams. Every lungful tasted of reeds and incense, of paper and tea and mud, and my heart hammered in the vicinity of my throat. Almost I preferred the smell of the sacks. I did not want to be here, but I forced my feet on.

Senet and Anouke were on guard duty outside the emperor's rooms. They straightened when they caught sight of me and murmured, "Welcome back, Captain," while averting their eyes from the sacks.

"Knock for me," I said, nodding toward Gideon's door. "My hands are rather full."

Senet grimaced and knocked.

"Yes?" came Gideon's voice from inside.

"It's Captain Dishiva, Your Majesty," Senet said.

"Ah, send her in."

Anouke gripped one door and Senet the other, and with a

flourish they slid them open, saluting as I entered with all the confidence I had left. Long strides, head high, chin lifted, and—

The sacks hit the floor with a squelchy thud, covering my shocked exclamation. For sitting across the table from Gideon, a tea bowl cupped in his long-fingered hands, was Leo. Leo turning to look at me over his shoulder. Leo smiling, a genuine smile like that of an old friend. Leo from whose face I could not pull my gaze even when Gideon spoke.

"You have news?"

Still staring, I managed a strangled "I am interrupting."

"Not at all." Leo smiled even more broadly as he gestured for me to join them. "I was just sharing with His Majesty the directions to the deserter camp you gave me before you left. *Shrine. Fork. Carved tree. Large boulder in a pool of swamp water.* I've remembered it exactly as you said."

He had been there, had still been alive when Jass had made me repeat the directions over and over to be sure I had them right. And now he knew. And Gideon knew.

Gideon's gaze slid toward the sacks oozing blood and stink at my feet. "Well, Dishiva? What news do you bring?"

And sitting across from the emperor, Leo smiled.

28. CASSANDRA

The cart stopped just south of the Rice Road and we climbed down, thanking the farmer with a forced smile and one of the empress's rings. He took it in his calloused hand and stared at it a long while, the stare of a man who would tell this story to his children and his children's children until the day he died. It was several long minutes before he drove on.

Rain danced through the pale morning as we left the track, lifting the hem of our robe to keep it from catching on the long grass. The rumble of the cart drawing away mingled with that of the distant thunder. Another big storm was coming, though the storm season would soon wear itself out and winter would be upon us. Already the air held none of its summer heat, and the damp linen against our skin left an uncomfortable chill.

You're used to having more padding.

"Padding? What am I, a chair?"

Come on, you know what I mean. It was a long night. Your body is—was—a lot more curvaceous than mine.

"I've noticed."

The empress lapsed into silence as we struggled on through the tall, clinging grass. It was like trying to swim through seaweed, and she was right—it had been a long night. She had travelled most of it while I recuperated in the darkness, but our body was worn out. At the edge of her thoughts, constantly pushed away, was the fear of another bad bout of illness. The last one had nearly killed her. And there was no Witchdoctor here to help.

Don't think about it. Just keep moving.

I walked on, having to yank my feet from the sucking mud and step over tall grass only to plant them in still more sucking mud. There had been plenty of other options. We could have travelled on toward the capital, have headed for the border, have hidden ourselves away in a farmhouse in the hope Leo wouldn't find us, but the mad vehemence with which he had sought the box had brought us back here instead, hoping to understand why. To understand his plans.

The hills and the misty morning rain swallowed the cart as it wound away along the track, leaving us alone in the middle of nowhere. A scattering of trees lay to the north while fields stretched south, and if we kept walking west we would soon reach the foothills of the Kuro Mountains. They rose as hazy peaks in the distance, edging Kisia like a city wall. I'd never wondered what was on the other side. Perhaps there was no other side and the mountains just went on forever. Or perhaps there was a whole other empire.

Tribes, mostly, the empress said. *We've had agreements with a few for trade routes, but it's no safe journey. Although neither is the summer pass to the south, I understand. The sea wind is as endless as it is bitter.*

As though summoned, a chill wind whipped across the field, shaking the grass and billowing the wet cloth of my robe. I crossed my arms over my chest. This was definitely where we'd met the scouts, where the hieromonk had called a halt and sent Captain Aeneas off with the box. He had been told to hide it, but where?

I walked on, stopping every few minutes to look back and check we were alone. Leo had been willing to kill for the box, but until I knew what was inside, I wasn't willing to die for it.

Sure no one had followed, we walked on toward the mountains

for a time, only to turn north toward the trees when we found nothing. Swiff had been gone a long time when he helped the captain, but they couldn't have gone that far burdened with a heavy box.

Stop.

I stopped, planting sandalled feet in the mud while wind blustered around us, pecking us with rain. The now distant track was still empty, as was every horizon. "What is it?"

Listen.

Wind and rustling grass, rumbling thunder and—

"A dead body."

The song teased my ears, so faint it might have been just a trick of the wind, but with nothing else to go by I turned west and followed its call toward the mountains.

You don't hear dead animals, do you?

"Never have before," I said. "So unless being an Otako grants you some affinity for . . . pikes or . . . dragons." I finished lamely with a flap of a hand, and Empress Hana deigned no reply.

A hill barred my progress west across the rainswept field, the sort of hill that from a distance looked like nothing but up close was a mountain. My knees protested just looking at it, but the death song was growing louder and stronger with every step, so west we had to go.

I tried to make it halfway up before stopping to rest but only made it a third. Already saturated, I sat in the wet grass and stared out at the grey morning, taking deep breaths to calm my racing pulse. But I couldn't seem to fill my lungs, my ribs too tight, and the more I tried the more uncomfortable it felt. Panic crept in from the edge of my mind, carried on dark thoughts. We could die here on this hillside, in pursuit of nothing, and no one would find us until animals came to gnaw the meat from our bones. Would we still be here, stuck in this skin while they ate? Sharp teeth ripping muscle and—

Cassandra!

Darkness closed around me as the empress took over, calming her body as only she knew how. Fear might catch at her attention, but she knew this skin, had lived with this illness, and so held the reins until our breath evened and our heartbeat slowed. Every part of her body still ached, but the worst had passed by the time she let me stand us up and continue toward the source of the song.

It must have been almost noon when we reached the top of the hill, so bright was the patch of cloudy sky overhead. The wind had died a little, but the rain continued to drizzle and dark clouds to the east promised more to come. Beyond the hill a slope led down to a muddy gully only to rise again to an even steeper hill, where rocks and twisty trees took over from the tall, waving grass. There was nothing to see, no sign of Captain Aeneas or the box, so we followed the song, half walking and half sliding down the slope to land in the mud. Our sandals sank beneath the surface, cold brown sludge creeping over our toes.

"Gross," I said. "This is why I like cities."

In a city it would be human refuse instead.

"Just call it shit, all right? None of this 'human refuse' business. It's not like there's anyone around to say it's un-empress-like." I tried to lift my foot, but the sucking weight of the mud was too strong and I could not pull it free. "Fuck."

Miss Marius—

"Shut up, we're stuck. Let me think." I tried to wriggle my foot, but it only invited the mud to close tighter around my ankle like a rabbit trap.

"Empress Hana?"

I looked up. Captain Aeneas stood on the slope, wet hair covering the scars around his eye. He had frozen mid-step, staring. "Hello, Captain."

The soldier looked from horizon to horizon without moving. "You're alone, Your Majesty?"

"As you see."

"His Holiness...?"

"Is dead."

His hand twitched toward his throat, touching an unseen pendant. "How?"

"This is hardly the place for conversation, Captain," I said, looking pointedly down at my stuck feet. "Why don't you pull me out of this mud and then we can talk."

Captain Aeneas folded his arms. "Why don't you ask your friend to help you?"

"Friend?"

"I heard you talking to yourself, so either you have a passenger"—he tapped the side of his head—"or you've lost your mind. Either way you're dangerous. Safer to leave you where you are."

"Passenger?"

"No need to pretend, Your Majesty," he said. "You don't serve the hieromonk for twenty years without learning things you never wanted to know."

Fear sparked at his words, but I tried to remain calm. My feet were stuck fast and I needed his help. I had refrained from reminding the empress that I'd told her going into Koi was a bad idea, and now she returned the favour with a deep silence.

The captain unclipped the scabbard from his belt and brandished it. "I can pull you out," he said. "But only if I like your answers. Understand?"

"Perfectly."

"Good. How did you know where to find me?"

"I didn't. I've just been walking around in the hope of running into you."

"God be damned, you're bad at this. I thought an empress would be used to lying. All that...court politics and"—he waved a hand—"backstabbing."

I scowled at him and set my hands on my hips. "You try lying with a new face and see how well it works for you."

Cassandra!

The man tilted his head. "Miss Marius?"

"Captain Aeneas."

"Where's Empress Hana?"

"Oh she's here, but it's beneath her dignity to talk to you so here I am."

Cassandra!

Captain Aeneas scowled at me and I scowled back. Truly it was brave of the raindrops to pass between us.

Eventually the captain grunted and looked away. "Her Majesty is to be pitied. Do pass on my condolences that she has to put up with you. Now you'll have to give me *very* good answers if you want my help. The world would be a much safer place without you."

I clenched my hands, hating that it made my knuckles hurt. "Safer with Leo in charge?"

"Oh? You think you know all about Dom Villius?"

"I know the hieromonk was afraid of him. I know he can do things no one should be able to do, and I don't think he'll stop at being lord and master of Koi. I also know you're going to need help getting that box out of here as fast as you can because he knows you have it and he wants it. I don't know what's in it, but whatever it is I think it's safer in your hands than in his, so here I am." I spread my arms. "Does that answer all your questions?"

He passed the scabbard from hand to hand. "No, you still haven't told me how you found me."

"I followed the call of the dead."

His brows rose. "The what?"

"Dead bodies sing to me," I said, looking away to avoid the sneer sure to overtake his face. "I think it's because they are empty vessels, a soulless container into which I can offload my extra soul."

Offload? Don't forget whose body this is, Miss Marius.

"A poor choice of words," I said aloud, not caring that he heard me. It had been a very long day.

"But there are no dead bodies here," the captain said.

"There must be. I can hear one." I pointed to where a short spur protruded from the hill behind him. "It's coming from the other side of that hill."

It was quite loud now, but as the captain turned to see where I pointed, I had to remind myself he could not hear it. I awaited his incredulous laugh, but like the mocking sneer, it never came. He turned back slowly. "From over there?"

"Yes."

He seemed as unwilling to meet my gaze as I had been to meet his, and for a moment he stared at the ghostly forms of the Kuro Mountains rising in the west and gnawed his lower lip. "And the hieromonk," he said, still not looking at me. "How did he die?"

"Leo killed him when he wouldn't say where you were."

"Is that true, Empress?"

She took over to answer, a catch in her voice as she said, "Yes. There was a fight and the castle caught fire." Her castle.

"And Swiff? Etus? Jovian?"

The memory of the hieromonk plunging his blade into the back of Swiff's neck replayed in my head, but I did not speak the callous words upon my tongue. Let him believe his master had been a good and pious man. "I'm sorry."

Captain Aeneas looked away again, but his lips twisted in wry amusement. Perhaps he had just realised I was his only surviving ally. An assassin in the body of an enemy empress. No doubt he had hoped for better.

Time dragged on, marked only by the thousands of raindrops that hit the ground while he debated our fate. Not liking his scowl,

I wriggled my feet again, trying to slide them out of the sandals and pull myself free.

Captain Aeneas thrust the scabbard out to me, a literal peace offering. "There's something you need to see," he said, not seeming to notice the sparkle of relieved tears upon my already rain-drenched face.

Not trusting my voice, I just gripped the end of the scabbard and wrenched first one foot then the other out of the mud. They came free with sucking squelches and brought so much mud with them they'd doubled in weight, but I was free and Captain Aeneas made no move to draw his sword. Instead he jerked his head in the direction of the death song and trudged away up the spur.

The effort of climbing yet another slope sapped all my remaining strength.

I need my body back, I said, even my thoughts sounding breathless as we neared the summit of the low spur. *We can't keep doing this.*

Empress Hana didn't answer.

Captain Aeneas waited at the top of the short hill, frowning as I joined him. The muddy gully ran around the spur like a river, leaving a small, flat piece of land like the webbing between a frog's toes. Someone had built a hut on it, nothing more than three ramshackle walls and a roof to protect whatever feed or tools were stored inside.

Captain Aeneas ran down the slope to the building and, without waiting, disappeared inside. I followed at an awkward, limping run, reaching the bottom to find him waiting beneath the overhanging roof. Whatever the original contents of the hut, it had been stripped back to a few loose mounds of straw. One had been covered with a blanket, while an untidy bundle of rations spilled from an open bag and the beginnings of a carving sat discarded in the middle of the floor.

The box sat at the back, covered in a smattering of straw—enough to confuse someone glancing in, but not someone who knew what they were looking for. I shivered, disliking the cold, clammy feel of the wet robes against my skin.

Captain Aeneas beckoned me toward the box Leo had been prepared to kill for. "Do you want to know how Leo Villius comes back from the dead?"

"Yes."

My breathless answer drew the captain's attention, but I shrugged off his concern. "The people whose heads I cut off don't usually come back for them."

"He didn't."

"Yes, he did. He took the sack from my hand."

The captain brushed the straw from the box and levered up the lid. Nothing leapt out, but my heart hammered as though it had and I didn't move until he jerked his head to invite me closer.

I saw the hand first, sitting upon undyed fabric like a body laid to rest. A body. In a coffin. My eyes darted to its face and I froze. It was Leo. It was Leo, from the fine-fingered hands to the pointed nose, from the soft, smiling lips to the pale eyes that seemed to look through one to something far beyond. They stared now at the dark roof with the same intensity, not seeming to know we were there.

"Is he...?"

"Dead?" Captain Aeneas said. "No. You can check his pulse if you want to be sure."

I had killed so many people, yet here at last was a body I couldn't bring myself to touch. But I didn't need to. Its chest rose and fell with the slow rhythm of someone in a deep sleep. "If he's not dead then why is he just lying there staring? Is that...a new body for when his current one dies?"

"No," the captain said. "This is Leo Villius. So is the one you just met in Koi. So is the one you killed there a few weeks ago. And the one who died at the hands of the Levanti. You are a Deathwalker. You have two souls in one body. Leo is... the opposite."

Kocho had mentioned such things when he sat sipping tea in my room that night. A single soul born into two bodies. The opposite of me. But this...

"How many bodies?"

"Odetta Villius gave birth to seven babies. All identical. I was a new recruit at the time, but I was there when it happened. One could not leave their service after that. They paid well for silence."

"Why?"

Captain Aeneas looked down at the still form of Leo Villius. "Why? Seven identical children, one of them..." He gestured to the body in the box. "It was unholy. The position of the church at the time was too precarious. It would have been used against them. Better to send six of them away to be raised elsewhere and keep one as their son. I was at the birth and so I made the journey out of the city with the six."

He passed a hand across his eyes as though made suddenly old by the resurgent memory. He was like a man unburdening his soul at judgement. "Of the six we had with us, five were normal, squalling babies, sucking their wet nurses dry and lulled to sleep by the movement of the carriage. The other..." He didn't look again at the unmoving figure in the box. Its eyes went on staring at the roof upon which rain drummed. "He's always been like this, ever since he was a baby. Doesn't talk. Doesn't move. If food is put to his lips he eats. If you pull him by the hand he walks. The body is alive, yet it has no... no..."

"Soul."

It was Empress Hana who spoke through her own lips and when I tried to back away her feet were planted upon the dirt floor.

We shouldn't have come, I said. *We should have gone after my body. Whatever this is, it isn't our problem.*

The empress stepped forward, and keeping our hands tucked beneath our arms, she leaned over the immobile young man. "Perhaps six is the limit to how many pieces a soul can break into," she said. "Torvash would know."

"The Witchdoctor?" It was Captain Aeneas's turn to look wary. "No doubt that . . . *man* knows as much as is possible to know about this particular Leo Villius. This is what the master traded you for. Both of you. The Witchdoctor came to study the seven boys when strange things started happening around them, but he would take no payment in gold or jewels or land. He only wanted a specimen. Septum has been with him ever since. I did not think to find him so well cared for."

"Septum?"

"They named themselves. Duos stayed to be brought up as Dom Leo Villius. Unus, Tres, Quator, Quin, Sextus, and Septum were sent away."

"The one I killed was Dom Villius then? I mean Duos, the real one."

Captain Aeneas looked grim and shook his head. "I doubt it. They are all the same, all with the same memories and the same thoughts and they know everything the others know at the exact moment they know it. It really is as though one person lives in seven bodies—seven bodies, one mind. One whole. It could have been any of them and you wouldn't be able to tell the difference. Except for Unus. There is something . . . extra, something different, something wrong about Unus. It's hard to explain but you'd understand if you saw him. And you'd know if you had."

The captain shifted from foot to foot, his eyes averted from the Leo he called Septum.

"You're afraid of him."

He went on staring at the floor some distance from my feet.

"The hieromonk was afraid of him too."

But I had travelled with Leo, had laughed with Leo, and had resisted the need to kill him as long as I could. He had been a sheltered, naive nobleman's son, a little odd, more than a little frustrating, but not evil. Not frightening. At least not then.

"So…" I trailed off, still trying to shape meaning into words. "The one I killed, whichever it was, he didn't come back to life at all."

"No."

"He's dead."

"Yes."

"And the one the Levanti turned on in Mei'lian?"

"Is dead."

"And what happens when they die?"

Once again Captain Aeneas didn't speak. The slight shrug he gave was answer enough. He didn't know. Of course he didn't know. It wasn't like you could pick up a book to find answers. No wonder Torvash had wanted this one.

I looked back at Septum, lying in his coffin. And he stared back. Not at the slanting wooden roof but at me. Right at me, with the clear, penetrating gaze his brothers had used like a weapon. "Shit!"

Captain Aeneas stepped back, breathing a string of colourful Genavan swear words. "Oh, fuck!" he ended, and retreating another step he dropped the lid with a reverberating bang. "Fuck!" He turned his wide eyes on me. "He's never done that before."

"Never?"

"Never."

Captain Aeneas and I stared at one another for a few seconds that I willed into an eternity. I shouldn't have come, should have insisted on going north, on chasing down Kaysa in my God-be-damned body. I should have run fast and far and never looked back.

Now it was too late.

We have to get out of here.

"We have to get out of here," I agreed aloud. "They all know we're here now, don't they? And that we're together."

"Yes. Yes, they do." Captain Aeneas paced the few steps from wall to wall and spun in the dry dirt to pace back. "Fuck!" he barked again, fingers running rows through his sodden hair. "We have to go. You have to help me get him out of here."

"Why not just kill him and run?"

The captain stared at me for a long moment, his jaw slack as though he had never even considered that as an option, but he glanced at the box and shook his head. "No. Septum could be the only way to stop Leo."

"What do you mean, stop him?"

"He's...You were right when you said he wouldn't stop at Koi, but it's not Chiltae he is conquering for. His Holiness went back for Septum because he knew Leo had been looking for the box and he couldn't let Dom Villius near the Witchdoctor in case...in case it only made him stronger somehow. He hoped..." He was babbling, pacing as he spoke. "He was sure the other Leos' sudden interest in finding Septum meant the...spare body must somehow be dangerous to them. A weakness." Captain Aeneas stopped and turned on me. "If you don't want to wake up one day and find Leo Villius the god-ruler of all that was once yours, Your Majesty, then I beg you to help me."

"I'll help you," she said, and I had to force my consciousness back to the surface to add, "But what about my body?"

We have to, Cassandra, the empress said. *This is our only way to save my daughter. To save Kisia.*

What do I care about Kisia?

You don't care about anything, but you are in my body and I am dying. Let me have this. Let me try to fix some of the mess I made before I am gone.

Her words cut fear into me that I tried to force away, tried not to dwell on, but it brought back the question that kept plaguing me. What would happen to me if this body died?

From the doorway, the captain glared, daring me to refuse, his very stare a reminder that he could have left me stuck in the mud. I didn't care about debts, but the empress was right. Leo had wanted Septum, which meant we couldn't let Leo have him. Not the Leo with wild eyes who had just tried to kill us.

I folded my arms and glowered at the captain because anything was better than admitting the empress was right. Admitting I was afraid to die here. "Fine, I'll help," I said. "But you have to say please."

A wary smile flickered upon his lips. "Really?"

"Really. No one ever asks nicely."

His smile twisted into a grimace. "All right. Please, Miss Marius, I need your help."

"We'll work on it. Let's go."

29. MIKO

The maid clicked her tongue as the comb caught on a knot of hair. There had been no time to bathe so she had sponged the blood from it as best she could, hurried along by the hovering figure of Minister Manshin. He had arrived like a whirlwind, picking things up and dropping them back in ways that better suited him. Pacing the floor before me, he said, "You remember all of that?"

He had been talking of Bahain and the Levanti, of war and revenge, of what it meant to be Kisian in our hearts. The words had washed over me, but all I could think of was Jie's staring eyes and fat, protruding tongue. Now I sat in his room wearing his robe, and with the dawn I would face his army for a far different show than what they had gathered to see.

Manshin stopped pacing. "Your Majesty? Are you hearing me?"

"No," I said, looking up and incurring another sharp *tsk* from the maid. "We need Oyamada."

"That is a dangerous proposition, Your Majesty."

"More dangerous without him, surely," I said, my voice sounding flat even to my own ears. "You said Emperor Kin sold the people a story they wanted to believe, but he could only do that because he was already someone they listened to. None of these soldiers have ever listened to me, but they have listened to Oyamada."

The minister chewed his lip. "There is much in what you say, but I don't think he will speak for you."

"Oh, I think he might. How long do I have?"

He looked out the window to where the first hint of dawn stained a night long torn by firelight. "Not long." He went out on the words, leaving me to the maid's ministrations. Her hands had shaken as she bound my wounded arm, but every moment helping me prepare had returned some of her composure. I had let her dress me in jewels, let her do up my hair and straighten Emperor Kin's imperial robe across my shoulders, and when I had tried to draw the line at paint, she had appealed to Minister Manshin with a level of entreaty that bordered on tears. One look in the mirror had been enough to make me relent. I looked terrible. Dark rings hung beneath my eyes and despite the maid's ministrations my hair was a mess, my face was pale and strained, and so many days walking Kisia without adequate food and rest had left me thin and worn out. I needed food. I needed sleep. I needed to scrub away the memory of that dead face. Of the child who would be emperor.

There would be time to grieve later. I had said that of my brother. My mother. Ryoji. How many lives would I have to grieve when the time finally came to rest? To stop.

With another click of her tongue, the maid fixed up some paint-work around my eyes with the tiniest of brushes. Outside the sun crept ever up and there was no going back.

After a time, footsteps reverberated through the house and Minister Manshin returned with Lord Oyamada. The man looked almost as bad as I did, dishevelled and bloodstained and pale beneath the blotching of tea-burned skin, but he straightened his back as he entered, his wrists straining against tight knots.

"Where's Jie?" Oyamada demanded as Manshin pushed him down onto the matting before me.

I inclined my head in a stately way that would have made even my mother proud. "Emperor Jie is dead."

Lord Oyamada said nothing. Instead he eyed my robe and my hair and at last turned to look out the window at the rising sun. "I see," he said. "And now I am to be executed."

"We could do that."

His brows lifted, disdain in every line. "Could?" He carried his pride like a mask, holding back his grief as I held back mine. "Your prattle about an alliance didn't work on me before, and now you've killed my grandson it is unlikely to have a better effect."

Excuses and explanations leapt to my tongue but I swallowed them all. They were a weakness no emperor was allowed. Kin had taught me that, had named it one of his lessons that night in Koi before Tanaka's return. *Lesson five, never beg forgiveness. Gods are never wrong.* It was not the lesson I needed now, however.

Lesson three, find their weakness.

I thought I had been doing so all along, but I had misjudged the man. I was not used to seeing familial love.

"I wish to honour Jie and continue on in his name," I said. "I wish to ensure it is known far and wide that he was Emperor Kin's son and heir, and that I, his sister, Miko Ts'ai, intend to avenge his passing and that of his father, by reclaiming their empire. I wish to give due honour and position to your family."

Lord Oyamada eyed me warily, his lips pressed tight against the spilling of grief or rage or both. Silence hung. The maid fussed with my hair. "A sentiment," he began at last, having mastered his first impulse, "that may sound hollow and false to any who saw you take the throne in Mei'lian."

"Not if they understand Grace Bachita acted without authority. I stepped in then, as now, merely to ensure the protection of Kisia."

A smirk quirked his lips, but though I couldn't doubt he wished to throw my failure in my face yet again, he did not. But nor did he decline my offer.

"We have lost all sense of unity," I said when he didn't answer. "Not only with half of the north bowing to the Levanti but with the south fractured into factions. Jie was losing them. Kin lost Bahain before ever the Chiltaens set foot across the border. We have to do better. We have to *be* better. Emperor Kin was divisive. My mother was divisive. My brother—" Words choked in my throat and I forced them down. "Even Jie was divisive. I have a chance to step out there as neither Otako nor Ts'ai, but as the last surviving member of any imperial family. And with a lord of the south and a minister of the north beside me, perhaps the generals and their soldiers will listen."

"And this position you offer, does it see me chained whenever I am not dancing upon a stage?"

"No. I said I would honour my brother, Jie, and his family. If you wish the same then I offer you the chance to stand with me, not against me."

The man sneered, but again he did not immediately answer. And as the silence stretched his sneer became a grimace and he looked away, afloat upon his undercurrent of grief. It drained as quickly as it had risen, and I couldn't but honour him for having a heart to break.

"I wish you had never been born, Your Majesty," he said at last, speaking without rancour as a man might observe a change in the weather. "Kisia would have been better off without your mother seeking to tear down Emperor Kin. And without you and your brother, nothing but the diseased remnants of an exiled madman."

"You are right," I said when he ended upon a sigh. "My mother, for all her professions of love and duty, was the worst thing that ever happened to this empire. But we cannot undo what has been done, we can only make the best of what we have and seek to build something bigger and better than ourselves. You have my word, Lord Oyamada, that I will seek to do this selflessly, for the good of Kisia, not myself. But to do that I need your help."

Behind the man, Manshin scowled, but he did not interrupt either my assurances or Oyamada's silence. Lord Oyamada's jaw worked as he sat with his thoughts, and again I waited. Not so many hours since this man had tried to end my life and now here I was appealing to his honour so I might spare his.

Eventually he fixed me with a narrowed gaze. "You'll name me minister of the right?"

"Yes."

"You'll let me send out proper announcement of Jie's ascent to the throne as well as his parentage? Even into the north?"

"Yes."

"You'll let me tell the story of his end as more...glorious than it was?"

I thought of the boy's dead, staring eyes and forced out a whispered "Yes."

I had given him a position of trust, and a proper place in history for his grandson and his family, yet still Lord Oyamada gnawed upon his thoughts. I acquitted him of being stupid enough to demand things I would never give, but as he was already rich in both land and gold, I held my breath. At last he spat out his final demand.

"And you'll not marry without our agreement?"

I had given no thought to marriage, but though I wished to snap that I would marry whom I willed, when I willed, I swallowed the words. Kisia had always had an emperor, not an empress. Because of that, whoever I married would gain more power as an imperial consort just by being a man than any woman had ever done. An eventuality Oyamada was right to fear.

"Yes," I said at last. "It is Kisia I want the people to fight for. I will do nothing to jeopardise that."

Lord Oyamada tilted his head just enough to glance up at Manshin standing over him. "Does that include having a minister of the left whose daughter is married to the Levanti emperor? I own I am surprised that Her Majesty puts so much faith in you, Ryo."

Cold fear gripped my heart. Sichi. Lady Sichi, who had been promised to my brother, who I had last seen in that bathhouse south of Shami Fields making a plea for information. Lady Sichi, who we had thought dead, married to the man who called himself Emperor Gideon e'Torin. Grace Bahain was her uncle. Had she known that day in the bathhouse? Had she begged for information because she stood upon a precipice I had never dreamed could be coming?

I forced myself not to look at Manshin as doubt flourished. He had served Kisia unfailingly and had turned on Bachita to protect it. If I ever stopped serving Kisia the way Manshin envisioned, would he turn on me too? Or could Bahain's plot already run that deep?

"That he married my daughter is all the more reason for me to be here," Manshin replied coldly. "It must be made clear that my daughter's betrayal of her empire is not my betrayal. I fought the Levanti. I stood up to the Levanti. I survived the Levanti."

Oyamada's only reply was a slight smile and an inclination of his head that seemed to mock even as it agreed.

"You sneer, Lord Oyamada," Manshin said. "But I remember what all you southerners forget. Every time we let someone step across the border and take our lands, we set a new and dangerous precedent. That same precedent has seen Chiltae shave more and more land off our border every year. If Kisia accepts rule by barbarians without a fight then invaders will never stop coming. We will be seen as weak, conquerable, and our border and our lands will never be safe again. Perhaps that doesn't matter to you down here because we northerners fight and die to keep your lands safe, but let the Levanti keep the north and your families and your way of life will never be safe again no matter how peacefully this Gideon e'Torin attempts to rule. I would fight for *that* before any child of my blood."

Impossible to answer such a speech, but his fervour quelled the strongest of my fears, even if it did nothing to allay my lingering doubts.

"We are running out of time, Your Majesty," Manshin added a touch impatiently when neither of us answered. "The sun is up. The generals have gathered."

Oyamada smiled with his lips alone. "Then let me go clean myself up so I do not present the wrong picture upon the stage."

Manshin looked to me, his way of asking if I was sure. I nodded, and he cut the sash binding Oyamada's hands and let the man rise. With nothing but a mock little bow, he departed.

"He will bury a knife in your back at the first opportunity," Manshin said.

"Then we must try not to offer him such an opportunity."

"We should be rid of him as soon as possible."

Again the thought of Jie stuck in my mind like food in my gullet and I could not answer. I had not spoken my fine speeches merely to win Oyamada temporarily to our side. If we were going to beat back a Levanti emperor supported by Grace Bahain, we would have to stand united.

———————◆———————

Today the soldiers of the southern battalions had expected to fight the Levanti. They had expected to march to death or glory in an attempt to wrest Mei'lian back from the invaders. They had not expected to stand upon the hillside and watch their city burn.

Lord Oyamada ordered them all to assemble before the stone plinth of the estate's shrine. There, in another life, another time, they might have gathered to see me executed before they marched to battle, but nothing had turned out quite as anyone had planned.

While they gathered outside, I stood inside the shrine and tried to calm the urge to be sick. I pressed my palms to my stomach, cupping the elaborate knot in my crimson sash—Jie's crimson sash. Kin's crimson robe had looked overlarge on him even with its hasty alterations. It fit me as though I had been born to it, but I could not stop thinking about what Jie had said, that all Kisia needed was a leader, not an emperor. Fear buried deeper. Fear that I, and any others who could claim imperial blood, were outdated, unnecessary, and replaceable. Fear that I had fought so hard and lost so much for nothing, because Kisia didn't need me at all.

The gathered mass of soldiers stilled to something approaching silence as Lord Oyamada stepped out to speak.

"As you have all seen," he began, shouting over the wind. "The Levanti cowards have burned the city rather than face us in battle. What you do not know is that they were so desperate to destabilise our army that they sent an assassin after our emperor. It is with a heavy heart that I must announce this assassin succeeded. My grandson, Jie Ts'ai, Emperor Kin, second of his name, is dead. Killed by a Levanti assassin."

The wind sought to carry away all outcry, yet it still rose through the gusts like thunder. Whatever the generals had thought about following Jie, their rage at the Levanti would be complete. Not only had they named one of their own as emperor, they had burned our capital and killed Emperor Kin's only living son.

"He will be farewelled as an emperor," Lord Oyamada said when the noise of the crowd subsided enough to continue. "But even as we mourn his loss we must keep moving forward. Fortunately, before the city was torched Emperor Kin's minister of the left, Minister Ryo Manshin, escaped imprisonment, killing many Levanti, and he is here with us now to fight this barbarian scourge."

Cheers rose and some of my fear escaped in a slow breath. He had been minister of the left for years, had been beloved by the army, yet still I had worried. Now I only had to worry for myself.

"The barbarians have taken his daughter and forced her to marry their false emperor"—boos and hisses rose as Lord Oyamada continued, his overdramatic play for the crowd exactly what the soldiers wanted—"but we will not be tricked into tolerating their existence with the theft of one woman, no matter how noble her family."

His words fanned their righteous fury, but even as that turned them toward our cause my heart ached for Rah and I wondered how many Levanti were just like him, not barbarians at all, just warriors far from home. But there was no space for such nuance when we needed these soldiers to fight, so I clenched my hands and awaited my moment.

"They think they have weakened us," Lord Oyamada went on, his voice rising with every pronouncement. "They think they can burn our city and kill our emperor and we will roll over and let them conquer our lands, but they are wrong! We are born and bred to the snow and the storms, to the stony plains and the bitter sea winds. Our southern skins are thicker than hide and it will take more than the thundering hooves of some foreign horsemen to make us bow. The Levanti may have killed Emperor Kin's only surviving son, but they did not kill his daughter." He waited out the sudden outburst of noise before he could add: "I, Lord Tashi Oyamada, minister of the right, pledge my allegiance to Empress Miko Ts'ai, last surviving heir of Emperor Kin, that we might stand united and see off these foul invaders."

"I, Lord Ryo Manshin, minister of the left," Manshin cried, adding his voice to the storm of noise, "pledge my allegiance to Her Majesty, Empress Miko Ts'ai, a warrior amongst women."

I could stay where I was. I could hide behind the altar or find a back door and run while they were all distracted. I could...but I would not.

I drew a breath and stepped out before I could recall my steps. Out into the light, out to face the avid stares of the soldiers filling the courtyard. Surely the farthest away couldn't have heard the speech, but Oyamada's words must have spread all the same, for silence fell. And there I stood, grateful for the wind that pulled at my clothes and my hair, hiding my trembling from rank after rank of soldiers waiting for me to claim their allegiance. Oyamada had played his part well. Now I had to play mine.

I parted my lips but nothing came out. Someone coughed. I had practised the words over and over in my head, yet I could speak none of them. So many lives could be saved if we just abandoned the north and defended the river, but then we would never be free of the Levanti or the Chiltaens or Grace Bahain's ambition, never be whole again, and bit by bit Kisia would weaken until it faded to nothing. For the sake of their children and grandchildren, for a future as yet intangible, lives had to be spent.

Kin had not had a lesson for this.

"Kisia will accept no rule by barbarians," I said, hating the high, nervous pitch of my voice as I threw it to the wind. "Kisia will not allow her borders to be infringed. I am the daughter of Emperor Kin Ts'ai and like my father before me"—I allowed myself a quirk of a smile, I alone knowing to which father I referred—"I stand before you ready to fight for the empire. For *our* empire."

Silence. The wind fanned my robe and pulled strands of hair from its elaborate crown of jewelled pins. Jewels hung around my throat too, making up for the absence of the Hian Crown. A few steps away Manshin stood in his armour, his sword at his side like the warrior we needed, yet I had been presented as a god because Kisia had always been ruled by gods, not men, not beings of flesh and blood who lived and died, who loved and hated and fought to their dying breath as every one of these soldiers was expected to do.

I tore the pins from my hair and scattered them to the watching crowd. One of my ministers choked in dismay as I tugged the necklace from my throat, but neither moved nor spoke as I stepped to the edge of the shrine's plinth. "I am no god," I shouted over the wind and the whispers. "I am flesh and blood the same as you, with a heart that bleeds and a soul that rages." I picked at the elaborate knot in my sash as I went on: "Rages for a Kisia that is whole again. United again. Strong again. A Kisia that can stand proud against all invaders, a Kisia that is everything our ancestors fought for and more." The knot came loose and as I threw my sash to the wind it flapped away like a flag let fly. "Power lies not just with me, but with you all," I cried, shrugging off the crimson robe so I stood before them in no imperial trappings, just a pale-hued half robe and breeches. "Power lies with every single person who picks up a weapon and fights for Kisia because without you there would be no Kisia."

Two steps took me to Manshin's side. I gripped the hilt of his blade and drew it free, lifting it to the heavens as the cheer of the soldiers lifted me. "I will fight for you if you will fight for me. I will fight for your families and your lands, your comfort and your freedom, for all Kisia's people. For her rich and her poor, for her city folk and her farmers, for her women and her children and her merchants and her weavers, I will fight. Are you with me?"

Upon their deafening cheers I soared, and in that moment, I was a god.

The story continues in...

WE CRY FOR BLOOD

Book THREE of the Reborn Empire series

Keep reading for a sneak peek!

ACKNOWLEDGEMENTS

Another book, another slew of people to thank for all their hard work, enthusiasm, and encouragement. So here we go!

NIVIA! I complain dramatically about the day edits arrive as being Ego Punching Day, but that you tirelessly rip through my work and see everything it can be helps to make it the very best I can write, so thank you. And to Emily Byron and James Long, my UK editors, for all their hard work. Also to my copy editor, Vivian Kirklin, for putting up with my inconsistencies and magically making sure I don't do anything truly foolish. Copy editors are magicians, if you didn't know.

Enormous thanks to Nico Delort for the stunning cover art; you continue to bring such energy to these books and I love it. Thanks to Lisa Marie Pompilio for the design that really makes it jump off the shelf/screen and into people's arms. And to Charis Loke for her amazing map with so many beautiful details. I think I forgot to thank her in the last book and feel MONSTROUS! (More magicians, these art folks.)

Thanks to Ellen Wright and Angela Man, my super publicists, and to Paolo Crespo and Nazia Khatun for all things social media, including just being fun humans to interact with. You are all amazing and I cannot thank you enough for your work getting me and my books out and about.

Also thank you to all the Orbit folks I don't know to name because you are secret ninjas working behind the scenes to make these things happen. I KNOW YOU'RE THERE! I see you. Thank you.

Once again, since this book was originally to be self-published and only pulled six days before its publication date, I would still like to thank the people who worked on that version. Without them it may not be the book it is now. So, some original credits...

...Ahhh, Amanda, one day I will run out of words to thank you for everything you do for me. You aren't just editor and best friend, but support staff, reading buddy, and occasional bed and breakfast. I would be lost navigating the shoals of this career without you.

A huge thanks to my whole production team. To John Anthony Di Giovanni for the art that captures scenes and characters I cannot see in my head, and to Shawn King for taking that art and dressing it so sharply and with such character that the whole thing speaks to all who look at it.

To Dave Schembri for continuing to lap up every design brief and turn out miracles; Dishiva's symbol is really something. And of course to John Renehan for always bringing so much energy and enthusiasm to any map project I throw his way...

...before I move on to the rest of the acknowledgements.

JULIE! My wonderful agent who always has my back, it's a huge comfort knowing you are there to fight for me whenever I need, so thank you!

Also, thanks to Belle for always being there for me and for reading everything I throw her way, even though it occasionally results in a campaign to include more smooching. And as many thanks to

Sam Hawke for sharing her experience and knowledge, but even more for always screaming back in all caps whenever I squee at her. To Jack for answering all my ridiculous medical questions about terrible wounds, Belinda Crawford for checking for glaring horsey errors, and to Matt McAbee for giving Itaghai such a cool name.

Thanks to Hiu and Petrik and Swiff and Lynn and Matt and Jordan and Esme and all the other early readers and reviewers who took a chance on the self-published version of *We Ride the Storm* and went on to shout about how much they loved it; I wouldn't be where I am now without you. And to Mihir and Lukasz at Fantasy Book Critic for all their support and for choosing *We Ride the Storm* as their finalist for SPFBO4; it has been quite the journey.

And to my Discord fam, too numerous to name (you know who you are), thank you for the safe, happy place where I can be my oddball self, thank you for celebrating with me, for laughing at *and* with me, for putting up with me, and for inviting me along in the first place. I love you all.

Thank you always to my parents for never suggesting I choose a different profession to pay the bills and for having so many books around as I was growing up. And to my kids who (for now) think I'm pretty darn cool for having my name on book covers even though they are too young to read them.

And thank you to my partner, Chris, for whom no words will ever be enough. For always being there to celebrate or commiserate, to listen or advise, and to hold the fort against the kids while I work. Without you there would be no books.

A book like this is such a long journey from start to finish that I always fear I will forget to thank someone at the end. If I do, I am very sorry and it does not mean your contributions were not valued. There are so many people who make this community such a joy to be a part of, and to all of you, thank you.

extras

orbit

meet the author

DEVIN MADSON is an Aurealis Award–winning fantasy author from Australia. After some sucky teenage years, she gave up reality and is now a dual-wielding rogue who works through every tiny side-quest and always ends up too over-powered for the final boss. Anything but Zen, Devin subsists on tea and chocolate and so much fried zucchini she ought to have turned into one by now. Her fantasy novels come in all shades of grey and are populated with characters of questionable morals and a liking for witty banter.

Find out more about Devin Madson and other Orbit authors by registering for the free monthly newsletter at orbitbooks.net.

if you enjoyed
WE LIE WITH DEATH

look out for

WE CRY FOR BLOOD
The Reborn Empire: Book Three

by

Devin Madson

*The empire has fallen and another rises in its place,
in the action-packed continuation of Devin Madson's
epic fantasy quartet.*

Chapter 1

Miko

I loosed the arrow, my heart thrumming in time with the bow's string. It hit the target with a satisfying thud, and while its fletching vibrated, I took another arrow from the barrel. At the other end of the courtyard, soldiers were busy breaking camp, while like two stiff statues, Minister Manshin and newly promoted Minister Oyamada stood watching me. Neither had addressed me since they'd arrived, but they kept up a stiff flow of conversation.

"And wine?" Manshin asked.

"Some," came Oyamada's reply. "We will have to be careful in its distribution, especially as we head into winter. Rice, too. Millet we have in greater abundance, also beans and dried meats, and we can make use of any river we pass for fresh fish."

Manshin grumbled as I loosed another arrow into the rapidly filling target.

"Steel?"

"Of course. And...arrows. Wood for defences, too. We are good for wood and metal in the south, you know."

"Too bad we can't eat them."

"We are not so poorly off for food," Oyamada said stiffly. "Wine will just need to be rationed. Wise when you want soldiers to be able to stand upright in a fight."

Minister Manshin shifted his feet and I could well imagine his scowl. "And never could you more clearly prove you know little about how armies work, Excellency."

"I have commanded—"

"Troops of guards hired for trade caravans do not count. You focus on maintaining our supply lines; I'll decide how to make use of them."

I loosed another arrow and turned before it hit the target, catching Minister Oyamada in the act of opening his mouth to retort, his features dark with colour. "Your caution is very wise, Minister Oyamada," I said, glancing a brief look of censure at Manshin. Of the two, I trusted him more, had been with him longer and needed his skills, but without Oyamada I would have no soldiers to command at all. We had seen Jie's body off only that morning, back to his mother to be laid to rest with all the imperial honours a country house could achieve. Under other circumstances he would have been buried in the imperial gardens, but smoke still rose from the burning ruins of Mei'lian.

Both men bowed, Oyamada with something of ironic thanks, Manshin in stiff apology, but neither spoke until I turned back to take another arrow. Lying at my feet, Shishi stirred, her tail twitching. "Majesty," both ministers said, their first sign of unity. "The meeting."

"It will not be wise, I feel," Oyamada added, "to keep the generals waiting. They may take it as a sign of disrespect."

"I am keeping no one waiting." I nocked the arrow. "We are having the meeting here."

"Here?"

I drew and loosed, the arrow hitting a free space upon the target. "Yes," I said, taking up another arrow. "Here. I do not wish to sit in a stuffy room and have men talk down to me.

They are my generals and they will come to me where I am most comfortable. I am sure you can make them understand, Minister Oyamada."

He received my confiding smile without returning one of his own, but taking it for the order it was, he bowed, shot Manshin a look, and departed in the direction of the house.

"You need to give him time," Manshin said as soon as he was out of earshot, the clack of his wooden sandals loud on the stones. "You killed his grandson only two days ago."

"And you need to not belittle the skills he is bringing to our cause."

A humourless smile turned his lips, deepening the dark rings beneath his eyes. "You mean the money he is bringing to our cause."

"His cause now too."

Manshin gave a little bow of acknowledgement and I took another arrow from the barrel. A gust of wind whipped through the narrow yard, flapping my surcoat about my feet and ruffling Shishi's fur. I nocked, compensated for the wind with barely a thought, and loosed—the whole process second nature, as meeting with his generals had been second nature to Emperor Kin. He had spoken and they had listened, his ability to hold the whole throne room still without a word impossible to replicate.

Despite the wind, the arrow hit more or less where I had intended—more than could ever have been said of my plans.

"You cannot rely on your prowess with a bow to impress them, Your Majesty," Manshin said as I reached for another arrow. "At best they will see it as intimidation, at worst as a reminder of your father."

"Of Emperor Kin? I do not see an issue with that."

"Not what I meant."

"No," I agreed. "But here and now I have only one father and he was Emperor Kin Ts'ai. Only one brother and he was Emperor Jie Ts'ai. My mother was a traitor. My twin a fool. These are the truths I have to live if I want Kisia to survive. But I also need generals who will listen to me, who know they cannot walk all over me as I am sure they plan to."

He nodded. "They will push to see how much power they have. Just remember it's a balance. They will hate you if you give them none and hate you if you give them too much."

"And hate me if I hit this target and hate me if I don't. Hate me if I act like a woman and hate me if I don't." I nocked the arrow. "I am under no misconception this is going to be easy, Minister. But the knowledge they will hate me no matter what is more freeing than you might imagine. I will do this my way. At least then I will look confident."

I drew and loosed, enjoying the thud of the arrowhead digging into the hemp coil. Minister Manshin observed me with pursed lips, his brow furrowed.

"I can do this," I said. "You took my armour that day in Mei'lian so I might live to fight another day; surely you did that because you believe in me."

"You, yes. Them, no." The distant murmur of voices sounded from inside the main house. "I fear they will not put aside old wounds, whatever the feelings of the common soldiers. Whatever the needs of Kisia. These are southern men whose homes and families have not been threatened." He lowered his voice. "Remember: To them the loss of Koi is something to cheer. Emperor Kin stoked the division in his ongoing war against your mother."

I glanced over his shoulder as the first of the southern generals stepped into the weak morning light. Wind pulled at his surcoat as it did mine, and he surveyed the yard with disgust.

Oyamada followed with the rest, most making dramatic shows of clasping their surcoats and huddling against the inclement weather.

I sighed. "I will not forget, but if I am going to rule Kisia that means all of it, not just north of the river. Please say nothing during this meeting unless you're directly spoken to," I added, and his brows lifted, no doubt as much at the polite words as at the request. "And refer as many questions to me as you can. They need to know they can't just deal with you. I am not your figurehead."

The whisper of my last words died as the generals approached across the damp stones. They formed something of a scowling semicircle as I took another arrow from the barrel, my heart thudding so hard I feared it might trouble my aim. But the arrow I loosed hit the target, its thud the only sound in the suddenly silent courtyard. Without looking at them, I took another arrow.

"Welcome to our first council meeting, Generals," I said, hoping they would mistake the tremble in my voice for effort as I drew and loosed again. "You all know me, but I am as yet unable to put faces to names. We will begin with you giving me your oaths, then your names."

Silence hung for several long seconds, until the man at the target end of the curved line cleared his throat. "Your Majesty, would it not be more proper to do this inside where the ground is not so wet?"

I had nocked another arrow, and with it held to the bowstring, I turned to look at him. "You are afraid of a little water, General?"

"Not afraid, Your Majesty, no, but—"

"You send soldiers to fight and die for you but you will not kneel on damp stone for your empress?"

His gaze slid to the arrow in my hands, before my face. He swallowed and drew himself up. "If my empress requests it of me, I will."

"I have requested it."

With a proud nod, he took a step forward and knelt on the stones, making no sign of discomfort though it would be like kneeling on ice. He lowered his head to the ground. "I swear on the bones of my forebears. On my name and my honour. I will mind not pain. I will mind not suffering. I will give every last ounce of my strength. I will give every last ounce of my intellect. I will die in service to you if the gods so will it. I will renounce every honour. I will give every coin. I will be as nothing and no one in service to you."

"You may rise and give me your name."

He got to his feet, more gracefully than one would expect of an old soldier, and he looked like an old soldier, worn and wary. Water had seeped into the cloth at his knees and his linen sleeves. "My name is General Senn Mihri, Your Majesty."

I turned back to the target and loosed the arrow. "General Senn Mihri, youngest son of the great General Mihri," I said as I took another. "As famed for his prowess upon horseback as for the quality of the horses bred on his estate west of Anxi. You were promoted to general after an engagement against the mountain tribes in 1370 and have been stationed there since, defending our western border."

Having loosed the second arrow, I gripped the bow in both my hands and bowed to him, low enough to be meaningful, not so low as to demean myself. "You served my father, the great Emperor Kin Ts'ai, with strength and honour, and I welcome your continued service to the empire."

The hardened soldier could not keep his eyebrows from lifting and, in a gruff voice said, "Many thanks, Your Majesty."

I took another arrow from the fast emptying barrel, but the next man seemed to need no such encouragement to play along. He stepped forward and knelt as General Mihri had, speaking the Imperial Oath in a monotonous voice. Head to the damp stones, he waited until I bade him rise.

"My name is General Moto, Your Majesty," he said. "Commander of the forces stationed at Ts'ai since the last border skirmish with Chiltae in 1385."

If he had given such details in the hope of leaving me nothing to say, he reckoned without the wealth of information Minister Manshin knew about each general long under his command. I mentally noted Moto was shrewd, adding to Jie's belief that he was one of the two southern generals most likely to take control of the empire in his place.

"General Tai Moto," I said, loosing the arrow I had been holding to take another. "First of his family to achieve the rank despite the second sons of the Count of Tatan having entered the Rising Army since the family first took the title in 1236." I owed too many hours of forced study and repetition of family names and honours to that one. "When you were a captain in Mei'lian's standing battalion, you defended my father against a pair of assassins who attacked while he was inspecting the plans for rebuilding the city's defences."

I loosed the second arrow, and as I had with General Mihri, I gripped the bow and bowed to him. "You served my father, the great Emperor Kin Ts'ai, with strength and honour, and I welcome your continued service to the empire."

No surprise this time, he had known it was coming, but with a shrewd little nod of a move well played, he said, "Many thanks, Your Majesty," before stepping back into line.

Next came General Joshi and General Taranada, both newly promoted from common families as had often been

Kin's way, and both eager to please. One after the other they knelt and took their oaths, before rising and stepping back into their places. Halfway along the line, I was beginning to think maybe I had overestimated their dislike of me, when I turned my attention to the first of the two southern generals with roots in the mountain tribes. General Bax stared back and didn't bow. All eyes were on me. I lifted my brows. "This is where you kneel and take the oath as your fellow generals have done."

"No, it is not," he said standing proud, his clenched fists white at the knuckles. "I give no oaths to conquerors who have done nothing to earn my allegiance. I will fight for Kisia, but I will not fight for you."

No fear in the words. No bitterness. Just honesty and honour no matter the cost. I ought to put an arrow through him, ought to defend my position with anger, but he had not threatened me, had not disrespected me, and I had not planned to meet such quiet defiance.

"I am Kisia, General," I said, confronting his calm with my own. "I did not conquer my brother nor my father; I succeeded them. But I will conquer the false Levanti emperor and retake what is ours."

"And I wish you all the best, my lady, but I cannot fight for you. I cannot order my men to fight for you. I gave my oath to Emperor Kin because he earned it, and I will give it to no other. As I told young Jie when he sought the same of me."

They all seemed to be holding their breaths, waiting, and though I wanted guidance I dared not look to either of my ministers. This had to be a decision I made on my own.

Never had a nocked arrow felt so heavy between my fingers, never had a man stood so fearlessly before me, awaiting judgement without making any move to defend himself. He ought to die; that was what I had decided would be the fate of any who refused, and yet...

"General Bax, you served my father, the great Emperor Kin Ts'ai, with strength and honour," I said, bowing the same to him as I had to the others. "Uphold your oath to him by making no war upon me. Go in peace."

The silence grew all the more tense, every man holding in an outcry he dared not let go. But General Bax bowed, the first sign of respect he had shown me, and taking his dismissal as immediate, turned to walk away. No one watched him go. No one spoke. No one moved at all. And still holding the same arrow, I stepped in front of the next man in line.

He was somewhere between the young General Joshi and the old General Mihri in age, with eyes heavily lined as though constantly narrowed in scrutiny. A moment of hesitation held him still. Followed by another and a third and as the seconds mounted up the rest of the generals once more held their breaths. Until he stepped forward and knelt. "I swear on the bones of my forebears," he began, and I was able to breathe again.

"My name is General Rushin, Your Majesty," he said at the end, his indulgent smile that of one preparing to put up with dull entertainment put on by children.

I tightened my grip on the bow, mindful to loosen it again before sending the arrow to be reunited with its fellows. "General Rushin," I said as I drew another, nocked it, and imagined the target was his face. "Another veteran of the ongoing battles with the mountain tribes. Named Hero of Giana after you and some twenty men held off an attack at the pass until the arrival of reinforcements and—"

"Twenty surviving men, Your Majesty," he said, still smiling. I wanted to split his lip with my fist. "There were two hundred of us at the beginning of the day."

"Indeed," I said, and bowing as I had to the others, added, "You served my father, the great Emperor Kin Ts'ai, with strength and honour, and I welcome your continued service to the empire."

"Why thank you, Your Majesty. The honour is all mine."

He stepped back and I turned my attention to the second to last general in the line, a heavy-browed young man, the most neatly dressed of them all and bearing his tribal crest as proudly as the Ts'ai dragon. "You must be General Yass," I said, taking a different opening with the southern army's other barbarian general. "Are you of the same mind as General Bax?"

The young man did not answer but stepped forward to kneel upon the wet stones and speak his oath. Once he had finished and I bade him rise, he said, "My name is General Yass and I am no different from any other Kisian. I would not have you treat me so, Your Majesty."

"That's a no, then," I said, turning to loose my arrow into the almost full target. "General Yass, the second member of your family to serve but the first to be named a general, after the battle of Chisit Pass in 1382, a position granted you by your men during battle and later ratified by my father. You also have the honour to be amongst the youngest generals ever named, along with General Ryoji and General Kin."

I bowed to him as I had to the others. "You served my father, the great Emperor Kin Ts'ai, with strength and honour, and I welcome your continued service to the empire."

"Your Majesty."

The last man in the line stood with his hands clasped behind his back and the look of a man who is nobly putting up with a great stench under his nose. By process of elimination this had to be General Onru, but he neither said so nor knelt. He glanced along the line with that same sneer and said, "How pathetic. Is this what we've come to? We will stand here being bullied by a girl? Not even a woman. Not even a true child of Emperor Kin, because no matter how many times she invokes his name, it was Katashi Otako's traitorous seed that made her, with not one ounce of southern blood. Who are you to demand our allegiance? Your mother was a witch. Your grandmother consorted with demons. Is that how you have Manshin and Oyamada under your spell? Well, none of your magic will work on me, girl."

I lifted my bow, heart pounding. "How dare you let such foul lies pass your lips. I am your empress and you will bow and take your oath or you will die."

He laughed. "You won't kill me."

"No?"

"You didn't kill Bax."

"He showed me no disrespect and himself no dishonour. The same cannot be said of you. Kneel."

Onru spat on the stones between us. "No."

Without thought, I drew and loosed for his throat. He rocked to the side, but neither of us was fast enough. The arrowhead buried deep in his shoulder, throwing him back. And as he spread an arm wide to steady himself, he pulled a knife from his sash. Shishi barked. Someone shouted, the cry of alarm muffled by the thud of my pulse. I had no more arrows. The barrel was half a dozen steps away. But as Onru lunged, I swung my bow at him like a club. He ducked, hissing spit onto his chin as the arrow in his shoulder bounced. The upper arm of the bow caught him on the leg on the backswing, but he leapt at me, knocking it from my hand. For a horrible moment I was falling and couldn't save myself. I hit the stones, head smacking hard enough to send a bright haze before my eyes. His knife sliced my hand and I howled, but when I tried to find some flesh into which to bury my nails, my teeth, my knees, I found nothing but empty air. And blinking back the daze and nausea, I hauled myself to my feet, head throbbing. A high-pitched wail cut through everything. Hot blood splattered across my face, and a body hit the ground with a meaty crunch.

I blinked, trying to dispel the haze, but everything looked wrong. Oddly flat and pale. Shishi licked my hand, her tongue rough and frantic.

"Your Majesty, are you all right?" Manshin's voice, and there he was seeming to float before me. "Majesty?"

Other voices asked the same question. More faces crowded.

"Onru?" I said.

All those around me turned, making space for me to see the body. Onru, his throat slit and his blood now pooling on the stones. A man knelt beside him in the plain robe of a servant, calmly engaged in cleaning a pair of daggers on the dead man's surcoat. Sensing my gaze, he looked up and bowed, so deeply his nose all but touched the dead general's navel. "Your Majesty, I am honoured to have brought this man's death for you."

"Who the fuck are you?"

"His name is Yakono."

I spun, breath catching at the sound of so recognisable a voice. There at the edge of the courtyard stood General Ryoji. Ryoji, who had trained us. Ryoji, who had been my mother's most loyal guard. Ryoji, into whom I had stuck a blade the night I had chosen to protect Emperor Kin against Mother's coup. For all the good it had done.

He didn't look any worse for it, but he looked older than when I had seen him last. I realised with a start of shock that I had never seen him in anything but one of his various uniforms. He looked strange in common clothing.

Despite the way we had parted, despite everything, it took all my self-control not to run to him, not to touch him to be sure he was real. Not to demand immediately to know what had happened to my mother and how he came to be here. The answers to those questions would hurt too much, I was sure, and better my new generals saw no weakness.

Instead of everything I wanted to do, I lifted my chin. "General Ryoji, it has been quite some time since I saw you last."

"Indeed, Your Majesty." He bowed and I could not but think of how long he had spent bowing to my mother and calling her by that title. "You are remarkably difficult to find."

I gestured at the man he had called Yakono. Having killed the traitorous general, he now stood beside the body, still and at ease. "And who is this?"

"Yakono," the general repeated, coming close enough for me to see how tired he looked. "He is a Jackal."

Whispering broke out amongst the generals and more than one stepped warily back. The man, Yakono, gave no sign he noticed. The Jackals were as much myth as history, and when I had learned about the elite assassins my forebears had maintained, I had envisioned something very different. The story was they had started out as elite guards under Emperor Tsubasa and slowly became assassins sent on special missions. There had always been twelve of them and each had taken an apprentice to ensure this would be the case, but Emperor Kin had executed them all, unwilling to risk their disloyalty. Yet here one stood, as unassuming and ordinary as any commoner on the street.

"Didn't Emperor Kin kill all the Jackals?" I said, breaking upon the continued whispering, and there the first sign of life from Yakono. He flinched, something of grief or anger crossing his features before they once more settled into calm like ripples fading from the surface of a pond. Ah, an anger I could use, perhaps.

"Not quite all."

I had so many questions, but the generals had gathered for a meeting and there was still so much to do and say. This distraction was losing them. "Well, I look forward to hearing more about it when we are finished here, General. Minister Oyamada? Have the body removed and see that General Ryoji and our new guest are made comfortable."

Oyamada hesitated only the briefest moment before breaking from the line of gathered men. "As you wish, Your Majesty. This way, please."

I pulled my gaze from Ryoji with an effort, setting aside all my unanswered questions. Back at the barrel I took up another arrow. It shook in my trembling hands.

I ran my gaze along the line of generals, each quieting now after the interruption. I could have let them know it was a warning for any who dared betray me, but they had seen all I had seen and to threaten them would look desperate and fearful.

"Now you have all given your allegiance," I said, nocking the arrow. "We may discuss what to do next."

The arrow thudded in amongst its fellows as I went on, "The Levanti are consolidating their hold on the northern half of our empire. There is a chance Chiltae may regroup and attack them, but it seems more likely after losing much of their army they will hold their borders and stay out of this." I took another arrow from the barrel. "It would be an easy enough battle to get these barbarians"—I winced at the word, but there could be no space for nuance now, no accepting they were no such thing when I needed to rally an army against them—"out of our land were they not allied to a number of northern lords. Lord Kato, Lord Rasten, and Lord Kiri we know for sure, and there are very likely others. Some may have joined out of a pragmatic wish not to be trampled, but others appear to have very deliberately made this choice, eschewing loyalty to the empire for power and personal gain. Chief amongst these being Grace Bahain."

No whispering followed. Of course they had all heard, but for a moment I was sitting across from Edo at Kiyoshio Castle as he wrote this treason for me to see. The realisation of having no allies left, of being wholly alone, had hollowed me with fear.

"We cannot strike at them head-on while they have such support," I said. "But we may be able to if we can lure Bahain away from his new emperor."

"Attacking Kogahaera would be suicidal," General Rushin said.

"Not Kogahaera. Not yet." I shook my head. "Syan."

A moment of utter stillness held the courtyard in its grip, before gazes started to flit to Manshin to be sure he had heard my mad utterance. When he gave no sign of surprise or derision, the complaints began.

"I'm sure you must realise Syan is one of the most fortified cities in Kisia, Your Majesty," General Moto said.

"The castle is behind at least three layers of walls."

"It has never been conquered!"

"Yes, even though pirates have raided the city for decades, the castle has never fallen."

I weathered their exclamations much like Kiyoshio weathered the furious sea and waited for them to die away. Eventually they did, perhaps because they had uttered every complaint there was, or because one by one they noticed I was standing, untroubled, waiting patiently for them to finish.

"We are going to take Kiyoshio," I said when they were all silent.

"May we ask how, Your Majesty?" General Mihri said. "You have a plan, perhaps."

"Yes. I do."

if you enjoyed
WE LIE WITH DEATH
look out for

THE UNBROKEN
Magic of the Lost: Book One
by
C. L. Clark

Touraine is a soldier. Stolen as a child and raised to kill and die for the empire, her only loyalty is to her fellow conscripts. But now, her company has been sent back to her homeland to stop a rebellion, and the ties of blood may be stronger than she thought.

Luca needs a turncoat. Someone desperate enough to tiptoe the bayonet's edge between treason and orders. Someone who can sway the rebels toward peace while Luca focuses on what really matters: getting her uncle off her throne.

Through assassinations and massacres, in bedrooms and war rooms, Touraine and Luca will haggle over the price of a nation. But some things aren't for sale.

Chapter 1

Change

A sandstorm brewed dark and menacing against the Qazāli horizon as Lieutenant Touraine and the rest of the Balladairan Colonial Brigade sailed into El-Wast, capital city of Qazāl, foremost of Balladaire's southern colonies.

El-Wast. City of marble and sandstone, of olives and clay. City of the golden sun and fruits Touraine couldn't remember tasting. City of rebellious, uncivilized god-worshippers. The city where Touraine was born.

At a sudden gust, Touraine pulled her black military coat tighter about her body and hunched small over the railing of the ship as it approached land. Even from this distance, in the early-morning dark, she could see a black Balladairan standard flapping above the docks. Its rearing golden horse danced to life, sparked by the reflection of the night lanterns. Around her, pale Balladairan-born sailors scrambled across the ship to bring it safely to harbor.

El-Wast, for the first time in some twenty-odd years. It took the air from the lieutenant's chest. Her white-knuckle grip on the rail was only partly due to the nausea that had rocked her on the water.

"It's beautiful, isn't it?" Tibeau, Touraine's second sergeant and best friend, settled against the rail next to her. The wooden rail shifted under his bulk. He spoke quietly, but Touraine could hear the awe and longing in the soft rumble of his voice.

Beautiful wasn't the first thing Touraine thought as their ship sailed up the mouth of the River Hadd and gave them a view of El-Wast. The city was surprisingly big. Surprisingly bright. It was surprisingly... civilized. A proper city, not some scattering of tents and sand. Not what she had expected at all, given how Balladairans described the desert colonies. From this angle, it didn't even look like a desert.

The docks stretched along the river like a small town, short buildings nestled alongside what were probably warehouses and workers' tenements. Just beyond them, a massive bridge arced over shadowed farmland with some crop growing in neat rows, connecting the docks to the curve of a crumbling wall that surrounded the city. The Mile-Long Bridge. The great bridge was lined with the shadows of palm trees and lit up all along with the fuzzy dots of lanterns. In the morning darkness, you could easily have mistaken the lanterns for stars.

She shrugged. "It's impressive, I guess."

Tibeau nudged her shoulder and held his arms out wide to take it all in. "You guess? This is your home. We're finally back. You're going to love it." His eyes shone in the reflection of the lanterns guiding the Balladairan ship into Crocodile Harbor, named for the monstrous lizards that had lived in the river centuries ago.

Home. Touraine frowned. "Love it? Beau, we're not on leave." She dug half-moons into the soft, weather-worn wood of the railing and grumbled, "We have a job to do."

Tibeau scoffed. "To police our own people."

The thunk of approaching boots on the deck behind them stopped Touraine from saying something that would keep Tibeau from speaking to her for the rest of the day. Something like *These aren't my people*. How could they be? Touraine had barely been toddling in the dust when Balladaire took her.

"You two better not be talking about what I think you're talking about," Sergeant Pruett said, coming up behind them with her arms crossed.

"Of course not," Touraine said. She and Pruett let their knuckles brush in the cover of darkness.

"Good. Because I'd hate to have to throw you bearfuckers overboard."

Pruett. The sensible one to Tibeau's impetuousness, the scowl to his smile. The only thing they agreed on was hating Balladaire for what it had done to them, but unlike Tibeau, who was only biding his time before some imaginary revolution, Pruett was resigned to the conscripts' fate and thought it better to keep their heads down and hate Balladaire in private.

Pruett shoved her way between the two of them and propped her elbows on the railing. Her teeth chattered. "It's cold as a bastard here. I thought the deserts were supposed to be hot."

Tibeau sighed wistfully, staring with longing at some point beyond the city. "Only during the day. In the real desert, you can freeze your balls off if you forget a blanket."

"You sound...oddly excited about that." Pruett looked askance at him.

Tibeau grinned.

Home was a sharp topic for every soldier in the Balladairan Colonial Brigade. There were those like Tibeau and Pruett, who had been taken from countries throughout the broken Shālan

Empire when they were old enough to already have memories of family or the lack thereof, and then there were those like Touraine, who had been too young to remember anything but Balladaire's green fields and thick forests.

No matter where in the Shālan Empire the conscripts were originally from, they all speculated on the purpose of their new post. There was excitement on the wind, and Touraine felt it, too. The chance to prove herself. The chance to show the Balladairan officers that she deserved to be a captain. Change was coming.

Even the Balladairan princess had come with the fleet. Pruett had heard from another conscript who had it from a sailor that the princess was visiting her southern colonies for the first time, and so the conscripts took turns trying to spot the young royal on her ship.

The order came to disembark, carried by shouts on the wind. Discipline temporarily disappeared as the conscripts and their Balladairan officers hoisted their packs and tramped down to Crocodile Harbor's thronged streets.

People shouted in Balladairan and Shālan as they loaded and unloaded ships, animals in cages and animals on leads squawked and bellowed, and Touraine walked through it all in a daze, trying to take it all in. Qazāl's dirt and grit crunched beneath her army-issued boots. Maybe she *did* feel a spark of awe and curiosity. And maybe that frightened her just a little.

With a wumph, Touraine walked right into an odd tan horse with a massive hump in the middle of its back. She spat and dusted coarse fur off her face. The animal glared at her with large, affronted brown eyes and a bubble of spit forming at the corner of its mouth.

The animal's master flicked his long gray-streaked hair back off his smiling face and spoke to Touraine in Shālan.

Touraine hadn't spoken Shālan since she was small. It wasn't allowed when they were children in Balladaire, and now it sounded as foreign as the camel's groan. She shook her head.

"Camel. He spit," the man warned, this time in Balladairan. The camel continued to size her up. It didn't look like it was coming to any good conclusion.

Touraine grimaced in disgust, but beside her, Pruett snorted. The other woman said something short to the man in Shālan before turning Touraine toward the ships.

"What did you say?" Touraine asked, looking over her shoulder at the glaring camel and the older man.

"Please excuse my idiot friend."

Touraine rolled her eyes and hefted her pack higher onto her shoulders.

"Rose Company, Gold Squad, form up on me!" She tried in vain to gather her soldiers in some kind of order, but the noise swallowed her voice. She looked warily for Captain Rogan. If Touraine didn't get the rest of her squad in line, that bastard would take it out on all of them. "Gold Squad, form up!"

Pruett nudged Touraine in the ribs. She pointed, and Touraine saw what kept her soldiers clumped in whispering groups, out of formation.

A young woman descended the gangway of another ship with the support of a cane. She wore black trousers, a black coat, and a short black cloak lined with cloth of gold. Her blond hair, pinned in a bun behind her head, sparked like a beacon in the night. Three stone-faced royal guards accompanied her in a protective triangle, their short gold cloaks blown taut behind them. Each of them had a sword on one hip and a pistol on the other.

Touraine looked from the princess to the chaos on the

ground, and a growing sense of unease raised the short hairs on the back of her neck. Suddenly, the crowd felt more claustrophobic than industrious.

The man with the camel still stood nearby, watching with interest like the other dockworkers. His warm smile deepened the lines in his face, and he guided the animal's nose to her, as if she wanted to pat it. The camel looked as unenthusiastic at the prospect as Touraine felt.

"No." Touraine shook her head at him again. "Move, sir. Give us this space, if you please."

He didn't move. Probably didn't understand proper Balladairan. She shooed him with her hands. Instead of reacting with annoyance or confusion, he glanced fearfully over her shoulder.

She followed his gaze. Nothing there but the press of the crowd, her own soldiers either watching the princess or drowsily taking in their new surroundings in the early-morning light. Then she saw it: a young Qazāli woman weaving through the crowd, gaze fixed on one blond point.

The camel man grabbed Touraine's arm, and she jerked away.

Touraine was a good soldier, and a good soldier would do her duty. She didn't let herself imagine what the consequences would be if she was wrong.

"Attack!" she bellowed, fit for a battlefield. "To the princess!"

The Qazāli man muttered something in Shālan, probably a curse, before he shouted, too. A warning to his fellow. To more of them, maybe. Something glinted in his hands.

Touraine spared only half a glance toward the princess. That was what the royal guard was for. Instead, she launched toward the camel man, dropping her pack instead of swinging it at him. *Stupid, stupid.* Instinct alone saved her life. She lifted her arms just in time to get a slice across her left forearm instead of her throat.

She drew her baton to counterattack, but instead of running in the scant moment he had, the old man hesitated, squinting at her.

"Wait," he said. "You look familiar." His Balladairan was suddenly more than adequate.

Touraine shook off his words, knocked the knife from his hand, and tripped him to the ground. He struggled against her with wiry strength until she pinned the baton against his throat. That kept him from saying anything else. She held him there, her teeth bared and his eyes wide while he strained for breath. Behind her, the camel man's companions clashed with the other soldiers. A young woman's high-pitched cry. *The princess or the assassin?*

The old man rasped against the pressure of the baton. "Wait," he started, but Touraine pressed harder until he lost the words.

Then the docks went silent. The rest of the attackers had been taken down, dead or apprehended. The man beneath her realized it, too, and all the fight sagged out of him.

When they relieved her, she stood to find herself surrounded. The three royal guards, alert, swords drawn; a handful of fancy-looking if spooked civilians; the general—*her* general. General Cantic. And, of course, the princess.

Heat rose to her face. Touraine knew that some part of her should be afraid of overstepping; she'd just shat on all the rules and decorum that had been drilled into the conscripts for two decades. But the highest duty was to the throne of Balladaire, and not everyone could say they had stopped an assassination. Even if Touraine was a conscript, she couldn't be punished for that. She hoped. She settled into the strength of her broad shoulders and bowed deeply to the princess.

"I'm sorry to disturb you, Your Highness," Touraine said, her voice smooth and low.

The princess quirked an eyebrow. "Thank you"—the princess looked to the double wheat-stalk pins on Touraine's collar—"Lieutenant . . . ?"

"Lieutenant Touraine, Your Highness." Touraine bowed again. She peeked at the general out of the corner of her eye, but the older woman's lined face was unreadable.

"Thank you, Lieutenant Touraine, for your quick thinking."

A small shuffling to the side admitted a horse-faced man with a dark brown tail of hair under his bicorne hat. Captain Rogan sneered over Touraine before bowing to the princess.

"Your Highness, I apologize if this Sand has inconvenienced you." Before the princess could respond, Rogan turned to Touraine and spat, "Get back to your squad. Form them up like they should have been."

So much for taking her chance to rise. So much for duty. Touraine sucked her teeth and saluted. "Yes, sir."

She tightened her sleeve against the bleeding cut on her left arm and went back to her squad, who stood in a tight clump a few yards away from the old man's camel. The beast huffed with a sound like a bubbling kettle, and a disdainful glob of foamy spittle dripped from its slack lips. Safe enough to say she had made an impression on the locals.

And the others? Touraine looked back for another glimpse at the princess and found the other woman meeting her gaze. Touraine tugged the bill of her field cap and nodded before turning away, attempting to appear as unruffled as she could.

When Touraine returned to her squad, Pruett looked uncertain as Rogan handed the older man off to another officer, who led him and the young woman away. "I told you to be careful about attracting attention."

Touraine smiled, even though her arm stung and blood leaked into her palm. "Attention's not bad if you're the hero."

That did make Pruett laugh. "Ha! Hero. A Sand? I guess you think the princess wants to wear my shit for perfume, too."

Touraine laughed back, and it was tinged with the same frustration and bitterness that talk of their place in the world always was.

This time, when she called for her squad to form up, they did. Gold Squad and the others pulled down their field caps and drew close their coats. The wind was picking up. The sun was rising. The Qazāli dockworkers bent their backs into their work again, but occasionally they glanced—nervous, scared, suspicious, hateful—at the conscripts. At Rogan's order, she and the conscripts marched to their new posts.

Change was coming. Touraine aimed to be on the right side of it.

orbit

Follow us:

f /orbitbooksUS

🐦 /orbitbooks

▶ /orbitbooks

Join our mailing list
to receive alerts on our
latest releases and deals.

orbitbooks.net

Enter our monthly
giveaway for the chance
to win some epic prizes.

orbitloot.com